LOST AND FOUND IN
Paris

Also by Lian Dolan

The Sweeney Sisters

Elizabeth the First Wife

Helen of Pasadena

LOST AND FOUND

IN

Paris

A Novel

LIAN DOLAN

WILLIAM MORROW

An Imprint of HarperCollinsPublishers

LOST AND FOUND IN PARIS. Copyright © 2022 by Lian Dolan. All rights reserved. Printed in the United States of America. No part of this book may be used or reproduced in any manner whatsoever without written permission except in the case of brief quotations embodied in critical articles and reviews. For information, address HarperCollins Publishers, 195 Broadway, New York, NY 10007.

HarperCollins books may be purchased for educational, business, or sales promotional use. For information, please email the Special Markets Department at SPsales@harpercollins.com.

FIRST EDITION

Designed by Kyle O'Brien

Library of Congress Cataloging-in-Publication Data has been applied for.

ISBN 978-0-06-290902-2

22 23 24 25 26   LSC   10 9 8 7 6 5 4 3 2 1

For those who have lost someone or something

LOST AND FOUND IN
Paris

Chapter 1

Pasadena
February 2011

My father always said that beginnings and endings were clichés. They couldn't help but be, with beginnings being bright and new and even the best of endings being painful in some way. He was right, of course.

Still, a cliché can crush.

Had I known what was going to happen, I wouldn't have spent my last twenty minutes of ignorant bliss talking about fruit. I would have had a drink and reapplied my lipstick for a little Chanel courage, as my mother calls it. But I was oblivious, so I carried on about produce. "One of the themes clearly defined in this piece is hierarchy. Power and privilege. Though the fruits and vegetables may appear to be strewn chaotically upon the table, in bowls or baskets, even upon the ground, the artist has actually imposed a well-defined order. They are arranged based upon their value and rarity."

A sea of glazed eyes greeted my observation; the well-suited locals who composed my listening audience were probably more interested in the food and drink outside on the patio than the pictures of food and drink inside the Wallace Aston Museum. The museum, known as the WAM, was a jewel box of art treasures from the private collection of industrialist Wallace Aston and his actress wife, Ashley Simonds Aston, ranging from European masters to twentieth-century abstracts to Asian pieces spanning two thousand years. Unlike some larger museums that used traveling exhibits with mass appeal to draw in visitors, at the WAM, it was the permanent collection that was the star. It was breathtaking to walk the galleries knowing that you were looking at a private collection on the grandest scale. Manet, Cézanne, Picasso, Van Gogh, Goya, Rembrandt, Zurbarán, Rodin, Degas, Frankenthaler, Fragonard, Nevelson, Kandinsky, Noguchi, Ruscha, Brâncuşi, Warhol—a greatest hits and then some. All displayed in a compact, well-composed space recently updated and turbocharged with fresh windows and new gardens. I loved it there—a clean, brilliant little burst of genius tucked in between the freeways.

My job was to develop lectures and other public education projects, write articles for the website and monthly magazine, and sometimes accompany the art to another museum as a courier. My work at the museum wasn't critical to the day-to-day running of the place. I had the words "Special Projects" on my business cards, because that sounded slightly less vague than "Employee-at-Large" or "Volunteered to Do a Few Things and Never Left." When I was hired nearly ten years prior, the museum was banking on my future contributions, and I was searching for an immediate distraction. It was a mutually beneficial relationship.

Tonight, I'd been assigned a VIP tour from the local hospital, a mix of doctors and administrators looking for some creative inspiration served with wine and cheese. Their fee would go into the children's education coffers. Usually I could command my audience's attention, but I appeared to be off my game. My feet hurt and even I had to cringe when I used words like "strewn" in a sentence, but I was nearing the end. Big finish. "You'll note the root vegetables relegated to the ground, while the prized peas and asparagus are elevated in status by their presence in baskets in the foreground of the painting. Questions?"

A hand went up, a childish gesture from a grown man wearing a checkered bow tie and a smirk. I knew exactly what he'd ask. He didn't disappoint. "How much is something like this worth?"

I answered like I always did, "A painting like Frans Snyders's *Still Life with Fruits and Vegetables* is a masterpiece of the Flemish baroque period. There simply is no price."

"But if there was a price?" Bow Tie Boy wouldn't give up. I bet he honed that overconfidence as president of his frat. And was that a slight Southern accent? Unusual here in Pasadena. The group twittered with laughter. I noticed my boss, the charming Caterina de Montefiore, standing off to the side but displaying her omniscience. Caterina was the director of communications, and she had tipped me off that there was a *New York Times* travel writer hiding among my corporate private tour. Half-Italian, half-Brazilian, and very competitive, Caterina was locked in a PR death match with other Los Angeles–area museums. She wanted the WAM to be the only one mentioned in this roundup of hot places to spend a Friday night in Southern California. She nodded and gave me the look that said in no uncertain terms, "Sex it up, Joanie."

I pointed to the painting, a riot of overripe fruit and luscious vegetables bursting with color and texture. "Let me ask you the price of a bowl of perfect cherries, deep red and glistening, begging to eaten. Now imagine their worth in the middle of a cold, dark Flemish winter after months of deprivation." Oh, I had Bow Tie Boy's attention now. "And what about this gorgeous plate of pears. Have you ever seen such lovely fleshy orbs, perfect in size and shape, bursting with sweetness? Finally, look at the longing in the woman's eyes. That's the look of a woman who wants to touch and feel and taste all she sees. This is not a painting of a table full of fruit; it's a masterpiece of desire. What's that worth?"

Bow Tie Boy conceded, "Well, I guess you got me there. Hard to put a dollar figure on that."

Caterina strode over, her steps making an authoritative pounding in the marble front gallery. She was ready to take over the tour, the museum, or a small country in Central Europe, wherever she was needed most. Caterina was always in charge.

I bowed like an idiot because that's how tired I was. "Thank you for your time and attention. The Blakely in the garden is best viewed right about sunset. Don't miss that. I'll hand you off to Caterina de Montefiore, who'll be happy to answer any questions about the museum or our programs." Caterina commanded the group into the Degas gallery with the wave of her hand.

Get me out of these shoes and get me home, I thought as I turned on my heels and headed toward my office. I felt a hand on my arm. Bow Tie Boy was offering his card, and up close, he was definitely more of a Bow Tie Man. "Mason Andrews. Thank you for the tour. I'm a doctor and I don't know much about art, but I'd really like a bowl of cherries right now."

That made me laugh. It had been a while since any man had made that happen. "That's what art can do. Make you want . . . experiences. I'm Joan Blakely. And, as you probably figured out, I'm an educator here at the WAM." It was the easiest way to describe my multifaceted job, especially to an emergency room doctor, as his card indicated.

I shook Mason's hand, a firm grip coupled with plenty of eye contact. Is now the moment when I tell him I'm married, or do I play this out a little longer because, despite the desperate bow tie, he's very attractive and, frankly, it's been a while since I've had a bowl of cherries?

"Blakely, as in '. . . the Blakely in the garden' Blakely?"

I nodded. "Yes, Henry Blakely was my father."

There was a flicker of recognition, then remembrance. "I went to the retrospective at LACMA a few years ago. Okay, I'll confess, an old girlfriend dragged me there, but I was blown away. The use of light and perspective. The colors. The space. It was amazing. Your father was amazing. You must get tired of hearing that."

"Never. It's a great gift to me. Really."

"He did that big thing in Central Park, right?"

"Yes. It was called *Castle Burning*. In 1993."

"My cool friend in high school had a poster from that exhibit," he said, like it was all coming back to him in that moment, and then, "I'm so sorry about what happened to him."

"Thank you," I said, meaning it, then changed my tone. "I guess you do know a little about art."

"I was about to make a lame joke about a 'private tour,' but that would really sound pathetic now. So, I'll go for it. Is there any chance, Joan Blakely, that I could see you again?" Sincerity, another quality my life had been lacking lately.

For one second, I wanted to say yes. This doctor in his blue suit looked uncomplicated and easily satisfied, not like Casey, who felt a million miles away these days, even when he was in the living room.

"Joan?"

No, now was not the time. "I'm married."

"Oh. I didn't see a ring. My apologies."

"No!" I practically shouted. "Don't apologize. I'm flattered. My ring is undergoing a few small repairs. But thank you . . . for asking." I assured him I'd keep his card, in case I had a medical emergency.

"I can't do anything about the wait time, but I do some nice stitches," Mason Andrews laughed. "Maybe I will see you around." He gave a slow nod and turned to rejoin his group, who had finally made it out to the garden and the patio for the wine, cheese, and sunset portion of the tour. I watched him walk off. *Men should go back to wearing suits.*

On cue, Casey came through the glass front doors of the museum in his photographer's uniform of blue jeans, black T-shirt, and a leather jacket. Needless to say, Casey didn't own a bow tie. He was on his way out of town to shoot a hotel in Kyoto for *Travel + Leisure*. What was he doing here? He rarely stopped by the museum these days.

Casey found me right away and barely said hello before launching into his common refrain lately: "I'm on my way to LAX . . ." And then to my surprise he added, "And I wanted to talk to you about something."

"Now? Here?" Casey usually preferred conversations over a beer on our back patio. But it had been a while since we'd even had one of those.

"Yeah, Joan. It's time."

"I can't do this anymore."

We stood in my tiny organized office, me leaning against the desk, arms folded across my chest, and Casey staring at the poster from an exhibit on the abstract painting from the sixties featuring Thomas Downing's *Red*, one of my favorite pieces in the museum, a grid of thirty-six hand-drawn but crisply rendered circles in red tones, from pink to burgundy, painted on a raw canvas. A study in color and form that was nearly perfect in my eyes. Casey stared at the poster as if his life depended on it, while I focused in on his statement. *I can't do what anymore?*

Casey Harper was not a guy who embraced confrontation; it was so much easier to get on a plane or hide behind a lens than to risk mixing it up emotionally. Plus, he'd developed a Teflon-likability that played well with clients, so easygoing and accommodating that you never noticed he always won. Over the years, what I had once considered as an asset, his laid-back style, had begun to annoy me. Tonight's vagueness was particularly tedious, as he was headed out of town for ten days. I felt enough confrontation for the two of us. "What are you talking about?"

Casey shifted on his feet. For the first time in our marriage, Casey looked scared. "What I mean is, I can't live like this anymore."

Now I felt the air sucking from my chest. "Like what?"

Without a word, he took out his phone, tapped it a few times, and held up the photo on the screen for me to see. It was two little boys. Adorable twins in matching striped shirts that looked to be in kindergarten, both smiling at the camera while sitting on their red bikes with training wheels. They looked exactly like Casey but with richer skin tone and wild curls. There could only be one explanation.

"These are my sons. Oliver and Will. They turn five in two weeks. They live in Eagle Rock, and no, I'm not with their mother anymore. But I was, for about six months." Casey had obviously re-hearsed his confession, because there was no stopping him. "And now I see the boys when I can, when it doesn't interfere with our lives. But it's time for me to be a real father to them. I'm sorry I lied to you. I have no excuse; I can't lie anymore."

I couldn't breathe. Last summer, after a couple too many drinks on the Fourth of July, I'd floated the idea of having kids like it was foreplay. Casey rejected me on all fronts, both for the sex and the baby making, gently suggesting I try water, aspirin, and sleeping in the guest room. The next morning, I was embarrassed (and hung-over) but not disappointed. I thought that's what we were supposed to do at this point in our marriage, but Casey's muted reaction made me realize that neither one of us was invested in becoming a par-ent. We never mentioned it again. Our marriage didn't look like it was pointing in that direction—at least that's what I surmised. But now, with Casey standing in front of me with his cell phone twins, I realized my ambivalence was a red flag. And his ambivalence was a white flag. He'd already surrendered to parenthood, and our mar-riage had been imploding long before this conversation.

I struggled to maintain an even tone. "How could you not tell me that you have children with another woman? Two children, in fact!" As if having one child out of wedlock was understandable but two crossed a line.

He hadn't rehearsed this part of the conversation. "I thought the reality would go away somehow. That I wouldn't get attached to them. But that was impossible."

For the past year, he'd been in demand, a new stage of his career, like he'd finally made it to the top of the heap in the competitive field of architecture photography. Alaska, Rome, Bangkok, Buenos Aires, and everywhere in between. He shot hotels, houses, offices, churches, all kinds of structures for editorial features, advertising, marketing. It was more glamorous than lucrative, but it was what he'd been trying to break into for years. Now he was rarely home. He'd even bought an extra rolling bag to keep packed, so he could simply swap out luggage without doing laundry between shoots. *Oh God, was he really even on location?*

"How deep is this? Did you even go to all those places to shoot? Or were you hiding out in Eagle Rock with the family?" I spit out.

He didn't answer. Instead, he actually hung his head. "I didn't want to hurt you; you've already been through so much already with your father. . . ."

"Do not equate this with my father."

"Fine. What I meant was that you'd been through a lot. In my heart, I knew the longer I let the situation go on, the worse it would get. But in my head, I couldn't find the words to tell you. I can't deny them anymore. They're my sons."

"I'm your wife." I saw it all unravel in my head, the decade we'd been together. The friends we had in town. "We've been married for almost ten years, and you've been lying to me for at least half that time."

"I know. I'm sorry." Casey's voice picked up in confidence, maybe even defiance. He was finally free of his double life, and he clearly felt liberated. *The asshole.* "I can't lie anymore."

"Well, good for you. You're Father of the Fucking Year." I squeezed my eyes closed to get rid of the image of my Fourth of July declaration and his rejection. How pathetic I must have seemed. "Now what, Casey? Now what? Do we start celebrating holidays with your second family? What's the name of my sister wife, anyway?"

"I know this is a lot . . ."

"It's not a lot, Casey, it's everything. Everything."

"I don't expect you to understand tonight." He was shutting down and shutting me out.

"Who knows? Do our friends know?"

Casey shrugged, and my heart sank.

I had to ask: "All of them? Amy and Dave?"

He nodded. Yes, Amy and Dave knew. Amy and Dave of the weekend-morning bagel tradition and vacations in the desert. Amy and Dave who gave birth last year to my godson, Frederick. Our dear friends knew that my husband had twins, and they showed up every Sunday with extra cream cheese and said nothing. I would deal with that incision later. "What's her name?"

"Marissa is the mother."

"Your old assistant? The one who charged your cameras? Oh my God." Beautiful Marissa Delgado with the dark curly hair, olive skin, and the best eyebrows in LA who traveled with Casey for several years, flying all over the world on assignments for shelter magazines. I recalled he complained about her not being able to schlep as much gear as the guys, but the extra feminist credit he earned by hiring a woman as his first assistant was worth it. Plus, she spoke several languages, including Portuguese and Spanish, and that was a bonus. I believed him when he said she was a little over-the-top but clients loved her. Turns out he must have loved her a little, too.

About five years ago she quit as Casey's assistant to focus on her own food photography. I'd spotted her credits in magazines and on websites. It never occurred to me that she could have quit for another reason other than bringing images of roasted grapes or blistered to-matoes to the Internet. Did I even know Marissa had kids? I don't think so. She would show up at various work-related holiday gath-erings over the years, barely making eye contact with me, saving all her energy for Casey or the other film and photo people in the room. That happened to me a lot with Casey's artsy friends, being looked over as a "non-pro," despite my museum job. I couldn't hire them, so I wasn't much use to them. Maybe the real reason she avoided me was because she was avoiding me. She had some nerve showing up at our house. But Casey had more nerve inviting her. "How great that she could find a sitter for your children when she came to the annual holiday open house. What the hell, Casey?"

"I'm sorry. Marissa and I are friends now, just co-parents, noth-ing more."

Co-parents? The nausea was gone, and I was starting to shake with rage, furious at his casual tone, as if we had some sort of open marriage agreement and this was a natural by-product of that ar-rangement. Casey continued, "If you want to do this together, then we can. The five of us can become a blended family. You, me, Will and Oliver, Marissa. She's fine with that. She thinks the more grown-ups in a child's life the better."

I didn't believe him for a second. A man who wants to create a cohesive blended family doesn't swing by his wife's office on a Friday night to drop a bombshell and then head out of town for two weeks. He thought I was an idiot. Or worse, he thought that I was the same lost twenty-two-year-old that he'd married. "That sounds like great parenting advice from the woman who slept with her boss, bore his children, and then lied about it for five years. Yes, the two of you make quite a team. I hope you're teaching Oliver and Will about your courage." My volume was escalating. *Could they hear me in the sculpture garden?* "And now what do I do? Announce to everyone I know that, surprise, I'm stepmother to five-year-old twins fathered by my husband on the side. No big deal. Maybe we can get the *New York Times* to announce it for us in the Style section. You know how they do those follow-up stories called Ten Years Later? They'd love this. Me, you, your former assistant, the kids, Granny Suzi Clements. One big happy family."

Casey seemed honestly shocked at my hostility. He started to back away. "Joan, please. I'm flying to Tokyo tonight, then on to Kyoto. I'll be back a week from Sunday. Think about it. We could let Will and Oliver into our lives in a meaningful way." He was back to his Dr. Phil script that Dave and Amy had probably written for him. "But if that's not what you want, if you can't let the boys into your life, then we'll need to end our marriage. I'm forty years old, and I need to be a man. Oliver and Will are my priority."

"Not me. Got it."

"You have no idea what's it's like to look into their eyes."

There was a large stone figure of Shiva from the eleventh century on a worktable next to my desk. I wanted to hurl it at his head. And so, that was it. We would end here, in the museum, where we started. What do you know? A cliché. "Please go."

In the cocoon of my office, with a glass of wine poured from the leftovers of last week's donor reception, I felt the anger fade to numbness, which dissipated to relief. Yes, I was relieved that Casey Harper wouldn't be the father of my children. He didn't deserve to be. He was a shadow of the man my father had been, a poor imitation and maybe I'd known that for a while. Honestly, I had. His defense that his deception was an attempt to protect me confirmed his character.

When my mother called me around six in the morning on September 11, 2001, and told me to turn on the TV, I had been sound asleep in my childhood bedroom in Pasadena. She was up in Ojai, at the weekend place, getting it ready for my father's return from a summer in Maine. He'd been there for months, working on a commission for a wealthy Boston tech executive who wanted a Blakely on the property of his Camden house. I'd been my father's research assistant on-site, having graduated from Smith that spring.

It was a fantastic summer, indulgent and invigorating. I was involved with my father's work on a daily basis and was finally gaining some understanding of his process. I dove deep into his notebooks, the beginning of what he hoped would be a full catalog of his work given to a deserving museum, most likely the WAM, right here in his hometown. My mother seemed to finally let go of the idea that I would become a model and accepted that my path would be more traditional, like a curator or gallery owner. Maybe even a writer. And, best of all, I was a hostess at a local restaurant and had a fast and furious summer romance with a local chef who swept me off my feet with seafood crudo and blueberry pie. When Labor Day rolled around, the relationship ended with a friendly high five and a gift of plum jam from the kitchen. It was as perfect as a summer could be.

As fall approached, we all headed back to Southern California on different schedules. I was off to various spots in Europe and Turkey to study the emerging Byzantine art market in Asia on a Watson Fellowship, a topic I'd cooked up to spend some serious time traveling, first in Istanbul and Hong Kong and then six months in Paris on somebody else's nickel. It was exactly what I'd planned during my junior year abroad with my friend Polly. At nineteen, we thought ourselves clever and sophisticated, gabbing endlessly over wine, bread, and fromage and acting like we'd invented Paris. Somehow, we'd return after graduation, we vowed. We'd share an apartment in Saint-Germain, trendier than our student dorm rooms. I'd conquer the art world and she'd write for *Vogue*. We cultivated an invincibility over the year that continued to strengthen during my final year at college as my plans fell into place. The world was our oyster. For a minute anyway.

My mother had moved on to the completion of my father's important commission, the Wallace Aston Museum. In addition, she was putting together her first small show of local artists in Ojai, a new hot spot in the California art scene. My father was set to return that day, after spending the weekend on a spiritual retreat with old friends, an annual tradition on the anniversary of his sobriety.

He'd boarded American Airlines Flight 11 in Boston. On the phone that Tuesday morning, my mother's voice registered pure terror, and when I saw the pictures of the North Tower, I understood why. "I think your father is on that plane," she whispered.

And he had been.

I met Casey a year after my father died. He was photographing the posthumous unveiling of my father's installation *Light/Break #47* in the garden at the WAM. I was there as the family representative to flip the switch, so to speak. As with many ceremonies after my father's death, I stood in while my mother stayed away. She had barely left Ojai since that day. I gave up my Watson Fellowship and Paris to become the de facto family mourner in an endless series of tributes and memorials.

Casey, the cute photographer trying to make a name for himself, was funny and solicitous, one of the few people at the time who made me feel normal, not like a cross between a helpless victim and a national symbol of grief. The courtship was three months. I was twenty-two and he was thirty-one, but I'd aged a decade in a single day, so it felt like we were at the same place in life. We married at Pasadena City Hall like my parents. I thought it was a tribute to them. My mother was suspicious.

After that, we settled into our lives as young marrieds. It was like I skipped the whole postcollegiate period of indecision and signed up for the full adult package: marriage, mortgage, couple friends with kids. Polly made it back to Paris, but the city slipped away for me. I wasn't the same person who had made all those plans over chilled Beaujolais or won the Watson.

When I was offered a job at the museum, I took it. It was a safe, easy career move that saved me from my grief. Casey focused on building his portfolio. I stepped right into my mother's shoes, managing his career like she had managed my father's.

No doubt, I was a lure for Casey's clientele, the only daughter of icon Henry Blakely and model-muse-manager Suzi Clements. The young, tragic Joan Bright Blakely.

The wine-soaked dinners we'd hosted for magazine editors at our house. The vacations in Santa Fe to drum up business. The constant socializing with his ad agency clients. Events where my parents' names invariably came up. *Your father did lighting for rock shows before his art career, right?* Yes. That paid the bills for a lot of years. David Bowie, Elton John, Kiss, Aerosmith, the Stones. *Is your mother still modeling for Ralph Lauren?* They are old friends, but my mother doesn't really get out much anymore. And she certainly doesn't model. *What was the name of your father's studio, where everyone who was anyone hung out?* The Motel because it had been an actual motel. Ever supportive, I answered their questions and told delightful anecdotes about my childhood memories of swimming in David Hockney's pool.

During our brief courtship, Casey had impressed me with his maturity, as if he truly understood his place in the world. Maybe it's because, up until that point, my romantic life had been limited to relationships involving boys who enjoyed beer, boys who enjoyed other boys but hadn't come to terms with that reality, like cute Paul, and the one chef in Maine. Casey seemed different, an artist with vision and a philosophy of life, well, at least a philosophy of his life, which is more than what most Amherst boys had. We'd sit on the porch of his run-down bungalow, drinking wine, not beer, and he'd explain that his work was temporal, limited, not art, but commerce. Photography was at its best when it captured a moment, but it failed at capturing a feeling. Leave that to the painters and sculptors and conceptual artists like my father. He'd take the paychecks and the precision of photography. His role was to translate an image, not an interpretation, and he was fine with that. I was undone by his self-awareness. I thought our life together would involve a million such discussions, a vibrant intellectual life as seductive as our sex life.

But it turns out, that was the only theory Casey had: one well-articulated position about photography. Other than that, he had nothing, like he never thought about the big picture at all. If I mentioned literature, he'd shrug it off, claiming that he "saw more clearly through a lens" than a book. Forget politics, economics, and religion. For a guy, he didn't even have a strong stance on indie music or steroids in sports. Other than an interest in food and a good eye for design, he bowed out of taking a position on anything that might involve conflict in the future. Mr. Neutral.

I guess that's what my mother meant when she let it slip that Casey lacked passion.

At parties, he'd trot out his one grand idea, expounding on image versus interpretation and the women would swoon, the men would nod, and the charade would go on. It got so that I had to leave the room when I heard him start his monologue. Is that why he slept with Marissa and, now I was pretty sure, countless others—because I was onto him?

My presence in the marriage was all for the benefit of Casey Harper, photographer, like a party trick in the flesh. I brought the kind of cachet that his safe Saint Louis upbringing couldn't match. And for almost the whole time, he'd had a second family—a warm, busy, happy family—tucked away less than five miles from our house.

I thought Casey was brave and strong. Turns out he was chicken-shit.

"Miss Joan? Are you okay?"

It was Javier, the head maintenance guy at the museum. He was pretty much the go-to guy for anything that was nonart related at the museum, from watering systems to excessive air-conditioning. We had a special bond because he loved my brownies and I constantly needed his help at my house, a midcentury architectural gem that was starting to show its age. During my childhood, my father had done everything in terms of home maintenance, a holdover from growing up in a small motel, from fixing toilets to changing light bulbs. I never appreciated my father's handiness around the house until the first time a pipe burst, and Casey panicked like a shipwrecked stowaway, more concerned about his photography gear than stopping the flow of water into the living room. His preppy upbringing in Saint Louis included lacrosse and crew but not chores. In retrospect, it should have been a red flag.

Fortunately for me, I discovered that Javier had a guy for everything. His brother ran a painting crew, his cousin did drywall, and his uncle's truck actually said "Senor Fix-It" on the side. Javier would know what to do. "I saw your husband leave and he wasn't happy."

After the long day, the scene with Casey, and a second glass of wine, I had no doubt my make-up was all over my face, along with a few stress tears. But the timing was perfect. "Javier, do you know a locksmith?"

"Yeah, I got a cousin in Montebello who does that."

"Can I get his number? I need the locks changed."

Chapter 2

The cool morning light flooded into my living room, illuminating the vast Sam Francis canvas on the dove-gray wall. Every morning since I can remember, I've looked at that painting, but it never looked more beautiful than on that sad, quiet Sunday morning after Casey's announcement. Sam had been a dear friend of my father's, and the painting was gift on the day of my birth. On the back of the canvas, the artist had scrawled, "For Joan Bright." The empty white space in the middle, the brilliant use of colors on the edges of the canvas. My father used to say, "It's your universe, Joanie. All brightness. Fill it up."

I thought that marriage and work would help me fill the hole, but it hadn't. My career, if you could call it that, was lackluster and accidental, not at all what I had intended on graduation day 2001. And now, it seemed my marriage was a sham almost from the start. Could the hole get any bigger? How would I ever fill it up? I was exhausted from the details of my life, the wills and contracts and agreements that had been a constant since my father's death. Starting Monday, there would be more clauses and tedium. I dreaded the next few months and I couldn't even imagine the next few years.

In the thirty-six hours since Casey's bombshell, I'd questioned every business trip he ever took, every supportive conversation we'd ever had, and every time he'd touched me in the last six years. A comment made several years earlier by my single friend Nina, a marketing executive who racked up as many frequent-flier miles as Casey, played over and over again in my head: "There's a lot of bad behavior on business trips. Those hotel lobby bars are the gateway to adultery. It's like everyone forgets their marital vows after a few glasses of whatever." Was that how it had started with Marissa? A couple of drinks after a long day of shooting and matrimonial amnesia set in? Or was she just more exciting than me, more exotic in every way with her Miami upbringing and her Cuban Brazilian heritage?

My mental torture led me to purchase and consume a considerable amount of red wine and wasabi-smoked almonds, the evidence of which cluttered the coffee table. It seemed the thing to do when your husband tells you he's a daddy and his twins are off to kindergarten in the fall. I can't say that I found the food and drink particularly helpful in crushing the humiliation of the situation, but the drama of stumbling through the grocery store, collecting my basket of heartache, and then curling up on the couch did kill some time: that first awful, awful day after a life-changing event when you realize that going back to yesterday is not an option.

On Saturday night, after the twenty-four-hour window had passed, I called my friend Tai from the museum, and he rushed over enough food for a football team. "It's my birthright," Tai explained. "We Japanese always bring food." That was true. Sometimes he'd show up with a single macaron, a perfect yet humble offering.

Tai handed me a postcard. It was an image of Joan of Arc with her famed quote, "I am not afraid. I was born for this." The visual was in the style of Keith Haring, and it was charming, perfect for my extensive collection of Joan ephemera, a collection that had started in childhood. My father had a thing for Joan of Arc, and he passed it on to me, along with the name. Postcards, children's books, prayer cards, any art with her image that I spotted in a bookstore or side-

walk art show. What had started as an inherited hobby became a ne-
cessity, a connective tissue to my father. The few friends that knew
about my collection were always on the lookout for me. "I found
this in the Village on my trip to New York, and I thought of you,
of course. Seems like you need some of that patron saint vibe right
now." I hugged him deeply.

Tai Takashita was a trusted confidant, a brilliant curator of contemporary art, with a serious demeanor and impeccable style. I knew
of Tai before I met him, as he was recognized as a leading authority
on the Light and Space movement and had actually written his PhD
dissertation on my father's work. We were friends from the second
we met in person at the WAM.

Tai lived his public life for his traditional and wealthy Japanese
family, who expected him to marry and have children someday, and
he lived his private life in private, sharing very little of his day after
he left the museum. But I knew it included a handsome "roommate"
named Anders and elegant dinners at home for the two of them,
as revealed to me late one night while we were in the final throes
of getting a show up. Occasionally I was invited to their downtown
apartment for drinks, and it was all very sophisticated, but we all
knew that the Takashita family clock was ticking, and soon Tai would
have to marry a woman and live a different life. There would be an
agreement and a wedding and some sort of life after that for Tai.
Until then, we never mentioned the inevitable.

As such, Tai had no use for indiscretion, and I needed his opin-
ion to back up my gut feeling.

"I know I should be heartbroken, but all I feel is stupid. Like I
am the biggest idiot, a total pushover. I want to punish him forever."

"You're too young to become this bitter. End it quickly and get
out ahead of the gossip," Tai said. "For lots of reasons, but mainly
because he doesn't deserve you. And, honestly, he never has."

It was exactly what I was thinking: I could never be a real family with Casey and his love children. Never. I would resent every moment of the next fifty years, having this ready-made family forced on me. I'd be an awful stepmother because I could never forgive Casey. I'd take that anger out on the kids, and they didn't deserve that. Not that I felt the slightest bit mushy about his sons, a fact which made me feel awful about myself, but I knew that I never wanted to meet them or spend one more minute in Casey's company. It was an extraordinary feeling of finality, a relief and a rush. I was done and it was over.

Moving on, to use a phrase I'd heard Casey say many times on set.

Now, in the light of my Sam Francis morning, I needed to pull myself together. It was my universe, all brightness. I'd start by cleaning the house. Then I'd call my lawyer. Maybe by Monday morning, I'd be ready to call my mother.

The doorbell rang around ten, as I had guessed it might. Another reason for pulling myself together. It was Amy.

Just two days ago, I might have found Amy's thrift shop boho ensemble to be a breath of fresh air in a world of cookie-cutter mommies. She had the excuse of being an animator; a gifted creative being whose whole world was a Technicolor dream, but my generosity of spirit had withered. *Grow up. You're somebody's mother. Enough with the overalls.* The thought made me smile to myself as I opened the door to the woman who had been my husband's friend, then mine, for the last decade. Maybe the New Joan would be Mean Joan instead of Cool & Lovely Joan. I decided to test the persona out a bit. "Amy, what a surprise. I thought you'd be bringing your bagels to Marissa's house from now on."

"Joan, please let me in so I can explain." She actually had a bag of bagels in her hand, but no kids and no Dave. Did she think we were going to break bread, shed some tears, and then have a laugh and a schmear?

I opened the door wider and let her into the front hall, as I'd done dozens of times before. But this would be the last time. "You can come in for a minute, but you can't possibly explain why you failed to tell me about the twins."

"I begged Casey . . ."

I cut her off. "Let's be clear: I do blame Casey, first and foremost. I have no words to describe my anger. But you, you've disappointed me more." It was harsh, but it was true. Because I'd married and settled down so young, I had lost touch with many of my high school friends in my early twenties. The girls I knew from Pasadena were young, unattached, and spending most nights at downtown happy hours or Hollywood screenings. They vacationed in Cabo and skied in Park City on the weekends. They lived uncomplicated lives, and my father's complicated death had made things very awkward between me and my hometown peers. Between me and most people, really. I went to a few parties and drinks occasionally, showed up at reunions and promised to keep in touch. I exchanged emails with a few old friends, but I didn't run with a crowd anymore. Possibly, the result of years and years of pauses after the words "I'm so sorry" made it too hard to connect to the past.

Amy and Dave were Casey's art school friends, an easy couple for us to hang out with. They were college sweethearts who moved out to Southern California together after graduation from the University of Minnesota to attend CalArts. They didn't know me before 2001, so they didn't come with the social baggage of having to mourn along with me. That was so appealing to me in 2002.

In terms of our backgrounds, Amy and I had nothing in common. She was from the Minneapolis suburbs, and her parents had jobs as a schoolteacher and a pharmaceutical salesman. Even her name, "Amy Asher," seemed so open and friendly that I never thought to second-guess her motivation for hanging out with me. But now, it was obvious that Amy was always going to be Casey's friend first, something

I hadn't seen before. "The hundreds of hours we've spent together. The walks, the coffee. I was there when your children were born. You were my friend, Amy. Casey cheated on me, but you lied every time you saw me."

Amy pushed back, "It wasn't lying. I promised Casey. And Dave. We all thought it was for the best, after your father and everything."

"Are you kidding me? Did you think it would break me? Am I that fragile to all of you?" The thought of the three of them sitting around discussing what was "best" for me was infuriating, as if their solid Midwestern upbringings, long-term relationships, and commercial art careers had been anything but predictable. They knew nothing about loss. Not a thing. "Don't pretend you had my interests at heart, Amy. My husband had an affair and there were consequences, serious ones, but you know what? Nobody died. We didn't lose thousands of people because Casey screwed his assistant."

She stammered, "Yes—yes, you're right."

"Do not mention Casey's infidelity in the same sentence as my father's murder in a terrorist attack." I rarely spoke about my father's death to friends or to Casey; I had a therapist for that. And I never used the 9/11 card as any kind of emotional weapon, but I was so tempted to let Amy have it, all of it. The shock, the terror, the nightmares. The pictures in my head of my father's last minute as he realized the horror of what was happening. (Though on my most positive days, I picture him absorbed in the paper, oblivious to the future.) Polite and stoic was the only way I could carry on for the first few years after it happened, with so many public appearances and statements demanded of me. Then polite and stoic became the way I carried on about everything. Did I appear fragile to them instead? Is that how other people saw me—my colleagues, my former classmates— as someone who needed special handling, as opposed to someone who handled the worst and made it through? Jesus, I hope not.

I felt a surge of sympathy for Amy, revealed as a pathetic sheep rather than the vital nonconformist I thought her to be. "You made your choices, Amy. And you all seriously underestimated me, which is astonishing to me. I think you should go."

"I'm so sorry, Joan. If I could do it all over again . . ."

"That's not really the way things work. Believe me," I said, imagining that a month from now, she'd be free of all guilt and be arranging playdates with Will and Oliver in their wreck of a backyard, where I'd spent hours painting with her kids. "Keep the bagels and don't worry about me. I'll be fine. Given the circumstances, I think it's best if you choose another godmother for Frederick." That's when Amy started to cry.

"We don't have to go there yet."

"I do, Amy. I do."

I was still shaking from Amy's visit when I heard the pitter-patter beats of a Skype call coming from my computer. My only digital pal was Polly, my oldest friend, who had made good on all our promises to return to Paris immediately after graduation. Evangeline "Polly" Davis, formerly of Pasadena, was now a glamorous Parisian resident married to a French lawyer name Jean-Michel de La Fontaine. The result was a name with so many syllables I had to snicker a little every time I saw it on her stationery: Evangeline Davis-de La Fontaine.

But she'd always be Polly to me.

Polly was living in the City of Light as a celebrity expat and international blogging sensation, creator of the site *Pasadena Meets Paris* with over a half million page views a month. According to an article in *Elle Decor*, it was the must-read blog for Americans abroad, Seven Sisters graduates, and midlife divorcées fantasizing about a year in Paris to rediscover themselves. Shockingly, I now found myself in more than one of those categories.

In high school at Sacred Sisters, Polly and I had been co-editors of the newspaper, an uneasy alliance with plenty of headbutting. We both had strong opinions, but not the same strong opinions, on what could be considered newsworthy stories. Polly broke new ground at the Catholic school by writing an op-ed about Eve Ensler's *Vagina Monologues*, pioneering the use of the word "vagina" in the newspaper and picking up the support of the nuns, several of whom had been anti-war activists in the seventies and now mainly sang protest songs with guitar accompaniment at Mass. Polly then made it a point to write about vaginas as often as possible for the remainder of her term as editor. I covered student council meetings; she covered body politics.

By senior year, she had checked out of the editor role once she made the Rose Court, ensuring that she would ride down Colorado Boulevard on New Year's Day, a mark of excellence and immortality that only a small circle of teenage girls achieved in Pasadena. She was one of the rare Black princesses in that era and made the most of her time in the sun, securing interviews with TV networks, scoring an internship at *Seventeen* magazine for the summer, and reeling in a debutante escort who went to West Point. After high school, we went off to rival women's colleges, keeping in touch but not going out of our way to see each other even though we were both in Massachusetts. When we discovered that we were on the same study abroad program, we rekindled our friendship in that way that Americans do abroad, out of desperation to speak English. But over the course of the year, Polly and I reached détente and then genuinely bonded.

After Wellesley, Polly established a thriving freelance career as a beauty and culture writer for a host of women's magazines with Paris as her hub. To fill the evenings while her then fiancé was studying, she started *Pasadena Meets Paris* as a personal blog focused on the basic how-tos of relocation, but her proper sensibilities, developed palate, and excellent sense of style quickly became the main focus of her writing. She was in early on the blogging gravy train. Her developed media instincts and unique writing voice, a sort of gushy socialite with warmth and a touch of superiority, served her well in the medium.

As her readership grew, Polly expanded her brand. She gave weekly tours of her favorite *Pasadena Meets Paris* haunts, spots where the cultured American woman would feel both a little daring and relatively comfortable, at the same time. She created a cottage industry out of her apartment in the 16th arrondissement, selling everything from the decorative pillows to linens to an extensive line of seasoned salt in her online store. Last time we'd spoken, a guidebook and app were on the way, plus she was in talks to partner with Target on a French-inspired product line.

Polly loved all things truly Parisian, especially wildly snobby Parisian, and she discovered an army of like-minded women around the globe. Why shouldn't Parisians be snobs? They live extraordinary lives, Polly argued. And Polly was cashing in on all that extraordinary.

When my father was killed, Polly delayed her return to Paris for months, essentially moving in with me to make sure I was fed and dressed, arriving at the right memorial service at the right time. It was the single greatest act of friendship I have experienced in my lifetime. This call may be the second. As soon as I picked up, she knew something was wrong. "Is this a terrible connection or does your face really look like that? What happened?"

There was no beating around the bush with Polly. "Casey has a whole other family. In Eagle Rock." The address alone made Polly shudder. As I gave her the blow-by-blow, she made the appropriate gasps and head shakes, tossing out the occasional "Merde."

When I finally took a break in my story, she was sympathetic. "The second family, it's so François Mitterrand. He, at least, was the president of France. Casey is not grand enough to deserve acceptance of this indiscretion. But that doesn't make it any easier for you, Joanie. I'm so sorry."

She never once said, "I told you so," because she'd also married young and after a short courtship, so I think she was genuinely rooting for us. Instead, she referred to our junior year abroad, and said, "Come to Paris. Please. We'll eat, we'll shop, we'll buy perfume, we'll gossip. It will be 1999 again." I appreciated the invitation, but it could never be 1999 again for me. Polly knew that, too. Her voice lowered, and her tone changed from life coach to old friend. "Listen, you've been through much harder stuff than this. You know that, right? You'll re-invent yourself. I know you will. You have plenty of time. But come to Paris."

"Soon. I promise. But I have a few things I have to take care of first."

"That's right, you do. Is his car in the garage? His custom shirts in the closet? You better light that merde on fire."

By the time Luther arrived that evening, the house was cleaned, the locks had been changed by Javier's cousin, and I'd packed the bulk of Casey's clothes into half a dozen cheap duffel bags I scored at a Big 5 sale years ago and hauled them to the garage. No fires, and none of these activities made me feel better, but I'd stopped feeling worse, so that was a small victory. I opened the door to Luther with a genuine half smile. Luther Mayfield was a family friend, attorney, connection to the past, and everything else in between: a rock, an uncle by choice, an adviser. He would know what I should do next. Luther would know.

Luther had been my father's next-door neighbor growing up, and they remained close until my father's death. My father's parents were ultra-strict Lutherans; he described them as formal and distant. He'd been an only child and, as such, gravitated to the lively, chaotic Mayfield household, where Luther was one of six boys. "Mrs. May-field taught me laughter," my father used to say.

Luther Mayfield was a gifted athlete, going to UCLA on a basketball scholarship in the golden John Wooden era, then onto UCLA Law. He knew nothing about the art world when my father started asking him about various contracts and such. Now Luther runs a successful management company for artists, actors, and athletes, taking on very few clients and providing them his full attention. Like my own father, Luther never strayed too far from his old neighborhood, creating a mentoring program that's been credited with lowering the high school dropout rate and increasing the number of kids that go to college from one of the roughest areas of Pasadena.

It was Luther that had insisted on the prenup for Casey and me. Add Luther to the growing list of people who knew that I was marrying a poor, poor imitation of my father. I'd given him the short version of the situation on the phone, so I skipped any repeat details. And I'd told myself not to get emotional in front of Luther. "How complicated is this going to get?"

"You're well protected, so it shouldn't be complicated at all, at least on my side. The house, the artwork, any IP related to your dad, that's all in the Henry Blakely Trust. He can't touch any of that. But he does get to keep half the Motel, as per the amendment to the agreement five years ago."

Goddamn, of course, five years ago when the twins were born! That's why Casey insisted that his name go on the deed when he pitched reviving the Motel, arguing that he deserved a piece of it for all the sweat equity and word-of-mouth marketing he'd be doing. That's why he oversaw every detail of the project to make it just right, a redevelopment hit. And that was the real reason Casey didn't tell me about the boys right away. Casey never would have walked away from his one chance to get a tiny slice of the Henry Blakely pie. Back then, I thought he had stored away some resentment from the initial prenup, and I wanted to smooth over any ill will by giving him half the property. A show of confidence in our future, I thought. But Casey wanted the Motel for *his* future, not ours. Any measure of acceptance I'd achieved by stuffing his extensive supply of Thomas Pink linen shirts into a duffel bag had disappeared. I repeated the facts slowly back to Luther: "Five years ago, when his children were born."

Luther nodded. It hadn't taken him as long to get there as it had taken me. "You got it. And now that he has heirs, if we try to nullify the agreement, I'm sure he'll push back," Luther said. He represented a host of athletes and actors, so he'd seen every complicated paternity situation known to mankind. "Couple of options: You buy him out or he buys you out. Or a third party buys you both out, which will be my recommendation if you want to move on, clean break. How's his cash situation? Do you know?"

I shook my head. "No, we always kept our finances separate. At least I did one thing my lawyer told me to do. None of my money was used to support his other family, so good for me!" Luther gave me a half hug. "But he has been working a lot lately. He doesn't tell me about his fees, but I think he's doing okay."

Luther nodded. "Another reason for the timing. His income is secure. I hate to admit it, but he did a good job reviving that place. He has added value. You'll find a buyer for sure."

A cultural historian had once called the Motel "an iconic headquarters for the vibrant Southern California art scene in the 1970s and early '80s." For my dad, it was his childhood home. My father had inherited his family's tidy, modest Mountain View Motel at age twenty-five, the year he lost his mom to a stroke and then his dad to lung cancer. The place was named for its foothill location and spectacular views of the San Gabriel Mountains. He quickly abandoned the idea of running it as an actual motel and set it up as studios and living spaces for himself and his fellow artists.

Over the years, with Luther's help, my father made some smart real estate moves and acquired an abandoned Department of Public Works garage next door and extended the footprint of the Motel to almost a full city block. Casey had spent three years renovating the building and bringing it back to my father's original intent, as studio space for struggling artists. Then he added a small gift shop and coffee bar that brought in actual income. And he thought to put in a ballpark-style concession stand that he used to host monthly pop-up restaurants, featuring young local chefs, that was a hipster magnet. I had to admit, the Motel under Casey's direction had been very successful.

The renovation put Casey on the map as a man with vision, a worthy successor to my father, though I knew he was limited. I should have paid more attention. I thought it was helpful he had a hobby, and secretly, I was thrilled that he was picking up the family mantle. I encouraged him to spend all his free time there, impressed he was finally getting his hands dirty doing physical labor. But now I wondered if he really was doing the hands-on renovations or if he was off playing daddy and planning his exit strategy? I tried to be un-emotional, but the realization of Casey's level of deception shocked me. "Oh, Luther, how can I tell my mother?"

Luther responded with the same wide berth he always afforded anything about my mother. "She'll understand. She never liked that place! It's why she insisted your father buy this house. Suzi Clements was not going to spend her life in a motel." We both laughed, a release. "If you want to buy him out, you might need to sell the Larry Bell in the bedroom. I think he gave it to your dad instead of a year's rent," Luther quipped. Most of the artwork hanging on the walls of my house was "rent," except for the Dennis Hopper series of photos. Those definitely covered "damages."

"I don't want any more contact with Casey. I can't."

"I think that's understandable. We'll reach out from our office to a family law attorney who I've worked with."

"Family law? Is that a euphemism for a divorce attorney?"

"Yes."

"I feel like I lost a decade of my life. I don't know how it happened." I was bone-tired, on the verge of tears.

"Things work out best for those who make the best of the way things work out," Luther quoted.

"John Wooden?"

He nodded. "It's true. You won't get the last ten years back, but you'll do something with the next ten. But take some time. And go see your mother."

Chapter 3

The drive to Ojai from Pasadena took about an hour and a half, just enough time to lose confidence, regain confidence, and then lose it again before seeing my mother. It's not that she was difficult—quite the opposite. My mother practiced acceptance every day, at least that's what she told me dozens of times on the phone, when she's called me after her hike to Meditation Mount, an Ojai landmark. "It is what it is," she'd say in response to almost any whine I might offer. Honestly, it was starting to drive me crazy, her ability to let go of conflict or pain. She used to be fiery, fully engulfed in the hustle and bustle, but now she accepted the bad with the good like it was her spiritual duty. If I'd learned anything over the last decade, it was that everyone has his or her own way of coping. Her retreat to Ojai, a small, lush artists' colony wedged against the mountains in between LA and Santa Barbara, had been her first gesture of acceptance that her life would never be the same after that day in September.

I knew I had to tell my mother the whole horrible story in person, especially the part about the Motel. It wouldn't be fair to tell her that over the phone. Casey's ten-day trip to Asia gave me a ticking clock, as if I had to have the whole thing settled before he touched down again, like a game show quest. Thinking about the tasks I'd have to accomplish like a simple To Do List (Change Locks; File

Divorce Papers; Admit to Family and Friends I've Been an Idiot) was the only way I could plunge ahead with life; otherwise, I couldn't keep the images of his other life at bay, the life where he already had everything I thought we wanted together. *When did he buy the boys those red bikes? Did he celebrate Christmas with them that year he told me he had the flu and was too sick to drive to Ojai? What did that mean, 'I'm not with their mother anymore'? When did that end? Or was he lying? Yes, he was definitely lying.*

That morning, I'd called work and had a short conversation with Caterina at the museum, explaining, "I have a few things I have to take care of this week, so I'm not coming in. Tai will cover anything that needs covering." Fine, she answered quickly, without asking any follow-up questions. Did Caterina already know about Casey's other family? She was so connected to everyone and everything, it wouldn't surprise me if some art director or stylist Casey had worked with had spilled the story to Caterina. How was I going to get my side of the story out? I'd deal with telling her and everyone else in town later, like Thursday. But first I had to break it to my mother, Suzi Clements Blakely—model, muse, photographer, manager, activist, widow.

My mother, born Susannah Claire Clements, was the daughter of a San Francisco lawyer and a socialite, a term that truly applies to my grandmother Adele, who still enjoys a gala and has her hairdresser come to the house on Nob Hill three days a week. In the early seventies, my mother headed off to Barnard to study art history and bite the Big Apple. According to her personal mythology, moments after registering for her freshman year, she was discovered by Eileen Ford in a coffee shop on the Upper East Side. A modeling contract quickly followed, and then she landed her first big Revlon ad about six months later. She was touted as "an American Catherine Deneuve," tall, blond, and patrician with a veneer of sophistication. By the time she was twenty-three, she was the face of the newly launched Lauren perfume, beginning a relationship with Ralph Lauren that extends to this day.

According to the story I'd heard a million times, she dropped out of Barnard after her freshman year and spent the rest of the decade traveling, modeling, and, as she told me on my eighteenth birthday, "doing many other things you'll never know about, some of which I hope you experience yourself. It was a singular time." Fittings in Milan, album cover shoots in Morocco, restaurant openings in London. There were lead singers and Kennedys and *Glamour* covers, but my mother got out before she got old. She picked up a camera in order to have something to do at parties other than drugs and started taking pictures, like an uber-insider photojournalist of the *Rolling Stone* magazine set. The camera gave her the freedom to approach anyone and the cover to hide behind the lens.

She met my father on what was supposed to be a long weekend in LA for Rod Stewart's birthday. She and another model, Annette from Sweden, made the trip from NYC. The birthday party was a dud, so they headed over to the Motel, an unlikely spot for artists and musicians to gather in suburban Pasadena, a stone's throw in distance but a million miles away in attitude from the Hollywood Hills scene. It was Annette who wanted to meet the owner of the Motel, artist Henry Blakely. "He's a genius. He does lighting design for big rock shows and then does his own stuff. And he works out of this old motel that his parents used to run. I hear it's crazy day and night."

But it was my mother that caught Henry Blakely's eye, not Annette. As she tells the story, "One hour after I met him, Henry told me I couldn't leave him and that was that."

That was in 1979, and my mother had stayed in Pasadena twenty years. When they met, Henry Blakely was a Light and Space artist, respected within his own community but not well-known outside the art world's elite because of the ephemeral nature of his work. You couldn't hang a Blakely on your wall like a Warhol. He was as much of a craftsman as an artist, building scale models of the light boxes and projection devices for each project that would later be sent to fabricators for giant versions. The studio was filled with metal cutters, welding tools, lathes, a wall of saws. He created his own filaments, experimenting with custom crafted paints and fabrics to get the reflections right. He conceived, designed, built, and installed every project with care.

Fifteen years older than Suzi and from a different world entirely, he was broad and barrel-chested, looking more like a blacksmith than a sensitive artist. He told Suzi that night that he was headed off to Paris for a year to stage what would become his breakout project, *Joan Bright & Dark*, a guerilla-style exhibit illuminating various public artworks that featured Joan of Arc, a commentary on war and faith in the streets of the City of Light. As he described his vision of "Art for the People" to my mother, in the concrete courtyard of the Motel, Steely Dan in the background, she was entranced. "In that moment, I knew one part of my life was over and another had begun," she told Barbara Walters once in an interview. My parents married at Pasadena City Hall three weeks later and set off for France. I was their honeymoon baby. They named me Joan Bright. Joan Bright Blakely.

By the time they returned from Paris, my father's reputation outside the art world was cemented. Henry and Suzi knew how to draw the crowds to them. The Motel became the place to congregate, create, and crash for artists, rock stars, and beautiful people of all stripes, despite its less than cool location in a modest Pasadena neighborhood.

The stories were legendary and well-documented, mostly by my mother's black-and-white photos that became pieces of art themselves, shown at galleries in LA, New York, and Paris in the mideighties as a series known as *Motel #1, Motel #2 and Motel #3*. She published a successful coffee table book by the same name, a collection of photos I knew as well as my own family photo album. When I was younger, I would page through the book over and over again, memorizing the famous faces. My father with a young Jamie Lee Curtis and Patti Hansen. The entirety of Aerosmith hanging out with Dyan Cannon and John Travolta. Ed Moses and Joan Didion playing pool with then rock star, now recluse Peter Beckman of the Ravens. Dennis Hopper, Carrie Fisher, and Ed Ruscha lighting a bonfire in the parking lot. And my favorite, a self-portrait of my parents kissing in my father's studio with Paul McCartney strumming on a guitar in the background. The photos looked like location stills of the coolest movie ever shot, except it was real.

Her natural poise and grace combined with everything she had learned in her time in the limelight became the building blocks for taking my father from visionary to successful working artist. Henry Blakely became almost a household name, thanks to my mother's acumen and his talent for thinking big. They didn't quite cash in like Christo, with T-shirts and coffee mugs, but all the more reason why my father's commissions were so highly coveted.

After September 2001, my mother had either thrown off the shackles of her previous existence—or thrown in the towel. There were no more runways or openings, deals to be made, photos to pose for in a vintage Halston number. Gone were the blinding flashes going off as she made her way into an AIDS benefit or a late-night dinner in Beverly surrounded by famous friends. Occasionally, she popped up in a "Where Are They Now" kind of article where my father's death was the main story or some fashion blogger posted a tribute to her as a style icon, but she never gave interviews anymore. For her, there was the quiet of Ojai and the area's famous lavender fields and the occasional white-wine-in-a-plastic-cup reception for a local painter she mentored. She retained a small, loyal circle of friends from the old days, but she lived her new life on a different scale.

My mother was only forty-eight when my father was killed, but as she liked to say, "I had a big life, then I chose to have a small life."

The full retreat from public life after his death may have been surprising to those who only saw my mother in her shining public persona, but not to me or to her close friends, who knew her complete devotion to and dependence on my father. All it took was one random photo on Page Six to send my mother to Ojai for good. About four months after my father's death, she was walking out of a Los Angeles restaurant and Jack Nicholson happened to be exiting the same place at the same time. A paparazzo's camera caught the two of them in the same frame. The *Post*'s headline read "A Merry 9/11 Widow?"

And, with that, she was done. No more limelight and no more public appearances, no more possible Page Six headlines. Though she later said to me, as she rolled her eyes, "As if I would ever date an actor."

The Ojai house was a bright, airy Spanish-style retreat that my parents had purchased before the movie stars moved down from Santa Barbara and invaded the town. My father rarely worked on a project in Ojai, save sketching and grinding out details in his notebook, but my mother's darkroom had always been there, out in a converted barn that was half art studio and half yoga studio. They loved spending long weekends nestled away at the end of the long driveway, shaded by eucalyptus, reading, walking, and talking by the fire until midnight. My mother instituted a "No Guests" rule in Ojai; after so many years of running a motel, she wanted nothing to do with overnight guests. You could come for dinner or drinks, but you had to stay in town.

I hated it as a teenager. It felt like the ends of the earth and the last thing I wanted to do on the weekends was go for a hike or have a glass of iced tea on the front porch. *Kill me now*, I used to say dramatically every time I was forced to spend more than one night there. But, of course, now I appreciated the serenity. The gravel crunched as I made my way down the driveway and my mother stepped out onto the porch, as if she'd been listening for my car.

Now, in her late fifties, my mother looked great, as always. Trim, fit, and pulled together, a testament to aging gracefully through diet, exercise, good genes, and very expensive clothes. Her style was more indicative of her San Francisco roots than her Ojai address. She hadn't given up her waistbands and tailored shirts in favor of gauze skirts and flip-flops. She favored clean, simple American designers in timeless styles. She could still wear her hair long, and thanks to expensive highlights, it was still blond. Her skin showed enough lines to look natural, but not so many as to look old. I'd inherited most of her physical attributes—the height, hair, and coloring— but only a fraction of her confidence. As I took in the visual of my mother, coffee cup in hand, dressed in denim and cashmere, casually waving from the front porch, it easily could have been a print ad, but instead, it was her life. Even in the darkest days after my father's death, she got up, got dressed, and put on eye cream and lip color. When I was little, I thought she was the most glamorous mother in the world. I still thought the same thing.

"Joanie." And that was all it took. I felt the tears the minute my mother put her arms around me.

The day had given way to evening and the cups of tea to a few glasses of wine, but I'd gotten it all out. The second family, Casey's calculated renovation of the Motel, and my signing it over to him, the sick feeling that ran through my whole body at the thought of having the awful story out there for the public to judge. From the ups and downs of my job to Casey's annoying habit of rinsing out the milk cartons and leaving them on top of the counter instead of simply putting them in the recycling bin, I didn't stop until my voice started to get hoarse. I even managed to take a swipe at Amy's overalls: "She's a grown woman and her clothes have painted flowers on them." I realized I spent so many years not talking about what really mattered in an effort to make other people more comfortable, that to finally get it out was exhausting and liberating. I ended my monologue with, "I have nothing to say to Casey. Not one thing. Isn't that odd?"

"No, not at all." At first, my mother listened, poured, and offered only sympathy. Now, she was ready to judge. "The man you thought you married left the building six years ago when the assistant entered the picture. What kind of a man has an entire family hiding in the wings? Who knows what he's really like now?"

"I don't even feel that bad about never seeing Casey again. I'm relieved. Like, thank God that chapter of my life is over."

My mother's blue eyes welled up. I knew where she was headed. "You had the opportunity to make a good choice. Be grateful you're in a position to do that." I knew she was referring to her sudden widowhood, and my eyes teared up, too.

My mother took my hand and we sat in quiet, until my mother started to laugh, slightly at first and then a roar.

"What's so funny?"

Her eyes lit up and she said, "Henry Blakely dies in a terrorist attack, and then his daughter spends the next ten years married to an asshole that has a whole other family with a whole other woman and somehow walks away with a chunk of the Blakely legacy. And his widow barely leaves the house, hasn't interacted with a straight man except her lawyer in a decade, and can't remember the last time she felt alive. Is that what's happening here?"

My punchiness matched hers, and I started to laugh.

Suzi was on a roll. "We're a sad, sad pair. What's wrong with us? What would your father think of us here, holed up in Ojai, drinking wine, and crying over some man?"

Then I started to laugh even harder. "What *is* wrong with us?"

We laughed like we hadn't in ten years, like we were expressing some kind of demon from our systems, the kind of demon that drags its victims down in a time-lapse drowning and then breaks their necks when they are just about out of air. It felt fantastic. We gasped and snorted. My stomach muscles hurt, and tears sprang from my eyes, the good kind, not the bad. I didn't even mind not being able to breathe.

Finally, my mother managed, "We have got to get over ourselves and get on with it."

I knew what she meant.

The next morning, I had a hangover, from everything, not the least of which was the laughing jag that resulted in sore abdominals. But I felt focused, liberated. I wandered into the kitchen, looking for coffee and finding my mother. "Good morning," I said, aiming for chipper.

The big farmhouse table in the kitchen was covered with letters, some hand addressed, beaten up, and yellowed, others in large manila envelopes with impressive seals on the outside. I poured a cup of coffee into the hand-thrown mugs my mother had used forever and added milk from the matching pitcher. "What's all this?"

"Getting over myself and getting on with it." My mother sat at the table in a sweater the color of oatmeal. Underneath was a light blue T-shirt that matched her eyes. She had on her reading glasses and a touch of lip color. She looked a little tired herself this morning. "Fan mail. Queries. Requests. People wanting to know about Henry Blakely. His work, his papers. Some are academics, others are fans, I guess. For the first few years, I swore I was going to read them and answer them all. But I couldn't. I read a couple, but then I couldn't open any more, there were so many. I tossed them into a plastic tub, then another tub. The guilt is unbelievable. It wakes me up at night, but I haven't done anything. I guess today's the day I start going through them."

I had no idea. I had gotten a few, mostly through the museum and all from book editors or writers looking for a quote or two, but nothing like the pile on the kitchen table. "How do they find you?"

I picked up a legal-size envelope and read the address. Suzi Blakely, General Delivery, Ojai, California.

My mother shrugged. "I guess people know I live in Ojai. The post office knows I live here."

I opened one from a small college in the Midwest, a query by a senior doing a thesis on my father's project in Central Park when he illuminated Belvedere Castle with enormous brilliant multicolored flares that he himself had handcrafted and giant projections, a technology way ahead of its time. The date on the letter was from three years earlier. "I hope this kid didn't fail his thesis. He wanted to know about the significance of the ratio of red flares to orange flares in the *Castle Burning* project. Good work, Mom. I think we can assume he didn't win the Art History prize at Wittenberg."

The former Barnard art history major didn't skip a beat. "I bet the kid's still there because he never graduated, thanks to his poorly researched thesis. Should I call the school and tell them that Henry Blakely always worked in prime numbers, and anyone writing a thesis on his work should know that? He was a mathematician first, artist second. Use a little algebra and you'll figure out the significance of the ratio of red to orange."

My mother was back. "Maybe you shouldn't answer these letters if we'd like to keep Dad's reputation intact. You know, as a generous man and humanitarian," I said. At times, my father was as intense and moody as the next gifted artist, and the last thing he wanted to do was share about his work with undergraduates. But thanks to my mother, he managed to pull himself together to be social and socially conscious when he needed to be. "It would be a shame if all those years of image management on your part went down the drain."

"You're right. Yesterday, I was still too sad to open these. Today, I'm too cynical." Plus, she'd never have the stamina to get through all the letters. My mother was a doer, not a writer. She'd be more likely to rearrange the stacks of mail into piles and photograph them than respond to them in writing.

"I'll hire someone. There's a young woman at the museum, she's one of those unpaid interns getting her masters at UCLA. Her name's Kiandra Douglas. I'm sure she can use the money, and she's sharp, really sharp. The least she can do is open them and see if there's anything significant in any of them. I'll make sure she puts together some kind of generic response that will work for most of the letters. We can send people to the foundation website, recommend the few good books on him. Maybe suggest that awful movie," I suggested, referring to an ill-conceived film starring John Cusack as my father and Robin Wright as my mother, based on a *Vanity Fair* article about the Motel. I could only watch about fifteen minutes of it.

"We should get more wine and rent that movie tonight to do a final purge," my mother responded. "Honestly, Joanie, thank you. These letters have been weighing me down. You better warn her, though, I'm sure there are quite a few from wackos and 9/11 deniers. I can't handle the conspiracy theorists." Weariness worked its way back into her voice again. "And honestly, some of the details about you father's work are starting to dim. Without his notebooks . . ."

"I know." We both knew. In many ways, the loss of the notebooks was almost as tragic as the loss of my father. Henry Blakely worked out the details of his projects in densely filled notebooks over the decades of his career. As he prepared to turn over his papers to a museum, probably the WAM after the completion of his commission there, my father had begun to go through the notebooks. To get them in shape, he'd told me, and to remind him of all he'd accomplished.

It had been my job in the summer of 2001 to help with the notebook project while he was on location in Maine, cataloging the contents of each for the fifty-plus binders. It was fascinating work, to see the evolution of his creative process, the advanced geometry, the painstaking design work that went into every project, from the epic public spectacles like *Joan Bright & Dark* and *Castle Burning* to smaller works, like *Light/Break #1*, which consisted of a single high-intensity circle of light in a closet-size room. To me, the notebooks were the documentation of his genius; to him, they were everything. The closer he got to turning them over to a museum, the more protective he was of the notebooks. He was afraid to let them out of his sight, so he checked the trunk containing the notebooks onto his flight that September morning, not trusting them to an airfreight company.

Or so it seemed, because the notebooks had disappeared.

For weeks after the attack, I held on to the irrational hope that the notebooks had survived, as if paper stood a better chance against a fireball than flesh. I could comprehend (barely) that my father was gone, but not his work. My father scribbling in the notebooks was my single strongest memory of him, more than any accolade or opening. He was always working, thinking, creating at the breakfast table, at the park where I played, late into the evening when I'd come home from a night out. His notebooks were everything. How could they not have survived?

My hope gave way to hysteria. Any day now, we'll get a call from authorities to tell us they've found the trunk, I thought. Before Thanksgiving 2001, when I finally had the guts to get on a plane, I flew back to Boston, thinking I could track down the trunk. Maybe he shipped it? Yes, I convinced myself, he'd shipped the notebooks, and the trunk was simply lost, like so many things in the chaos after 9/11. I was sure the trunk was out there, still in existence. Maybe he took it to FedEx or UPS before he got on the plane and sent the trunk home all on its own, instead of checking it onto the flight. A college friend picked me up, and we drove around to shipping sites and post offices from Boston to Maine, like amateur private investigators asking desperate questions about whether they remembered a man with a booming voice and salt-and-pepper hair shipping a trunk on September 10. Nobody did, of course.

I even tracked down a few of the people that had been on retreat with my father before he boarded the plane, a collection of artists, writers, and musicians who supported one another through sobriety for years, but none of them remembered seeing the trunk of notebooks at any time during their weekend in the Berkshires. But they all sobbed and told me how much my father had meant to them over the years as they kept the demons at bay. "A rock," one Pulitzer Prize–winning playwright said to me, as he choked back tears. "An absolute rock."

Only then, on the nearly empty flight home, as airports were ghost towns that fall, did I finally accept that the notebooks and my father were gone. I came back to Pasadena, found a grief counselor, and threw myself into the WAM project, the last *Light/Break* that would ever be created, taking up where my mother had left off, as she was too devastated to care if the commission ever got finished. Working with my father's assistants off the plans that the museum had on hand, and by memory from the discussions I'd heard over the summer, we completed *Light/Break #47* for the museum's garden. I met Casey the night the exhibition opened.

I'd never told my mother about the notebook chase. She thought I was at a friend's wedding, a nonsensical excuse she never questioned. No point in mentioning it now, either. The memory only stood to remind me how much time I felt I'd lost. Gathering up the letters, I told her, "Let's put them all in a box. I'll take care of it. I'll have some free time now, you know, because I have no husband and no future."

"Yes, that does free up the hours," she agreed. Before last night, I would have felt terrible about saying such a thing, but now we could both smile. My mother poured me some more coffee and said, "You know, I was thinking, you should just go someplace. Take a few years off, go back to school. Do you think you could cash in on that fellowship you won? You should go to Paris! You haven't been back since college, you lost all of that. Go. To. Paris!"

"That's what Polly said, too. I'll think about it. I need to get a lot of things in order."

"Stop! Don't think. Go! Take that time you never got when you were twenty-one. You got cheated. Your twenties should have been much more fun. Make your thirties what your twenties should have been! Throw some caution to the wind! Let life come to you." I know my mother viewed her wild twenties as some sort of sacred rite of passage that everyone deserved. Now that I'd solved her Letter Guilt, she seemed determined to repay the favor.

But I knew time didn't work like that. You don't get a do-over on loss. "I will get there. I promise. But in my own time." Besides, even driving to Ojai had felt like a journey of a thousand miles. How could I pack up and start over somewhere? "But, the house . . ."

"Please, it's a house. And, technically, it's *my* house; I should be the one worrying about the HVAC system, not you. I can take care of it for a few years, and then we can decide what to do with the real estate and the paintings and everything." I knew she meant the memories, too. We'd both delayed so many decisions in favor of emotional expediency. "I wouldn't mind moving back to Pasadena. I miss . . ." She hesitated. "Life."

I was happy to hear her say that, thinking about how my father described her need to see and be seen as combustible. "Let me think about it. Truly. I feel like I need to get through the next six days before Casey gets back from Tokyo. If I'm still standing and can still show my face in public by next Monday, then maybe I will go someplace."

My mother's expression turned very dark. "Casey's lack of courage will come back to haunt him. He'll pay more for this more than you."

"What do you mean?"

"Nobody admires a liar. What he did to you is all about him. Put the truth out there, and then disappear for a little bit. His reputation will be far more damaged than yours." My mother's mind was working on the kind of strategic level I hadn't seen in years. "I had an idea this morning on my hike. You remember my friend Candy?"

"Of course." Candy McLean was a former Rose Queen, disgraced soon after her star turn down Colorado Boulevard by a few tasteful, but half-nude photos in the "Women of the Ivy Leagues" edition of *Playboy*, the kind of photos that high school girls now routinely post on social media without the blink of an eye. But in the late eighties, the photos led to a social purgatory for Candy in Pasadena. She rebuilt her reputation as an on-air TV anchor in LA, donating her emcee skills to every charity event in town as penance. Unfortunately for Candy, she lost her last bit of collagen at exactly the same moment that HDTV came into being. It could have been a career-ending coincidence, but Candy was smart, and she saw the future: online gossip. She left TV and became a society reporter and web entrepreneur.

Her website, CandysDish.com, had started as a Pasadena society page but quickly gained traction by including favorable puff pieces on the Hollywood elite, both those in front of the cameras and the bigwigs behind the scenes, like agents, studio executives, and producer types. My story, at the intersection of society, the arts, and personal tragedy, was exactly the sort of reportage at which Candy excelled. "She's the perfect person to put this story out there in the public for you. She'll be discreet behind the scenes and kind in print. And now, this week, before Casey gets home and has any chance to speak to the media."

I had a hard time envisioning Casey speaking to the media, given his role in the situation. Then again, he did seem confident in his convictions, like he was doing the right thing, and, thanks to my support and name, he had more of a career to protect than I did. But I had no idea where to begin. "I'm not sure I can sit in front of someone and say, 'I've invited you here today to talk about my crap husband and his other family I didn't know about until last week.' I'm not ready."

"Of course not. But this conversation won't be about that, it will be about something bigger," my mother said. She had clearly been doing a lot of thinking. "I'm getting all kinds of interview requests for the tenth anniversary. Are you?"

Yes, I was. The *New York Times*, *LA Times*, CBS News, *Good Morning America*—almost every major news outlet and a bunch of documentarians had requested an interview as they "look back" at the attack ten years later. September was still months away, but producers were lining up their segments. They all promised a sober, reflective tone that would be a tribute to our loved ones lost that day. I hadn't even responded to the emails. Like the letters on the kitchen table, the prospect of reliving the events of the day on a national scale filled me with dread and guilt. "Yes, but what does that have to do with this?"

"I think we should tell Candy you'd like to talk to her in advance of events, a chance to catch up with you and what's happened since that day. But mainly, about what's happening with you in the future. Then you slip in the fact that you are newly single, your life has changed abruptly again, but you have a bright future."

"I do? Have a bright future?"

"We'll make up something. Come on, you're not my daughter for nothing. I spent years staring into a lens pretending to be somebody else—somebody stronger or sexier or sluttier. You can fool Candy for five minutes."

Flickers of the Suzi Clements Blakely of yore. I liked it. And she was right about the sooner, the better before the reality of the situation really set in. "Fine. Can you set it up? But I do have to tell the museum first."

"Of course. I'll call her and catch up first, then debrief her on the situation and suggest a lunch between the two of you. Sound good?"

Nothing sounded good. "Super."

"Well, this has been a productive day already." My mother stood up and began gathering the letters backs into the tubs from whence they'd come. "How about a massage at the Inn?" My mother's one indulgence, besides good clothes, was lavish spa days at the Ojai Valley Inn and Spa, a nearby oasis of tranquility. "Lavender Sugar Body Polish or Rosemary Sage Scrub?"

Chapter 4

I'd sat in dozens of hotel bars by myself. In the early days of our marriage, when Casey was trying to transition into travel and architecture photography after an unsuccessful run at lifestyle work, I'd travel with Casey on assignment if my schedule allowed. The cities were domestic, usually West Coast, and the hotels were modest, but I used the time to slip into galleries, artists' studios, picking up pieces I liked.

In the evening, I'd sit patiently in the hotel lounge, waiting for him to wrap for the day. I never minded the wait. I was comfortable alone, cloaked in anonymity and nursing a beer while taking in the comings and goings of fellow guests. At the time, I adored my husband, and his career made me feel worthwhile somehow. A couple of nights in a Courtyard Marriott in San Diego seemed like a real perk.

When had I stopped traveling with Casey? About the time Marissa started working with him, I recalled. The newness had worn off, and my work at the museum intensified. He was getting better gigs, but so was I. My work took me to Munich, Venice, Abu Dhabi, and Dallas, all great cities with world-class hotels and bars perfect for people-watching.

But this was the first time in years I'd sat in a hotel bar alone and was actually *alone* alone. What the hell was I doing here sitting at the Tap Room at the Langham Pasadena drinking a gimlet by myself?

Tai, who had been checking in with daily calls and texts, had promised to meet me at the bar to shepherd me through the next few hours. "Like an AA sponsor. But with drinks." Unfortunately, he begged off at the last minute, something about his sick grandmother, an oft-used excuse. I'm sure she was sick, but does the whole family have to rush to her side every time she coughs? I'm the one who needed a minder, not his *obaasan*. I'd just have to go it alone.

I was hiding out. My ten-day countdown to exterminate all signs of Casey Harper from my life was over. A text from Tokyo informed me that Casey would be home around eight that night and he wanted to talk. *You're about five years too late for that conversation, buddy.* When he arrived at the house tonight, he'd find the locks changed and a manila envelope taped to the door with an official letter from my new lawyer, a Russian female divorce attorney highly recommended by Luther. Valentina Lugonova didn't think much of marriage in the first place and even less of Casey when I told her the facts of my situation. She'd been briefed by Luther's office, so I didn't have to go into too many gory details, but still, Val wasn't impressed by Casey Harper. "Not one penny. Not one," she promised.

The letter stated that he must vacate the premises immediately and contact her office for any future communication. There was also a key and a map to a storage unit, home to everything he ever owned and brought into the house, including a half case of terrible light beer and a tub of old trail mix he insisted on buying the one time we went to Costco. Thanks to Javier, the storage unit was inconveniently located in an industrial park in the Inland Empire.

I didn't trust myself not to open the door to Casey, not to give in to the subtle manipulation that he was so good at, so I packed a few things and checked into a local hotel for a few days. I know it would have been more imaginative to strike out for a glamorous room on the beach where I could stand on the balcony with a tearstained face and windswept hair, but the past week had drained every drop of drama out of me. I'd faced the music at work, telling my tale of marital woe to Caterina, who was both incredibly sympathetic and incredibly outraged on my behalf. I'm also guessing she had heard about the twins because she made a comment that hinted at prior knowledge: "Now it all makes sense."

I didn't ask what made sense. I really didn't want to know what she knew and when. I felt foolish enough.

In a gesture of sisterhood, Caterina took me to lunch, talked very loudly about all the terrible men in her life, including her current much-older boyfriend, drank three glasses of wine while I had seltzer, and then proceeded to delete Casey's name from our official mailing list when we arrived back at the offices with some pageantry, like a direct mail exorcism. She vowed to support whatever changes I needed to make in my life but made me promise not to move too fast in leaving town altogether. "We can't let you go yet."

After that, I lunched with disgraced Rose Queen Candy, someone I'd met a few times in high school and spotted at social events over the years, but it had been a long time since we'd been face-to-face. My mother and I had worked out an outfit that said "calm and in control," which wasn't hard because most of my closet said "calm and in control." I arrived at the Parkside Grill in a simple blue sheath dress, Ferragamo pumps, and my favorite short trench. My mother loaned me a vintage silver cuff to wear for some sort of secret protection, like Wonder Woman. When I hung up my coat, Candy recognized the bracelet right away as an Elsa Peretti piece from the seventies. "Your mother's, right? I miss seeing her around town putting the rest of us to shame as we all desperately chase style and she simply is style. How is she? She was always a bright light here in Pasadena."

"She's well. Ready to come back to town more and be part of the scene. That's why we thought it would be great to catch up. Big changes in my life and hers." That was a little more desperate and direct than I'd intended to be in the first two minutes with Candy. I'm sure my mother would have pulled off that opening line with a lighter tone and a self-depreciating reference, but, as I'd always told my mother, acting was not my thing. I *was* desperate.

Candy quickly waved the waiter over; we both ordered the salmon salad, and then she took out her tablet. "So, what's happening?"

"As you know, it's been almost ten years since Henry Blakely's death. My mother and I thought it would be a good time to do our one and only interview with someone we trusted as the anniversary approaches." I'd gotten used to referring to my father by his full name for interviews like this. I only used "Dad" or "my father" when I really wanted to make a point about our connection. It was my therapist who suggested I use that language as a way to acknowledge a public loss versus a private loss. I planned on using the same tactic with Casey, never again referring to him as my husband, soon-to-be-ex-husband, or ex. He'd simply be Casey Harper.

I spun the tale my mother and I concocted, a confection of vague statements on the Blakely legacy, art for the public good, and the family's commitment to the Wallace Aston Museum. I worked in the personal changes I would be making as our salads arrived. "It's an exciting time for me. After so many years of looking backward, I'm looking forward to the next decade of personal growth. I am ending my marriage to Casey Harper, as we've grown in different directions, but that's no surprise. I was only twenty-two when we married, and it had been a really emotional year prior to our wedding. We have different priorities now. My plan is to take the next few years to further my education and branch out in the art world, maybe open a gallery. And Casey Harper will be focusing on his global photography business and his five-year-old twins who live in Eagle Rock with their mother. We both look forward to new directions."

Candy's eyebrows shot up, or at least as much as they could, given her close personal relationship with her dermatologist. "His twins are five?"

"Yes." End of story.

Candy nodded in complete understanding of the situation. "I see. It's very trendy now in Hollywood, you know."

"What?"

"The family on the side. You're not the only woman I've seen go through this. You're smart to get out." Candy was on my side. One down, a town to go.

"Just my luck, I'm trendy at matrimonial disaster." We both laughed, then I remembered that she was press. "Oh, can you keep that off the record?"

There was a vague nod, like maybe that would be the headline and not off the record, so I improvised like my mother suggested. I could fool Candy for one lunch and be someone stronger and sexier. "Once everything is settled, I'll head to Paris for a sort of reinvention sabbatical. According to my mother, thirty-one is the new twenty-one, and I'm looking forward to taking all of Paris in. And by that, I mean *all* of Paris." I considered winking on that last line to imply something sexier than patisserie, but I couldn't pull off that sort of wink. "Of course, I'll be under the tutelage of Polly Davis-de La Fontaine, my dear friend and expat extraordinaire. You know Polly, don't you?" This conversational jag was right up Candy's alley: name-dropping, foreign locations, and personal reinvention.

She bit. "I love this! Tell me more." And I made up some more details about freshening up my French and working in a gallery to satisfy her word count.

"This is great stuff!" she said, quite possibly forgetting that the impetus for the meeting was the tenth anniversary of my father's death. Then, like a true Pasadenan, she turned to the one true topic of interest to all readers at CandysDish.com. "Tell me, what's happening with all your wonderful real estate? The house here, the Motel, the house in Ojai?"

And with that, the conversation about Casey Harper and his

"bonus" family was done. Onto the much more titillating details, like what's going to happen to the Buff & Hensman house in the hills, because that's what people really wanted to know: When's it going on the market and for how much? At that moment, I was grateful to be a Southern Californian. Candy's piece would post tomorrow, another reason to stay in hiding for a few days.

At Caterina's suggestion, I was planning on spending the day holed up at the hotel with my phone off working on a new salon talk I'd proposed to the museum about our deacquisitioned pieces. The museum held "salons" on various topics throughout the year. They were structured lectures held in the theater with slides and a lengthy discussion afterward, no wandering around the museum showing off the artwork. So, the topics could be more varied and should inspire engagement.

There had been controversy in the press lately about museums selling off donated artwork, sometimes in order to pay off debt and salaries, though that was against museum ethics. Though that was never our situation at the WAM, because of a huge endowment and tremendous foundation support, we did from time to time sell, trade, or barter pieces of our collection for various reasons. Often, we wanted one piece but had to buy a lot of five to get the one we wanted, or we had similar or duplicate pieces. Other times, we simply didn't want what had been bequeathed to us and sold it to purchase a piece we did want, which was the most controversial, families taking it personally. I thought it would make for a lively lecture topic to expose what the museum had sold and why. We could highlight what had come our way as a result of deacquisitioning.

Caterina loved the idea, especially the notion of pulling back the veil to explain that deacquisitioning was sometimes good business. "It's controversial and edgy. I love it!" It was why she was so adamant that I not leave town, retreating to Bali or Phuket just yet. I agreed to keeping plugging away at the topic to see what I could put together. The research gave me a great excuse to bury myself in something esoteric after ten days of excruciating pragmatism.

Plus, I was sure that Casey would show up at the museum to confront me. We both decided that a Caterina and Tai combination provided the perfect human blockade.

So, a few nights at the historic Langham and a gimlet or two it was. I took in the scene. It was crowded on a Sunday with both locals and out-of-towners wrapping up the weekend. The Tap Room was dark and cozy, dimly lit by candles and a roaring fire. Everyone looked good in such low lighting, even after a long week of work and commuting. The official happy hour was over, but the crowd of twenty- and thirtysomethings didn't appear to be going anywhere soon. I glanced at my watch. Casey would be at the house in a half hour. I didn't want to go back to my room and stare at my cell phone, even though I'd turned it off. Much better to be among the bar patrons than alone with my doubts, I reasoned, when I heard a familiar voice.

"Drinking alone on a Sunday night? Is this the medical emergency you promised me?" a gentle Southern accent whispered in my ear. It was Dr. Bow Tie; except this time, he was tieless. He appeared to be freshly showered, like he'd come from the gym with his brown curly hair still wet and combed back off his face. He wore jeans, a gray fitted T-shirt, and blazer. He was only a few inches taller than me, but had a lean build that made him seem taller. "Mason Andrews. We met at the museum a little more than a week ago. Seems a little curious I'd be seeing you again so soon, Joan Blakely. Are you stalking me?"

That encounter felt like another era. "It does seem curious," I said. "But we had a ninth-century Buddha from Thailand go missing that night. That wasn't you, was it?"

"I tried, but it didn't fit in my messenger bag. I did pocket a paperweight from the gift shop, though."

"We know. We billed insurance."

Quite pleased by our repartee, we both laughed.

Mason gestured to the stool next to me. "Is your husband meeting you here? I assume that was him last week I saw walking into the museum after you turned me down. I heard him ask the security guard about your whereabouts. That guy that looked like Matthew McConaughey's better-looking brother?"

"No, I'm solo tonight," I hedged, and then plunged in. Why not? I had to get used to telling people why I was suddenly single, and this relative stranger was excellent practice. "Yes, that guy you saw last week *was* my husband. In fact, he stopped by work to tell me that he fathered several children, twin boys, with another woman five years ago and that I had to learn to deal with it or the marriage was over. In case you didn't get all that, let me repeat: My husband told me last week that five years ago he had twins with another woman, but thought it would be a good idea now if he started being their father. My choice: stay or go. So, he's not meeting me here tonight. Or any night. And, henceforth, will only be known as Casey Harper."

"Whoa." Mason Andrews nodded slowly. "Casey Harper is an asshole."

One more gimlet for me and something called a Dark 'n Stormy for him, plus a couple orders of portobello sliders later, most of which Mason ate, and I had laid out the whole story, including the manila envelope taped to the front door and Casey's impending arrival back in Pasadena. Mason reacted with shock, disgust, hooting and hollering at some of my actions, and just the right amount of attitude so my story didn't dissolve into misery with company. By the time I finished the drink and the diatribe, it was well past zero hour, as I sneaked a look at my watch and saw the time. I made it. Casey would have come and gone, and I was still standing. I wanted to stop talking about me, so I started talking about Mason. "What have you been up to since we met?"

"Saving lives," Mason said, and then gave me a little more

background. He was from Jackson, Mississippi. His father was a doctor who practiced family medicine and taught at the med school there, and his mother was a nurse who worked in the public schools. He picked emergency medicine as a specialty because the hours were predictable shift work and when he was done for the day, he was done for the day. No office to maintain, no insurance forms to fill out. He loved his work. "I was never going to be anything else, except maybe Batman, and being an ER doctor is about the closest to Batman you can get in the medical profession."

He went to undergrad and med school at Ole Miss and wanted a change of scenery for his residency. And then there was the old girlfriend. "She's an actress, so we moved out here together. But she's, um, intense, so that didn't really work out. Or maybe I'm a terrible boyfriend, which could also be true, so there are no hard feelings. But I liked it here well enough, so I stayed."

"Will you ever go back to Mississippi?"

"Sure, I miss SEC football and humidity." I was skeptical, not about the football because I know nothing about sports, but about the humidity. "No really, I do. My skin is so dry here." In that minute, Mason Andrews seemed like the opposite of Casey Harper: genuine and charming, not a whiff of manipulation about him. If Mason Andrews said his skin was dry, it must be dry.

My own skin was starting to feel warm, and then the reality of the situation hit me: I had a room upstairs in the hotel. I could make a night of this chance encounter. I was single again, and the rules that governed our interaction last week at the museum no longer applied. I could weigh myself down thinking about how that could possibly change in a week or I could "let life come to me," as my mother suggested. Which creeped me out a little because I didn't really want to think of my mother at a time like this.

I immediately felt self-conscious, as if I must look like the most obvious on-the-prowl near divorcée in the place, and I certainly wasn't the only one, as the crowd had aged up considerably in the past hour. Mason and I were now on the younger end of the scale, as Pasadena regulars filled the tables, mixing and mingling like the old friends they were. *Really*, I wanted to shout, *I'm just here so I don't hear my cell phone buzz. I'm not looking for anything else.*

"I think I need to call it a night," I told him. Okay, no more gin for me, no matter what he suggests. "Thank you, Mason, for keeping me company. I'm so glad I ran into you again. You've been very helpful."

Mason waved down the bartender by calling out his name. "Helpful? Well, that is quite a compliment." He paid our tab, quietly without fanfare. I acknowledged the gesture. He explained, "I live nearby and use the gym here, so this is like my neighborhood bar. I like to take care of things here."

"That explains the wet hair and the fact that you know the bartender's name."

"I'm walking home. Let me escort you to the valet," Mason said with mock formality as he stood and pulled back my chair, offering his arm.

I accepted. "I'm staying here tonight. I have a room in the hotel."

There was a slight pause in Mason's step, and then he offered to walk me up to my room. I didn't object, mainly because after nearly a decade of being attached to someone else, I was caught off guard by the offer. "Sure."

On our way out, I spotted a familiar face seated on one of the couches near the fire, in a big group of women. It was Candy, of course. And she gave me a thumbs-up.

"This is me." We reached the door of room 301. I turned to face Mason, whose eyes were focused on mine. I noticed that his hair was dry now and looked incredibly soft. "I don't know what I'm doing."

"Don't worry, I do." He leaned in and kissed me. His hands

rested on my shoulders, then pulled me gently into him. He smelled like fresh laundry and sage, and tasted like dark rum. The kiss felt wonderful. I had missed moments like this, the ones filled with promise. But I wasn't ready. Not at all.

Mason pulled away slowly. "I can't do this," I whispered, almost hoping he didn't hear me.

But he had. And, in his richest drawl of the night, he said, "I'm going to let you get some sleep, Miss Joan Blakely. But if you change your mind, you can find me here most Sunday nights." He reached out and ran his finger across my cheekbone. His hands were rough, like they'd been washed a million times, and they probably had, given his work. I liked the friction. "Sound like a good plan?"

I smoothed his hair because I'd been tempted to do that all night. It was soft. "That could take a while. How do I know you'll still be . . . hanging out at this bar?"

"I told you, I'm a terrible boyfriend. Don't worry, I'll still be here."

I checked my phone. There were three calls from Casey and a single text. I deleted the voice mails without listening to them but read the message. Clearly, Casey felt as relieved as I did in that moment. It read: It looks like you've made your decision. I understand.

Chapter 5

I soaked in the silence of what we at the museum called the "Birthing Room," a spectacular gallery of eighteenth- and nineteenth century European paintings, many of which featured Madonna and Child. I enjoyed sitting in the quiet gallery after hours for contemplation. On my mind today was a question about why a total stranger at the nail salon gave me a little "Fight On" fist and declared, "We're all rooting for you!"

Thanks to CandysDish.com, my situation had gone public, and my mother was right, support was staunchly on my side. Lydia, my favorite guard at the museum, whose grasp of art history rivaled that of some of the curators, had given me a thumbs-up when I entered her area, then, using her gallery voice, whispered, "Bastard. Let's do that to him." She pointed at Picasso's Cubist masterpiece *The Ram's Head*, a disorienting still life featuring an animal skull surrounded by deconstructed fruits, vegetables, and fish tails. She made the international sign for decapitations, saying, "Say the word." I thanked her, fairly confident I'd never look at that painting the same way again.

From the outside world, kind notes flooded my inbox and mailbox. There were invitations for happy hours and coffee on my voice mail, from old friends and emboldened acquaintances, all of whom wanted in on my misery. Casey's betrayal had made me a folk hero of sorts, especially to the squads of women who'd been done wrong. I couldn't leave the house without a Pasadena matron accosting me to confess her husband's longtime mistress, her father's secret family, or an uncle's illegal tax scam that resulted in the loss of a family fortune and the country club membership. Apparently, everybody's got at least one skeleton.

As the mother of a high school classmate said to me at the gym, "We used to think that your life was so perfect, but now we know you're one of us."

Sure, my life was perfect. Except for that little "terrorist attack" glitch. "Um, thank you?"

She nodded and, of course, patted my arm, which I'd come to understand as the international symbol for "I'm sympathetic but still your social superior."

"You should think about taking up bridge," she said. "We have a lot of fun."

I wasn't quite at the point where bridge sounded like a life goal, but maybe in six months.

The sound of footsteps interrupted my meditation.

"So, Joan, are you still interested in polishing up your French and working in a Parisian art gallery?" David Weller, director of collections, said as a greeting, referring to Candy's column of a few months ago. "Yes, I read CandysDish. I have to know my donor base, don't I?"

"I was trying to get ahead of the gossips. And I think it worked, but I can see where it may have surprised you. It never occurred to me you read that column. Please don't take it as a resignation!"

"I didn't. Plus, Candy can get anybody to say anything. I've learned the hard way." David had been at the WAM for decades, a well-regarded art historian who combined that with arts management and business savvy. He was confident and warm, but never chummy. It was hard to picture him getting carried away at any time, with anyone. He refers to himself as "the guy in charge of the art" and he was, from maintaining our current collection to acquiring new pieces. "But we did have an unusual call, and I thought of you."

"Oh, really, why's that?" I tried to make my voice cheery, even though my mood wasn't. Final paperwork for the divorce had come through that week. In record time, my divorce lawyer had informed me, very proud of her expediency. I didn't expect the legal finality to hit me so hard, but the end triggered random acts of sobbing all week. I didn't want to cry any more in front of work colleagues, especially a serious and sober man like David Weller. "Did the Chagall stained glass acquisition happen? Are we celebrating?"

"Unfortunately, no. I believe as long as the owner is alive and kicking, we'll have to wait for our Chagall. But I did just get a call from a dealer in Paris at Margot & Fils. Do you know of them?"

I shook my head.

"They have a small gallery in the Marais, and most of their work is done in discreet transactions. European royalty selling off some of the family treasures to pay the bills. Midlevel works of art usually, particularly decorative pieces, furniture, sculpture, and manuscripts. The business has been in the family for generations, that's how I know about them. It seems they have someone interested in our Panthéon Sketches."

My ears perked up immediately. The Panthéon Sketches were a treasure to me. A collection of pen-and-ink drawings that came to the museum in the early sixties, as part of the sweeping Duveaux Gallery purchase, an acquisition of about eight hundred pieces of European art and the New York City building that housed the gallery. Collector Wallace Aston had wanted to make a quick splash in the realm of European art, doing so with the purchase of a well-regarded New York gallery. All the art, the building, the reputation—lock, stock, and barrel—was acquired in a single transaction. Aston was mostly interested in the paintings, but along with masterwork oils, he acquired furnishings, decorative arts, ceramics, some ephemera, and many sketches of famous works. The museum had sold off the majority of the acquisition to cover the cost of the initial investment, but about a hundred pieces remained in the collection, most archived because of condition, age, or irrelevancy.

The Panthéon Sketches were the work of Jules-Eugène Lenepveu. They were never-shown pieces, due to their delicacy. But, because of my personal interest in Joan of Arc, I'd seen them many times, allowed to page through the collection like the latest issue of *Allure*. A museum perk.

Jules-Eugène Lenepveu was a barely known but respected French painter of the late 1800s who specialized in vast historical canvases. His work once decorated the ceiling of the Paris Opera and the theater of Angers, though, in each case, those paintings had been covered over to make way for another artist. His most famous paintings were eight panels depicting the life of Joan of Arc at the Panthéon in Paris, four huge portraits of Joan as shepherdess, warrior, and martyr and four friezes depicting corresponding scenes of Joan during the Hundred Years' War. Richly detailed, vibrantly hued and skillfully painted, the Joan of Arc Wall is an unexpected pleasure for those who wander into the church in the Latin Quarter.

Unlike some muralists who worked on the surface of the ceiling or wall, Lenepveu painted on canvases that were then attached to the wall with glue. Like most artists, before Lenepveu painted the canvases, he sketched. The WAM owned these simple, delicate sketches, studies of Joan, at once both intimate and powerful, as Lenepveu clearly viewed Joan with awe and reverence. Joan in armor. Joan in peasant's clothing. Joan clutching a cross at the stake. The sketches were on eleven-by-fourteen drawing paper, all the panels rendered both in pen-and-ink and then again in watercolors. Sixteen in all, the sketches were loose in a black portfolio case protected by an archival sleeve. The collection of sketches didn't constitute a priceless piece of art, but for the few admirers of Lenepveu, and the many, many more admirers of Joan of Arc worldwide, owning the drawings of the patron saint of France would be worth several hundred thousand dollars.

My interest in the sketches has always been personal. My father had used the Panthéon Wall of Joan as one of the settings for his *Joan Bright & Dark* display, lighting up the inside of the church with golden light. Then he named me after the saint, like a devotion to the woman who had become a symbol of strength and honor to him. He thought of Joan as the one who led him to sobriety and the one who kept him there. I felt connected to the drawings on many levels. Sometimes I would remove them from the portfolio and lay them out on the worktable portfolio, just to soak them in. I wasn't ready to let go. "Who's the buyer?"

David shrugged his shoulder. "We don't know. I spoke with a Beatrice Landreau, and she said the buyer would like to remain anonymous for now. Apparently, the buyer doesn't fly but would like to look at the sketchbook in person, so asked us if we could bring it there. Of course, I thought of you to be the courier. And, if it sells, it would be a great first-person story to add to the lecture you're working on. Here's a case where it makes sense to sell off a piece of the collection. We'll never show it. It belongs in the hands of somebody who'll appreciate it. If going to Paris is of interest to you . . . at this time . . . the job is yours."

At this time. That was kind of David, to be aware, but not obvious, about my personal situation. In the few months since the bombshell, the revelation at CandysDish.com, and the subsequent legal work, I'd spent most of my days at work and most of my nights home alone, barely leaving my zip code, never mind the country. My mother kept asking me about my plans, an unrelenting drumbeat for getting out of Dodge. *Go to Paris! Go to Morocco! For God's sake, at least go to Hawaii!* But I'd taken refuge in work, finishing up my research that was now ready to go public in print and as a scheduled talk and video series. This opportunity seemed like a sign of some-thing, like the trip was more than a work boondoggle.

I felt a pit in my stomach, but the phrase "at this time" echoed in my head. I couldn't say no. I was ready for this.

"When do I leave?"

The term "art courier" has glamorous connotations. Who wouldn't want to escort a priceless piece of art to a famed museum or high-value art dealer in London or Tokyo or Saint Petersburg? That sounds like a first-class ticket to adventure. But in reality, it's a lot of paper-work, a lot of standing around in cold warehouses monitoring the packing and shipping process, talking to shipping agents, who are, for some reason, all loquacious Irishmen, spending endless hours in customs offices in airports and then long days on your feet as the artwork is secured and displayed at the destination point. There is a reason that senior curators don't raise their hands for the job. It's schlepping, albeit culturally inspired schlepping.

My first courier gig had been a bit of a fluke; I was a last-minute sub for an associate curator who came down with a case of adult chicken pox so severe she required hospitalization and a year's worth of dermatologic follow-up thanks to the scars. Poor thing. The mu-seum was loaning the painting *Allegory of Touch*, part of the *Five Senses* series by Spanish artist José de Ribera, to a show at the Prado. Ribera, who painted in the early part of the seventeenth century, was a follower of Caravaggio, and his work features the same depth as the master, but in smaller scale, with greater warmth and humanity. The *Five Senses* series featured a single subject exploring taste or touch or the rest of the senses in gritty composition. Our painting featured a blind man trying to re-create a face in a painting by touching a three-dimensional bust. Simply put, it's a beautiful piece, just beautiful.

So, when Gwen went down with the pox, I raised my hand to go as a stand-in. I was happy to do my part to reunite all of Ribera's *Five Senses* at the Prado. Frankly, I wanted to see them all in one room.

I'd had a lifetime of traveling with art, one of the skills you soak in as the daughter of artists and travelers. My father's "work" was unwieldy, not the kind you could shrink wrap in a four-by-six-foot box. We would travel to shows and commissions with trunks of materials for him to create his pieces, with strong black-and-stainless cases, more like a film crew. My mother managed the logistics like a general, and I spent half my life standing in lines with her, much to the amazement of shipping agents who were struck by the fact that a woman who had once been in a sexy Gillette ad was now filling out forms in their unheated warehouse. Eventually, my mother turned over those duties to assistants, but during my childhood, she did the hands-on work, and I stood next to her, bored but learning, apparently.

I executed the Prado job without a hitch, staying awake for thirty-six hours straight to get the painting from Pasadena to the walls of the Prado. Then, I collapsed in my room at the Ritz, one of life's truly glam moments. I had a knack for being both in charge and incognito, one of the key attributes of a successful courier. You can't go blabbing to the nice woman next to you on the plane or chatty cabdrivers that you're carrying a piece of art valued at millions. You have to blend in, keep your head down, and get the job done. After that, much to Gwen's chagrin, I became the go-to courier for the museum.

Unlike many museums who loan out works on a regular basis, the WAM was a reluctant participant in this grand art tradition. When the opportunity arose, once or twice a year, I viewed it as a treat and not a chore. I'd safely escorted works to the Frick and to the National Gallery over the years. The curators were happy to let me do the physical labor, and they would swoop in after the piece was settled to make sure the museum and the art was well represented and then attend the fabulous openings. I also got the nod for assignments like the Panthéon Sketches, when pieces of the collection were being sold off and the art needed to get to the new owner. Those courier jobs were executed with less fanfare, but the same amount of paperwork, hassle, and attention to detail. I'd delivered lesser medieval tapestries, minor modern sculptures, and a gorgeous seventeenth-century footed silver serving bowl to new homes in Aspen, Milan, and Berlin.

Casey used to tease me, that I fancied myself some sort of secret agent, and called the trips my "missions." It's true; I often thought up new identities and wore a wardrobe that featured a lot of black and leather. (I stood out in all the wrong ways in snowy Aspen; leather isn't a wicking fabric.) But role-playing made it fun, and I wasn't having a lot of fun in other areas in my life at the time. As I packed my bags for Paris, my mind wandered back to what Casey might have been doing while I secured a truck in Berlin or stood in the Italian loading docks. *What does it matter now.*

I pulled out my black leather jacket. Perfect for late April in Paris.

"I put together this list of galleries you should check out. Some great shows happening now. There's a great group show with some Marcia Hafifs at Le Plateau gallery. Didn't your father know her? And, please, check out the new Luna space by the Pompidou. It's just opened and they are putting up a new show like every week to attract press coverage. But a lot of their stuff reminds me so much of your mother's work. Street photography, black and white, rock and roll, and fashion from the seventies and eighties. Ask for Guy and tell him I sent you, and you'll get a private tour." Tai handed me a neatly printed sheet of paper with names, addresses, phone numbers, and his personal notes. He'd come back from a week in Paris earlier in the month, so he felt up-to-date enough to tell me what to do. "I'm so glad you're taking a few extra days. You won't want to come home. Wander around and explore. The art market's starting to pick up, so the gallerists might not be friendly to random Americans, but you have the right look." I don't know who was more excited about my trip, Tai or me. My mother was definitely the most excited, but second place was pretty much a tie. "And the Messerschmidt exhibit at the Louvre is great if you feel the need to experience a roomful of angry Germans, both in lead and in the flesh. It was packed when I was there a month ago. Real Germans looking at sculpted Germans. Redundant, right?"

"I'll skip the Germans, thanks. But I saw the Cluny has a show up about the Virgin Mary I thought I'd go to. Illuminated manuscripts. Looks good."

"Sure, cut loose with the Virgin Mary. That's the way to see Paris."

"I like blue."

"I know. You have that medieval thing, which is fine, and the Musée Cluny is a gem, but get out of the fourteenth century if you can. I wish I could go with you, instead of to the retreat." The curatorial staff was off to the desert for a long weekend of visioning and professional development, courtesy of a wealthy board member who hosted the event at his compound. Tai wasn't really a team player, so the thought of being trapped for four days with his fellow curators like Robert the Whitest Guy in LA going on and on about the Near Asia collection and its relevance to Asian hip-hop scene was not his idea of a retreat. "Think of me, dehydrating, while you're enjoying an aperitif in my name. Have some fun, okay?"

If one more person told me to have fun, I might scream. I knew everybody meant well, but really, I wasn't a sullen twelve-year-old headed off to AstroCamp. I had taken some pretty big shots lately, and if I needed a few months to get my feet under me, why all the pressure to have fun? Though all the mandates made me wonder if I even remembered how to have fun anymore. What does fun look like for a thirtysomething divorcée who prefers cathedrals to clubs? Every time someone said the word "Fun!" an image of Euro Disney popped in my head, manufactured merriment served up by corporate conspirators. I had no ideas for fun. The constant encouragement only made me feel worse about the tame and mundane life I was leading. "Planning on going nuts. First, I have to do my job, though."

Chapter 6

The international terminal at LAX was a madhouse as usual. It never seemed to matter what time you arrived or departed, day or night, the place was packed. I'd arrived hours early for my flight, surprisingly nervous. My anxiety had nothing to do with the portfolio of Panthéon Sketches in my carry-on. I was nervous to be on my own, solo, leaving the country without a significant other waiting at home. Well, my mother had essentially moved back into the Pasadena house, so she was there, but it wasn't the same as having a husband in the wings.

I was scheduled on a midmorning flight to Paris on Air France. I had a coach ticket for the flight over and a business class ticket for the flight home. Ideally, I'd be keeping a low profile en route to Paris, traveling like the thrifty tourist I was meant to look like. I was dressed in black: jeans, boots, and leather jacket, with a black cashmere wrap for the plane. I hoped it was nondescript enough for the flight because I knew I'd blend into the crowd as soon as I landed in Paris, the Capital of Black Clothing. I'd worked up my cover story: heartbroken working girl spending a weekend in Paris with an old high school friend, now a glamorous Parisian. Some parts of that were true, so I could stick to my story, even under duress, but I doubted there would be any. The thought made me laugh, a grilling from a French customs agent or a car hijacked by a crazed Joan of Arc devotee.

Polly was thrilled when I told her some business would be taking me to Paris. I hadn't been specific about the nature of my business, of course, but she was my cover should I encounter a nosy grandma wedged in coach. *I'm so excited to see my dear friend Polly in Paris*, end of story.

Because the portfolio of drawings was on the small side, the shipping department decided it would be best if I carried it right on the plane, wrapped in protective covering, of course, and slipped into my wheelie bag. Hand-carrying is always the safest option if available. The fewer hands on the art, the less chance that it would go missing. It doesn't happen often, but enough, so that theft is a concern. All it takes is one truck driver or customs agent or warehouse foreman to be on the take, and an entire shipment disappears en route.

I had the proper paperwork with me as well. All I had to do was get the sketches to Paris, go from the airport to the offices of Margot & Fils, and then arrange for a time to meet the prospective buyer. The agent in Paris was being a bit cagey, but that wasn't unusual. Sometimes the agent's "sure thing" was really more a "vaguely interested" collector, so there was some stalling on their end as they softened up the buyer. They did inform me that the buyer was "rather well-known" and "skittish about public contact." Frankly, these details just made me feel even more like a CIA agent.

My nerves were starting to subside. *I got this.*

Until I didn't. Standing in line at curbside check-in with a suitcase filled with my actual clothes, I locked eyes with Casey, my Casey, one entrance over. Casey and his whole damn family: Marissa, the twins, and a woman who was clearly a nanny. My eyes darted around the scene, taking in the reality of what I was seeing. Casey stood next to Marissa, who was dressed like she was headed somewhere tropical, in a printed maxi dress and a complicated head wrap. He was holding the tickets and the passports; she was typing into her phone and not paying any attention at all to the two boys, who were wearing pajamas, an odd choice for midmorning. The nanny was simultaneously encouraging the boys to settle down and shuffling the five bags along in the line, because clearly Casey and Marissa were too grand to manage their own bags and their own children.

That's when it hit me: no camera gear. There were none of the telltale equipment cases that accompanied Casey on every work trip I'd ever taken with him, just five suitcases and a golf bag. A golf bag! My outrage was mounting. Marissa and the boys weren't tagging along on a work trip; they were going on a family vacation. So much for Casey insisting they weren't together.

And, if the airline was any clue, the Harper Delgado clan was headed to Belize. Freaking Belize, where Casey had refused to go with me a few years ago, calling it "a yuppie version of a Central American country, not a real Central American country like Nica-ragua." All because they spoke English and had luxury resorts with spas. And, really, "*yuppie*"? Who even said that word anymore? But there it was, right in front of me, Casey and the fam headed to Be-lize, complete with a nanny and golf clubs. Who's the yuppie now?

I added up the plane fare alone in my head and realized that Casey must have been doing much better than I'd suspected, thanks to the decade I supported his career, charmed potential clients, and subsidized his housing and lifestyle. Other than when I tagged along on work gigs, he'd never taken me on a real trip out of the coun-try, except a long weekend in Cabo years ago. I needed a second to process all of it: this is what it feels like to do the heavy lifting in a relationship for years and then see the girlfriend reap the spoils.

It was brutal.

I stared at the scene, catching a nasty exchange between the two world travelers, the sort of low-volume hissing that couples engage in when they don't want to draw attention. Marissa was shaking her phone at him, like she was armed with a lightsaber. Casey looked tired, beaten down, and middle-aged, as if this insta-family had worn away his last shred of hipness and he'd headed down the path of Weary Dad. Marissa snapped at the nanny, instead of at the children, who were spinning like tops and annoying other travelers.

It had been eight weeks since that night in my office. Eight weeks! And I was out of his life completely. My eyes circled back to Casey. Now he was staring at me, his expression slightly ashamed, like a dog caught with a shredded shoe in his mouth. Marissa noticed his gaze and turned my way. She had no shame at all, pulling her spinning children toward her, creating the illusion of a protective wall around Casey. I nodded at the two of them and walked into the terminal.

"Miss Blakely, are you okay?"

I guess I wasn't if the Air France gate agent thought to inquire. I couldn't seem to control my shaking hands as I handed her my passport. Was I hyperventilating a touch, too? "I, I . . ."

"Nervous flier?"

"No, just, just . . ." Just what? Furious? Jealous? Humiliated? Yes to all three.

"Do you need me to call someone?" Now she had that "national security concern" look in her eye.

"No, I'll be fine. I saw my ex-husband with his new family all together for the first time. He, he . . . had an affair and fathered these twins like five years ago but only told me two months ago. And there they all were with the nanny. They were going to Belize. Where he would never take me." My voice cracked.

The gate agent nodded. Her perfectly tied red, white, and blue silk scarf looked like it was holding her head on. "I remember when

I saw my ex with his new wife at Home Depot. They were ordering new kitchen cabinets. For my old house. For my crappy kitchen that I cooked in for years, but he was too cheap to renovate. I wanted to ram them with my new stepladder. Big splurge for me in my crappy condo." Not exactly the professional behavior they expound in the Air France employee handbook, but I appreciated the sharing. "Let's see what we can do to make you feel better." The gate agent pounded away at her computer keys until the very thing came up: a business class upgrade.

"Thank you. That's so nice of you . . ." I read her name tag. Lisa Wagner, not the slightest bit French. "Thank you, Ms. Wagner."

"You're in 10B. Looks like 10A is a man. I hope he's cute and single. By the way, you look great. I love that leather jacket." She handed me my boarding pass with a smile of solidarity. "You have *fun* in Paris. Maurice here will walk you to our Executive Level security line. No waiting!"

The VIP treatment reminded me of a trip to Reykjavik I'd taken with my parents in high school, when air travel was still glamorous and benign. My father was receiving a medal of honor from the Icelandic government, and we were flying the national airlines. I recall multiple escorts to the gate, early entry onto the plane, branded earphones offered by immaculately dressed flight attendants. So much fuss. I loved it then, and this little bit of fuss improved my mood considerably. But nothing made me happier than spotting Casey and his entourage at the end of the long security line, one twin already lying down on the ground refusing to move, the other hanging on to the nanny's leg for dear life. Again, eye contact. I checked my posture, straightened my shoulders, and smiled at Maurice as he unhooked the rope and let me through to TSA, like I was walking into the VIP lounge. I'm sure Casey was watching.

—

Well, he was cute, in a tweedy coat with leather patches kind of way. Not that he was wearing that, but he looked like he might if the weather turned tweedy enough. Neatly trimmed dark hair, pleasant face, throwback khakis, and an earnest sweater vest. Not exactly the bad boy Gael García Bernal fantasy I had cooked up in my head as I charged down the Jetway, but he did hold some potential for flirting. I was suddenly aware that my all-black ensemble might intimidate a guy who favored wool. *Why do I care*, I scolded myself. This is a random guy on the plane, not my destiny.

He didn't seem to care at all. He was clearly not interested in striking up a conversation, not even looking up as I deftly stowed my carry-on in the overhead in one strong motion, stashing my leather jacket on top. Oh well. My plan was to pound a few glasses of champagne, then pull out my battered copy of the Blue Guide for France, 1997 Edition, and relearn the city I hadn't visited in ten years. I wasn't going to let one sighting of the Happy Harper Family throw me off my intended course.

I was proud that I had an actual book in my hands; I'd been on a TV jag of the worst sort. *How had I never watched* Damages *before?* Prior to Caseygate, I filled my free time with reading or at the very least, paging through magazines. But since Casey left, I'd barely cracked a single spine, TV my drug of choice. But it was time to get back to being me again, and the Blue Guide returned me to a time before anything was complicated and everything was beautiful.

My phone pinged, reminding me to turn it off. I looked at the screen expecting a message from Tai or my mother. Instead, it was from Casey: You looked great, Joan. On a mission? I hope it's someplace cool. Maybe we can get a drink when you get back. See ya.

See ya? Is he fifteen? My only reply was no reply. I pressed the "off" button with a vengeance, then glanced to see if my seatmate was suspicious about my cell phone abuse. But my seatmate was absorbed in work, with a full display of devices working overtime. He was talking on the phone, staring intently at his laptop screen, and tapping away fluidly. Not even a nod as I slid into my seat. So much for any mile-high magic. What did it matter? Business class was so much better than coach in every way. I could make the upgrade work with my cover story if it came to that. Gate agents must have a long history of taking pity on recently dumped girls headed to Paris to get over the heartbreak. But it didn't seem like my seatmate was going to grill me on my background; he was clearly a very busy man.

When the flight attendant came by with a round of champagne, I took advantage of the bubbly. That got a look from Sweater Vest, who had ended his phone call with a quick "Gotta go. I'll call you when I get there."

"Would you like some champagne?" I asked him, as if I were personally hosting the flight. I took the liberty of grabbing him a glass and putting it on the tray table between us. I was a little worked up, actually, quite a bit worked up, and I thought the champagne would have a calming effect.

"Thanks. Trying to finish up some stuff before we have to turn off our electronics," he said.

"That's the beauty of a paperback. You never have to turn it off."

He wasn't impressed. I took a big slug of champagne.

"Yeah." Back to work he went. Of course, it took all my strength not to peek at his screen. My eyes were drawn to the glowing laptop like it was a visual siren song. All I could make out were spreadsheets of some kind, not the sort of information that I could easily decipher, like the usual stuff of outbound LA flights: screenplays and marketing PowerPoints. I gave up trying to snoop, closing my eyes and attempting to clear my mind. The image of Casey & Co kept popping into my head, so I refocused on the night at the hotel with Mason Andrews. I had been tempted to go back to the bar at the

Langham and try to find him several times but held off because it still felt "too soon." Well, not after today, it didn't.

My schedule in Paris would be my own for the weekend. I was set to drop off the notebook at the art agent's office in the Marais when I landed. I'd made plans with Polly for some time on Sunday but had an open schedule for the rest of the weekend. Sleep, coffee, and wandering were my plans. Alone. The meeting with the mystery buyer was set for Monday. I opened my eyes and absentmindedly reached for the extra glass of champagne. As I took a sip, Sweater Vest shot me a look. "You know, they give that out free all flight."

"Oh my gosh. I'm so sorry. What's wrong with me? I'm not used to flying business class," I lied.

He looked embarrassed that he'd busted me. "Well, then by all means, have another glass. But it's a long flight." He went back to work.

After feeling the effects of the second glass of champagne, I'd given up on reading and was watching *Toy Story 3* instead, thinking it would be a breezy way to spend a few hours. A friend's dad had worked on the original *Toy Story*, and going to the premiere on the Disney lot was a vivid memory for me. But I loved the movie so much, I made my dad go see it in the theater with me. He identified with Woody completely. I had no idea that the latest addition to the franchise was such an emotional minefield as those damn toys made it back to their person, Andy. I pretty much cried for two straight hours because you'd have to be made of stone not to cry at that movie. It was a poor choice for a plane.

After a trip to the restroom to wash my face, with my own wipes, of course, and to apply a thick layer of La Mer like my mother had taught me, I wandered back to my seat. I rewrapped myself in cashmere and settled in for dinner. Sweater Vest had filed away his devices and was staring straight ahead as he ate his beef Wellington, an ambitious entrée for in-flight cuisine. He nodded at me as I sat down.

"Really sad movie," I explained.

"I could tell."

"Should have gone with *Gnomeo & Juliet*." Apparently, he didn't realize I was kidding because an awkward silence ensued. "Did you finish your work?"

"I did. I have to speak at a conference this weekend, and I hadn't put together my speech. I have an outline now."

"Oh, what kind of conference?" Maybe he was a doctor. They have conferences all the time in glamorous places like Paris. Or worked for a think tank. He had that think tank look.

"I work in tech, mainly with robotics and artificial intelligence. It's a conference about the future of AI."

"Oh," I said weakly, unable to think of a single informed question, except to inquire when the robot army was going to take over, so I left it at nothing.

A little smile from Sweater Vest. "That's the reaction I usually get."

"I don't know much about artificial intelligence. What does your work look like to dopey real people like me?"

"In short, I started in software that works in robots who help build cars, slit steel, that sort of thing. Assembly-line work. Now I'm working on an application for artificial limbs."

"Oh, that must be fascinating," I said, apparently unconvincingly.

Sweater Vest laughed. "It is to me, but not to everybody." The flight attendant came over with more red wine, and I made the hand gesture for a swallow more. "Are you going to Paris for fun? Or work."

"Fun. A little treat for myself. To visit an old friend. And do some shopping." Perfect, vague, believable.

Sweater Vest wasn't looking for fashion tips. "What do you do for work?"

"I'm a dental hygienist."

Here's the thing about dentistry: nobody asks any follow-up questions because the thought of staring into people's mouths all day is revolting to most human beings. Other than the occasional "Why did you want to become a dental hygienist?"

To which I answered, "My parents are dentists." If there's anything scarier than one dental professional, it's a family of dental professionals. Sweater Vest completely changed the topic after that, and for the few hours after dinner and before giving in to sleep, we covered every topic but teeth. One of those intimate and far-ranging conversations that you only have on planes because you know you'll never see the person again. Sweater Vest was surprisingly talkative once he put away his family of Androids.

He'd grown up in Portland, Maine, was forced to learn to sail, and never got comfortable on the water, much to the disappointment of his outdoorsman father. He much preferred sitting in a dark room, playing video games and writing code, for which his two older brothers teased him. He'd received a PhD in artificial intelligence from the University of Washington and then made his way down to Silicon Valley after that. As far as I could tell, he worked at, with, or near Stanford at some point, which I think is the law in that field, and developed some patents, sold them to some entrepreneurs, and had just relocated to Santa Monica, or Silicon Beach as the Chamber of Commerce dubbed it, because of a particular deal and was trying to get used to the constant sunshine. He wished he had a dog, but he was never home. His favorite city was Hong Kong, but he also loved London. He was a terrible cook, couldn't boil water, but was really good at ordering in restaurants. He was in Paris for the weekend but may have to stay longer if some meetings he was trying to set up worked out. He was staying in the conference hotel, the InterContinental, because it was convenient and Paris geography confused him.

I managed to avoid most personal information, except the fact that I was allergic to dogs, thought driving was overrated, and wished LA had a more cohesive public transportation system—and that I was staying at my favorite hotel on Île Saint-Louis, but I hadn't been in the city for years. I mentioned that my relationship status had recently changed but didn't go into details.

I had the vague sensation that he had a girlfriend somewhere, because he kept referring to "we," as in, "We're renting a place near the beach, but we never have time to sit in the sun." I guess it could have been a roommate, but he seemed way too old to live with somebody he wasn't sleeping with. He had one-tenth of the charm of my former husband, unless you find the qualities of seriousness and intensity charming, which I was beginning to, thanks to my encounter with Casey earlier. Though I could never be 100 percent sure again, my seatmate didn't look like a guy who would hide a secret family in a nearby neighborhood. The more he talked and the more wine the flight attendant poured, the more attractive he grew, khakis and all. I switched to water.

Finally, about two hours later, he handed me a card and said, "I'm Nate, by the way." Now that I knew his life story, it was time to learn his name. His card read "Nathaniel Redmond, PhD, CEO Green Town Industries."

"I'm Joan. I don't have a card." Of course, I did, but not one that said "Dental Hygienist." I was starting to really regret my cover story when a recollection hit me. "Green Town Industries? Is that a Ray Bradbury reference?"

Nate was clearly surprised. "It is. Are you a Bradbury fan?"

"Um, my father . . . ," I started, then stopped, hoping Nate wouldn't notice the incomplete sentence. Of course, what I really meant was that my father was not only a fan, but a friend. Two Angelenos, they met regularly for lunch over the years, both creative visionaries with a love-hate relationship to new technology. My father was always forcing Bradbury books on me, explaining that Bradbury put down in words what my father created in light and color. I read Bradbury's last novel, *Farewell Summer*, set in the fictional Green Town, Illinois, after my father's death. It was bittersweet. But Nate didn't need to know that. "You must admire his work."

"Yes. I wasn't much of a reader growing up, but his books always made me think." Nate looked a little embarrassed by his confession.

I was tempted to confess that I wasn't really a dental hygienist, to make him feel less exposed. By this point, I was pretty sure he wasn't a threat to my Panthéon Sketches, and I probably could drop my cover story, but then how pathetic would I look? I slipped his card into my bag. My eyes were starting to get heavy. "I think I need to doze off now. Or I'll sleep through my first day in Paris."

Nate smiled. "You wouldn't want to do that." He held my gaze. *Well, that was a little bit of something.*

"Do you need a ride to your hotel? I have a car waiting. I can drop you anywhere," Nate said in a matter-of-fact manner. We were walking through the airport, en route to baggage claim, then customs. I realized I was going to have to ditch him. As soon as we landed, I went into work mode. I had to get the sketchbook safely to the dealer, and then I could relax for the weekend. Until then, I needed to be cautious. I didn't want him following me through customs.

"Oh, that's so kind of you. My friend is coming to pick me up." Not true at all. I had a car coming as well. "In fact, I have to make a detour here to the restroom. I guess this is it." I pulled up my wheelie bag and reached out my hand for a parting handshake. "I enjoyed talking to you, Nate."

"Thanks, Joan. Me too, with you. Usually I work the whole flight. It was a good break." There was a pause as he slowly let go of my hand. "Joan, I have reservations at this restaurant tonight. It's supposed to be very good and very hard to get into. It's called Passages or Itineraries or something like that. Left Bank. I have the address in my calendar."

"Itinéraires?"

"That's it. My sister is a foodie, and she was going to come along but had to cancel at the last minute. She's my business partner, too, and usually the one to force me to leave the conference hotel no matter where we are. She made me promise that I would get out, and I don't want to disappoint her."

Oh, the "we" was not a girlfriend, but a sister. For some reason, that made my skin prickle a bit, and it felt good.

"I don't know if you're free tonight, but I would love to have a dinner companion. Seems a shame to waste the reservation."

Yes, it did, especially to such a hot spot. I'd read about it on Polly's blog, of course, where she praised the "sleek design and the market-fresh menu." There were a million reasons I could come up with to say no, including fear of exhausting my knowledge of dental terms pretty quickly should the conversation turn to my work. But after seeing Marissa in that maxi dress, headed out on my dream vacation, and then that stupid text from Casey, like I was still pining away for him, I knew I had to do something a little reckless with a guy. And here was a guy right in front of me asking me out to dinner at a trendy restaurant. I didn't have to sleep with him, but a Paris street make-out session would do the trick. The thought stirred up some genuine and unexpected sensations in my body. Why not go to dinner? After all, it was Paris. This could be categorized as fun, right? "I'd love to."

"Great. Does your cell phone work here?"

"It does. I'll text the number on your card. Then you can let me know the details."

Nate looked pretty pleased with himself. "I'll see you tonight."
"Yes."

From PasadenaMeetsParis.com

Good Morning, mes petites! I'm so excited! An old friend is
coming to visit and nothing but bouquets of ranunculus from
the market will do to welcome her to La Maison de La Fontaine.
I'm even making a dash to Bellota-Bellota for some jambon and
manchego to stock the fridge with nibbles and wine. I know,
Spanish food in France! I should be ashamed. No worries,
PMP'ers! My friend Joan Blakely is nothing if not sophisticated.
She can appreciate a little cross-cultural noshing.

Joan of Art, as I like to call her because of her *très important* job at the Wallace Aston Museum in Pasadena, has
been a friend since elementary school days when we both
wore enormous bows in our hair and the trademark pinafores
of our school. We reconnected during our junior year abroad
stints here in Paris. What fun we had, drinking gallons of coffee and Beaujolais, scouring Paris for secrets haunts to buy
perfume and the perfect shade of red lipsticks. We walked
for days, taking in the City step by step. Because of Joan, I
only wear Gerbe tights and understand the Importance of
Navy Blue.

Like her spectacular mother, photographer/model Suzi
Clements Blakely (Trust me, even more beautiful in person,
if that is possible), Joan could make sackcloth look chic. But
there was no sackcloth in Joan's closet, just clothes with simple lines, wonderful construction and heritage. While it took
me years to absorb the Frenchwoman's style, Joan got it right
away. She spent the year in good shoes, Breton sweaters and
a vintage Hermès coat in charcoal gray with lines like a cape. I

covet it ten years later. Even French women deigned to stare at Joan as she walked down the rue de Buci.

Welcome back to Paris, mon amie!

NB, lovely readers! Where does such an on-point Pasadenan spend her nights while in Paris? At a perfect petit hotel on Île Saint-Louis. Totally charming, totally Parisian. *Tennis, anyone?*

Chapter 7

Had it not been drizzling, I would have stuck my head out of the car window like a happy golden retriever as we drove through the streets of Paris. The city represented so many befores for me: before adulthood, before September 11, before Casey. Before I'd taken on the responsibilities of so many other people's lives besides mine. How I'd missed a return visit here in the last dozen years surprised me, but that's the way life is. My mother always said, "Travel like you'll return someday, but understand that you may not." In other words, don't fill your schedule with must-sees and miss out on sitting in a café for hours or wandering aimlessly through the streets visiting tiny shops and churches far from the beaten touristy path, but make sure you see a few of the top tourist sites because you never know if you'll really make it back. Never in a million years did I think that it would take me so long to return to Paris, but now that I was back, I wanted to breathe it all in.

I couldn't help but think about the time my parents surprised me my junior year, showing up unannounced at the campus of College Year France in the Latin Quarter on a Wednesday in October. (As my apartment mate Polly said, "Close to the Sorbonne, but not really the Sorbonne.") The plan was that I would be gone for the whole year, not that my famous parents would show up eight weeks into the semester and commandeer my time. I knew one thing for sure: I didn't miss my parents. Since landing in France, I felt like I'd shed my entire skin and assumed a new identity as Experienced Expat, leaving behind the Uncertain Undergrad I'd been at Smith. But I wasn't ready to share New Joan with my mother and father. Chatty, once-a-week emails were all I could handle. This felt like an invasion.

I was furious when I saw them ingratiating themselves with the stone-faced dean, who treated her American students with equal parts endearment and disdain. I was even more annoyed when I heard my mother rattling off my whole life story to Madame in French more fluent than mine. I could barely hide my feelings when I greeted them, "Quelle surprise." I was awful.

"You look beautiful, dear." My mother did the once-over. If you didn't know her, you wouldn't recognize that with a barely perceptible eye flick, she was completing a full inventory of my person, like a sci-fi movie cyborg. Height, weight, bust size, hair volume, neck length, prominence of clavicle, degree of ear protrusion. And, of course, a quick cataloging of clothes, shoes, bags, and accessories. (Extra points for vintage silk scarves and simple jewelry.) I'd like to say it was for informational purposes only, but there was some judgment involved. "Paris agrees with you. All the walking has been good for your cheek-bones."

Though I wanted to object on the basis of my art history/feminist studies class, Reexamining the Male Gaze in Twentieth-Century Painting, I hopped off my high horse. I was happy to pass muster in Suzi Clements Blakely's trained eye. It would be easy to mistake my mother's commentary as weight related, but she was really all about bone structure, once rhapsodizing about how the clavicle was a woman's greatest accessory. She was right; the endless walking had narrowed my face and toned my legs. I'd never match my mother's height, but I was taller than most women I knew. My straight blond hair was naturally streaked, and I was wearing it in a high ponytail. I had on the black turtleneck my mother had given me before I'd left Pasadena, assuring me that I could wear it anywhere and every day in Paris, and I had. "We walk everywhere," I explained, less combative now.

"You always look lovely, Joan," my father said, true to form as well.

My mother had spun a fantasy in her head that we'd all go to Fashion Week together, the highlight of which was a party in honor of Halston, the late designer, thrown by some old model pals of my mom's, collectively known as the Halstonettes. But I had other plans because it was our midterm break. "You couldn't have emailed? Let me know you were coming?"

"We thought it would be special this way," my mother explained. My father raised his eyebrows. He wasn't quite throwing her under the bus, but he was making it clear that he would have emailed, but Suzi does what Suzi wants to do. "Come on, Joanie, don't you want to go to this party? It will be something."

Honestly, no. I'd been to that party before, except in Hollywood and New York and once in Miami. My father, who'd been sober about two decades, was very selective about accompanying my mother to these fundraisers. But when I turned seventeen, I was deemed old enough to be my mother's plus-one. For about two minutes, right before we got out of the car, when I looked at my mother and she squeezed my hand in anticipation, the whole scene was thrilling. *Pop! Pop! Pop! Pop!* Exiting the limo. The flashes of strobes. Photographers yelling, "Suzi, over here! Suzi!" Learning from my mother to shimmy-shake my shoulders and embrace the chaos.

Until it wasn't thrilling. The photo line, the fake smiles, the tedious chitchat. Beautiful people screaming over the throbbing music, looking over my shoulder during conversations because nobody really wanted to talk to "daughter of," or any teenager, for that matter. If you couldn't gossip about your worthless agent, an asshole director, or your celebrity therapist, the other guests weren't that interested in you. I had no interest in a life on the runway or the screen, despite my mother's encouragement. I mostly stood in the corner, forced to make conversation with other "children of." I spent a lot of time in ladies' rooms.

My father says that my mother tolerates her time in sleepy Pasadena until her need to see and be seen builds up to a frenetic crescendo with hair and makeup. That's when she would coerce us into openings, galas, and fashion shows to blow off steam. But I didn't feel like indulging her at the moment. Plus, I had plans. And cute Paul, my crush from Swarthmore, was involved. "I'm going to Oktoberfest."

My mother looked confused. "What is that? A bar?"

"No, *Oktoberfest* Oktoberfest. In Munich. Germany? You know, with the beer and the hats and dirndl skirts. Our fall break starts tomorrow. A bunch of us are going. We made plans weeks ago. Remember Polly from high school? Well, she's on this program, too, and we're staying with her friend from Wellesley who's in Munich for the year. We're taking the overnight train tomorrow after our last class."

"Can't you go another time?"

"It's called Oktoberfest for a reason."

"You don't have to be so snippy."

My mother always went to the "snippy defense" when I pushed back on anything, from adding long layers to my hair to going to her choice, NYU, versus my choice, Smith College. I looked at my father for backup. "Dad?"

"Nobody parties like the Germans." Clearly, my father did not want to get involved. But I could have used some backup.

"The whole thing will be American college students drinking beer," my mother spit out as if she were describing the least desirable trip she could imagine. "I thought we could do Fashion Week as a family. When will this happen again, that we're all here in Paris the same week?"

I didn't even know where to start with this statement, so I started at the beginning. "Is Fashion Week really something you need to do as a family?" My father laughed; my mother did not. I was trying hard not to apologize, because it wasn't my fault that my parents failed to send a single email or leave a message at the office for me about their plans. I no longer lived on their schedule. "It's really more your thing than mine."

"I don't know why you say that. You could walk in any show you wanted. Look at you. That Kate Moss is only five foot seven." My mother really struggled with Kate Moss's success, like it was a personal slap in the face to all the models who'd come before her and had not trashed hotel rooms. But Kate Moss aside, I could tell she was losing steam. Her picture-perfect vision of the two blond Blakely women in vintage Halstons flanking the great artist Henry Blakely on the red carpet was dissipating with every second.

"Remember that charity fashion show I was in when I was ten. And I threw up as I left the stage. That was enough for me, Mom." I put my arm around her. "I think I'd look better in a dirndl skirt than Halston."

"That's not true." She would get over it the second she stepped in front of the cameras on the red carpet, but not a minute sooner. "I can't believe we came all the way here and you're leaving." I stared silently, having learned over the years that my mother eventually draws the right conclusion, but it takes her a while to get there. "Let's at least get out of here and find a café. Then we can wander through some shops this afternoon. We're trying to stay awake today so we can sleep tonight."

"I have class."

"Of course you do," said my mother, the college dropout, perpetually dismayed by my sense of responsibility.

"It's a site visit to Sainte-Chapelle to see the stained glass windows. You'd love my art history professor. He's a funny, smart Brit who has zero interests in tests and papers and just loves to show us Paris. Why don't you come with us?" My olive branch, having purposely avoided talking about my parents to any of my Paris classmates. I didn't add that Professor Goodspeed, or, as we called him, Jamie, would probably drop dead when I arrived at the meeting spot with Henry Blakely. "Please."

"My favorite windows in the city." My father was ready to move on. "Let's make the most of the time we have together this trip. And next time, some advance conversations might be advised before we plan a Parisian family vacation."

"Big idea, Dad."

"The two of you," my mother said, as she pressed my shoulder back to straighten my posture, a familiar gesture.

Looking back, going to Oktoberfest was one of my biggest regrets. We should have done Fashion Week as a family. Instead, I took a packed train to Munich, drank way too much beer, a beverage I didn't even really like, and had to watch cute Paul make out with a guy in lederhosen from UVA. All in all, a bust.

Don't let this trip be a bust, I thought. *Make it be the start of something.*

As the car made its way through the maze of le Marais, my attention returned to the present. The offices of Margot & Fils were tucked into a seventeenth-century building on the rue de Trésor in le Marais, the area of the city that can transport you back to medieval Paris, if you squint and block out the sounds of car horns and cell phone pings. Beautiful buildings and houses, cobblestone streets, and a labyrinth of alleyways and hidden courtyards. Pre-Revolution, the Marais was home to some of the city's wealthiest inhabitants; post-Revolution, it was abandoned until the poor Bohemians moved in, including Victor Hugo. In recent decades the gay community had moved into this longtime Jewish quarter of Paris and kept up appearances, maintaining the painted windows and antique adornments.

I loved le Marais, the narrow streets jammed with fashionable pedestrians and motorbikes, the cafés with cheerful red awnings bustling with noise and diners, bright flower boxes and micro balconies of wrought iron defining the densely packed apartments on the floors above the shops. Even in the April drizzle, the neighborhood hummed with activity. As a student, I had spent many afternoons getting lost in the tangle of streets, always finding my way back to the Hotel de Ville metro. But now everything looked new and unfamiliar to me. I felt lost. I hoped it would all come back, like my rusty French.

Margot & Fils was equidistant between the Centre Pompidou and the Place Des Vosges, in an area dense with design shops and restaurants. My plan was to meet with our agent, Beatrice Landreau, see the sketches secured, and then have the car take me to my hotel on Île Saint-Louis. I'd tried to communicate this to my driver, with limited success. I did manage to direct him to the gallery, but as he double-parked, I noticed the shop looked closed. The dark interior was a concern. "Attendez, s'il vous plaît." I hopped out of the car with my rolling bag, hopeful that my contact was simply working in the back.

I rang the bell several times and peered in the window. I could make out a few grand vases, some simple tapestries, and a case of polished silver against the back wall, but not a soul inside. I rapped on the door, louder this time, and called out, "Hello?" Nothing. I motioned to the driver to hold on a minute or two while I checked my phone and texts on the sidewalk. Nothing from the office, but it was the middle of the night in California, so I went into my email and spotted a message from a B. Landreau with the subject line "Family Emergency."

To: Joan Blakely
From: Beatrice Landreau

Hello, Joan,

I am so sorry. I have a family emergency outside of the city and cannot meet you today. I am unavailable on Friday and have informed the buyer. But we will see you Monday. Je regrette.

Beatrice

Unbelievable. Granted, I wasn't walking around with a Pissarro in my pocket, but the casualness of her email seemed unprofessional. *Oops, sorry, family emergency.* While not priceless, the Panthéon Sketches had some value, and I was much more comfortable with the idea of the portfolio locked in a gallery with a top-notch security system than riding around town with a sketchy livery driver. I stared down at my roller bag, as if some solution might materialize. But the only solution was simple: head to the hotel and hide it.

Île Saint-Louis is one of two natural islands in the middle of the Seine near Notre-Dame. Accessible only by bridge from both the Right and the Left Banks and connected to Île de la Cité, it's an oasis of quiet and culture. Developed as a master-planned urban center in the seventeenth century by Henri IV and Louis XIII, it's both an elegant residential neighborhood and a tourist magnet, with high-priced apartments and a few select streets of restaurants, boutiques, and shops. ISL is also home to the best ice cream store in Paris, maybe the world, called Berthillon. As Breezy, one of my roommates during my junior year who happened to be a blond Amazonian field hockey player from Greenwich, described Île Saint-Louis, "It's like French Nantucket! I want a summer house here."

A spread of Breezy's wedding in *Town & Country* confirmed that she was in for a life of whatever she wanted thanks to that blond ponytail and those legs. And, though it looked nothing like Nantucket, Breezy was right that Île Saint-Louis has a pristine, step-back-in-time quality. Crossing the bridge was like walking into another century. I'd been enchanted by the area as a student, jealous of the Americans who had snagged homestays on the ISL, but they all complained it was too boring and didn't have enough nightlife.

When the trip to Paris came up, Beatrice Landreau offered to make reservations at a nondescript hotel that catered to tour groups. But I told the museum that I'd take care of my own reservations. The first place that popped into my mind was a little hotel I remembered on ISL because, according to my Blue Guide, it had once been the sight of a royal tennis court. The hotel was in a converted four-hundred-year-old wooden-framed building with towering ceilings in the common area and a glass elevator. I made my reservations at Hôtel Jeu de Paume, thinking it would be the perfect spot for me, but I hadn't planned on bunking in with my Panthéon Sketches.

I didn't want to ring our security people from the car because I wasn't sure how much English my driver knew. Better not to let him know I had valuables in my roller bag, so I asked him to pull the car over before we arrived at the hotel.

I took the call in an alley and was assured by Mike Danbretti, our longtime security specialist, on the other end that my hotel checked out. Mike, a former FBI agent, had started a high-end art and antiquities shipping company about ten years ago. He spent his time at the FBI tracking down stolen art and now was on the other side of the equation. With offices in Los Angeles, it wasn't unusual to run into Mike at the museum or art opens where outside security might be needed. We had a good relationship. He appreciated my embrace of the cloak-and-dagger; I liked his buttoned-down tough-guy act.

"Does this happen a lot? No contact on the other end?" I asked.

"All the time. Buyers that are no-shows. Dealers that forget the delivery, or usually, something bigger and better comes along, so they stall. I'll check this gallery out on a deeper level, but I don't see a major problem, Joan." It still struck me as odd, but Mike was good at his job, so I let it go.

He explained to me how to use the dummy portfolio as a decoy and where to hide the real one. "Good location, actually." I could tell Mike was sitting at his computer, checking out the Hôtel Jeu de Paume, entering the address into whatever database a security company might have. "Off the beaten path, small hotel where the front desk can keep an eye on the comings and goings. I would keep the information to yourself, but feel free to let them know that you don't expect any visitors. And decline maid service, the usual stuff. I wouldn't spend too much time away from the room, but the piece is safer in the hotel when you go out than wheeling it around with you when you go shopping."

"Thanks, Mike. Because pretty much all I do is shop," I razzed. We both laughed. Mike was forever telling me I should expand my wardrobe, suggesting that I "wear some pink" or "try yellow every once in a while." Meanwhile, I stuck with the classics, black and blue. "There are more black clothes in Paris per capita than anywhere else in the world. Did you know that, Mike?" I apologized for waking him up and then hung up. I hopped back into the car and was pretty sure that my phone call had raised some suspicions. The driver gave me a long look. Now I was a touch paranoid, which comes with the job.

"Île Saint-Louis, s'il vous plaît. L'Hôtel Jeu de Paume au 54 rue Saint-Louis."

The jet lag was starting to hit me. I was looking forward to a hot shower and then a walk around town when my phone pinged. It's Nate. Our reservation is at 8. Can you stay awake that long?

Damn. I had already forgotten about dinner. At least the restaurant was within walking distance from my hotel, which made me feel better somehow, like a mother running down the street for a quick errand while her child napped. I texted back, I'll meet you there. Pajamas okay?

—

The hotel was as charming as I remembered it, with walls of stone, timber beams, and coved ceilings in the breakfast room. My room was simple and clean with high-quality sheets and contemporary art on the wall. There was even an old yellow lab that lived on-site named Monsieur Scoop, sprawled on a rug near the front desk. Everything about the place felt cozy and safe. Even still, I was cautious. "I'm finishing up a project for work, so I'd appreciate no interruptions for a few days. Thank you."

The front desk clerk, a man in his fifties with a crisp white shirt and a name tag that said "Claude," shook his head and said, "Ah, you Americans. All work."

"Only a few days, then the city is mine," I assured him.

Before hopping in the shower, I did as Mike had instructed me on the phone. I had been provided with a duplicate black portfolio, a standard-issue case, filled with fake sketches. It was covered in Bubble Wrap and completely taped up. In theory, anyone looking to snatch the drawings wouldn't bother to spend the time to open and check to see if the real Panthéon Sketches were inside. It had been inside my roller bag in the most obvious place, buried a few layers underneath the top, in case anyone had followed me through customs and gotten any ideas. I put the fake in the safe in my hotel room, just big enough to hold the yearbook-size piece.

The portfolio with the real sketches stayed in the hidden compartment in my roller bag where it had been since I left Pasadena. The false bottom was undetectable: our own little bit of spy craft. I unpacked my clothes, shoes, and sundries and stowed my bag in the closet, just as a normal tourist would. The Panthéon Sketches were hiding in plain sight.

I felt like quite the operative as I triple-locked the door and got in the shower. It was good to be here.

—

It was Paris, so I had packed one decent black dress in addition to my low-key jeans, jackets, and lifetime supply of scarves. Actually, it was more than decent: it was a fitted Roland Mouret number with a deep square neckline my mother had bought for herself a few seasons ago but then claimed was "too young" for a woman of a certain age. "It was a weak moment. Me, a good cabernet, and the Neiman Marcus catalog." She forced it in my bag along with that Elsa Peretti cuff, insisting, "You never know who you might meet."

After a walk up and down a good stretch of the Seine to take in the skyline and stay awake, I felt refreshed. Being back in the city I loved was like a jolt of energy running through my brain. Seeing the jagged profile of Notre-Dame against the background of gray sky was all I needed to shake the jet lag—from the travel and the last few months. Everything had changed and nothing had changed. I popped into several markets on the way back to the hotel to assemble a light lunch of bread and cheese and more bread. I did one of those idiotic American gestures, taking a theatrical breath as I walked into Boulangerie Julien for a baguette. The locals paid no attention, but I knew I needed a few more days here before I acquired the cool shrug of belonging that Parisians shared.

I spent the afternoon babysitting the sketches, attempting to give myself a professional-looking blowout, and checking my email. My brain nearly short-wired when I saw a message in my inbox from Casey with the subject line "You look great. Can we meet?" First a text, now an email? He must need something, a favor or introduction to someone. The gall, I thought. But was even more shocked when the email itself hinted about a reconciliation with a line about meeting so that we could "heal together." The ego and the gall. I deleted it in case I might be tempted to answer it after a few glasses of wine. Then I retrieved it and stuck it in the folder labeled "Casey

Sucks" with all my divorce-related emails. Maybe one day I would respond.

But my rage led me down a rabbit hole of searching for images of Casey and family online, like the paparazzi was going to care if a second-tier photographer and his baby mama went on vacation. One quick search did bring up several photos of the two of them together at various restaurant openings and art shows. There was even a shot of the whole family at the Eagle Rock farmers market four years ago. I didn't even want to do the math on that one, triangulating my location in relationship to his lies. I shouldn't have looked. I clapped my laptop closed to spare the further shredding of my self-esteem.

A message from Tai saved me from myself: How's Paris?

I replied: Glorious. But Art dealer flaked! No show. How weird is that?

Tai came right back: Weird, for sure. Will ask around to my sources and see what people say about her. Send me her details again.

Mike was already on the official channels to find out if Beatrice was legit, but I thought Tai might have some off-book sources who might know some scuttlebutt, so I did as Tai asked. I hadn't bothered with due diligence prior to getting on the plane, unusual for me. I was too excited to anticipate any issues with the art agent. Better to have more information now so that I was ready to meet with Beatrice on Monday.

My watch alarm went off, telling me it was time to get ready for dinner. I was afraid I'd fall asleep and miss dinner, so I'd set a reminder. The image of Nate on the plane popped into my mind, earnest and polite. There was something there or else he wouldn't have invited me to dinner, right? I checked myself in the mirror. *No way my mother bought this for herself,* I thought. She was always going to give this to me. The dress fit perfectly, and I felt halfway to okay for the first time since Casey confessed his deceit. *Not bad for a dental hygienist.* I'd be wildly early if I left now, but sitting in my room was getting claustrophobic. I gathered my coat and bag and headed out the door, determined to have some fun.

Nate was at the tiny bar inside the bustling restaurant, which was, as Polly had said, a modern spot with warm white walls and pristine white tablecloths, filled with attractive young people, laughing, drinking, passionately engaged in conversation. He was sipping on a beer and checking his phone, either a nervous habit or a genuine device dependency. Given his occupation, I was betting on the latter, but then he slipped the phone into his coat pocket, not leaving it on the bar like Casey would have. Score one for Nate. The sweater vest was gone, replaced by a proper shirt and jacket. I have to say, I didn't miss the sweater vest.

He stood to greet me. There was no buss on the cheek or faux hug; he just started to talk. "I didn't want to fall asleep in my room, so I walked the whole way here to wake up, and then I was thirsty. Sorry for starting early." He paused and took me in. "Hello."

I removed my coat, a little more dramatically than I had intended, but my mother would have been proud, especially at the shoulder shimmy. I'm not in the business of turning heads like she was, but I managed to turn Nate's—the wrong way. "Wow," Nate said, and immediately looked away, pretending to flag down the bartender. When he finally got the nerve to address me face-to-face, he said, "You don't look like the same woman who was crying at *Toy Story*."

"I've never done this before."

"Done what?" He looked worried.

"Met a seatmate after deplaning."

"Right. Me neither."

I had never done this before either: slept with a seatmate. I don't know if it was the champagne followed by red wine or the long, slow meal that included a "mousse de chou-fleur" and something called "crumble chocolat" that we shared while making a significant amount of eye contact. Maybe it was the clack of the cobblestones under our feet on the walk through Saint-Germain to my hotel reminding me that I was a single girl in a foreign country. It certainly had something to do with the fact that Nate was focused on me in a way that resonated through my whole body. And then there was the drumbeat of whispers in my head of everyone who told me to cut loose, enjoy life, have a wild love affair. Maybe a one-night stand with a man possessing a doctorate in computer science doesn't sound like a wild night to everybody, but it worked for me.

Once Nate relaxed into the evening, he told some engaging stories about life at a start-up, the quirks of colleagues, and the endless hours of coding. I listened intently because the last thing I wanted was to have the conversation turn to my alleged work, but also because Nate's earnestness was disarming. He spoke about the mythology of failure, a concept he thought was bogus until one of his start-ups was a spectacular fail, and then he became a believer. "Failure doesn't only make us stronger; it makes us smarter and grateful and . . . more humble."

Amen. Not a classic pickup line, but I wanted all those things after my failed marriage. At least the smarter and more grateful part. I felt I was pretty humble already, thanks to being the average child of a great beauty and a great artist, but I was totally on board with moving into the next part of my life with more intelligence and gratitude. "That's a good theory. Do you have others?" I thought of Casey and his limited intellect, then I pushed him out of my mind. This night was not about him. *See ya.* It was about me.

"Am I talking too much?"

"Not at all. Your work is fascinating. And I mean it this time," I said, referring to our in-flight conversation. I leaned in and gently pushed the dessert plate toward him, brushing his hand as it held a wineglass. "Though I think you better eat some of this amazing 'crumble chocolat' before I finish it."

He picked up the spoon. "Your French is much better than mine."

"Well, your French is nonexistent, so that's not much of compliment."

"Touché." Then Nate stared straight down my dress. Ah, merci, Roland Mouret. "That's French, right?"

Whatever the special concoction or secret ingredient, the entire evening had me hot and bothered. By the time Nate quietly paid the check, I had stopped listening to what he was saying, focusing entirely on what might happen next. It was exciting to feel excited, on edge. I felt ready to start taking back my life, and a night with this decent man seemed like a good place to start. While we walked back to my hotel, arm in arm, I was working on my pickup line. "I have incredibly soft sheets. You should see them."

Nate really enjoyed the sheets.

The note on the bedside stand read: *Joan, I had to leave early for my conference. I think I've forgotten my whole speech. Thank you for last night, Nate.*

And that was that. No promise to call, no plans for later. *Oh, thank God.*

I wanted simple, complication-free, back-on-the-horse monkey business, and I got it. Yes, I did. Checking the next step in my "recovery" off the list, adding it in with "announcing break-up to press" and "signing divorce papers." One of the many things I had to do to move on. Though, I have to admit, for a math nerd, Nate had pretty great shoulders and unexpected take-charge manner. I lingered in bed thinking about his hands running down my back, my body on top of his.

I was so nervous. Being with somebody new was surprisingly

exciting and intimidating at the same time. The bravado I had felt on the street dissipated by the time we rode up in the tiny elevator. *Breathe. Enjoy. Dammit, relax.*

Nate seemed to understand and went very slowly. He made quite an event of unzipping my dress, clearly an admirer of French fashion designers. Taking his time to move from back to front, he traced my collarbone with his finger a dozen times while brushing his lips to my neck, forehead, cheek, earlobe. His attention steadied my breath while ratcheting up my desire. He slipped the dress over my shoulders while his eyes dipped down to my breasts and back up to meet my eyes. His lips followed where his eyes had been, and I responded immediately. I could feel the fabric pooled around my feet while his hands moved strongly across my hips and down my thighs. "You are very lovely," he whispered, stepping back. I stepped out of the dress and Nate rescued it from the floor, taking care to lay the dress over a chair back before we fell onto the sheets.

Thank you.

And that's the way I felt in the morning—lovely and smug, having pulled off such a night. Nate was the perfect choice for undoing the damage that Casey had caused. *Somebody thought I was lovely. Somebody thought I was enough.*

I did have a slightly foggy head, so there was that. But I was sure a cup of coffee and brisk walk through the Luxembourg Gardens would take care of it. I had a whole day to kill, most of it in my hotel room, so I didn't even mind the hangover. I checked my cell phone; it was almost nine.

It was only when I hopped out of bed that I noticed my closet door ajar. *Had I left it open last night? I didn't notice it open when Nate and I stumbled through the doorway, wrapped up in each other. Maybe because he was really a good kisser.* My heart sprang into action, and I could hear the pounding in my ears. I scrambled over the bed and pulled back the clothes on hangers in my closet. The safe was open and the duplicate portfolio had been unwrapped, bubble paper tossed on the floor and the copycat sketches scattered on the closet floor.

Jesus.

Now I was really panicked. My roller bag was pushed into the back corner of the closet where I'd left it. It looked undisturbed, but I pulled it out anyway to check the contents. I unzipped the top flap, then the felt for the hidden closures in the false bottom and snapped them open. The space was empty. The portfolio was gone. The sketches were gone. Time slowed to a standstill as I repeated the motions, thinking that maybe the sketchbook would magically appear if I checked the false bottom a second time.

Still gone.

This is totally what I get for having a one-night stand.

Chapter 8

Even worse than the walk of shame is the call of shame. My first instinct was to run downstairs like a bad actor in a B movie, yelling, "Stop that thief!" while taking in the questioning looks of the Australian tourists in the breakfast room. I managed to quell that instinct and stay put, knowing full well that Nate had been gone for hours. I tried to slow down the surge of adrenaline by throwing on some jeans and brushing my teeth. After regrouping, I strolled downstairs as casually as I could, mainly to get coffee but also to see if Claude at the front desk might have spotted anything suspicious.

"I see it was not all work and no play," he said with a wink. Apparently, he has spotted Nate on the way out.

"An old friend. You know how that goes," I explained, trying to sound casual and confident. "Did you happen to notice what time he left?"

"About seven. I came on duty then, and he stopped at the desk."

"Was he carrying anything?"

"Ah, yes!" Claude's face lit up. He reached under the desk as he said, "Your old friend asked me to give you this." Claude handed me my scarf; I must have left it at the table in the restaurant. "He said it was in his pocket. Very good to get it back, yes?"

Merde.

I grabbed some coffee and two croissants and headed back to the scene of the crime. I dialed Tai's number out of habit, but there was no answer because of course it was late and he was six thousand miles away. I didn't bother to leave a message because really, what was there to say? Besides, of course, a giant scream and maybe some crying, and poor Tai had had enough of that already from me. Then I remembered that the curatorial staff was on a weekend retreat in Palm Springs, assessing their work from the previous year and planning for the next. Essentially, if I confessed to one curator, I confessed to all.

I pictured the disappointed look in the stern face of David Weller, director of collections, as I dialed the phone once again. When Mike Danbretti picked up the phone for the second time in two days, there was no joking around. "The Panthéon Sketches are gone, Mike. Stolen from my hotel room."

First came the painful, cringeworthy series of questions involving where I was, who I was with, and how could I possibly have slept through the robbery. It was like confessing to my uncle Mike the Priest, if I had an uncle who was a priest, which I didn't. And it was excruciating. Mike handled my one-night stand like a pro; I was the one with issues.

Then, Mike went to work on what I knew about Nate Redmond while he tapped away into his database. Fortunately, Nate had a real paper trail and reputation, as an inventor and entrepreneur, not as an international art thief, so at least I hadn't been totally hoodwinked. Stealing art must be a side gig. "I can't believe he took it, even if all the evidence points that way," I said.

"Well, you can't say for sure that the portfolio was there when you came home from dinner, right? You were otherwise occupied. It's entirely possible someone was in your room while you were out. Probable, really, because they had time to open the safe and check the fake portfolio. Is there anyone else that knew where you were and what you were doing?"

I recalled the driver's suspicion when I made my phone calls. I told Mike. And then I turned on poor Claude and his dog Monsieur Scoop. "He knew I had work to do—maybe he put two and two together?"

"That's not really two and two, Joan. That's one and nothing. How about the Beatrice Landreau at the gallery? Have you been in contact with her since she was a no-show?"

"No, nothing. She had suggested a completely different hotel to me, but I booked my own travel, so I don't even think she knew where I was staying." I was still bothered by her no-show yesterday, knowing I had valuable artwork. I thought about mentioning that Tai was also looking into her but didn't. I was pretty sure Tai's sources would run more to gossip than facts when it came to Beatrice. Then I thought of my boss at the museum. "David knew of her reputation. Maybe he'd have some insight . . ."

Then, I stopped. Admitting to David Weller that this piece was stolen out from underneath me, or should I say, while Nate was underneath me, was both embarrassing and demoralizing. Everything about David said Venerable Father Figure, and he'd been such an important source of strength for me over the last decade. Plus, this wasn't any piece of art; it was something special to me. "Mike, do we have to tell David right away? Is there any way you could give me twenty-four hours to try to get the sketches back?"

In my mind, I'd waltz into Nate's conference, toss my hair around a bit, and suggest an afternoon rendezvous in order to get his hotel key. While Nate finished up his keynote telling the world about his plans to make artificial limbs on 3D printers and give them "brains" all at a low cost for the good of humanity, I'd rifle through his sweater vest collection and steal the portfolio back. He'd be cold, lonely, and stunned when he returned to his room. And I'd be long gone, having saved the day.

"That's going to be tough. For insurance purposes, we have to document a timeline. You at least have to call the police, tell them what happened, and have them question the hotel staff, look at security footage. That will give us a paper trail." Mike was on my side. Plus, if I managed to recover the sketches, it was a lot less hassle for him. "Why these sketches, Joan? What was special about it?"

"Honestly, not much," I answered. Lenepveu was a midlevel painter who had long fallen out of fashion. I doubt there were more than a hundred people worldwide that even knew they existed. But they were special to me, so maybe they were special to someone else. "But I can tell you this: the value's not in the work; the value's in the subject. Joan of Arc means a lot of different things to a lot of different types of people. She inspires a religious fervor and has a cultlike following. Military historians revere her, so maybe there's something there. And for the French, she is the symbol of their true national identity. It would be hard to pinpoint any other motive for stealing such a piece, except Joan of Arc's appeal to a variety of people."

"Okay, I'll look into that angle from here, any recent activity in works of art concerning Joan of Arc. Maybe there's a pattern."

"On a scale of one to ten in terms of art courier stupidity, how bad is this, Mike?"

"It's a seven. Max. At least you didn't leave a Degas dancer in the cab. I had one courier do that. And, other than the art theft, this Nate sounds like quite a catch." Mike added, "Okay, Joan, I can give you twenty-four hours before I inform David Weller. But don't do anything stupid. It's not up to you to recover the sketchbook. That's what insurance is for."

Yes, for the artwork, but not for my reputation.

The Paris police treated my situation like an everyday event, on par with criminal mischief or using an English word when a French one would suffice. Inspector Didier Angier, a tall, thin man in a dark blue suit, took my information. He signaled to Claude that he'd need to interview the staff and review the hotel security tape, and then turned to me and said, "Art goes missing every day here in Paris. C'est vrai. This is not life-or-death. It may turn up, but I wouldn't count on it, at least, not anytime soon. A piece like this could take a decade to surface. But I will go talk to Monsieur Redmond at some point."

That's when it hit me. The cover story, *my* cover story, was a huge liability. I had lied from the second I met Nate. If he was the thief, he knew that and could exploit it. He could turn my stupid contrived happy-go-lucky dental hygienist from Southern California against me. At face value, I created a false identity, flirted with him on the plane, plied him with food and wine at the restaurant, lured him to my hotel room (*My sheets are so soft . . .*), and now was accusing him of art theft.

If he wasn't the thief, the fact that I had created a cover story, left the artwork unattended, drank heavily, and then invited a stranger back to my room made me look guilty of conspiracy. Like I was trying to frame Nate and sell the sketches myself. This could be a real mess with French authorities, never mind the museum.

One thing I knew, I had to get to Nate and question him myself before Inspector Angier.

The InterContinental in Paris is a big, grand hotel built in the mid-1800s in the Opéra district. Recently renovated, it gleamed with gilt, silk, and dozens of brilliant chandeliers throughout. On this weekend in late April, it bustled with tourists, many from Asia drawn to the prime shopping location near le Printemps and Galeries Lafayette.

A flash of memory came over me as I took in the historic lobby, done in a soft green, cream, and gold color scheme, rich with gilded chandeliers, potted palms, and enough toile upholstery to satisfy any

Francophile. Back in my student days, it was the time-honored place to meet one's parents who may be in town, and I'd spent a few afternoons having tea at the hotel's restaurant La Verrière with Polly's mother and Breezy's parents. We devoured those tea trays while the mothers watched enviously, remarking on our "active metabolisms."

I made a beeline for the conference rooms. A small sign in the lobby alerted me to the Association of Advancement of Artificial Intelligence conference in the Mozart Room. Obviously, I had no conference credentials, but I was hoping security was lax. It was early afternoon, and I figured the panels would be letting out, with hundreds of men in sweater vests milling about. Back in my jeans, leather jacket, and cashmere, blending in was not really an option with this United Nations of scientists and engineers. So instead, I was going for the time-honored Girlfriend Locked Out of Hotel Room gambit. I figured I could talk my way in past any badge monitors to track down Nate. If he was even here and not halfway back to Los Angeles with my sketchbook.

But I didn't need to talk my way in. As I walked down the long hallway toward Mozart, I spotted Nate holding court in a circle of fellow PhDs and one bespoke guy I presumed to be a venture capitalist, standing out in an eggplant V-neck sweater and gray blazer. I scanned the circle of men and focused on my man.

As Nate spoke, others nodded. He looked so engaged and intense; how could this guy have possibly been the one to rifle through my closet while I slept a few feet away? Then I thought about the soft hairs on his chest and felt my cheeks blush. I could never have a career in intelligence. Clothes, body parts—where was my focus? Just then, Nate looked up and saw me. His expression fell somewhere in between curiosity and terror. "Hi, Nate. Sorry to interrupt, but can I talk to you?"

All eyes turned on me, the fish out of water among the mathematically gifted. One guy in crepe-soled shoes had clearly never been this close to a female before and started making small snorting noises. I tried to look away but couldn't. Nate recovered. "Joan. Sure. Yes, let's step over here." He took my elbow and steered me away from his adoring audience, much to their admiration.

We made our way around the corner in silence and found a pair of chairs in the wide hallway for our conversation. "I'm surprised to see you here," he said cautiously as we sat down, more of a question than an exclamation of excitement.

"I'm surprised to be here." Why beat around the bush. I was determined to be the tough guy. "Did you take something from my room last night?"

"What? No. I left the scarf at the front desk. Is that what you mean?"

"No. Something went missing from my roller bag. In my closet. It was there last night when I went to dinner and gone when I woke up."

"Are you accusing me of stealing money from you?" An edge seeped into his voice.

"No, not money. Something else."

Now he looked at me like I was nuts. "I don't know what you're talking about. Are you okay?" He was either a fantastic actor or he was genuinely worried that I was having a disassociated event. Then again, con men are good liars.

I started vamping for time. I really hadn't thought this through. "If this isn't a good time to talk, then we can meet later. But I know you know what I'm referring to." Yes, I would have been a terrible spy.

"Riddles are not really my thing, Joan. I'm going to go back to my colleagues. Maybe it's best if we don't have any further contact." His voice was stern.

"Wait!" I shouted, which made the cohort of nerds look our way. I lowered my voice and grabbed his arm. "Do you mean to tell me that you've never heard of the Panthéon Sketches?"

He shook his head slowly, backing away. "I have to get back to my conference. Don't follow me or I'll call security."

"Please, call security and then I can ask them to search your hotel room for the valuable work of art you stole from my hotel room. I know you took those sketches. You were the only one who had access and time. Is this a side gig for you? Art theft. Does your artificial limb company need funding?" I was losing it now, but he was cool as a cucumber. I changed tack. "Why did you invite me to dinner?"

The question seemed to catch him off guard, so he answered it directly. "I asked you out to dinner because you have a wonderful laugh and I was alone. I came back to your room because"—he looked down—"you're very pretty and a good listener, and women like you don't come into my world very often. And because you asked me." Then his face reddened, like a shy middle schooler.

Oh God, he was telling the truth. There's no way he took the drawings. What a mess I'd made. "That was very nice of you to say. I'm sorry for the confusion." I handed him my business card.

He read the card, still fully confused, and said, "The Wallace Aston Museum? I don't understand."

Poor Nate. "I work for the museum as an art courier. Sometimes I come up with cover stories to explain my trip to anyone who might ask—like a cabdriver. You . . . us . . . our evening together required me to carry on with my cover story longer than usual." More silence from him, so more explaining from me. "Here's the real story. I flew to Paris with 150-year-old drawings, artist renderings of the Joan of Arc panels at the Panthéon. The work has been in the museum's collection for decades, but there was supposed to be an interested buyer here. I ended up keeping the sketches with me longer than anticipated when the sales agent left the city suddenly. At some point last night, they were stolen from my hotel room by someone with experience in art theft. Someone who knew exactly what they were looking for. Someone like you who had access and opportunity. Was it you? We can work something out if it was."

He burst out laughing. "I'm in Paris trying to buy another tech company. I like art, but I don't really have time for international art theft." The mirth ended. "Plus, I don't steal stuff, Joan."

"The whole dinner, wine and dine, the dress thing—that wasn't a setup?"

"You're the one who wore that dress, so it kind of seems like you were trying to set me up." Right, of course he'd get to that conclusion quickly. He was a guy who worked in artificial intelligence. "Honestly, I don't know what you're talking about, and I'm starting to get offended."

"A valuable collection of art was stolen on my watch, and I'm screwed."

"Do you work for your parents' dental practice and the museum?"

"My parents aren't dentists."

By the time I'd finished explaining the whole story in a compressed version that included highlights like my cheating husband and his secret family, my famous mom and dad, the September 11 tragedy, a down and dirty divorce, Pasadena gossip mavens, and Amy's freaking overalls, I could see that Nate was putting me in the category of Psycho Ex-Girlfriend. As I listened to myself, I couldn't blame him. He thought he'd had a perfect Paris night with a carefree American in a sexy black dress and soft sheets. Turns out, he'd hooked up with a desperate divorcée with a dark backstory and somehow wandered into a crime scene. From the many, many times he checked his phone during my explanation, it was clear he wanted nothing more to do with me. He hadn't swiped the sketchbook. It was time for me to get out of there and leave the poor guy alone. "I'm sorry I had to lie. Part of the job. Then, I just had to keep up my cover story. I never expected to see you after we . . . deplaned."

Nate stood up abruptly. "Understood. I should be getting back to my colleagues." He offered his hand, like we'd concluded a minor business deal. I shook it. "Well, Joan, I hope this works out for you."

Then Nate added sincerely, "I admire your father's work. I came across an article about him and his fascination with astronomy. It's an interest of mine, too, so I went to see one of his pieces in Copenhagen when I was there for a meeting. It was something. Eye-opening. Breathtaking."

I nodded, remembering. "He loved that piece at Arken. It spoke to his interest in the creation of the universe. The origins of light, he used to say. It was symbolic of his version of faith, that we can know a star without touching it. I haven't seen it in a long time." I was sixteen when he did the installation. My mother and I had spent a few days in Copenhagen after the opening. I was more interested in cute boys than art, and I found Danish men to be extremely tall and attractive, not that I talked to many. But I remember how blue the sky was there and how my father had used that same blue in his piece to illuminate a spherical opening. Talking about my father's work only made the reality of losing the Panthéon Sketches worse. First him, and then his notebooks, and finally these sketches of Joan that he would have loved. It felt like all my connections kept slipping away. I couldn't seem to hold on to anything that mattered. "I'm sorry for the awkward situation, Nate. I know I must seem like a very unreliable person right now, but I did have a wonderful time last night. Take care."

Nate softened. "Let me walk you out. Do you need a taxi?"

The valet station was a madhouse, so we wandered out onto the street to flag down a cab. We didn't say anything. I took a step into the street to get a clearer view of any available cabs waiting at the light a half block away. Just then, a black sedan came wheeling around the corner, slightly out of control, but heading right toward me, there was no doubt about that. Complete panic washed over me and froze me in place. I heard Nate shout something and then felt him violently pull me back onto the sidewalk. The car missed me by inches, swerving back into the center lane and disappearing into traffic.

Nate recovered more quickly than I did. His eyes were wide. "What the hell? Was he trying to kill you?"

Chapter 9

The hot chocolate was rich and delicious, but my hands were shaking so badly, I could barely get the cup to my mouth. I sat alone at the café in the hotel, waiting for Nate to return. He'd steered me back to the InterContinental so he could gather his gear from the conference and stash it in his room, but not before seating me at a very public table and ordering me the drink. He asked if I wanted to speak to hotel security, but I waved him off. I didn't need any more officials involved in my mess.

I checked my phone and saw that Tai had texted back his intelligence on Beatrice: Sources say she is not well-regarded. Questionable provenance on pieces. Then another: I am literally dehydrating to death during this break out session. Send Evian. In Tai's world, "not well-regarded" was a damning slam. And "questionable provenance" was tantamount to being in the pocket of the Russian mafia or some other organized crime syndicate laundering money with art. This was bad news. It made me wonder what else Mike would come up with on Beatrice. I couldn't tell Nate.

He intended to personally escort me back to my hotel. Whatever happened out on that street had rattled us both. How could I be a target? The portfolio of sketches was gone; why did anyone need to intimidate me? Nate asked me the same question two or three times as we made our way back to the hotel. My initial response was this: "I don't know. I'm just the courier."

"Are you sure?"

"I mean, obviously my name is a connection. Joan of Arc and Joan Blakely. But I'm hardly the second coming. Maybe it was random?"

Nate wasn't buying it. "Joan, this is what I do, sequence events, from A to B to C with a finite number of detours. From what you've told me, none of this seems random. You being here with these specific sketches at this time."

"You're sorta random."

"True. I'm a variable." Nate smiled. "But somebody knew when you were out of your hotel room and had some idea of when you'd be back. And now it seems that somebody knew you were here at this hotel." He left me in the café pondering his observation.

I thought about the course of events: the out-of-the-blue inquiry from an anonymous buyer; the missing, and now-questionable, art dealer Beatrice; the theft of the sketches themselves, executed with skill and precision during the three hours I left the room; and of course, the near-death experience. Maybe Nate was right. The whole thing was starting to feel bigger than the individual incidences.

As I waited, I started to text Mike about the car and then thought the better of it. I wanted more time to follow up, to find the missing drawings on my own. If Mike knew that my physical safety was in jeopardy, he'd pull the plug. I was on my own here. But I did tell him about the information Tai had given me about the missing Beatrice.

Nate rejoined me at the café. He'd swapped his jacket for a more casual suede shirt. He looked like a guy ready for action, not a panel discussion. He hung his messenger bag on the back of the chair and swung into his seat. He'd told me at dinner that he was a distance runner and a novice yogi. I surmised that made him more graceful than the average coder. Something I'd noticed the night before, too, as my fingertips glided down the backs of his legs, up the front of his thighs. *Yes, he was very fit.* A little wave of heat seared through me.

Nate flagged down the waiter and ordered a coffee in perfect English, not even attempting a slight French accent. Why pretend? He started in on me. "Okay, so if the artist isn't anything special and the sketchbook is of modest value, then what's the deal with Joan of Arc? I don't really know anything about her."

Obviously, he'd used the last few minutes to scrutinize the situation, as I had. He'd asked the exact right question, but I was hesitant to go into detail. The less he knew, the better because eventually we would wind up at my father's exhibit in Paris, a fact that was starting to creep into my own consciousness as a possible connection. I couldn't connect any dots yet, but there was no reason for Nate to even try, as I'd already involved him in way too much for a one-night stand.

I gave him the middle school tour version of Joan of Arc. "She is an important figure in both the political history of France and the religious history of France and the Catholic Church. Joan was a peasant girl, uneducated but a hard worker, who grew up in rural France in the fifteenth century during the end of the Hundred Years' War. In short, the Hundred Years' War was an epic battle of control for France between France and England, with both sides laying claim to the French crown and both sides having cause. But France having a little more cause because they were, you know, *France*. As a teenager, Joan heard, or as some would offer, claimed to have heard, the voice of God, instructing her to crown the son of the French king, the Dauphin, and return France to the Catholic Church. Let's remember, she was an uneducated French teenager with a bad bowl haircut, and this was a preposterous notion. How could she do that? She kept her conversations to herself and waited four years before beginning her task." Nate listened intently, so I continued. Here I really was in my element.

"As you can imagine, there was disbelief, skeptics and tests from authorities of church and state to prove her sanity, her faith, and her virginity. Because virginity—that's important in your military leaders.

Ultimately, Joan prevailed, first accompanying and then leading the French army, defeating the British in key battles, crowning the French king, and winning the hearts and minds of the French people. But she overreached, went rogue, and headed to Paris to conquer the city for the French. Not part of the instructions from God, FYI. On the road to Paris, she was captured by the British, put on trial for heresy, and ultimately burned at the stake. Twenty years later, Rome and the French state embraced Joan as a martyr and leader. And in 1909 she was beatified in a ceremony at Notre-Dame, then canonized by the Roman Catholic Church in 1920."

"And what's her appeal now?" Nate said, like a scientist, apparently unimpressed with one of the great "unlikely hero" tales of all times.

I scoffed a little because he was so serious. "Well, that is a pretty incredible tale, even if only half of it is true. And we know much more than that is true because of the copious documents surrounding her trial, including the transcript of her testimony. She has a well-documented life and it's an extraordinary story. But to answer your question, people are drawn to her because of her faith and the manifestation of that faith. They are drawn to her because of what she overcame and her strength in the face of doubt. They are drawn to her as someone who put it all on the line and delivered. She is considered a brilliant military strategist, a leader of warriors who continues to inspire. According to documents, Joan's image appeared to French troops in World War I, and they defeated the Germans in a key series of battles, giving her full credit. And of course, there are numerous feminist story lines that still inspire. To women around the globe, she is the symbol of strength. To millions, she is one of God's soldiers. Joan has a lot of fans. Of course, to others, she is symbolic of women's hysteria, manipulative ways, and general instability, but that's a small subset of male academics and misogynists." A small head shake from Nate was a welcome sign. "Now that I think of it, next year is the six hundredth anniversary of her birth. That would add value to any Joan ephemera, like the Panthéon Sketches."

Our eyes connected. For the first time since I stormed the conference, he looked at me like he had last night at dinner, when he lingered over the tastefully revealing neckline of my dress, a look that made my cheeks warm and my defenses relax. He looked at me with desire, not like I was a psychopath who'd come to stalk him. "You know a lot about history . . . for a dental hygienist."

"Again, I'm really sorry about that bit. They are true professionals, and I didn't mean to besmirch their good name," I countered, then I reached out to touch his hand gently. "I wish we could have met on different terms."

"Me too." There was a long pause, and then Nate went back into information-seeking mode. "Joan, somebody followed you to my hotel. They waited for you to exit. Then they informed the driver you were leaving the building and exactly where you were standing on the street. There must be some reason, and it must be tied to these sketches."

I shook my head and shrugged my shoulders.

Nate now appeared eager to get moving, like he was determined not to let my drama become his drama. "First, I don't think staying in that hotel is a good idea. You're in danger there."

For one tingling moment, I thought Nate was going to insist I stay with him. A picture of the two of us napping in his suite with Eiffel Tower views popped into my head. And the next moment, I was annoyed he was telling me what to do.

"What about your friend? The one who married the lawyer? Can you stay with her?" I hesitated one instant, and Nate said. "Oh, is she made-up, too? She's not real, is she?" No mistaking the edge in his voice. We wouldn't be napping together anytime soon.

"No. Polly is real, a real person with a real backstory. We did go to high school together and she did marry a French lawyer. She's out of town this weekend, but I'm hoping I can at least stay at her place and regroup."

"Good. You need to alert the authorities and get out of Paris as soon as you can. There's no other solution." Nate's voice had taken on the tone of a concerned adult.

I could think of a hundred other options, starting with tracking down art agent Beatrice and getting the name of the mystery buyer out of her. If Nate wasn't the crook, and I was 98 percent sure he wasn't, maybe the mystery buyer had lured me to Paris and waited to steal the piece rather than buy it outright. That didn't explain the attempted murder, of course. I know Nate meant well, but I felt like if I could wait it out until Monday and talk to Beatrice, I still had a shot in recovering the sketchbook. No way I was getting on a plane to go home. I'd watch my step and be fine. As chilling as the last hour had been, I was starting to get my groove back. Invincible Joan circa 1999 was on the rise.

I took a sip of hot chocolate as a stall tactic. "You know, Nate, I've done this before. I mean, not the part about losing the artwork and the car almost running me down, but I've handled a lot when it comes to logistics . . . and life. I can handle this. I'll go back to my hotel and call my security team in California, too. They have resources and will be able to tell me the best course of action."

"You're right. This is your call." Nate signaled the waiter and signed the check to his room. "But I insist on taking you back to the hotel."

Back at the Hôtel Jeu de Paume, Claude was not particularly happy to see me, as if I had brought a contagion to the place, when here I was thinking that I was the victim. "Mademoiselle, you have several messages. Please let me know if I can be of any assistance."

I took the pile from Claude, some paper slips and an envelope. I looked through the messages, one from Inspector Agnier and one from the car service I used yesterday. It seemed like a throwback to call the hotel and leave a number when I had a cell phone and email, a sign that they wanted to talk to me but not really. "Thank you, Claude."

Gallic Shrug with Lips Pursed.

My guess is both calls were to tell me they knew nothing about the theft—the car service as a courtesy and the police as a follow-up to the call to the car service. I'd call them back from my room, as even Claude seemed like a suspect now, someone monitoring my movements. I turned to see Nate sitting in the small lobby bar, scrolling through messages on his phone. He'd done what he said he would do, escorted me back to the hotel safely, and now he wanted out of this circus. "I guess I'll go up and make some calls. Thank you for seeing me back to my hotel, Nate." I shifted the envelope from right hand to left in order to shake hands.

"What's in the envelope?"

It hadn't even registered that I was holding it. "Probably something from the police. A report of some sort." An address label on the outside was printed with my full name, *Joan Bright Blakely*. That seemed odd, as if the police had gone back to the precinct, or whatever they call the damn place in French, and Googled my full name. Then I remembered handing Inspector Angier my passport. *Of course, my passport had my full name on it*. I relaxed as I opened the closure and pulled out a piece of eight-by-eleven paper, a copy of something. I focused on the lines on the paper. It was no police report. It was a page from one of my father's notebooks.

One of the notebooks that I thought had been destroyed on September 11.

Chapter 10

My parents didn't fight very often, but when they did, they could get loud. I don't recall specifics from their arguments, but the general gist of most of them seemed to be that my father would get lost in his work for days and weeks on end and ignore my mother and me. I didn't notice his absence because I was used to him being gone, but my mother would begin to get restless and resentful after a week or so. I realize now that she must have felt abandoned and frustrated in a suburban town, driving carpool and wondering what had happened to her jet-set life. But at the time, I had no perspective on what my mother gave up being the wife of Henry Blakely. It was only when she became the widow of Henry Blakely that I understood her sacrifice.

If he was in the middle of a project, my father would come and go at odd hours, if he came home at all. There was very little conversation, and what there was centered on the logistics of married life. *Will you be home tonight? Did you call the eye doctor about an appointment? Can you take a look at my car? The engine light is on.* My mother would ask the questions, and my father would answer vaguely.

During one particular fight, the night of my tenth birthday, the issue was my father's absence. He had failed to make the after-school party at a bowling alley, the dinner at home, even the cake cutting. He was in the midst of a museum commission, but from the vitriol in my mother's voice, she didn't care if he was designing the Taj Mahal. In fact, I think she said that: "I don't care if you're working on the Taj Mahal; you could have shown up for ten minutes." When my mother really wanted to get under my father's skin, which wasn't often but occasionally, she'd compare his work to some tourist attraction. Caesars Palace! Times Square! The Taj Mahal! It made him furious.

I was brushing my teeth when I heard the arguing start. I crouched behind a wall on the upstairs balcony, listening to the noise, my mother's clear frustration and my father's resistance. This was it, I thought.

I was sure they were going to get divorced because my friend Jessica's parents had split up and she had to go visit her father every Saturday in downtown LA where he was living at his fancy club with the Oriental rugs. Sometimes Jess begged me to go with her so she didn't have to be alone with her father, a partner at a big law firm, because she'd never really spent any time alone with him, and it was uncomfortable to all of a sudden have to spend an entire day with him. We'd swim at the indoor pool, then have lunch in the dining room, where they served mac and cheese on china. Then we'd go home, smelling like chlorine. I was sure my parents were en route to that sort of break-up because of the volume of their fight. As an only child, I had no one to talk with about my parents, so I closed myself up in my room and lay in bed listening to music until I fell asleep.

The next morning, my father knocked on my door, and I was sure he was going to announce that he was moving to the same downtown club, because I didn't understand then what "private" meant or that my parents weren't club-type people. Instead, my father announced that we were all playing hooky and going to Disneyland.

Never in my life had we done something so normal. Disneyland? As a family? On a Tuesday? I'd accompanied my parents to art openings and cocktail parties, backstage at concerts and to designer showrooms. My parents would pull me out of school for weeks at a time to go to New York or Tokyo or Houston while my father installed projects. The nuns at Sacred Sisters would wag their fingers and warn that I would never learn cursive or multiplication. But then my mother would work her charm, and my father would offer to light the chapel for Christmas Eve Mass, and off I would go with their blessing. The nuns were right, though; I never really did learn cursive.

But Disneyland was a whole new experience for us as a family. It was one of the best days of my childhood. We rode It's a Small World three times because my father was fascinated by the ride, as if it was a message from another universe. We stood in line for Space Mountain, ate some giant turkey legs, and watched a parade on Main Street. We were almost like every other family, except for the times when my mother was asked for her autograph and my father's insistence that we stay for the fireworks, even though we were exhausted, because he wanted to see the "color palette."

After the trip to Disneyland, my father disappeared for eight weeks. I would later learn that he went to Betty Ford and got sober for the final time after a relapse. When my mother explained it all to me at sixteen, I joked about that maybe he was high at Disneyland and that's why we did It's a Small World three times. She did not confirm or deny my allegation. But at age ten, I had no idea what it meant when my grandmother Adele, who came down from San Francisco for an extended stay, told me he went to the desert to dry out. I thought he literally got wet somehow and went to get dry.

I don't recall my parents ever fighting like that again. Whatever they worked out that night stuck for the duration, as did the sobriety. He went to meetings, sponsored his fellow artists and creatives, and avoided triggering situations. The work was still intense and there were long periods of silence from my father, but my mother's anger and resentment faded. Her ultimatum, or whatever bargain they struck, was life changing for both of them. First, an iconic Gap ad of the two of them shot by Patrick DeMarchelier debuted in every magazine on the newsstand. After the world was reminded of Suzi Clements Blakely, her modeling contracts picked up, giving my mother her identity back. Finally, my father created *Castle Burning* in Central Park, establishing him as one of America's best-known artists. But it all started that day at Disneyland.

Several months after the epic Disneyland trip, my father, home and sober, created a piece called *It's Not Really a Small World After All* that the *New Yorker* once called "a tiny, tinny miracle." Housed in a stand-alone tin-sided building measuring about twelve by fourteen, *It's Not Really a Small World After All* paid homage to the immensity of the universe, using forced perspective and natural light to bring the galaxies down to the viewer. A slab of black marble kept the floor cool, as the piece was meant to be experienced over an hour as the moon rose during certain days of the cycle. Viewers would lie on their backs as the moonlight came in through a carefully engineered slit in the roof. Hundreds of pinpoint mirrors reflected the light in mesmerizing patterns. My father created a mock-up of the piece at his studio, and I loved lying in the dog-kennel-size box watching the light show.

It's Not Really a Small World After All now stood on a bluff above the Marin headlands in Tiburon at the home of a private collector. But there, in the lobby of a hotel in Paris, I held a copy of my father's initial sketches in my hand. It was dated the day after we went to Disneyland in 1990. Notes in my father's hand read "The most incomprehensible fact about the universe is that it is comprehensible"—his favorite Einstein quote.

I broke down.

Nate guided me to the glass elevator and walked with me to my room. Wisely, he didn't ask any questions, waiting for me to regain my composure. I was now officially his worst one-night stand ever, a complete basket case as the spontaneous tears gave way to full-blown sobbing. He fetched me a glass of water like a good boy. Poor Nate, he was thoroughly out of his element, clearly not something he was used to. I managed to hand him the piece of paper.

"What am I looking at?"

There was a long pause as I took some deep breaths and drank some of the water. I spoke slowly. "A page from my father's notebooks. He wrote down every idea, every thought he had for decades in these simple black-and-white notebooks. We thought they were lost on 9/11. But maybe not."

"Wait, is this different than the Panthéon Sketches?"

"Yes, completely. The Panthéon Sketches belongs to the museum. A different artist, different time. But this is from my father's personal notebooks." My voice rose in volume and frustration. Poor Nate kept nodding. "I don't quite understand the connection between the Panthéon Sketches and this page from my father's notebook, but there must be one, right?"

"I feel I'm about ten steps behind in all this, but not necessarily. It could be a coincidence. Statistically, that happens more than you think. The two incidents, three if you count nearly being run down, they may not be connected at all. For sure, though, a lot of people know that you're in Paris and exactly where you are. I wonder how that is?"

I was glad one of us could reason. I sat down on the edge of the bed, and Nate sat down next to me. "Are you okay?"

"I can't tell you what this means to me."

Nate put his arm around me as I buried my head in his shoulder. He soothed my hair and we sat quietly for a few more minutes. His suede jacket smelled like pine needles, rich and woody. I wanted to kiss him, be naked with him again. I was exhausted from lack of sleep, the stress, the mild hangover and jet lag. I wanted Nate to make it all go away for an hour. "It's like a ghost. Or some kind of miracle."

Nate released his arm from around my shoulders and created some distance between the two of us. "Isn't there someone you should call?"

"Umm . . ." A shrink, my mother, the police, Luther—yes, I should call all of them. "I can't think."

"Is there anything else in the envelope?"

I reached into the envelope and pulled out another piece of paper, a page of cream-colored stationery, almost rough and ragged in its texture. On it, there was a paragraph of crisp handwriting. I scanned the page. "What the hell?"

"What?"

I read it out loud:

There she rode on horse with sword
And led her men without a word
Here's my book that tells me so
Here's my faith that lets me know
I'll see her again, oh yes
I'll see you at six, sweet maid
Come meet with me at six, sweet maid

There was no name, no signature, just a hand-drawn sketch of a black bird.

"What is this?" I handed the paper to Nate. "A clue? An invitation?"

Nate studied the page, then read it aloud to himself, as if hearing the words might make more sense than reading them. "It's both. But it's unusual. It's not a riddle. It's like a poem. What's this drawing? Do you recognize it?"

I shook my head. "A blackbird?"

"Yes, but, I mean, does it mean anything to you?" I shook my head.

Nate was agitated. "Okay, now you call the police and then your friend and her lawyer husband, because I don't like this at all."

He was right. Circumstances had taken a turn for the creepy. It was one thing to get nearly run over on the street, but another layer of disturbing to have a treasured artifact with a poem be delivered to my hotel. This was beyond personal; it was intimate. Still, seeing the copy of notebook page gave me a sort of hope, like I was safe.

I reread the clue again and again. "Whoever sent this has my father's notebooks and maybe the missing sketchbook. Obviously, he wants to meet with me somewhere at six. I can't pass that up. What time is it?"

"No."

"What do you mean no?"

"You can't meet this guy, this person. Joan, he's dangerous."

"We don't know that."

"He tried to run you over."

"We don't know that. It could have been coincidence, right?" Obviously, Nate didn't appreciate the turnaround, but I didn't have the leisure to worry about his feelings. I took out my phone and checked the time. It was almost five in the afternoon. I had to get going. I fired up my computer. "I don't want to lose this opportunity."

"You can't be serious. You don't even know where to go." Nate was determined to be the brakes on the operation.

"The Panthéon. The Joan Wall. From the sketchbook. That's what he refers to in the clue: 'And there she rode on horse with sword . . .' That's one of Lenepveu's panels, a frieze actually. It depicts Joan accepting the sword on horseback surrounded by her men. See?" I brought up the image on my computer. "He or she, or let's just call the person Blackbird, must want me to meet him there. Maybe he'll have the notebooks. Look, 'Here's my book that tells me so . . .' That must refer to my father's work. Or the Panthéon Sketches. In either case, I'm going." My voice rushed to get all the words out before Nate could shut me down.

"How many notebooks are there?"

"Fifty-three exactly."

"Joan, whoever sent you this has a copy of one page from your father's notebook. One page from one notebook. Something he could have gotten at any time, well before 2001. Don't get ahead of yourself. You have no idea if this person has even a single complete notebook, never mind all of them. You need to turn this over to the police and let them do forensics or whatever they do and figure out who sent this." Damn logic.

I could fight back. "The police told me crimes like this are a dime a dozen in Paris. They don't run down every piece of missing art." I started to unbutton my shirt. All I could think about was getting in a quick shower and then getting out the door. I do my best thinking in the shower, and I needed a jolt, a fresh start on this dilemma.

But Nate kept reasoning. "Maybe that's true. But this guy added attempted murder, exhortation, and stalking. This sounds like something Interpol might be interested in. Not that I have any experience with Interpol. And this page? Is this related to Joan of Arc?" Nate said the whole name as if she were some mythical creature. Clearly, he was uncomfortable with the idea of a spiritual warrior or the fact that I was down to my camisole.

"No, not exactly." I was with him on this. I wanted all the dots to connect, but the reference to *Small World* seemed out of context.

"What are you doing?" he asked finally as I stood in the doorway of my bathroom.

"I need to take a shower. I do my best thinking in the shower. Then I need to go to the Panthéon."

He was exasperated. "I don't understand your thought process. I would think maybe calling the police is a better use of your time than showering. Or checking out of this hotel that art thieves and stalkers seem to know that you are checked into." Nate glanced at his watch. "One more question. What is this with the Einstein quote?" He pointed to the drawing on the page. Of course he knew it was an Einstein quote.

"That's another piece of my father's from 1990. Later than the Joan series." *Shit.* I hadn't wanted to get into all of that.

He cocked his head, as if to say go on.

"My father did a guerilla exhibit in Paris in 1980, illuminating the public works of Joan of Arc in order to tell a story of war and faith and hope. Five nights, five different Joans, all over Paris. It was the talk of the town. It made his reputation internationally. He called it *Joan Bright & Dark.*"

"So, before when you said you had no connection to Joan of Arc, that was not exactly true." Edgy Nate was back.

"Nate, it's all so far-fetched, it's hard to know what matters. But this notebook page is from much later. This piece is called *It's Not Such a Small Word After All.*"

"Funny," Nate conceded. "That's a funny title. Is it connected in any way to the Panthéon Sketches? And don't bullshit me."

"No," I admitted. "And it's not related to Joan or Paris or anything that's happened in the last twenty-four hours. But it is related to a really special day in my childhood, so this is very personal for me. I can't explain." Damn. Maybe it was a coincidence, a cruel joke. "Nate, maybe we can talk about this all later? I feel like I need to get going."

He surprised me with an abrupt answer. "Me too. I have a dinner tonight. I can't miss it." Nate threw his bag over his shoulder. I moved toward him and he reached out, running his hand across my collarbone. He sighed. "Joan, I know you want some answers. But be careful. Stay in public space. Don't get in any strange cars. Stay alert. Don't do anything . . . risky."

Nate was the second guy to tell me that in twenty-four hours. I

guess he didn't know that I never ever did anything risky. "I won't."
I stepped toward him.

An alarm went off on his watch. The mood changed immediately. Time to go, for both of us. "I guess this is it, then. I feel the
need to say out loud that I think this is a terrible idea." I nodded so
he knew that I understood. "Good luck with everything, Joan." Nate
sounded like I'd interviewed with him for a job I was never going to
get. Then he patted my shoulder in what must have been the Most
Awkward Gesture of All Time. "You know where to reach me. . . ."

"Yes." But clearly, I shouldn't try.

I stood under the shower for as long as I could afford, about three
minutes. Why that page? Why *Small World*? It meant so much to me,
but who would know that? The water did the trick. And a thought
raced across my brain. I hopped out of the shower and sent an email
to my mother. It was too early to call her, and I didn't have time for
a long explanation. I did several rewrites to strike the right tone, not
alarming but believable.

I checked my phone and saw I'd missed a call from Mike while
I was in the shower. His message said that he had some information
on Beatrice, the art agent. I would call him back later after I'd done
exactly what he'd told me not to do: get in the middle of this.

Then I put on clean clothes. All black for Blackbird. I looked in
the mirror and a thought popped into my head: *I wish Nate were here.*

To: Suzi Clements Blakely
From: Joan Blakely

Hi, Mom. Paris is wonderful, of course. Wore the dress already—
killer. Thank you so much. Quick question: the dealer who is
brokering the deal for the Panthéon Sketches implied that the

buyer may be a collector of Dad's work. He referenced *Small World* in a note, which is such an obscure piece, but he wants to remain anonymous, so that's all I know. Wondering if you and Dad had any friends who ended up living in France. May have Joan of Arc interest, too. Just curious! Let me know. xoxo

To: Joan Blakely
From: Suzi Clements Blakely

Morning, sunshine. Happy to hear the dress has already been out and about. You'll have to fill me in when you get home. Re: French friends. We did have a few friends from our year in Paris that we stayed in touch with. Ian and Nicola Forster, an English couple who worked at the embassy as cultural attachés. They live in London, but have a home in Provence now, of course. They do collect, so maybe it's them. I haven't heard from them in a few years, but they sent a lovely note and made a donation after your father's death. They were very upset.

Then there are a few of my fashion friends like Ines de la Fressange and Carole Bouquet, but I don't think they'd be anonymous or have a JoA thing. Patrick DeM & Mia have a place in Brittany but I just saw him for dinner in Montecito—shooting guess who—and he would have mentioned something about this, I'm sure.

Good mystery. Let me check my Rolodex and see if anyone else pops out at me. Yes, I still have one!

xoxoSCB

Chapter 11

The drizzle was turning to rain and the light to dark as I raced to reach the Panthéon before the doors closed to tourists. The air was cool; dodging and weaving through the Latin Quarter got my blood going. Dodging students and tourists and locals took me back to my junior year. I loved the chaos of this neighborhood with cafés on every corner and markets tucked here and there. Narrow sidewalks packed with people and the occasional quiet block where you could catch your breath. The Panthéon in Paris was a massive structure with the facade of a Greek temple complete with imposing Corinthian columns. I was invigorated as I climbed the steps to the ticket window.

It was built as a church dedicated to Saint Geneviève, the patron saint of Paris, by Louis XV but then rebranded by the people after the French Revolution as a temple to intellectuals. The main floor was vast and cold, as if stripping the building of its religious affiliation had also stripped it of its humanity, in an odd sense. Now it served as a crypt to some of the most revered minds in French history, from Voltaire to Jean-Jacques Rousseau to Alexandre Dumas. It's also the final resting place of Marie Curie, one of five great women entombed in the Panthéon. I guess the French must consider Madame Curie to supersede her gender, as the inscription over the entrance reads "Aux Grands Hommes La Patrie Reconnaissante." *To Its Great Men: A Grateful Homeland.*

I'd only visited the Panthéon once as a student, in Jamie Good-speed's architectural history class. There was so much else to see in Paris, and tombs of dead guys weren't very high on my list, even though my father had made his mark here. Jamie made no mention of *Joan Bright & Dark*, which was a relief because at the time I was in denial of my father's work. In previous classes, I tended to throw up my hands when a professor asked me about it. "It's what he does," I would say, as if his work were on par with plumbing or floor re-finishing. Maybe because that's the way my father acted most of the time, like his art was a J-O-B.

I hadn't recalled how imposing the Panthéon really was. How would I ever find Blackbird? I bought my ticket to go in. The ticket seller reminded me that I only had a half hour to see the entire Pan-théon and its many wonders, then gave me a stink eye, as if to say, "What else to expect from an American?"

I answered in French, "Je suis ici pour voir le mur de Joan seulement." *I'm only here to see the Joan Wall.*

"Ah, très bien." And a half smile to boot.

As I entered the interior of the dome, my eyes darted around frantically. What exactly was I looking for? I had no idea.

I heard a voice. "Hey."

It was Nate, standing against a slender column waiting for me to arrive. He was reading the visitor's brochure. I felt complete relief. And a tingle down my spine. He looked like he'd run through a wind tunnel before arriving. He was a long way from the slicked-back, button-down guy on the plane.

"This is a big place. What do you call this . . . style?" he said as he waved his hand around and walked toward me. He brushed my cheek with a kiss, then gave me a squeeze, like he was trying to let me know everything was going to be fine. He must have seen the worry in my eyes. "You smell clean."

"Thank you," I said, staying close to him. "It's neoclassical. It was the first of its kind in Paris. The building ushered in a design simplicity in the architecture of the city, a refreshing turn after the baroque style. But honestly, it's a little boring, isn't it?"

Nate shook his head and laughed. "Where did that come from, Susie Tour Guide?"

"College art history class meets museum guide. I'm nervous."

"Well, did you know the first experiment with Foucault's pendulum was held here in 1851?" He held up his handy-dandy brochure as proof. "At least I think that's what this says. They only have guides in French, so I'm using my high school Spanish to translate."

"I really don't even know what that means."

"Foucault's pendulum? It's a simple device to demonstrate the rotation of the earth. First demonstration here in 1851."

"See, we all have our obscure areas of expertise."

"I wouldn't call physics obscure."

I didn't want to let him go, but I did. "Thank you for being here. I thought you couldn't miss your dinner?"

"I realized in the cab back to the hotel that the dinner tonight was work. Talking to the same sort of guys I talk to every day about the same stuff we always talk about. I'll have that same dinner twenty times this year. And twenty times next year. My sister made me promise to get out and see the city. I think this qualifies. Plus, art theft and international intrigue? I don't get a chance to do a lot of that. I thought I'd tag along."

"To make sure I don't get into any strange cars?" I was starting to relax.

"Exactly. You have very questionable judgment when it comes to men." He reached out and touched my cheek, then glanced at his watch. "It's 5:54. We should find that Joan Wall, right?" Nate took in the cavernous interior, still dotted with a few tourists. "That could take a while."

—

The Joan Wall runs along the north transept of the Panthéon. There are four major panels, each more than fifteen feet high, that depict Joan's life, from peasant girl to martyr. Above the panels are four additional friezes with more scenes from Joan's life as warrior and leader. Eight or ten massive columns create a visual and physical maze that a viewer must navigate in order to take in the entire wall. The Lenepveu oils peek out from between the columns, the colors deep and glowing from the low, warm lighting. I hadn't seen the Joan Wall in person in over a decade, but I'd been through the sketch-books so often in the basement of the museum, that I was struck by its familiarity.

According to my father's own account in a piece from *Interview* in 1981, for the first installation for *Joan Bright & Dark*, he lit the columns in front of the panels with lights that changed from green to smoky gray to orange that he'd placed around the interior during the day with the help of a few art-loving guards. The paintings themselves were lit by a golden wash, and pastoral images were projected across the ceiling. An art critic writing for the *International Herald Tribune* said that the work made the columns, walls, and ceiling crawl to life and created the effect of Joan rising from the dead, as if she were a crypt buddy of Marie Curie's. For some reason, the image made me laugh despite my nerves as we approached the Joan Wall. All I could think of now was how those giant columns made it impossible to see if Blackbird was hiding in the shadows. And the half dozen tourists milling about in front of the wall were an innocent distraction. Nobody looked the slightest bit suspicious in their fleece jackets and blue jeans.

"This is a lot to take in," Nate observed. "Bigger than I expected." He lowered his voice, as it was clear that everything echoed. "What do you think we're looking for exactly?"

The same question I had asked myself. "In my mind, it's a guy in bird suit with a wheelbarrow full of notebooks, but I think that's unlikely." Suddenly we both cracked up.

"Right, look for feathers," Nate said. "Seriously, this *Blackbird* could be dangerous. Here's what I'm going to do. See that last pillar thing on the end? I'll hide there and keep my eye on you. And on everyone else wandering around. Sound good?"

Nate and I were certainly not pulling off high-level surveillance techniques, but it sounded as good as anything else I could come up with. "Okay. Now that I'm here, I'm glad you're here, too. Take this so you look like a tourist." I handed Nate my Blue Guide.

"Like a tourist from 1985," Nate said, assuming his post behind the pillar and opening the book to the handy paper-clipped section on the Panthéon. I stood in plain view in front of the wall hoping to attract someone's attention.

The lights flickered in the building, two big dips that left us in temporary darkness. I heard the guards in the building announce in French, "Quinze minutes jusqu'à la fermeture." Fifteen minutes to close. Floor traffic picked up as visitors headed toward the doors. It seemed like bodies were coming out of the woodwork to leave. Not exactly a stampede, but a rush. My eyes were trying to take in the scene. Then there was a tug on my arm from behind. I whipped around.

A young male security guard in a sharp blue uniform was holding a large envelope in his hand. "Excusez-moi. Avez-vous déposez ce?"

The envelope read "JBB," my initials only. I looked around to see who might have given him the envelope. Nate was at my side in a second. He spoke sharply to the guard. "Who gave you this?"

I translated as best I could. "Cette enveloppe, qui vous l'a donné?"

The guard pointed toward the exit, where dozens of people were headed out the grand doors and out onto the streets. "Un homme."

Nate could barely stand there. "Oh, a man. That's helpful."

I said quickly, "Une description de cet homme?"

The guard did a tiny head shake and answered in half English. "Tall. Pale. Veste noire." Tall, pale, and in a black jacket like half the men in Paris after a long winter. I turned to see Nate headed through the crowd in an attempt to spot the right tall, pale guy in a black jacket.

I slipped the envelope into my backpack, then started toward the exit to follow Nate. Remembering my manners, I turned to the guard. "Merci. Merci bien."

The lights flickered again as I made my way across the transept and out onto the steps in front of the Panthéon. Where was Nate?

The drizzle had stopped, and the late-April night sky was streaked with the last bit of sunlight cutting through the clouds. I stopped on the top of the Panthéon steps and searched for Nate but got caught up in the view. The Panthéon's setting on the top of a hill provides a startling vantage point across the neighborhoods of the Left Bank all the way to the Eiffel Tower. I wasn't prepared for the sight of the lights of the city stretched out toward the iconic structure, and for a moment, I forgot my mission. I must have stood at this spot more as a student. I thought of my father, too, making the city his canvas. How had that all slipped away?

"Joan!"

Out of the corner of my eye, I saw Nate at a street corner, waving his hand to grab my attention. He was alone, no Blackbird in sight. But a half dozen heads turned to stare me down as I waved back, as if we violated some code of Continental cool. I didn't care. I wanted to get across the street to him as quickly as I could and rip open the envelope.

Nate turned and, still clutching my guidebook, threw his hands up, clearly unsuccessful in his attempt to spot Blackbird. As a consolation, I held up the large envelope in my hands.

—

"Wait. Don't open it here. Too many people. We should regroup. Plus, I'm starving," Nate said, gently taking my elbow and guiding me away from the street corner with purpose. The traffic, of both people and cars, was heavy, and I didn't want anything to happen to the envelope. Neither did Nate.

"Me too." We ducked into a doorway, and I slipped the envelope in my bag. "Let's find a café, order some drinks and food, then open the envelope. Sound good?"

It was logistics first and then we'd discuss what had just happened. Nate was on his phone, searching for cafés in the 5th arrondissement, the labyrinthine neighborhood surrounding the Panthéon. With the Sorbonne and other universities nearby, the area was loaded with cheap ethnic restaurants and signs for souvlaki hiding some architectural gems from the fifteenth century. While my main concern was opening the envelope and scrutinizing its contents, I wasn't too keen on eating cheap student food, either. I wanted to sit, order a glass of wine, and take my time with the contents of the envelope. Nate was beginning to work his way through the Yelp reviews when abruptly he stuck his phone in his pocket. "Let's just walk that way. I'm sure we'll find some place." Serendipity over crowdsourcing.

I couldn't wait until we sat down, even though the streets were crowded, and the traffic was noisy. "Did you see him?"

"I don't think so. I saw a tall pale guy in black leather jacket walking down the steps and crossing the street, so I followed him, but he met a woman on the other side of the street. Clearly, it was a date or something, because they looked very happy to see each other. I don't think he had even been in the building, now that I think of it. Probably just using the steps as a lookout spot." We crossed the street indiscriminately. Nate seemed to be in a hurry to somewhere.

"Well, at least we know Blackbird is a man," I said, dodging a large group of American students. Nate made another quick turn off boulevard Saint-Germain and onto a tiny side street. It was nearly impossible to talk and keep up with Nate's blistering pace. Parisians walk quickly and with purpose, but Nate was in a league of his own.

"Likely, yes. But the tall pale guy in the black leather jacket could have been a go-between to a go-between. We don't know for sure it was Blackbird that handed the envelope directly to the security guard."

I chuckled.

"What's so funny?"

"I've never used a code name in a conversation before. Have you?" Nor had I ever gotten my heart rate up to the red zone looking for a place to eat, but I tried to breathe deeply and keep up.

"Yes, I have, but usually for projects that involve highly valuable intellectual property, not guys in black leather jackets." Nate stopped in front of a wine bar named Le Porte Pot. "This looks fine," he declared. By then, I would have agreed to McDonald's. I needed to sit down and catch my breath. We pushed through the front door together.

Nate ordered a beer even though it was a wine bar, and I chose a Sancerre, plus a bottle of sparkling water and a couple of dishes to share, ordering as quickly as we could. The restaurant was warm and inviting, with beamed ceilings, giant maps of wine-producing regions on the wall, and simple wooden tables and chairs. If Nate and I had simply been tourists taking in a few sites, it would have been the perfect post-Panthéon spot for happy hour. Instead, Nate's eyes darted around the place like he was checking for the nearest exit, and I felt like a covert operative who'd just failed a meet. *How did we get here?* Once the drinks arrived, I felt settled enough to open the envelope.

"Wait," Nate said.

"Did you want to sprint somewhere else first?" I said, alluding to his distance-runner pace setting.

"No, but let's try something. Why don't you tell me what you think is in the envelope? What might be the next page from the notebooks? The next location to meet up, if there is one?"

"Is this some bogus exercise you do at Green Town Industries?"

Nate didn't appreciate my skepticism. "My sister leads the brainstorming sessions. She went to business school, so there's a method to her madness. It works. It gets your brain pumping before you have to zero in on the question at hand. When we're trying to anticipate what might go wrong or right with a project, it opens us up to other avenues of inquiry when we think about all possible scenarios."

"That makes no sense to me."

"Think about what we know about Blackbird now and how he or she works and thinks. What connections have we learned so far? Not what we think we know, but what we know for sure."

I wasn't in the mood for this. I was in the mood for quick answers and the big bowl of mussels we ordered. But I could tell by the serious look on Nate's face he was going to see this intellectual exercise through, so I indulged him. "That Blackbird is familiar with my father's work and, well, we can even back up and say that he knows who my father is. And, we know that at some point, he had access to my father's notebooks and made copies of certain pages."

"Or discovered those pages in someone's files, right?"

"Oh, right. He seems to have a network of people willing to do his bidding, like maybe Beatrice or the security guard at the Panthéon, so he must have facility with the language, knowledge of the area, and persuasive techniques." This was kind of fun. The waiter put down a small plate of olives and roasted nuts, along with some cheese puffs, and both Nate and I reached in at the same time. "Or a lot of money."

"Good answers. So, knowing these things, what do you think

might be in there? For example, today we met at the first location of your father's Joan exhibit. What's the second location? If he is trying to lead us down that path, where do we go next?"

Now I was starting to get the point of the exercise, but that didn't make my brain work any faster. "Give me a sec." Nate looked surprised. "You know, I'm not a Henry Blakely scholar; I'm his daughter." It was a line I'd used many times before, but saying it to Nate made me hear it with fresh ears. It's true that most of what I knew about my father's career was anecdotal or observational, not academic. I'd never studied him properly or written a thesis on his early work. But I'd heard him tell the stories of his work, witnessed the process, cataloged the notebooks, and, in general, been along for the ride. Occasionally, I'd Google his name and read an article about him, if I had time to kill at work. Or, because of his depth of knowledge about my father, Tai and I would wander into a conversation over lunch about my father as easily as if we were discussing the films of Martin Scorsese or modern chair design.

I wanted to protest to Nate that I didn't have any kind of comprehensive timeline of his work stored in my brain to access at moments like this, but that wasn't true. I lived in his shadow during his lifetime and taken on his legacy after his death. Now was the time to make all the effort pay off, so I corrected myself, "I'm not a trained Blakely scholar, but I'm the next best thing."

In my mind's eye, I conjured up a series of photos that lined the walls of a hallway in the Pasadena house, taken by my mother during that week in Paris long ago. I had stared at them for decades, absorbing the images, but now I had to recall the exact order. Next to the Panthéon was . . . Notre-Dame.

"If that's a pattern, then the next place to meet would be Notre-Dame," I announced, remembering the image of a stone statue bathed in white light. "There's a simple statue of Joan praying. It's very pious, very straightforward. It's by a French sculptor. I'm so hungry I can't remember his name. Des- something. My father used this piece to represent Joan's steadfast faith, her simple belief in what she was doing. He lit the statues and that whole area of the church in white light, using various sources from candles to lanterns. I think there was also sound in that installation, a choir of some sort, chanting. It was said to be, um, reverent, that's the word most often used to describe the installation. At least in what I've read."

"So, if Blackbird is leading us on a wild-goose chase inspired by *Bright & Dark*, Notre-Dame would be the next logical stop." Now it was my turn for skepticism, because I objected to the phrase "wild-goose chase." Nate plowed ahead. "Any idea what page from your father's notebooks corresponds to the Notre-Dame location?"

"No. There are dozens of notebooks. But there doesn't seem to be a connection to *Small World*, so why should there be a connection this time?"

"True. Anything else you think might be in inside?"

"Nate, I'm opening this envelope."

"This makes no sense."

I handed the paper to Nate. He read the words aloud, in some vaguely Shakespearean cadence. It made the poem even more nonsensical, almost comical.

If the gilded light should fade
When you hear house men have strayed
Here's memory that tells me so
Here's golden hair that falls below
I'll touch the line of her chin
Like steel and glass from within
Come cut those locks at three, sweet maid.

Nate had no future in community theater, that was for sure, but I had to give him an A for effort. He stared at the paper, and then at me, asking, "Does anything jump out? Anything familiar to you? Any Notre-Dame reference?"

"No obvious ones. There are a lot of metal references—golden, gilded, steel. Maybe it has to do with the famous golden Frémiet statue of Joan at the rue de Rivoli. But even that's a stretch. I'd have to see it again to understand the steel and glass references. It could even be the I. M. Pei pyramid at the Louvre, but I can't think of any connection there to Joan or my father."

"Especially because the lines before seem to be about a woman's head of hair. Did Joan of Arc have golden hair?"

I thought about the hundreds of pieces I'd collected over the years with depictions of Joan, from master painters like Rossetti and John Everett Millais to the pop depictions like Kate Bush as Joan. Joan's hair color was all over the map, depending upon the artist. "Sometimes. Depending upon the cultural orientation of the artist."

"Anything else in the envelope?"

I reached in and pulled out a photocopy of another page of my father's notebooks. This time, there was no recognition. It didn't look familiar to me at all. It was a rough sketch of the facade of a stone building with arched windows and a grand doorway. Maybe a church, maybe an academic institution. There were some measurements and numeric notations, but no quote, no signature, no date. "This isn't helpful, either. I don't recognize it. Do you?"

Nate shook his head. "Looks like a campus of sorts. But it could be any campus. Did your father do any commissions on college campuses? Churches?"

"One finished piece at Lewis & Clark College in Portland. I've never been to the campus, so it could be a building there, I guess."

I had a thought and pulled my trusty Blue Guide out of my backpack. I turned to the index to look up House *of anything*. House of

Steel? House of Gilded Light? I heard Nate snort. "Sure, that should be a lot more helpful than this," he said as he waved his phone around.

"You never know. History doesn't change that much in a decade, Nate. And books are another way of organizing data, still a legitimate source of information." I actually used a lot of books at work when I was researching topics. Being Internet-free kept me focused on the task at hand, and we had an extensive library of books in the back office, annotated in the margins, filled with Post-its from curators and researchers adding their own two cents. The waiter set down a steaming bowl of saffron-scented mussels and a basket of bread. It smelled divine. I closed up my old-school guide. "I'm starved."

Nate was considering my words and then made a circle motion with his finger, indicating another round of drinks. He even managed, "Encore, merci." He slipped the drawing back into the envelope for safekeeping. "Let's eat."

The walk back to the hotel had been quiet, but the setting special, with the spires of Notre-Dame lit against the dark sky, first in the foreground, then behind us as we crossed the bridge to ISL. Young, beautiful city dwellers claimed spots along the Seine and benches on all the bridges for impromptu picnics with wine and food, a casual Parisian happy hour. I remember doing that many evenings during my student days when the weather allowed, bringing the American college tradition of kicking off the weekend on Thursday nights to France. I started to tell Nate about the memory but couldn't muster the energy. Clearly, we were both tired.

When we arrived at my hotel, there was a moment of hesitation. I had no doubt that I could figure out the meeting place in the morning with a good night's sleep and some focused research time. But despite today's heroics, I had some lingering doubts about Nate. In a previous life, like two months ago before the Dawn of the Twins, I might have blindly trusted a man this thoughtful and thorough, who had pushed me out of the way of a speeding car and chased down a stranger in the street for me. But now, I couldn't quite manage it.

"I have to ask again, Nate. Are you involved in this in any way? I've lost a lot lately and taken a lot of punches to the gut. It appears my instincts have been off for a long time. You seem sincere, but one more betrayal . . ." I couldn't even finish the sentence.

He looked right into my eyes. "I am not in involved in this in any way. I promise. Like you said earlier, I'm entirely random. But I do understand your hesitancy. None of this makes any sense. Does it?" He leaned in and kissed me gently on the lips. Salty. Sincere. Then his hands ran down my arms, across my lower back. I stepped in to meet his touch, his mouth, with newfound energy. The kiss on a Parisian street corner I had dreamed about a decade ago was finally happening. Every inch of my body responded.

But I wanted more. I pulled back slowly. "I never had a chance to say it, but remember last night? You know, before the felony? I had a wonderful time."

"Was that only last night?" he said as he brushed my hair back, shaking his head a bit, then tracing my jawline.

I knew what he meant. The last twenty-four hours felt like a hundred years, but I didn't want the day to end yet. I found my key card and let us in. I took his hand. "Stay with me tonight, Nate. Please."

Chapter 12

There was another note on the pillow from Nate. *Went out. Back soon. Best, Nate*

Best, Nate. Classic. It was almost eight, and I felt rested and ready. Satisfied. And, for the first time in many months, I felt capable.

It wasn't the most glamorous of terms, but ever since Casey's announcement, I'd been unsure of almost everything, from my decision to divorce him to my choice of nail polish. My failed marriage had left a big hole where my modest confidence had previously resided. Even though the stolen sketches were bad, I mean, *really bad*, I felt like everything else was going pretty well. I had handled the aftermath capably. Security was alerted, I had a sense of purpose, and I nailed the first meeting spot even though Blackbird had slipped away.

Then there was Nate, who was turning out to be like some kind of sexual Spackle, gluing my confidence back together. And I was about 99.9 percent sure he wasn't a con man with a PhD, which was a risk I could live with.

Casey's infidelities had shredded me. Once I got over the initial shock of his abundant affair, things only got worse. I lay awake in the middle of the night dissecting our sex life, from our first time—a coffee date that lasted all weekend—to our last—an early-morning nonevent. The more I thought about my role, the more I found myself wanting. Even though I knew the kind of deception that Casey had maintained for five years was not really about my lack of adventure in the sack, the thought that I had bored him out of our marriage messed with my mind. Being with Nate was the beginning of a new chapter, if not for Nate, then at the very least for me. I had never thought of myself as a needy person, requiring another person's presence to validate my own. But feeling Nate's body move over mine gave me strength.

I rolled over, threw on my discarded nightgown, and grabbed my laptop. Time to check my emails and face some music. I knew I had to connect with Mike today, and there was an email from him in my inbox.

To: Joan Blakely
From: Mike Danbretti

Joan,

Not getting any response to my calls. Time difference. Please contact ASAP when you get this, as I am concerned.

Checked into connection between theft of Panthéon Sketches and any other Joan of Arc–related pieces that may have been stolen in Europe. There doesn't seem to be any sudden uptick in such thefts, but there was a small statue of Joan of Arc lifted from a church in Donremy along with some other items. The artist was Dubois if that means anything, and it was a copy, so not that valuable. Let me know if you think there may be a connection, but it looks doubtful.

I also checked out Beatrice Landreau and Margot & Fils. There's something there, as Tai indicated. The gallery is in some financial trouble and she's had three sales reversed this year due to forged documents of origin. The works in question were all tapestries that appear to have been looted from Poland by the Nazis, then surfaced in France forty years later. No connection to Joan of Arc or Panthéon. It looks like Beatrice could be vulnerable to a bribe of some sort. Can you confirm any recent contact with her?

Nate Redmond checks out. From interviews and additional sources, it appears all he does is work. Nothing about his background indicates an interest in art or knowledge of the art world. Unlike some tech guys with $$$, he does not collect art. He collects Star Wars figurines, but I don't think that counts as fine art. It's a fairly valuable collection, though. He's into music and has a large album collection. Mentioned in a profile of him in SF Chronicle. In case you are wondering, he is truly single— never married, no kids. He contributes money to the Boys & Girls Clubs and is on the board of SheCodes, a nonprofit that encourages girls to go into tech. His last known girlfriend was in 2009, a programmer.

The work he's doing with artificial limbs is pretty impressive— low-cost, 3D printed limbs with smart chips for kids and veterans. According to Wired, he was inspired by a story he heard on NPR and it's been named one of the "Do Good" start-ups of the year. Sounds like a good guy.

Finally, I will have to go to the Museum on Monday to inform them of the theft. You have until 10 a.m. PDT.

Call me. Mike

I read Mike's email quickly and ran though the answers to his questions in my head before responding. No, there would be no obvious connection between a copy of a Dubois statue and the Panthéon Sketches. No, I hadn't been able to reach Beatrice, despite repeated calls and emails to her. And thanks for the thumbs-up on Nate and the *Star Wars* collection. I told him I'd keep trying Beatrice's cell to see if she would pick up and answer questions about the buyer. I decided not to tell him about the appearance of the mysterious envelopes, or that Nate was still in the picture. But I told him enough to show him my gratitude for his discretion until Monday.

There was no follow-up email from my mother, but the intern Kiandra had sent a message. She'd been thrilled to get the extra work of responding to the Henry Blakely letters. I think I bought her undying loyalty with the generous twenty-dollars-an-hour salary. Relieving my mother's guilt was worth at least that.

She wanted to let me know she was working through the pile of mail my mother had ignored for ten years and would let me know if there was anything that concerning or personal. I thanked her for getting on this task so quickly, asked her to scan anything that seemed suspicious, and wished her a happy weekend.

I hopped out of bed feeling a thousand times more clearheaded than yesterday. My plan was to inspect the clue again with the help of a map of Paris after some coffee. I threw on a white shirt, black jeans, boots. I caught a glimpse of myself in the mirror. Happy weekend? Yes, somehow, yes.

My phone buzzed. A text from Polly. Home early. Brunch? My Place? Bring hometown gossip.

Something in my gut told me that brunch with Polly might be the right call. It dawned on me that my instincts hadn't been all that fired up over the last six months. Or six years. But apparently, they were back.

"No sugar, right?"

Nate handed me a mug of coffee from the hotel's breakfast service. He had a plate of bread and jam with him that he set on the table next to the window. I turned from the charming view to see that he'd also changed his clothes from the night before. The sweater vest was back, and it looked good. I put the coffee down and reached out to touch him, which seemed to catch him off guard. I didn't let go. "Did you go back to your hotel already this morning?"

Nate moved closer. "I did. I'm an early riser. Plus, I had some work to catch up on. I have a few meetings this afternoon, so I didn't check out . . . but there's a room available here tonight. I can book that, you know, depending on what happens today. The front-desk guy here is really getting to like me. I can tell."

It was such a grown-up thing to do, make separate sleeping arrangements in the same hotel. I was compelled to caress his chest. "Did they drum you out of the International Society for the Takeover of the Human Race because of your failure to show up at the dinner last night?"

"Yes. I'm now left to the same fate as the rest of you sad sentient beings. Subjugation by the AI Overlords."

"I'll protect you. I know Pilates." Was tempted to work my hands under the wool and a layer of cotton to skin when Nate announced with enthusiasm, "Hey, I think I know how Blackbird found you. At this hotel, I mean."

"Really?" I pulled away, interested in the answer. "How?"

"Your good friend Polly. She didn't actually name the hotel where you were staying in a blog post about your visit. But she ended her piece with "Tennis anyone?" which is a pretty short mental walk for Blackbird to a place whose name is literally Hotel Tennis Court."

"That's not cool. How did you find that out?"

"I Googled you. It popped up near the top. Along with your bio from the museum. Your wedding announcement in the *New York Times* and your divorce announcement from a site called Candy-Kane or something. Oh, and a photo of you in high school with the president of Iceland."

"Sorry you didn't Google me thirty-six hours ago, aren't you?"

"Not really. I would have missed a great meal, a great dress, and some other great things." Nate blushed. I'm not sure morning-after talk was a specialty, but he continued. "We all have a past. I feel better knowing your former mother-in-law sells real estate. That's the most normal thing about you."

"Like your *Star Wars* collection." I worked on his buckle.

Nate laughed. "You Googled me, too?"

"So beyond Google. Got my high-priced, former FBI security team on it. Remember, you were the prime suspect for this crime twenty-four hours ago, but the chance of you collecting both Yoda figurines and nineteenth-century French art is pretty slim," I said taking a sip of perfect coffee. "Do you think Blackbird actually reads Polly's blog? Or was searching for me on Google and found it?"

"I don't know. But if Blackbird read it, anyone else could have, too."

"Right. Like Beatrice. Her silence is beyond suspicious. When did it post?" I brought up Polly's website on my laptop. Despite her lapse in judgment, I loved the photo of me in my cape standing in front of the Rodin Museum from 1999. That girl had style, I thought. That girl had big plans. I needed to dig that cape out of storage when I got home.

"Thursday morning. A day before the sketches disappeared."

"I like that you said disappeared and not stolen. I think I'm winning you over with my conspiracy theory."

Nate looked over my shoulder at my screen. "You haven't changed at all."

You're wrong, Nate. I've changed completely. "Maybe a bit. I'm seeing Polly for brunch. She knows Paris inside and out. Maybe she can help figure out the next location."

"You trust her? Even with the information breach?"

I laughed at his choice of words. "She's a blogger, not CIA. I'm sure she didn't intend to . . ."

"Blow your cover?"

"Again, with the aggressive language."

Nate wasn't done with his theories. "Maybe Polly is Blackbird. She knew you had the sketches, paid off the maid to watch your room, and when you left, stole them. Probably sold them to a Joan of Arc enthusiast who has enshrined them in his man cave already. Right below his unicorn poster."

"That is dismissive. Faith is powerful. Plus, I never told Polly specifically what the nature of my business was in Paris. She has no idea about the sketches."

"Any old boyfriends out there?"

"What's this about? Curiosity or jealousy?"

"Thinking of possible suspects who might want to get your attention." He stepped away, giving me room to stand.

"Ah . . ." I closed my screen, stood, and turned to face him. "It's a pathetically short list that includes my escort to the debutante ball, a friend's brother who later came out, but boy, could he waltz. He holds no grudges. I seemed to specialize in pining after gay boys for a while. Then, there was a chef, a couple of college flings, and an Australian. That's all you're getting." I started to gather up my devices and stash them in my bag. I debated changing for brunch with Polly but changed my mind. I'm sure I had nothing in my carry-on truly worthy of her, so I stuck to all black.

Nate watched me put on my jacket. "It's not a bad idea to think back on old acquaintances. Maybe somebody will stand out as trouble."

"Will do. I wish you could come to Polly's. I think you'd like her."

"I wish I could. But I really can't miss this meeting today. It's with a Swiss firm that Green Town is hoping to acquire. Plus, I need face time at this conference to send a message that we're in good shape."

A light bulb went off. "Maybe we can use Polly's blog to send a message to Blackbird. We can plant something to see if we can get his attention."

Nate stopped for a second. "Smart. You're pretty good at this, Agent Blakely."

"Thank you."

Chapter 13

"Sweeping" is the word I would use to describe just about everything in Polly's Parisian apartment: the view across the Seine to the Eiffel Tower; the hemline of Polly's cream-colored palazzo pants across her polished parquet floors; and the motion of her manicured right hand with the sapphire bauble as she gave me the two-dollar tour of her flat that was in painfully good taste. There was even a uniformed domestique in the kitchen with the broom. Yes, everything was sweeping at Polly's place.

She squeezed my arm as we stood at one end of her living room, looking back toward the grand windows and her husband, Jean-Michel, mixing cocktails. Here in the 16th arrondissement, Polly was among her people—the well-heeled, tennis-loving, and Baccarat-collecting upper crust of Paris. She looked right at home in her home.

After an inquisition about the impressive black sedan that dropped me off at her place, I was forced to explain that it was not a museum perk, but the ride of my seatmate Nate. Naturally, Polly jumped to the conclusion that Nate's gesture was romantic in nature, not a safety precaution. "You are glowing! I expected sad sack Joan, but you look great. Good for you!" After a few details on our meeting and subsequent interactions, Polly was impressed by my take-charge action, being in the "good sex is the best revenge" camp of getting over a bad breakup. "So, you actually met someone on a plane? I thought that was one of those women's magazine myths, like limiting yourself to four ounces of wine or doing your own at-home facials. I think I contributed to that mythology in the early aughts writing for *Glamour*." Polly was putting the flowers I had brought into a vase, arranging the blooms with ease.

"All I can say is that I put nothing out there but anger and disgruntlement, and the universe rewarded me with a business class upgrade and Nate." My eyes danced around the room, a design-magazine photo spread in real life. I had always admired the ability to mix antiques with abstract art, prints, and stripes, Danish side tables with medallion rugs—but this apartment was really in a class by itself, another level. Polly had it going on. I could see why her readers hung on to her every accessory. True to her Pasadena-meets-Paris brand, there was a pink-and-green needlepoint pillow on a side chair that read "Nouveau Riche is better than no riche at all."

I'm sure her French in-laws loved that.

I had real estate envy for sure. It struck me that I'd never really had my own place. My childhood home became my adult landing spot, thanks to tragedy and circumstance. When Casey moved in after the wedding, he dropped all of his student furniture off at Goodwill, happy to trade up. I had inherited my style; Polly had created hers all on her own. Truthfully, her own with a few behind-the-scenes designers who traded service for blog mentions and ad placement, but still, the place said "Polly." Suddenly I wanted to start fresh, somewhere new. "This apartment in amazing."

"Merci. JM lets me do anything I want, as long as I don't get rid of that reading chair in the corner." Polly nodded toward a well-worn chocolate-brown leather chair, acceptable by any standards but Polly's. "I added the orange pillows as a distraction. Does it work?" I nodded. "But, pretty soon, we're going to have to do a little redecorating."

I looked around and didn't see a single nook or cranny that could be improved. "What's left to do? Paint the ceiling?" I looked up. Never mind. There was trompe l'oeil on the twelve-foot ceilings.

Polly leaned in and whispered, "I'm pregnant! You're the first non–medical professional I've told."

I surprised myself by being genuinely happy for her, not a hint of jealousy. I was even curious in a way I hadn't been with other friends. My news about everything that had happened in twenty-four hours could wait. A bit. "Congratulations! When is the baby due?"

Another round of Bellinis had materialized thanks to JM, and the magical kitchen produced brunch of a bacon and onion tart, an herb salad with vinaigrette, and a tomato confit. Toast and various marmalades accompanied the main course, with Polly claiming to have made the fig-and-orange one. I had my doubts because I knew her area of expertise was shopping, not canning, but I didn't get into it with her because I was trying to be a good guest. Plus, my personal countdown clock was ticking. I only had a few more hours to decipher the next meet-up spot, so I couldn't really linger on marmalade or have another Bellini.

The clue ran through my head. *If the gilded light should fade . . . Here's golden hair that falls below . . . Like steel and glass comes from within.* I had spent some time researching buildings of steel and glass, and of course, the Louvre's pyramid was the first on the list. It came from within, sort of, bursting through the courtyard of the Cour Napoléon. What did it have to do with "golden locks"?

I checked my phone. Two more hours before the scheduled rendezvous. Polly was setting down a cheese course when I changed the subject from politics to stolen art. "So, I need your help."

Polly froze. "Is it about the *Marie Claire* piece?"

"What *Marie Claire* piece?" JM gave the barest head shake, and

Polly bit her lip. I imagined the worst—a hatchet job on my mother's career, a brutal think piece on my father's work, maybe even something scandalous about the museum that mentioned me. "I'm beyond shocking. Seriously. Nothing penetrates my hard shell now except these Bellinis."

"Oh, some slideshow with captions about Casey and his family, air quotes, and the show he has opening in Belize at some eco-resort. I'm mean, really, who goes to the jungle to see art? *Personne.* Nobody. And a collection of photos about water? Yawn. Plus, the online edition only, so clearly someone owed him a favor. Or *her.*" Polly refused to say Marissa's name in solidarity.

Of course he was in *Marie Claire*. Publicity-seeking Casey cashing in on the multicultural family to further his own career, heading off to some trendy thatched-roof lodge. I thought they were stealing my dream vacation, but no, it was all about Casey. "Believe it or not, I saw them at the airport checking in for their flight. He looked like every cranky forty-year-old dad on a forced vacation. It was shocking to see him with his family, no air quotes. They are a family. He looked like a dad with his kids. He texted me right before I took off, something about how he could tell I was on a mission because of my leather jacket. And how he thought I looked really good. Then he emailed and used the phrase 'heal together.' I didn't even respond."

"That must have been hard. To not want to get one good zinger in there."

I nodded. "Yes and no. I don't really miss him, but I wanted him to miss me."

"Since when does he do art photography? I thought he was in it for the money?"

"He dabbled. I never saw much of it. He always wanted a gallery show to prove himself to his art school friends. Now he's got it." A decade of tedious conversations about his work not being taken seriously came to mind. The bitterness that popped up whenever a good friend enjoyed a successful show and a sale or two. He was a working photographer, and he begrudged his starving artist friends their one glimmer of limelight. Casey seemed to get everything he wanted, including an opening night and an online slideshow of his fabulous family. "Were there pictures of her, too?"

"Unfortunately," Polly said. "The write-up and photos were totally contrived. She was referred to as his 'manager.' Clearly, the post was sponsored by Cost Plus because there was a cheesy picnic set up with melamine wineglasses and bamboo coasters. In the shot. It was atrocious."

That was the laugh I needed. "Paris has healed me. I don't wish them well, but I don't wish them ill."

"Really? Not even a little ill will?"

"Okay, a touch of ill will. But only to Casey. Not the kids. I'm not a monster."

"Très bien." Polly waved her hand around, and the woman from the kitchen began clearing our plates. "That seatmate of yours must really be something."

"He is. But I do have a situation here in Paris, and I need your help."

"I love situations." Polly was laser focused.

I filled Polly and JM in about the theft, the clues, and the chase thus far. JM, the lawyer, asked all the right questions about police procedure, insurance, and liability. He was also quite concerned about my personal safety, even though I'd fudged the details about the car in front of the InterContinental. Before I had a chance to show them the latest clue, JM declared, "I need to sit in my chair with a brandy to take this all in." It was early afternoon, and a brandy seemed extreme, but I went on as we moved into the living room. Polly brought along the cheese, some cookies, and an urn of coffee.

I took the latest envelope from Blackbird out of my bag, and Polly clapped her hands in anticipation. "I have a new clue that I can't figure out. I thought you might take a look at it. You both know the city so much better than I do. And here is the page from my father's notebook. It appears to be a random drawing of a building, but maybe you'll recognize it, if it has a Paris connection."

"This is like those art history treasure hunts my English friend hosts for large groups of suburban ladies from America. She makes a fortune taking all those Garden Club Sustaining Members to the same ten spots in Paris, convincing them it's a hidden gem! But this is so much better! It's real!"

Did Polly miss the part about art theft, attempted murder, and me losing my job, I wondered.

"This doesn't look familiar at all. It could be any one of a million buildings here—or anywhere in the world, really," Polly said, handing the page to JM, who also shrugged.

"Also, Polly, I want to use your blog as a message board. I think Blackbird is reading your posts. He knows where I'm staying." I spoke the final part slowly and carefully.

"That's incredible!" Polly gushed, as if having a potentially dangerous art thief as a reader were the equivalent of a *Vanity Fair* mention. Then she realized the dark side of the statement. "Oh dear."

"How is that possible?" JM asked, his nose out of joint un peu.

"Oh my God, Joan. I am so, so sorry. I." Polly cringed. "I didn't mention the name of the hotel directly, but I gave a hint. I was hoping the hotel might appreciate the publicity so much, they'd comp a few rooms for my brother and his wife when they come to visit this summer. I'm so tired of having them show up every August, you know, like they live here or something. Nobody entertains in August in Paris, except us, because my sister-in-law likes to pretend, she, quote, has a place in the sixteenth. I've heard her say that, Jean-Michel!" Polly patted her belly just to make sure her husband understood. "I thought sticking them in a hotel on the other side of town on an actual island seemed like a good idea this year."

JM wasn't happy. "So, you traded Joan's safety for free stuff?"

Polly's apology was sincere. "I'm a terrible friend. Forgive me, Joan."

"Did you get the free rooms?" I had to ask.

"Four nights! They loved the offhand reference. Now I'll do a proper post on them." JM was horrified, but I assured him that there would be no legal retribution. Or emotional fallout. Polly was grateful. "I owe you. Anything you need, Joan. Anything."

"Let me show you this first, and then we'll figure out what to say."

I opened up Blackbird's envelope and dug my Blue Guide out of my bag, which was peppered with Post-its of possible locations. I slid the paper across to Polly and picked up a perfect palmier to go with my coffee.

Polly read the clue aloud for all to hear, slowly and softly, ending each line with a question mark in her voice.

> If the gilded light should fade
> When you hear house men have strayed
> Here's memory that tells me so
> Here's golden hair that falls below
> I'll touch the line of her chin
> Like steel and glass from within
> Come cut those locks at three, sweet maid.

It took her all of about twelve seconds to unravel the next Blackbird meetup spot, lest I'd forgotten that she was our high school valedictorian and magna cum laude Wellesley graduate. "It must be the site of Antoine's, the famous Parisian hairstylist. He was the world's first celebrity hairdresser. And his salon was at Galeries Lafayette, on Haussmann. See 'house man'? Haussmann. And the steel-and-glass reference? That's clearly the spectacular atrium there."

Compelling but not complete. "Aren't there other steel-and-glass atriums in Paris? Maybe even on Haussmann?"

"Of course, but not as famous or a spectacular as GL. And Antoine created the Joan of Arc haircut. It was his first claim to fame. Not exactly sexy, but a very good start. His real entry to grand society was the creation of the bob, and it became *the* cut of the Jazz Age. He charged hundreds of dollars a haircut *in the twenties*. Before Vidal Sassoon or Sally Hershberger, there was Antoine!"

Dr. Polly Davis-de La Fontaine expounds on the History of Hairdressing. I felt like an idiot that I didn't figure this all out. Maybe Nate was messing with my brain, because when Polly laid it all out, it seemed obvious. "You're amazing! How do you know all this?"

"Oh, ladybug, I've been blogging for years now, and the number one question I'm asked by expats is about finding a decent salon with stylists who speak English. Well, that and how to find a gynecologist who looks like Olivier Martinez. But I've done dozens of posts about hair, haircuts, hair products, hair balls. I know my hair. I know my white girl hair and my Black girl hair. It's like fate that you brought this to me." Polly started dialing her phone to set up appointments and then paused. "There are three salons inside GL. What do you think we should do?"

Considering the complex choreography of Blackbird's moves over the past thirty-six hours, I took an educated guess. "Call around. I bet one of them has an appointment on the books for me at three."

Sure enough, the call to salon number two hit pay dirt. "You have a blowout scheduled at Franck Provost," Polly reported and then added, "You know, you kinda need it. You have a little bedhead."

—

I'd forgotten how thrilling it was to walk into the historic department store with its glass-and-steel dome and art nouveau staircases. Shopping magic, impossible to resist. The store was crowded with both Parisians and tourists, mobbing the makeup counters for French skin-care treasures. Even though we were focused on a possible meet with Blackbird, we stopped by the perfume counter, like old times. Polly bought me a travel-size bottle of Nina Ricci perfume. "To make up for the security breach. Please accept my apologies. L'Extase—ecstasy. I think Nate will like it."

We hustled up to the third floor and found the salon. By late afternoon, I had a head of smooth, shining, extra-conditioned hair booked and paid for by Blackbird. The appointment almost passed with no sightings of the mystery man or a new envelope, despite the fact that Polly kept a close watch on all the comings and goings by keeping her sunglasses on inside and talking out of the side of her mouth whenever a suspicious type entered the salon. When I asked the receptionist with the streaked blue hair if anyone had left anything for me, she said in perfect English with a British accent, "This isn't FedEx."

While it was impossible to relax completely, Polly and I chatted as we sat side by side, like we were at home in Pasadena, running down a list of our former classmates' current statuses. Tinsley Madden: single lawyer, possibly gay, in process of adopting foster child. Kristy Lynch Newhauser: divorced from high school sweetheart, now in rehab, raising two boys, living in rather sad town house, dating younger guy with emerging man bun, and back to using maiden name. Tiffany Tang: dermatologist married to thoracic surgeon, living in an enormous house in San Marino with three Maltipoos and full-time help for the dogs. Bethie Sims: class officer, wife, mother of one adorable baby boy, and salt of the earth, working in development at the old alma mater. Val Neely: off the grid since college, returning with a vengeance, including a boob job, a Russian fiancé, and a lost decade on her résumé. Of course, Polly was the source for most of this information, maintaining her hometown network, even though she lived six thousand miles away.

"Why don't I know any of this? I live there. No one tells me anything."

"People are intimidated by you, Joan. They always have been. The parents, the cheekbones, your access to backstage passes."

I think Polly was exaggerating, but I said, "They're not scared of me anymore! Since the whole betrayal thing, I'm getting high fives in the parking lot from people who haven't talked to me in years."

"You're one of them now. Flawed."

"I did run into Bethie Sims and her blue blazer at Whole Foods a month ago. She was buying the world's most expensive baby apple-sauce, and I was buying a bottle of wine, a sushi snack pack, and a pair of yoga pants so I didn't have to do laundry. She was truly sorry about Casey, and I swear, Polly, she looked at the yoga pants in my cart and said, 'Are you okay?' Like buying clothes at Whole Foods was the sign of a mental health crisis."

"Well, let's face it, it is." Polly reapplied her lipstick as she studied my coif. "Hair, nine. Front desk service, two. How do you think I'm doing with the pregnancy bloat? Trying to hold the line. French-women have no mercy when it comes to baby weight gain."

"That lipstick shade is very slimming," I responded, and thought maybe Blackbird had wanted me to have some girl time with Polly. Then I realized that maybe I had a variation of Stockholm syndrome, endowing the guy with a little too much humanity, considering his actions. I texted Nate to let him know we were finishing up. He wanted to send his car back for me.

To my surprise, the surly receptionist informed me that she had received an envelope at the front desk. She apologized for the mis-understanding earlier and added, "Delivered by messenger."

The envelope had arrived after my service, as if the messenger was keeping an eye on the place to make sure I'd finished up before delivering the item. There was no credit card record for the payment; it had been cash, also delivered by messenger prior to my arrival. "Don't you think it's strange that we've gone from the Panthéon to the hair salon? What is this game?"

"It seems very personal. And whoever Blackbird is, he has a sense of humor, a sense of fun. Who doesn't want a blowout? Picking the spot known for the Joan of Arc haircut is kind of funny, don't you think?"

I had to give her that, even if my personal and professional reputations were on the line. "I guess. I might find it more hilarious if the sketchbook materialized."

"Well, you look amazing." Polly was due back for yet another social obligation, so I promised to email her the clue when I got back to my laptop, along with the message I wanted her to embed into her blog. I didn't know quite what it would be yet.

As we parted with a double cheek kiss on boulevard Haussmann, my car and Polly's taxi waiting, she squeezed my hand and said, "I know this is all crazy stuff and you've been through so much, but remember this: you will always have great hair. And that is worth something."

With that, Polly swept into the cab and disappeared into the Parisian sunset.

The driver explained that we had to swing by the conference hotel to retrieve Nate, and I felt my blood rush a little thinking about seeing him again. I'd wait to open the envelope with Nate; I liked the way it felt to work out the clues with him, like foreplay, if you were the type to find crosswords sexy.

I checked my emails in the back of the car, looking for anything from Beatrice. Nothing. She was still MIA. But instead, I skipped to the next one, another email from Kiandra at the museum.

To: Joan Blakely
From: Kiandra Douglas

Hi, Joan . . .

Hope you are having a blast in Paris. I have received several desperate texts from Tai in the desert, begging me to bring trashy novels and gossip magazines to the curators' retreat. He's so funny. He sounds bored. I think it sounds like a dream to spend the weekend talking about what art to buy next, but, oh well.

It's freakishly hot here in SoCal and my apartment has no AC, so I've spent the weekend at the office in the air-conditioning going through your mom's mail. Win-win. Paid work & regulated body temps. Thanks again for your trust. I've made it through most of the letters.

First, let me say that your father has a lot of fans (still) and most of the letters are people reaching out to say how sorry they are. The letters go back ten years, but there are some as recent as last Christmas. It's really touching how meaningful your father's work is to people all over the world. I've never lost anybody significant to me and I know I'm lucky, but I think you'd find a lot of solace reading some of these notes. They are amazing reminders. Your choice.

Also, I wanted to alert you to one series of letters that seem both personal and urgent, even though they were sent in 2003 to 2005. There are six typed letters sent over a two-year period, addressed to your mother, who is referred to as "Suzannah." The letters seem to be from someone both your parents knew and they include personal details about shared memories, like "the time we all swam in the Pacific at midnight" or "closed down that club in SoHo." Unfortunately, they aren't signed. Instead the sign-off is always *Best* and then a scribble of a black animal or bird or something. The reason they stand out is that he repeatedly asks your mother to contact him/her (although he writes like a him) about something of your father's that he has in his possession. The details are vague, like the fact that he leaves no contact information, but it seems legitimate. In the last letter, he says that he won't contact your mother again if he doesn't hear back. I've gone through the stacks of mail looking for letters after 2005, but there aren't any additional ones.

Oh, and it's kind of weird because he makes reference to you and asks how you are coping. Sorry to dump all this on you when you are out of town, but you said to contact you if anything stuck out. These do, for sure.

Do you want me to send them to your mother? Or scan and send to you? Let me know. At the office most of weekend. Standing by . . .

Have a glass of Bordeaux for me.

Kiandra

Chapter 14

Occasionally, my mother would take me on location with her, if it meant we could spend a weekend in New York or a school vacation in another exotic locale, courtesy of somebody else's expense account. Her regular clients, Ralph Lauren and Longines, each needed her once or twice a year for shoots to cover everything from print ads to in-store collateral. In a few days of shooting, the ad agency had everything they needed for a year, and my mother got her mojo back for a few months, like a shot of adrenaline to her personality. These long-term contracts were the glue that held her together. She knew it was a gift to be employed after the age of thirty in her business.

She loved me, but I never got the sense that she loved driving me to dance class or attending parent-teacher conferences. She never volunteered at school like the other moms, preferring to raise money for AIDS awareness. I don't recall her ever baking for a bake sale, bringing snacks to soccer, or waiting in line to sign me up for, well, *anything*. This was celebrity parenting in the days before it was good PR to have a baby and churn out quotes to magazines about how your children "kept your grounded" and "gave you a new set of priorities." My mother clearly found the business of motherhood much less interesting to her than the business of modeling.

She wasn't exactly Suzi Clements Blakely, PTA president.

For a couple of weeks a year, while in front of the camera in Aspen or Montana or Manhattan, my mother had a life beyond her family. She would pretend that she dreaded everything about the assignment—the frantic dieting and facials beforehand, the fittings and the fuss on set, the travel and hotel hopping—but she didn't hate it at all. She loved every second. My father and I would share eye rolls when she complained about "eating cabbage soup for two weeks straight." But every time we headed to LAX in a town car, she'd shake her blond head and say, "Suzi Clements, back in action."

I found the endless hours of hair and makeup and lighting to be incredibly dull, but when I was a cute tween, everyone made a big deal over how much I looked like my mother, patted my head, and smiled. Usually the manicurist offered to do my nails, or the stylist would trim my hair. For a few years, it was special, something I could take home and tell my friends about. Their moms were lawyers or accountants, not supermodels. I was special because she was special.

But eventually, the magic wore off. I liked being with my mother, but not being on location. Mainly, I sat in a corner with a book and watched Suzi Clements operate as the center of attention. She thought it would make me want to follow in her footsteps, treating it like a Take Your Daughter to Work Day with a side of Look at Me, How Fabulous Is This? But the trips had the opposite effect, convincing me that the last thing I ever wanted to do was be a model. The sheer number of people touching her face, head, and body at the same time was a turnoff to me.

As Suzi Clements, my mother flirted with everyone, from assistants to the art directors, but especially with the photographers. I remember a Ralph Lauren shoot in Montana once, seeing my mother cozy up to the handsome, but very young, photographer, and being shocked by the complete personality change. Who was this laughing, touchy coquette? Around Pasadena, my mother was all business, all the time. Warm enough, but never inappropriately attention seeking.

She kept people at arm's length, partly because she liked her ice-princess reputation and partly because she didn't have to feign friendships with others. She was Suzi Clements Blakely, after all, a tad too good for the average mother.

Once, after a few glasses of wine, I told Tai about my mother's set behavior, and his jaw dropped a bit, because Tai revered both my parents for different reasons, and he wondered aloud, "Oh my gosh, it's hereditary. Do you think that's why you fell for Casey? The whole photographer thing?"

Maybe, maybe not. But I know when I stopped going on location with my mother: after a brutal few days in London where my mother was shooting a watch spread in various locations from Wimbledon to the Victoria and Albert Museum. She was styled as a glamorous jet-setter that loved life and sipped champagne at all hours. By day three on set, I thought I was going to lose my mind. I had recently started in on an early feminist phase combined with eco-activism, and the whole modeling world was the opposite of what I believed in at the moment. Plus, I was at the height of my awkward stage, at age fifteen—tallish, flat chested, wearing braces and a permanent scowl all set off by my purple glasses I'd seen a character wear on *Full House*. The cute was gone. Nobody wanted to do my nails or trim my hair anymore.

As I read *Women Who Run With the Wolves* hidden behind a rolling wardrobe, I heard a young, impossibly chic British assistant stylist whisper about how I must have gotten the milkman's genes, because I couldn't possibly be "the spawn of the two most attractive people in the world. How do Suzi Clements and Henry Blakely create such a dreary being?" When another assistant stylist suggested that I might blossom, Snarky Stylist said, "She's no swan. And she's probably no Blakely."

The swan bit, I understood; the Blakely bit, less so. My mother adored my father, didn't she? I literally hid in the bathroom of a posh town house the rest of the day, refusing to come out, alternating sobs and screaming at my mother about wanting to go home. I could never tell my mother exactly what the stylist had said, but I know she suspected that it was deep and cutting. The stylist was gone by lunch, but her comments were enough to undermine my self-confidence throughout most of high school and beyond.

And now these letters addressed to "Suzannah." Not even my socialite grandmother called my mother Suzannah. She was Suzi from the minute she was born. There was something more intimate, jarring even, seeing my mother called by her full name. Polly was right; this was personal.

Who on earth called my mother "Suzannah"?

The driver and I had been parked out in front of the InterContinental for a half hour, waiting for Nate to finish up his meetings. I'd texted him a few details but not many because I knew he was in meetings. His only response was "Out by 5." Not an emoji kind of guy.

When Nate opened the door of the car, I was startled. "Wow, look at you." Nate climbed into the back seat of the sedan. The driver hopped out to handle his bags. "Oh, sorry. Didn't mean to scare you. Is everything okay? Did something happen?"

"Blackbird knows my parents. Or knew my dad and refers to my mom as 'Suzannah,' which nobody does, by the way. She has always, always, always been Suzi, except to my dad, who called her 'Love.' And Blackbird claims he has something of my father's, which he was desperately trying to return to my mother five years ago, but my mother never bothered to open the letters. Six of them over three years that she never even opened. This makes no sense. Is that what this is all about?" It all came out in one breath.

Nate took it in stride, considering he'd been talking about

advancements in laser technology all day. "You know you have to start at the beginning of this, right? Walk this all back a bit so I know what's going on."

"Of course. I'm overwhelmed with information. How were your meetings?" I tried to sound interested, but Nate wasn't fooled.

He shook his head. "You don't have to pretend to care about my business, Joan. I get it. Now, what happened?"

The driver pulled away from the hotel into the light Saturday-night traffic.

"Polly figured out the location in seconds. It was a hair salon, and she's like a salon savant. It had nothing to do with art or architecture, but everything to do with hair. A salon at Galeries Lafayette." Nate shook his head. "A very famous department store—all gilt and glass and steel on boulevard Haussmann. Get it? Like the clue. Courtesy of Blackbird, I had a wash and set at the salon where the Joan of Arc bowl cut was created."

"Ah. That's unexpected. And pretty clever. I gotta give that to Blackbird. And to Polly. We weren't even close." Even Nate was susceptible to warm and fuzzy feelings for the guy.

Then I filled Nate in on the latest, from JM's concerns, to the series of messengers monitoring my movements at the salon, to the unexpected email from Kiandra. "It must be the same guy, right? A signature that looks like a small bird, those were Kiandra's words: that must be our guy."

"It sounds possible, even probable. But one step at a time." *Oh, here he goes again with the alternate theories*, I thought, and Nate read my mind. "Now hear me out. Maybe that Blackbird signature is a common sign-off, like an acknowledgment of being a member of AA or some other group your father might have been associated with. Did you check with your mother? If nobody called her Suzannah except this letter writer, then she might know who it is right away."

Damn. I hadn't thought of any other possibility besides the most obvious. Maybe it was some secret society sort of thing. And no, I hadn't checked with my mother, because the last thing I wanted to do was give her any hope about anything—my father's work, some lost papers, whatever it is that this guy was holding on to. For the second time in two days, I made the decision to keep my mother in the dark. "Why do you have to be so logical? It never occurred to me that the bird thing might be a symbol. That actually sounds plausible. And I don't want to say anything to my mother yet. I'd like to see the letters first, so I asked Kiandra to scan and send them to me. It's early on the West Coast, but she'll be up and at the office in a few hours. I want to make sure the letters are legit before I bother my mother. It's hard to go back to that place again, do you know what I mean?"

"I don't really know, but I imagine it is."

There was a moment of silence between us, not awkward like so many others in the past when the circumstances of my father's death came up in a conversation with new acquaintance, but a genuine moment, like Nate was truly trying to imagine being in my place. As we crossed the Seine, the spires of Notre-Dame came into view. Almost home at the hotel. Nate gestured toward the envelope in my hand. "Anything new in there?"

"Let's open it together. Over a bottle of something."

Nate had checked into his own room at my hotel, much to the amusement of Claude the Front Desk Guy, who seemed to be the Hôtel Jeu de Paume's only employee. Still put out that he'd been interrogated by the police, Claude enjoyed baiting me as he handed Nate his own room key. "I see you and your old friend are very close, but not that close." To which Nate had answered, "I have restless leg syndrome." We laughed, but Claude didn't. He did manage to recommend a neighborhood spot tucked around the corner when we requested a quiet, authentic place for dinner. "It's a little early for dinner, but you Americans . . ." Then he added, "Maybe some wine will help your leg calm down."

For the third night in a row, Nate and I were tucked into the booth of a bistro, ordering drinks and food and looking, I imagine, like a regulation tourist couple on a Paris getaway. Nate had showered, shaved, and changed in record time, and I had put on a fitted dark gray sweater and a touch of makeup, as long as my hair looked so good. Our knees touched under the table, and I ran my hand over his thigh. He didn't flinch. For the tenth time in two days, I wished the theft had never happened, and Nate and I could have spent the weekend any other way but chasing clues. "Shall we?" Nate said, nodding toward the envelope on the table.

While Nate waited for his beer, I opened the third envelope— two sheets of paper, just like the other ones. I removed them carefully and laid them down on the table. One was another notebook page and the other a handwritten clue written in verse. Drawn to my father's scribble and scratches, I studied the notebook page first. Nate waited patiently. He didn't grab the other paper or ask questions; he let me be with the material. The drinks arrived, and Nate managed a "merci" for the waiter.

It took me a while to place my father's drawing, but then I recalled seeing it in one of several notebooks that my father labeled "On Tour." It was a drawing of the set for David Bowie's Serious Moonlight Tour. In the corner, there was a tiny notation that read *01/83*. The rough sketch was of four tall columns, an oversize hand, and, of course, a moon. There was another note on the top of the page. *Moonlight = Sunlight + Starlight + Earthlight*. And then a notation that just said, *Purkinje Effect*. I didn't know what the Purkinje effect was, but the sweetness of my father's equation for moonlight made me tear up. I would have been two years old when my father did this sketch. I handed the paper to Nate. "My father did the lighting design for several of David Bowie's tours. According to the date, this sketch is from the 1983 tour."

"Serious Moonlight."

"I'm impressed. Very nice."

"It's a recurring *Jeopardy!* category. And my mother is a Bowie fan. I can't believe your father did the lighting for David Bowie. That's very cool."

"He was cool. He did lighting for about two dozen tours, especially when he was young and wild. Sometimes he did one-off shows when the bands played in LA or Vegas; sometimes he did the lighting design for the whole tour. The Eagles. Stones. Rufus & Chaka Khan. Elton John at the Hollywood Bowl. A bunch of others. That kind of work paid the bills for a lot of years. But once he got married and I was born, he really cut back because it was grueling. And it wasn't great for his sobriety. Besides, he didn't need to do it for financial reasons."

"Because his artwork started paying off?"

"Yes and no. Yes, he made a modest living from his art after *Bright & Dark*. But also, because he married my mother. She comes from some money and made more modeling than my father did making art. She had some long-term contracts that were fairly lucrative for decades, but not zillions of dollars. My mother used to say, 'We don't have Live at Wembley money'—because many of their friends did. Rock and roll made a lot more money than conceptual art. Doing the lighting on tour was his bread and butter for years. I know my parents were able to buy their house in Ojai because of Serious Moonlight. My dad often referred to it as 'the house that David Bowie built.' The original tour poster is still in our guest bathroom. They stayed friends, got together occasionally in New York or here. They had a lot in common, including their model wives. And no, I never met Bowie. I had a chance my junior year abroad, but I went to Oktoberfest instead. Me and every other American student in Europe."

Nate was quiet for a second, then said, "That's appalling."

"You have no idea the regrets." I handed the page to Nate.

"Where is this all taking us? Murals, hair salons, Disneyland, moonlight. I feel like I should understand the significance of the Bowie reference or the date should mean something. But it's another random moment from my father's life."

Nate studied the page and then said, "Do you know what the Purkinje effect is?"

I shrugged. "It sounds vaguely familiar."

Nate tapped away on his phone, then read, "According to Wikipedia, it's 'the tendency for the peak luminance sensitivity of the eye to shift toward the blue end of the color spectrum at low illumination levels.' I guess that has to with how we see moonlight—a little blue."

Of course, that's the kind of physiological fact my father would take into account in his work. I should have been listening more closely, as I'm sure he lectured me on the Purkinje effect at some point. It would come into play while lighting a rock concert, accounting for the eye being able to see blue in low light instead of just throwing up a few blue gels and calling it a day. "That makes sense. My father understood how the human eye and the brain perceived light. It was essential to his work. I guess he wanted the audience to see David Bowie bathed in real moonlight, not just blue gels."

"That sounds like a difference Bowie would appreciate. And, does this have anything to do Joan of Arc?"

"No, I don't think so." Then I recalled some photos of the Notre-Dame installation that my mother had taken from *Bright & Dark*. There was a serious moonlight quality to those images as well. "Now that I think of it, there may be a link to Notre-Dame, but I don't know."

I lifted up the second piece of paper, containing what we now knew would reveal the next location. It had the same rough quality, same handwriting, same black bird at the end of the verse as the others. I read on:

Soon the pictures, black & white
Captured maid, prince, and silent knight
Here's my eye that tells me so
Here's my sight that lets me know
I'll see her sacred heart ignite
Be there at the stroke of midnight
Come meet with me then, sweet maid
Come sing with me then, sweet maid

"We need to be somewhere at midnight!" I handed the paper to Nate. *Maid, prince, and silent knight? Black & white? Sacred heart ignite?* Nate read it to himself several times as I watched him. "This is really out of my element. I don't see a Notre-Dame reference. But, I gotta say, I like this one. Poetic and romantic. Once you set aside the criminal aspect of the enterprise."

I felt a burst of warmth for Nate. *Sacred heart ignite*, indeed. He was right. "It is well crafted."

"We can do this. We have time. Anything jump out at you?"

I studied the words again, and it was like my vision came into focus. Phrases popped. I was getting good at this. "Of course, 'sacred heart.' That's a reference to Sacré-Coeur, where the last night of *Bright & Dark* was staged. That's pretty obvious."

"Maybe to you."

"Sorry. You're right. Obvious to me."

"What about 'Captured maid, prince, and silent knight'? Is that Joan and the French prince guy?"

"I would assume. Yes, Joan and Charles, the Dauphin. The Silent Knight could be Henry of England. Or Archangel Michael. Some scholars think he taught Joan military tactics."

There was a sharp laugh from Nate, followed by incredulity.

"Really? Some scholars actually think an angel taught Joan military tactics?"

"Well, it is hard to explain how an illiterate peasant girl defeated the English army without any training. Angels make as much sense as anything, really, once faith is in place," I snapped. I didn't feel like debating this point, but I felt like I needed to represent Joan's integrity.

"Sure, so 'taught by an angel' makes a lot of sense. Military training by a guy with fluffy white wings. Got it."

"Let's debate that later. Ticktock. The important thing to note here is that there is a statue of Joan at Sacré-Coeur, so I think we're in the ballpark."

"All right, nearby Sacré-Coeur at midnight. What do you think that means? Is that a big area?"

Ah, Nate. Stick to artificial limbs, I thought. But his earnestness was so appealing, sexy even, and my mind skipped back to Friday evening when he had run his hands over my hips in the elevator of the Hôtel Jeu de Paume.

"Joan?"

My name shook me. "Um, what we have is pretty vague. Sacré-Coeur is a basilica on top of Montmartre." I gestured in the general direction. "You may have noticed the white building at the far side of the city. The church itself is enormous and dominates the neighborhood. As I recall, there are hundreds of steps leading up to the church on one side and a wraparound plaza. Great views of the city from there. But 'nearby' could mean any of a million places. It's impossible to say exactly where. The surrounding area is packed with streets, cafés, apartments, and stores. It's a busy, dense neighborhood with a bohemian tradition, where all the artists hung out in the twenties. Crazy charming. Imagine if Greenwich Village was built on steep hill, with winding streets, a million cafés, and hidden staircases. That led to more charming streets. Moulin Rouge, tons of tourists. I don't know the area well enough to even guess what's 'nearby'—we should study a map and maybe something will pop out at me. I didn't spend a lot of time there as a student." The food arrived, duck for me and beef for Nate. I stared at the paper again. "'Black and white.' That's a specific phrase, isn't it?"

"Could be colors. Or names. A commentary on contrasts."

"Listen to you, a commentary on contrasts!"

"Hey, I took a literary criticism class to get through one of my pre-reqs in college. You know, you don't really need to understand literature to criticize it."

"True of so many things." A sip of wine and a bite of cassoulet au canard later, a thought popped into my head. "It's 'pictures, black and white,' not just 'black and white.' That could be photos, right? We're looking for photographs possibly."

"The references to seeing and sight would back up that theory. That's a good guess. Or, as we say in my business, a conjecture with merit." The daylight was gone outside the restaurant, and Nate's eyes shined in the candlelight. He was enjoying this. "So, we need to find a place near Sacré-Coeur that has a black-and-white photo of Joan of Arc and some guys. Pretty straightforward, I imagine."

Immediately I picked up my phone and searched for photo galleries in Montmartre near Sacré-Coeur. It was nearly impossible to tell from the vague or outdated gallery websites which one might have a photo exhibit up and no way to tell which one might have photos of a maid, a prince, and a knight. "These websites are rubbish, especially the mobile sites. We may have to walk the streets of the neighborhood and hope to get lucky. We should start right after dinner," I said, only half-joking.

"Do you know anyone here that is a photographer or photo dealer? Maybe they could steer us in the right direction. Maybe Polly knows someone."

A tiny wave of juvenile jealousy went through me at the mention of Polly's name as some sort of all-knowing genius. *Seriously, still in competition after all these years?* Then I remembered the list of galleries Tai had given me before I left Pasadena, a million years ago or last Wednesday. I recalled that he said one specialized in black-and-white prints. "Nate, you're a genius."

I dug though my bag and found the list in an envelope filled with other Parisian tips from curators and friends with restaurant suggestions and the like. Tai's note mentioned Luna, a gallery with branches in several cities all over the world. *Street photography, Black & White. Fashion, Rock n' roll. Beautiful people. Like SCB's work. Ask for Guy. Drop my name.*

I explained, "My friend Tai is a curator. He gave me a list of galleries to visit while I was here. None are near Sacré-Coeur, but one is a place that specializes in black-and-white photography. And Tai made a note that the photos are like my mother's. Street. Rock and roll. Could that be the Bowie reference?"

"Was Saint Joan in a rock band, too?"

"Okay, buddy, that's verging on heresy. No, she wasn't. But today some fangirl site would call her a rock star." Luna wasn't that far from the hotel. "It's Saturday night, though. I'm not sure the gallery will be open." I found the phone number, hit "call," and mumbled a short prayer to my patron saint as I waited for the connection.

The list of what I had to do was long: talk to our security expert Mike and art dealer Beatrice and probably my mother; come clean with the museum about what had happened to the Panthéon Sketches and the current goose chase I was on for my father's notebooks or the sketches or maybe both; plant a message for Blackbird in Polly's blog, but what message? But in the charming restaurant with the warm yellow walls and the brass wall sconces, I couldn't focus on anything but Nate's jawline. It was quite good.

Just then, someone on the other end picked up the phone. "Allô? Galerie Luna."

—

"Why are we stopping at the hotel? Shouldn't we get going? We don't have a lot of time here." Nate was tossing some euros on the table to pay the bill. We had quickly finished our dinner as soon as I'd hung up the phone.

"Nate, it's an art opening in Paris. One that we don't have an invitation to. I'm not going dressed like this." I indicated my jeans and boots. "Tai would kill me if he heard, and believe me, he'll hear." Plus, I had a feeling we were going to need a bit more subterfuge than a "lost invitation" excuse and the first name of a curator. The voice that answered the phone had not been very encouraging about entrance. I'd texted Tai to ask if he could get us on the list at the gallery but hadn't heard back, so I could only assume that he was trapped in a visioning session. We were going to have to wing it. "Pray for us, Joan," I whispered to myself.

"Do I need to change?"

"Not at all." I had a plan, and Nate's tweed jacket was part of it. This was going to be fun.

Chapter 15

From across the street, the scene at the Galerie Luna looked like a still life painting in action: a glass-fronted gallery lit from within with warm hues and track lighting, giant photographic prints of race cars visible in the background, and in the foreground, a swath of beautiful people of all colors, dressed in black and gray with the occasional pop of red. Each time the door opened, a wave of conversation and the beat of EDM made its way out onto the sidewalk across the street where we stood. A few paparazzi were hanging around outside, suggesting the guest list was as exclusive as the woman on the line had said when she'd answered my call an hour earlier. "Invitation uniquement. Invitation only. Pas de public."

My heartbeat quickened, and I realized it wasn't just because of our task at hand—to find Guy and get some information. It was because I'd been shut off from events like this for so long. This is what I thought my life would be like when I graduated from college, a mix of day-to-day scraping out a living in the art world punctuated by heady openings with handsome men, but that reality never materialized for me. My work at the museum was safe and steady; my evenings with Casey, the same. I could have used a little bit of glitter.

I wished for a second that Nate and I were simply here for the art and the scene, me back in my black dress and Nate in tweed. Then

I felt Nate take my hand. "This looks amazing. I think it was that prayer." Nate winked a sloppy wink. "Yeah, I heard you."

"We're going to need a little help getting in. Play along."

"Got it." We crossed the street, dodging traffic. "You're killing me in that dress, by the way. And you smell really good."

"I know."

We were stopped at the entrance by a phalanx of gallery girls looking like all gallery girls the world around: thin, stylish, and dressed in black, black, and black with their hair pulled back tightly and grim expressions on their young but serious faces. I approached the first gatekeeper at the table, attempting what I characterize as a haughty nod to acknowledge her existence. She returned the haughty and upped me boredom and distain. "Votre nom?"

I presented the young woman with my card and then attempted some French. "My name is Joan Bright Blakely, and I'm an art consultant based in Los Angeles. I'm not on the list but heard about the opening from my friend Tai Takashita, a curator at the Wallace Aston Museum in California who knows Guy. We were hoping to get a look at the work and a word with Guy."

Apparently, I didn't completely botch the syntax or accent because Gallery Girl replied in French, "You are not on the list. This is a private party."

I bent in and stage-whispered, "Yes, I understand. But I have a very wealthy private client here from Silicon Valley. And I know he's interested in investing in this sort of art. So, I'm hoping you can make an exception." I gestured toward Nate. Gallery Girl gave him a once-over. Nate, totally tweedy, stood there unsuspecting, with an all-American grin on his face that was perfect for the ruse, and he gave her a little wave. I appreciated his efforts, but Gallery Girl did not. She shrugged. "I don't know where Guy is. I'm sorry.

You'll have to come back another day with the gallery is open to the . . . public."

So I threw it down, using all I had left. "I believe Guy will be disappointed. He is an admirer of my father's work. And my mother's. Perhaps you know of the work of Henry Blakely and Suzi Clements?"

Gallery Girl #2 sprang to attention. I knew that even though she was staring at her list, head down, she'd been eavesdropping the entire time. She looked to be the oldest in the group at about twenty-five. "Ah, of course. You look just like your mother. I, too, admire the work of your father." She pressed a button on her headset and said, "Guy to the front, please." Then she spoke in English while turning her back on Gallery Girl #1. "One moment, please, we are happy to accommodate you." Gallery Girl #1, either embarrassed or indignant, refused to even make eye contact with me and literally brushed us along with her hands.

I wished I had a little of her self-absorbed confidence at thirty-one, never mind twenty-one.

As we waited, Nate peered through the windows like a schoolboy. The opening was for a photographer who specialized in oversize prints of race cars in action, portraits of shirtless drivers staring at the camera, and a few shots of naked women posed strategically with car parts. The prints were huge, vibrant, and very solid in terms of technique and artistry. Not my kind of thing, but I could see that Nate was wowed. "These F1 cars are amazing specimens of engineering, masterpieces. I can't believe what the engineers achieve year after year. Come on, look at that exhaust system. That's a thing of beauty."

Nate pointed to a five-by-three-foot photo of an unnamed naked woman, a lot of metal and carbon fiber pieces, and a prominent tailpipe. Luna did a robust business online selling limited-edition prints, and this photo was actually labeled "Bestseller," which struck me as funny and demoralizing. "All the genius in the universe can't compete with a naked woman," I said out loud, quoting my mother. Nate turned and I explained. "My mother said that once when she was trying to console my father after one of his pieces was ravaged by the *New York Times* while that photo Demi Moore, naked and pregnant, was the talk of the town. Do you remember that *Vanity Fair* cover?"

Nate shook his head. "You appear to have had a very different childhood than I did. Pretty much all we talked about at my house in Portland, Maine, was sailing and the weather."

Just then, a well-groomed, slim Frenchman emerged from the front door to the sounds of Afrojack and a few pops of flash from the paparazzi. "Hello, Joan. I am Guy, the gallerist here. So happy to meet you. Tai texted me that you might come tonight. Bienvenue." There were introductions all around, a brief declaration of admiration for both my father's work and my mother's, and then some chatting about the health and welfare of Tai and his work at the museum. Guy's English was fine, but I wanted to set the stage, so I switched to French, telling him about Nate, my wealthy tech client and neophyte collector. Could we please go in, take a look around, and then ask him a few questions about the photography scene in Paris?

"Mais oui. Bien sûr." Guy bowed slightly to Nate. "I understand you are just starting a collection, Nate. Please. Let me introduce you to the photographer, Didier Durand, and maybe some of the drivers?" Nate nodded his head enthusiastically, and we were inside.

What surprised me most was not how out his of element Nate was, but how *in* his element he was. He chatted with the rugged photographer, asked questions of the drivers, all of whom he recognized, and sought out some of the engineers who were present to ask questions, even collecting a few cards and promising follow-ups. "Believe it or not, some of this technology is relevant to my work," Nate said. "This event is better than that conference!" By the time Guy circled back to inquire how we were enjoying the show, Nate had already made up his mind to buy one of the prints, a shot of a car on a track rounding a corner in the pouring rain, a gray-green affair with strong composition and a sense of mystery, like a beast emerging from the deep woods. It was the most understated of all the shots.

"Why that one?" I asked, thinking that some of the others in bolder colors and close-ups were a little sexier.

"Driving in the rain really separates the great drivers from the average drivers. There's only so much the engineers and the technology and the car can do, and then it's all about the human element. Man, not machine. It's a good reminder for me. In my work." In that moment, I had a flash of Casey and his false humility, constantly replying to people who praised his work, "It's all about the camera." Maybe it was all about the camera after all. An average man with an above-average tool. Nate was proving to be the opposite of my ex in every possible way. I took Nate's hand, and Guy noticed. I guess most art consultants don't do that. Oh well. So my cover was blown a bit. He led us over to his desk to settle up and get the shipping information.

Watching Nate buy the piece of art, I felt giddy for him. Whatever happened to us tomorrow, he'd always have this photo as a reminder of our weekend. An incredible self-indulgent thought, I know, but it made me want my own sort of souvenir. Art can make you want experiences, I said on my museum tours, but experiences can also make you want art.

I tried not to be rushed and rude, living up to the stereotype of Americans, but I was aware of the ticking clock. We only had a few hours to make it to Montmartre and find the "pictures, black & white." Now that Nate had ponied up for print, a total surprise purchase, I felt I could pump Guy for information. "Guy, I have a question for you. It's going to sound a little vague. We're looking for a gallery in Montmartre that has photos—black and white, street photography, maybe some religious overtones, maybe a little Bowie feel. We don't know the name, only that it's in the eighteenth somewhere near Sacré-Coeur. It's hard to explain, we're on a . . ." I struggled to find a word for what exactly we were "on."

"A treasure hunt," Nate piped up as he signed his credit card bill.

"Oui, exactement. Une chasse au trésor. We need to find a similar gallery to Luna near Sacré-Coeur."

"Comme c'est amusant. Well, there is no similar gallery, of course, because we are the best," Guy said with pride, and made his way around to his computer, entering a few details in a search engine. "Ah, yes. I think this is a good place to start. There is small atelier on rue du Mont-Cenis run by Jacques de Baubin. Do you know of him? He is a very influential writer in the arts since . . . forever and is someone who brings people together to talk about art and music and philosophy. He sells art, yes, but uses his atelier as a salon as well. He knows everybody and he loves street photography and fashion. I don't know if he carries religious items, but I know he's a great advocate for photography. His atelier is right next to a famous record shop, so there is lots of rock and roll in that neighborhood. I am guessing he could be helpful."

Guy showed us his computer screen. "Do you know the streets behind Sacré-Coeur? They are very old with great history. Take a look at the map." While Nate leaned in to study the map and entered the address into his phone, I studied the website itself. Simple, more of a web page than a full site, but right away I noticed something on the page above the type, used as a sort of logo. It was a heraldic shield with two fleur-de-lis and a sword. Clearly the coat of arms of associated with Joan of Arc. *What is the French word for* bingo?

Guy handed us a slip of paper with a street address for Atelier

Artemesium. "C'est ça. I hope you find what you are looking for. Come back when you have more time! I would like to buy you a coffee. When it is not so much chaos!" There was a round of double kissing and handshaking, and I could see right away why Tai liked Guy. Not too many questions, but full of answers.

There was still an electric vibe in Montmartrc, and wc could feel it, even from inside the car. Nate looked at his phone and said, "Let's walk from here. We still have an hour to kill. It's only two hundred and seventy steps to the summit of Sacré-Coeur." He sounded like a kid on summer vacation. Then he looked down at my shoes and said, "Oh, never mind."

I pulled out a pair of boots from a bag under the seat. "Eh, voilà!"

"I'm impressed."

"If Blackbird shows up, I want to be able to run that bastard down."

"Don't turn around until we get to the top. Save the view." Nate was taking the steep stairs up to the top of the hill like a Sherpa, and I thought I might need oxygen. The dress had a compression system that made the most of my figure but not of my lung capacity.

The white basilica gleamed in the lights, and the steps leading up to the front doors were crowded with laughing groups of twentysomethings from all over the world drinking and talking, a couple of guys in dreads on guitar playing Bob Marley, of course. I'm sure there were a few petty thieves and pickpockets, too, despite the lateness of the hour. There was something inspirational about the crowd and the setting that kept me going, despite my shortness of breath. I looked up and focused on the Joan of Arc statue above the right portico, a mannish interpretation of Joan on a horse, once bronze, now green with patina. "Give me strength," I prayed for the second time that day.

The Basilique du Sacré-Coeur was constructed in the late 1800s and early 1900s as a sort of offering for France's future protection after the Prussians whooped the French in 1870. The basilica wasn't completed until after World War I, when the French turned it around and beat the Prussians' cousins, Germany, so I guess it worked. The Romanesque-Byzantine style was dramatic and fit the site, sitting atop the highest point in Paris. Joan of Arc earned her spot in the front as patron saint and war hero.

Nate slowed his pace to accommodate mine, and when we reached the top, we both caught our breath before turning around. The whole city of Paris, from the Right Bank to the Left, from the Seine to the Eiffel Tower to the Arc de Triomphe was lit up before us. Nate actually gasped. "Spectacular."

"Worth the climb?" I asked.

"A hundred times over," Nate responded. "You?"

I turned back toward the basilica, thinking of the photos I'd seen of the *Bright & Dark* installation with the church bathed in warm white light, a spot of red flare on the statue of Joan. I realized that I'd always thought of those installations as static, because I'd only seen photos. But taking in the hundreds of people, the singing, the cell phone flashes, I understood now that each night was more than just a moment in time, it was crowds, noise, light, and maybe even faith. "A thousand times over."

There was a long pause, and then Nate said, "We should get going."

Chapter 16

There are beautiful streets all over Paris, cobblestone surprises that delight with evocative buildings, romantic balconies, riots of color from flowers and blooming trees that look and smell like spring. The streets behind Sacré-Coeur fall into the category of "unexpected delights." While the streets in front of the basilica had given way to T-shirt emporiums and overpriced cafés frequented by tourists, behind the dominating structure, on the backside of the hill, the neighborhood had retained its "village" charm. Once filled with vineyards and gypsum quarries and home to working-class Parisians and artists who discovered cheap rents and large studio space, now it was filled with expensive lofts and homes with private gardens, but not as shiny as other parts of Paris, like Polly's neighborhood. There was still a little Bohemia to be found here.

"No phone service here, no GPS. I think I can wing it. I studied the map."

Of course he had.

Nate took the lead, marching toward our destination on rue du Mont-Cenis. There was life on the street, people in the café on the corner. It was a lively block, filled with shops and signs. There was one sign indicating a bookstore, and a tabac, and a smaller directory to the handful of studios, or ateliers créatifs, and artists' homes situated there. We spotted the record store that Guy had mentioned, and then Nate pointed out the red-and-orange sign to Atelier Artemesium. "Looks like it's down this way. Narrow streets in here," he said, checking out the surroundings. "Should Blackbird come busting out of one of the doors, I feel like I have a shot at him. I like it. I think I can take him." He made a few crouching-tiger moves, which made me laugh despite the pit in my stomach.

What a difference thirty hours can make. Nate had been wound like a top at the Panthéon; now he was loose and joking. Why was I so nervous? Because I wanted it all, that's why. This really was a treasure hunt to Nate (I didn't blame him), but to me, it was more. It was about reclaiming pieces of my life, from the Panthéon Sketches to my father's work. The art opening had been energizing, but I wasn't ready to let my guard down yet. "Let's focus."

Nate gave me a look. "Yes. I am. I meant that it will be hard for him to get by us in this environment."

"Sorry, I'm tense."

"You don't have to be sorry. Let's find the gallery. Hopefully, we'll get lucky."

We headed up the block as the sign indicated and stopped in front of a deep-purple door with a brass plate that read "Atelier Artemesium." There was light pouring out of the shopwindow, a good sign. We peered in the window first and scared an enormous orange cat asleep up against the spotless glass pane. There were stacks of art books beautifully arranged, several framed watercolors of Paris landmarks, and right smack in the middle of the tableau was a black-and-white photograph on a gold easel. The hair on my arms stood on end. It was a photo of my father, my mother, and a brutally handsome young man in a T-shirt and jeans caught in a moment.

Captured maid, prince, and silent knight
This must be the place.

—

I have a hard time remembering the first few months after my father died. Not the sadness and grief, that I can go back to in a second, like anytime I happen down the ginger ale aisle at the grocery store or past his favorite taco spot. Those are the times I'm overcome by the smallest reminder of his time here on earth. But the specifics, I can't recall at all, like what happened when, how the first few weeks unfolded, when did we find out who perpetrated the attacks, and when did we all realize that nothing would really ever be the same.

In the years since, when I overhear other people talk about that day, they remember the sort of details I think of as the "Where were you when you heard?" details. That they were standing in line for coffee at Starbucks or watching weeping newscasters. It all sunk in with the first big press conference, they say, when the authorities announced the deaths of all those first responders. They have sharp clear memories of the hours, days, and weeks after the attacks; the closer they were to New York or DC the more definitive their recall seems to be. But when I listen closely to their stories, I can hear that most of their memories are shaped by images they saw on TV, what they read in the papers, what they heard on the radio, memories made by media, not by circumstance. And I get that. For them, September 11 was a historic event; for me, it was the day my dad died.

For the people who lost family members and friends in the towers, there was some sense of hope for the first few days, as if thousands of people would be found alive in the rubble, and that was totally understandable. But for the people on the planes, there was no hope.

The first call I made was to Luther. His office arranged for a car to pick up my mother in Ojai and bring her back to Pasadena. The second call I made was to Polly, who came over for a few hours and ended up staying months. The four of us sat in our living room, waiting for the phone to ring. Our call came on the evening of the eleventh from the airline, confirming my father's death. Once my mother hung up the phone, we turned the TV off. We didn't need to watch the news; we had gotten our news already.

Then the press calls came. As my father was one of the earliest and most well-known victims identified, a short obituary was in the papers two days after the attack, on the front page of the *LA Times* and then a longer one a day later in the *New York Times*. Our grief wasn't delayed by false hope. It was right there in black and white for the world to read. We were plunged immediately into the normal business of mourning—sitting with family, receiving friends, crying and saying over and over again, "How did this happen?" We couldn't make any more sense of it than anyone else, but we were too actively involved in the rituals of mourning to notice the details of the disaster.

Within weeks, we received all sorts of invitations to ceremonies, memorials, and official events, some honoring my father specifically for his contribution to the arts or local charities, others honoring all the victims on Flight 11 or the first responders. That's when it really hit me that my father's death was part of something larger.

My mother fled to Ojai and surrounded herself with old friends. My grandmother Adele came down from San Francisco and stood guard, acting as her corresponding secretary for all the flowers and casseroles and calls. While my mother gave herself over to the exhaustion that is grief, I got caught up in representing the family as if it was my duty. I'd get up, put on a simple sheath dress, and accept the condolences of complete strangers. Polly essentially moved into the house, getting me up and going, and somehow kept me upright. "We're going to get you through this," she must have said a million times.

I was self-conscious of the expectations of others, the public, friends, the media. When I went out to the store or an event, did I look sad enough? Strong enough? Should I wear makeup and comb my hair to project a "they're not going to beat us" mentality, or would people criticize my use of mascara so soon after a national tragedy? Was wearing black too severe? Wearing white too juvenile? Was it too soon to laugh or too obvious to cry? The scrutiny was exhausting, and I felt like I couldn't win.

It was also disorienting, feeling the obligation to mourn with strangers and receive commendations and American flags. I was still having a hard time accepting that my father had died over the skies of New York City when he had gotten on a plane in Boston bound for Los Angeles. I couldn't relate to what was happening at Ground Zero at all. That didn't feel like his burial ground to me, but at the time, I couldn't articulate that because I was swept up in the enormity of the event. I was trying too hard to hold it together for the sake of our family name.

At first, I said yes to everything because it seemed like the proper thing to do, even these awkward counseling sessions offered by the airline for the victims' families in Southern California. At the counseling sessions, I felt forced to care about others, when I could barely dress myself. Mostly, the talk consisted of conversations about insurance and lawsuits and conspiracy theories. I couldn't connect with anyone there, even though I wanted to on some level. We had nothing in common except one rotten coincidence, no matter how many times the counselor talked about "the connective tissue of shared loss." *What bullshit*, I thought at the time.

The last public ceremony I attended was meant to honor my father but ended up being more of a patriotic rally. It struck me as all wrong, like I didn't need to be there at all, because I didn't. Luther had come with me and was standing next to me as he had done so many times that fall. Halfway through a boys' choir rendition of "America the Beautiful," I stood up and left.

There seemed to be national mourners all over TV, on the cover of magazines, honored by the president. I didn't need to be one of those people. Then came the group of widows fighting for victims' rights and proper memorials, but I had no interest in their cause. They were coping the way they needed to cope. I was done with that part of the process. After that, I declined all invitations for years, except when the WAM dedicated my father's final piece of work. The night I met Casey.

In the days after Casey left, I thought maybe I should have kept going to that counseling group with all those people who'd lost family members. Maybe I wouldn't have clung to Casey so hard if I had acknowledged that "connective tissue of loss." I'll never know.

In between my official appearances and my wild trip to New England to track down my father's notebooks, my mother pulled herself together long enough to hold a memorial for my father, mainly at the urging of friends who needed to gather in one place in Henry Blakely's memory. He had touched a lot of people with his talent and drive, mentoring, teaching, and encouraging young artists for decades, and they wanted to come together and remember. It was over Thanksgiving weekend. My mother invited about one hundred people to share a meal and memories in the courtyard of the Motel. My grandmother hired a caterer, of course, because there would be no potlucks on her watch. There were long tables, white lights, and lots of candles, art directed by my father's assistants, and yet somehow it struck the spontaneous "we are all here out of love" tone that my mother had wanted and my father would have appreciated.

As my father's oldest friend, Luther said a beautiful grace and we all cried. Old drinking buddy J. D. Souther sang, and we all cried. And then Dennis Hopper, a onetime resident of the Motel, stood up and eulogized my father, reminding us all of the importance of his work, of the generosity of his spirit in taking in lost souls and making them whole, and of the love and pride he had for me, and the love and respect he held for my mother. Of course, we all cried, but no one harder than me, because finally, *finally* after all the hollow words from strangers and official citations, these three men who had known and loved my father had laid him to rest.

I had no doubt that the photograph in the window of the Atelier Artemesium was one of Dennis's. I'd never seen this one, but the composition was unmistakable. Three figures walking down a cobblestone street slicked with rain. The location was hard to place, and the era looked like the late seventies, maybe early eighties, based on the clothing and hair. My father, wearing his typical carpenter pants and wool sweater, looked confident, focused. He has a full head of salt-and-pepper hair and dramatic sideburns. He's striding forward while tugging my mother's hand. My mother is in a slinky white jumpsuit with a gold chain belt, sandals on her feet even though the street was cobblestone. Her body is facing forward, but her head is turned behind, her famous blond hair caught midflight. She is staring at the lost young man in the jeans and the T-shirt. He's standing flat-footed, unable to keep up with the likes of Henry and Suzi. His face was so familiar, but I couldn't place it. Where had I seen it before? I stared at the photo for a few seconds, and then pointed. "That's my parents. And some guy."

Nate leaned in to take a closer look. "Is that Peter Beckman of the Ravens?" Once again, Nate surprised me with his recall. He explained. "I had a cool babysitter. She had a Ravens thing and I had a babysitter thing."

Of course! There were several photos of Peter Beckman in my mother's books about the Motel, but those photos were grittier, of a man who'd been on the road for a few hard years, banging out a lot of groundbreaking music and Jack Daniel's, I suspected. This Beckman was young and beautiful. "I think you're right. I'm pretty sure it's a Dennis Hopper print. But that's definitely Peter Beckman."

Nate looked at me. "Peter Beckman . . . of the Ravens. And ravens happen to be black birds."

"Oh my God." I had no idea what this meant in terms of the

sketchbook or my father's notebooks, but I felt some sense of relief that this old family friend, this man familiar to me from the many times I paged through my mother's books, was involved.

Nate pulled out his phone and started typing furiously into the search feature. "No service."

The atelier door opened. Clearly, Jacques de Baubin had been expecting us.

"Jehanne." The Old French name for Joan, a name I had seen in print but never heard spoken out loud. It was pronounced in two syllables. The first with the soft "J" as in the French phrase, "Je suis . . ."; the second with a hard "H" and rhyming with "yarn." *Je-Harn*. A peasant's name, but when this elegant older man said it, it sounded elegant as well. "Hello, dear Jehanne."

The atelier was a surprise: a clean, bright space with shelves of books, two entire walls of contemporary oil paintings, and black-and-white photos for sale, most featuring religious iconography. There were modern tables and chairs arranged in groups for conversation. Obviously, at some point, the place had been nearly gutted and remodeled, but a few original touches remained. Oriental rugs added warmth to the room, the soft colors of the paint glowed in the lamplight, and a number of well-done oil paintings hung behind the desk and dominated my sight line. A still life that popped with red pomegranates and green apples caught my eye. An abstract work that looked like it could have been a midcentury French artist was of some value. And then I studied the portrait in the middle, a depiction of Joan of Arc as a peasant girl. It looked to be the oldest and most accomplished of the oils. Joan of Arc. Jehanne. One and the same. *What is going on here?*

"Is he here?" Nate spoke first.

"Who?" said our host, feigning ignorance to buy time.

"Blackbird. Is it Beckman?"

"Nobody is here but us," said Jacques de Baubin, making himself busy by pouring some red wine into green glasses. Clearly, he didn't want to get into anything with Nate. He was taking his time, welcoming us like guests, not treasure hunters on a deadline. Jacques was tall and thin with very little hair left but a vibrant look in his blue eyes. I guessed he was in his early seventies. "I understood you to be coming. And I know that I need to give you something. That is about all." He paused and looked at me for a good half a minute, not speaking. Then he said, "That dress. You are your mother."

He gestured that we all take a seat at a Saarinen tulip table. The chairs were high-backed Parsons covered in a soft gray. I only noticed because we had a similar table and chairs at our house in Pasadena, and the familiarity was unsettling. "Please sit and we can talk." He lingered over my face, taking in the details. "I must say, you look so much like Suzi. How is she? I miss her." I noticed he said Suzi, not Suzannah. I had thought for a second that he might be the author of the letters, but apparently not.

It was like this Frenchman, in the blue jeans and navy-blue sweater, put some sort of hex on me because I answered like I was on a typical Pasadena social call with a friend's dad. "She's fine. Busy as she wants to be in California." Ease seeped into my mind, like everything was going to be fine. No questions had been answered, but the pieces were coming together in a manner I could understand: the photo of my parents, a familiar face in Beckman, this lovely man Jacques. It was all connected, right?

But Nate snapped me out of it. He was still standing and searching the place with his eyes. "Okay, I have to say, enough with the small talk here. I'm Nate. I'm here with Joan. It's midnight, and we want to know who you are and what you know about this situation. And where can we find the guy that stole the sketches and tried to run over Joan?" Nate's buoyant mood was over. I guess he felt like we had closed in on the mystery and he wanted answers *now*.

"Is that true?" Jacques looked straight at me, ignoring Nate. "Did the Panthéon Sketches get stolen?" Apparently, my near death wasn't that concerning to Monsieur de Baubin, but anything in regard to his beloved Saint Joan was shocking. And suspicious. The Panthéon Sketches weren't the sort of piece that qualified in the "household name" category. It was hard to believe that it held any name recognition at all, even for an aging French art critic. Jacques set down the wine and a charcuterie platter as he took his seat.

"Yes. The sketches were in a portfolio that was taken from my hotel room on the first night of my trip. We believe that whoever stole them is the person who directed us to come here."

"That I did not know. I would not be involved in theft of any kind. Unless, of course, it was a Braque. I have a soft spot for his work." Clearly, this was a bit of a game for him. "Bread? Cheese? Are you hungry?"

Nate took a tore off a piece of bread and helped himself to some cheese because, honestly, it all looked amazing and our early dinner had been a while ago. He ate standing up, which I'm sure horrified our host but seemed to calm Nate down. He jumped back into it. "Well, then, what do you know? What are we doing here? And what does that photograph in the window have to do with all this?"

Jacques turned to me. "Do you recognize it?"

"Yes. Sort of. Obviously, it's my parents, and I think that's Peter Beckman, but I don't know where or when it was taken. Is it a Dennis Hopper?"

"Yes, very good. It was taken in Paris. When your father was here for *Joan Bright & Dark*. That was a wonderful time. There was a tremendous sense of energy every night for that week, as your father brought his beautiful light to Paris. It seemed like everyone was here—writers, artists, musicians, philosophers, actors, chefs. After each public event, we had a party every night with music and food and wine. Lots of wine. Lots of . . . everything." Jacques shook his head, like he still had a hangover from 1980. "Your father made the art, but your mother made it magic. The photo was taken not far from here. You can see my little atelier in the background. It's not always in the window, but when I put it there, it draws people in. It was a gift from Dennis to your father. And from your father to me."

Maybe Nate noticed that I had tears in my eyes, because he stopped pacing around the room and came to sit at the table. I felt like I had stepped back into another life, like my mother's, and a sense of comfort washed over me. Nate's voice softened, but his mission was clear. "I'm trying to look up information on Peter Beckman, but there's no signal. Do you have Wi-Fi?"

Jacques laughed. "I did for a week, and all my customers, all my friends, they stopped talking to each other and only stared at their phones. So, I got rid of it. Here, we talk and then you can go back to your hotel and tap, tap, tap."

I wanted to listen to Jacques for hours, but I thought Nate was going to pummel him. Apparently, Nate was immune to his charms. He kept up the questioning. "Do you have an envelope for us? And can you tell us who gave it to you?"

Jacques took the crazed American in stride. "I do have an envelope. It arrived via messenger this morning. There was a note attached that said I might enjoy meeting the daughter of Suzannah and Henry. At first, I was confused. Who is Suzannah? But then I realized it should have said the daughter of Suzi and Henry."

Nate and I exchanged glances. "Who sent it?"

"It was unsigned, but there was a little drawing of something."

"A blackbird?" I said

"Yes. Exactement."

"And it didn't strike you as odd that you would receive such a request from, from . . . nobody?" Nate's tone was so unmistakable that I almost laughed. He was right. Who accepts envelopes from strangers anymore? Didn't that go out with anthrax?

Jacques dismissed Nate and patted my hand. "Not odd, exciting. I am an old man now and I did want to meet this daughter. You, Jehanne." His use of the medieval name of Joan of Arc touched me. "The note said I should expect her and her gentleman friend today around midnight. It all seemed so exciting and mysterious; of course, I thought I must play along." Jacques stood up and walked to the desk at the front of the store. He unlocked a top drawer and took out the envelope, slowly as if he was torturing us on purpose.

Nate looked at me and rolled his eyes; I held up my hand to say "Relax." Jacques blocked out Nate on his way back to the table and handed the familiar yellow rectangle to me deliberately. "Why don't you open it later, after we finish our talk, yes?"

I was willing to wait, despite Nate's obvious impatience. This was a chance to understand a slice of my father's life I hadn't even considered before tonight—his brilliant success in Paris, the catalyst for his entire career. I had a million questions on how the photo, the painting, the Panthéon Sketches, and this man, Jacques, all fit together. But I had to start with the portrait of Joan. "Can you tell me about that painting?"

"Of course. It's by a little-known female painter, Virginie Bovie. She is from Belgium. Late twentieth century. I found it at Les Puces one Sunday, many years ago. A little treasure. I have admiration for the Maid."

Joan of Arc. The maid. *Sweet maid.* How had I missed that in all the clues?

Nate read my mind and caught my eye. He mouthed, "*Sweet maid?*"

I nodded to Nate and turned back to Jacques. "That's something you shared with my father. I noticed her shield on your website."

"Yes. Your father and I shared many things—good and bad. It was something to know him. Now, why don't you tell me about this Blackbird, and maybe I can help?"

—

By the time we had finished telling Jacques the details, we'd made it through a half dozen minicourses, from fruit to cheese and tapenade to chocolate and more wine. Jacques made me start at the beginning, with the request from the art agent Beatrice, and walk him through everything from Nate and I meeting on the plane ride to our car ride to his atelier. Jacques asked a hundred questions in between as he stood to fix little plates of food and clear away others, wanting the details on everything from what I wore to dinner to the demeanor of the Parisian police to the make of the car that nearly ran me over.

After he'd heard the details, he declared, "This is not the work of Beatrice Landreau. I had dealing with her years ago. She is a crook, that's true. But she's not clever enough to plan anything this intricate. She is a shill, not the master thief. Take her off your list."

But he saved his greatest interest for the Panthéon Sketches, displaying a depth of knowledge on Lenepveu, the original paintings, the life of Joan of Arc, and the sketches themselves, even though to my knowledge they had never been photographed or written about in any publication. To him, the Panthéon Sketches were gold, not the work of a minor artist of an overlooked series of murals. "I go see the murals as often as I am in the area. The depictions of Jehanne are simple, but beautiful. They are the only thing in that dreadful building with soul. Well, Jehanne and Marie Curie's tomb."

It made me reconsider the theft of the drawings. "Jacques, we were starting to think that the theft of the sketches was simply to get my attention for the rest of this . . . quest. But you seem to think that the Panthéon Sketches have a much higher intrinsic value that what the insurers say. Why?"

Jacques poured a touch more wine for the two of us, but not himself. "The fascination with Joan, Jehanne is deep. Not only here in France but around the world. Your father tapped into that with his work, but that is just the tip of the iceberg. That's the saying, yes?"

I nodded and he continued.

"What do you know of *Joan Bright & Dark*? Have you ever seen photos of the crowds that your father's work drew here in Paris during that week?" Once again, he got up and wandered into the back of the atelier to a set of galvanized steel shelves that stretched across the back wall. He went right for the bottom shelf and pulled out a bound photo album. Returning to the table, he handed the book to me. "I took these. They are terrible. But beautiful for the memories."

As I paged through the amateur snapshots, Nate moved his chair over and studied them, too. The first dozen had been taken in the room we were sitting in—photos crammed with beautiful people, including Charlotte Rampling, Christina Onassis, Peter Gabriel, Mick and Jerry, Iman and Esmé all laughing, drinking, smoking. Next came shots of crowds of people on the streets staring up at Sacré-Coeur, young and old, but all glistening with light. "Your father seemed to take over the whole city, shining his light on our Joan. It was amazing to see all of Paris out to watch his creations. The beautiful candles at Notre-Dame. The fire that engulfed the magnificent Frémiet statue at Place de Pyramid. But my favorite night was here at Sacré-Coeur, of course. Your father wanted to symbolize courage that night. The statue of Joan at Sacré-Coeur is so simple and strong, and that's the image of Jehanne he created for all to see. A young but very brave woman who acted on faith. Thousands of citizens of the world crowded the steps and streets. Your father used these beautiful white flares to light up the whole front of the basilica. But the light around Jehanne, it was white and gold. The red! There was singing and music from the crowd. The whole night glowed like . . . heaven."

I thought of the scene I'd witnessed on the steps tonight and tried to imagine it magnified exponentially. I had no words. "It must have been something."

"It was *miraculeux*. At the end, a red light appeared, starting like a small dot and then expanding. I don't know how your father did it from the crazy ladder he was on. But the red symbolized Michael the Archangel and Jehanne's new committed faith. At least, that's what I thought. But art, as you know, means something different to everyone."

"It sounds like it had a profound impact on you," Nate said.

"Jehanne had always been a central figure in my understanding of God, of France. But after talking with your father, she became something more for me. A symbol of courage in many areas of my life. Of strength in personal struggles. And I have found so many others who turn to her for all kinds of courage. But some who turn to her, they are . . . very extreme."

Nate perked up. "Like cult extreme? Dan Brown Knights Templar extreme?"

"I don't think so. But you never know. There are two groups now, I'd worry about. I've noticed a rise in the use of Joan imagery from people who are anti-immigrant. It's a new wave here in France. It's something to keep an eye on."

"I wasn't aware of that," I said, thinking how sad that would have made my father.

"And then there are the people who turn their fascination with Joan into something material. There are so few genuine relics of her, that something like an artist's sketches would be very appealing, very valuable to their worship of her."

"My father wasn't in the extreme category, was he?" I had to ask. Because if not now, when?

"No, of course not. Your father was spiritual, you know, but not susceptible like that. He was a scientist of sorts. He believed in math and order, the workings of the universe as a complex system circumscribed by rules, equations. But, he found personal strength in Joan and used her as a talisman. For his sobriety, his work. She was important to him. That is why he named you Joan. To remind himself.

And, when those of us who knew him gave up all our bad habits, too, she became important to us. He made sure."

With that, Jacques took something out of his pocket. It was a pewter-colored medal, the size of a half-dollar, like something you'd find in a religious gift shop. Not valuable by any monetary standard, but I recognized it right away, because my father kept the same trinket in his pocket every day. How I had forgotten about it? One of the many little habits of my father that had slipped from my memory.

Staring at the talisman in Jacques's hand, I could see my father as clear as day, sitting at the kitchen table with his coffee, flipping it over and over again in his left hand as he read the paper. I must have gasped, because Jacques asked, "Do you recognize it?"

"Yes."

"I had a problem with some very bad habits. When I gave them up, your father sent me this. I have kept it with me every day ever since."

"My father had one, too," I explained to Nate. "He rolled it over and over in his fingers whenever he thought no one was looking. But sometimes I was. When I was little, he never let me play with it. He said it wasn't a toy."

Jacques handed me the medal. It was a mundane rendering of Saint Joan of Arc on one side and engraved on the other: *St. Joan of Arc, give me the courage and the fortitude to defeat my fears and give me the strength to fight for what I believe in* . . .

A dime-store prayer, but Jacques had worn the medal down with his touch. Clearly, the prosaic words meant something to him. I handed it back. "How long have you had this?"

"Since 1999. A very long time. And I know that I'm not the first or the last to get one of these from your father." So, my father had visited Jacques on the same trip to Paris when I'd ditched my parents. Fitting.

"So you were some kind of secret society," Nate said.

"Maybe we were. The Sons of Joan or something like that. Les Fils de Jehanne! And our leader was Henry Blakely." Jacques laughed to himself.

"Was Peter Beckman part of this group?" Nate was back on task. I saw him look at his phone to check the time. I felt his anxiety to open the envelope, read the next clue, and then get to someplace with service so we could do the research we needed to do.

"I don't know. I've only seen Peter Beckman once or twice in person since that week in 1980. The week that photo was taken. But, I think he lives here."

I was astounded. "In Paris?"

"No, somewhere in the country outside of Paris. He used to be in the newspapers. He dated Carla Bruni before she married our president." Jacques stood to clear the table for the last time. "You should go somewhere and tap, tap, tap, and figure it out. Yes?"

"Yes, we should. It's late. We have to get back and make sense of all this." Jacques double kissed me and held my hands for a few extra seconds. I squeezed them. "Merci pour tout. It was one of the loveliest nights I've had in a long time." I meant it. This polished, warm gentleman reminded me so much of my father that I ached. His intensity, his curiosity. The fact that he was about the age my father would have been in 2011 made my heart hurt. I felt like I'd witnessed how my father would have aged, mellowed. My father would have accepted an envelope from a stranger, I was sure.

Jacques seemed to feel some special connection, too. "Come back and tell me what happens with everything. And, if I hear anything about the sketches, I will let you know." I handed him my card with my number. Jacques slipped it in his pocket with his medal. "Goodbye, Nate. Off you go. Tap, tap, tap."

Nate and I were in the back of the car, headed back to the hotel. He was distracted by the site of the brightly lit windmill as we passed the real Moulin Rouge at the edge of Montmartre, patrons exiting after a midnight performance. Then he pointed to the envelope. "Ready?"

I wasn't. "I need a second. That was intense." There were a million question marks floating around in my brain: Beckman, the ticking clock, the cult of Joan and the Panthéon Sketches, the coin, the letters to my mother, the comforting familiarity of a total stranger. I couldn't shake this feeling that a giant sinkhole of understanding had opened up in Atelier Artemesium. "My parents never told me much about that time in Paris. Why have I never heard of Jacques de Baubin? Obviously, that was a relationship that my father kept up. He gave him the Joan coin, sent him that Hopper print. Jacques has kept that photo album for thirty years. That year I lived in Paris, my mother sent me all these letters of introduction to her friends here, like I was a Victorian traveler, but she never mentioned Jacques. It seems so strange that this is all new to me."

"You were pretty young when your father . . . died, right?" Like most people, Nate didn't know exactly the right word to use about what happened to my father. You could tell a lot about people's religious and political point of view from their word choice. The most outraged used "murdered by . . ." and then tossed in names of various terrorists, political figures, or movements. One time I even got "Murdered by deteriorating standards and loose morals," which stunned me into silence. My religious white friends used "passed away," while my religious Black friends said "passed," which had made me laugh inappropriately, thinking that my father had escaped through some rip in the universe, a fate he would have enjoyed. I usually said that my father had been killed, but "died" struck the right tone to me in this circumstance. "I mean, did your parents tell you everything about their lives? Probably not."

He was right. At least, not in the sense that they confessed or came clean. My father would go quiet for months if he was working on a piece, and my mother was a spinner of stories, with her memories having a beginning, middle, and end, full disclosure optional.

Entertaining, pitch-perfect, but not necessarily honest. Maybe a detail like a long-ago friend didn't seem worth the trouble to explain.

Or maybe I should have asked my mother more questions. "I had just graduated in May of 2001. I was pretty self-absorbed, like most college kids. And my parents, even though they had public lives, they were very private people. Despite what you think, Nate. They weren't open in that 'let's all get in the hot tub together' way. They had barriers with me, for sure. I was an only child raised around adults, but it wasn't a free-for-all. And now? My mother has higher walls than ever."

The streets of Paris were quiet, and we were making quick time back to our little secret spot in the middle of the Seine. As the light whizzed by, my mind was still on what Jacques had told us. "I've read textbook descriptions of *Bright & Dark*. Seen photos. The last summer I spent with my father, we went over timelines of the exhibition in a clinical fashion, but he never talked about the people he was with. And he never, never talked about the audience response, how the viewers perceived the event. I never even thought to ask about the impact on the audience, people like Jacques, watching the different events unfold."

I thought again about the week they visited me in Paris and I'd gone to Munich instead. Maybe I would have learned this history, been introduced to Jacques, relived *Bright & Dark* in some way. But I'd chosen to go to Germany and drink beer because I thought I had all the time in the world to ask my father the important questions. We'd all come to Paris again, right? My father had hinted at some sort of official twenty-fifth anniversary of *Bright & Dark* sponsored by the French government in 2005. There would be time. I felt no sense of urgency at age twenty to know everything about my parents. "I asked my mother in an email the other day if she had any friends in Paris, and I got nothing back, except the names of her modeling friends. But not Jacques. None of the other people in those photos."

"And not Peter Beckman?"

"No."

"Maybe these two were really friends of your father's, not your mother's?"

"That could be. Connected to my father through his . . . secret boys' club. No girls allowed except Joan of Arc. Or maybe the people in those photos were never friends in the first place, only people in the same place at the same time."

Nate put his hand on my thigh and said with all sincerity, "Later, when it's appropriate, can you tell me what Mick Jagger's really like?"

"Absolutely." My phone pinged several times. We were back in service. Nate immediately got on his phone to search for Peter Beckman. All I could think about was that photograph in the window. *Captured maid, prince, and silent knight.* I thought I knew my father's story, but maybe not. Was he the prince or the silent knight?

"I'm ready." I ripped open the envelope. This time the notebook page was unexpected. No calculations or dimensions, just a sketch of a woman who looked to be my mother. Or maybe not. The truth was, my father wasn't very strong at figure drawing. Most of his sketches had a generic quality, like it could have been anyone. In this sketch, the human figure was not accomplished, half-drawn, but the background was complete with a café scene, some buildings, and a street sign that read "Impasse." It was dated 4 April 1980. I didn't recall having ever seen this page, but there were thousands of total pages in the notebooks, and I'd done only cursory cataloging. Something like this could have easily slipped by me.

But the date stood out. April 1980, the same month as *Joan Bright & Dark*. My parents would have been in Paris. I handed the page to Nate.

"Your mother?"

I nodded. "I think so." Then I reached in and pulled out the now-familiar thick white paper with the handwritten clue. I clicked on my phone's flashlight to see the words.

When the pure white light should fade
When all that glitter starts to stray
We're at an impasse, aren't we girl
Down the alley love unfurls
I've seen the last of her lips of gold
I'll see her again when we are old
Come say goodbye at dawn, sweet maid

Staring down, a thought popped into my head, something Nate had said when we read the first one. *Not really a poem, not really a clue.* Looking at the black ink on the white paper in full, I could see exactly what they were now: song lyrics.

Beckman was Blackbird.

A tidal wave of relief passed over me. It wasn't the Russian mob or nationalist extremists or over-the-top Joan acolytes. It was an aging rocker who knew my parents back in the day. This I could deal with. I might not understand the why of it, but I understood the who of it. And I was going to get those sketches back. "Call your babysitter. Tell her you're finally going to meet Peter Beckman."

From Wikipedia
The Free Encyclopedia

The Ravens (Band)

The Ravens were an American rock band formed in Los Angeles, California, in 1974 and are considered pioneers of alternative rock. The band was composed of vocalist and guitarist Peter Beckman, guitarist Dean Lawrence, Lawrence's brother, bass guitarist Nick Lawrence, and drummer Colin Beardsley. Peter Beckman and Dean Lawrence met at Santa Monica

College in an accounting class. They dropped out of college six months later, after a demo single became a radio hit. It would be several years before Righteous Records released a full album. Following several critically acclaimed albums, including *Here & Now* (1976), *What Was the Point* (1978), and *Yes & No* (1981), the Ravens disbanded in 1984 with the individual members pursuing their own careers. Though the band never experienced any significant commercial success, they did enjoy critical respect and have been cited by many bands as a key influencer. *Yes & No* was cited by *Rolling Stone* as #12 on the Most Influential Albums of All Time in a 2008 list.

The Ravens were influenced by the Rolling Stones, Faces, Big Star, and Lou Reed, as well as punk bands such as the Ramones, the Clash, and Dead Boys. Unlike many of their Southern California contemporaries like Black Flag and Germs, the Ravens were noted for their melodic rock, self-deprecating lyrics, and songs that lasted longer than two minutes. Lead singer and songwriter Peter Beckman was both the heart and the face of the band. With his intimate songwriting and raw singing style, Beckman is often seen as the precursor to Kurt Cobain. Cobain himself noted in a *Rolling Stone* interview in 1991, "There would be no Nirvana without the Ravens."

The Ravens were a notoriously inconsistent live act, sometimes showing up onstage too drunk to perform or storming offstage if the crowd wasn't paying enough attention. In 1978, they were kicked off the Rolling Stones tour when they failed to complete a single song as the warm-up band, playing only snippets of cover songs instead. In 1982, lead singer Beckman was charged with being drunk and disorderly on a plane, one of the first documented cases of air rage. Beckman did three months in jail for destroying a drink cart. By the end of the band's run, they had matured as performers, and before disbanding, the

Ravens did fourteen straight nights of live shows in Southern California, performing everywhere from the Hollywood Bowl to the Motel in Pasadena to the parking lot of a 7-Eleven in Montebello. This send-off tour is known as the Fortnight.

The band broke up in late 1984, releasing a statement that read, "It's been real. Thanks for the memories." They were sued by their record company for breach of contract, a suit that was settled out of court. They never reunited for any reason. In 1995, brothers Dean and Nick Lawrence were killed in a plane crash while piloting their own single-engine aircraft over Napa Valley where they owned a winery. Colin Beardsley currently works as a producer in New York City and has worked with bands like Blink-182, Green Day, and Hole.

Peter Beckman solo career

Though all the Ravens' songs are credited to all four of the band members, it's long been known that Peter Beckman was the primary writer of the band's material. In the early 1990s, Beckman released two solo albums that garnered some attention. *Nice Try* (1991) reestablished Beckman as a songwriter of substance and his solo acoustic tour was well received. *Yes, It's Me* (1993) was a commercial success and received four Grammy nominations, but no wins, in the Rock category where he lost to Eric Clapton, as did Nirvana. Beckman did not attend the ceremony, nor did he tour with the record. In a profile piece in *Spin* magazine in 1993, Beckman stated that he became a "colossal asshole as a touring rock star. Being onstage made my ego grow and my self-esteem shrink. I drank so I could get up onstage and be huge and then I drank more when I got offstage so I could be invisible. I could not handle any aspect of being famous. Not one. It all brought out the worst in me." Beckman has rarely been seen onstage or in the media since 1995. It is said that the deaths of his former bandmates that year may have sent Beckman from the limelight.

Peter Beckman now lives outside of Paris in Rouen, France, where he runs Fortnight Studios. He is a versatile and successful songwriter for pop signers like Pink and One Direction. Beckman also cowrites, working with such bands as Good Charlotte and Fall Out Boy.

Beckman is unmarried, but had a longtime relationship with singer/model Carla Bruni that ended in 2007. Since 2007, he has been romantically linked to several women, including jewelry designer Maeve Kincaid and painter Estelle Martine.

Chapter 17

Oh, the game was on now. "Impasse Ronsin in Montparnasse. That's the next meetup spot. It's a famous alley where a bunch of artists had studios in the early-to-mid part of the twentieth century. This one was obvious." Blackbird's losing his edge. I thought about the drawing of my mother in the envelope. That must have been done during *Bright & Dark*.

Nate checked his watch. "That gives us about four hours to sleep." He wasn't exactly enthusiastic.

And neither was I. "You know what? Screw this. We're not going to run around all night trying to figure out this clue and wait around at dawn for another envelope. This has to stop. Now that we know who he is, we get to be in charge."

"I like Fired-Up Joan," Nate said as we entered the hotel lobby and strode past the desk. No Claude. The hotel managed to find another employee to work a shift. It was two in the morning and we were done, on every level. "We can call the police on this asshole and let them go after him. Attempted murder and theft are crimes, not games."

"Well, it's a little bit of a game, don't you think?" The whole mess had gone from a professional nightmare to a personal one. There were certain facts about my parents that even I didn't want to know, and the relationship between my mother, my father, and Peter Beckman was starting to look suspicious. My new goal was to prevent family secrets from spilling out in front of Nate or the French police, or the museum for that matter. "I'd like to see this through on my terms, without involving the police. And frankly, they haven't been any help so far. I want to get the Panthéon Sketches back to the museum, or into the hands of the interested buyer, if that person exists. And, if there is any chance that this Beckman guy has even one of my father's notebooks, I don't want them confiscated as evidence or anything like that. The French government may feel they have some claim to them now, if they've been in this country for a while. I know that sounds unlikely, but everything about the last seventy-two hours has been unlikely. And countries appropriate art all the time. Ask the Greeks about their marbles."

We were in the elevator again, what I'd come to think of as our elevator. I turned to face him, placing my right hand on the middle of his chest. I could feel his heartbeat, his frustration. I felt the same sort of tension. I moved my hand up and down gently. Nate started to relax. I pressed two buttons, one for my floor and one for his. "I don't want you to feel obligated, you know, to stick around if it's too intense. This is not your problem to solve, Nate."

"You sound like my sister. When we come up against something at work, I go into this tunnel until I can figure out how to fix it. But she says that I should accept and understand why the issue arose before I try solve it." I stayed silent because I could tell Nate wasn't done. He was working out his end of this whole charade. "This Beckman guy seems to be on this power trip that I don't get."

Ah, yes. "Don't meet your heroes," I said quietly.

"What?"

"I see now. You are a Ravens fan. You're a Beckman fan, and this is not the guy you learned to love to impress your babysitter. It's the old 'don't meet your heroes because they'll disappoint you' scenario."

"I thought of him as a guy with integrity. His music is honest. He stood up to the labels. He left when it wasn't working for him anymore. Why he would put you through this ego-driven bullshit, jumping through hoops? Did he steal the sketchbook instead of buy it? If he has the notebooks, why doesn't he arrange a meeting and give them to you?"

For the first time since I'd met Nate, I felt like I had some wisdom to offer him, not vice versa. "I can't explain his motivation. But I do understand where he's coming from. Because it's where I came from. These people—the artists and musicians I met growing up—they can be brilliant. And they can be very, very small. Their insecurities can equal their talent. They need to know where they stand in comparison to others all the time—the charts, the awards, how much did that sell for, how big is your contract, where did your last album chart, why did she get the cover of the *New York Times Magazine* and not me. The comparisons can kill them. It comes with the territory."

"I don't understand."

"It's the exposure. It's putting yourself out on the ledge, inviting people to judge your work. Every day. In the most public way. Now, it's 24-7 with the Internet. That doesn't happen in most jobs. The constant scrutiny. I work at museum, and I get an annual review, a few action items to work on to improve my performance, and then I go back to my tiny office for twelve months. Like most people. We're not being constantly deconstructed publicly. It's brutal. No one was surer of his vision than my father. But his drinking was a crutch, his wall against the judgment of other people, of himself. After he stopped drinking, my mother became the wall. They all need protection in some way." My brain scrolled through flashbacks of all the pep talks I'd given over the years to Casey, moderately talented Casey. It was exhausting being someone's wall. *I won't miss that*, I thought.

"That doesn't explain Beckman's behavior toward you. I'm mean, what is the point of this? I don't get it."

I kissed him. "It's not yours to get. This whole thing may get weird, Nate."

"This whole thing already is weird, Joan," Nate laughed. "From that first glass of champagne on the plane until right now." Nate's right hand was on my face, my neck, my collarbone, while his left hand found my hip. He pulled me closer. "I'm sorry. I'm not great with so much chaos. This"—he gestured back and forth to indicate the two of us—"has a lot of variables."

I recalled how Tai had teased me for looking forward to a Virgin Mary exhibit. Now look at me! I started to really laugh. "Neither am I!"

"It was supposed to be one dinner, you know."

"Yup." We were both struggling to define what "this" was.

"I didn't mean anything by that, except that I was looking forward to one dinner with a pretty girl and then getting back to my normal life."

"Of work, work, and more work?"

"I can be a little intense about what I want. At least that's what . . . other people say about me."

"That's clear from the last few hours. One minute you're buying art *like a playah* and the next minute, I think you might deck an old man for serving us a cheese plate."

"I didn't think the Camembert had softened enough." Ah, there we go. Nice Nate back in action. "By Monday, you either have to have the sketches back or tell the museum. Or that Mike guy is going to do it for you. We don't have much time to find Beckman, this poor suffering artist with the outsize ego. I'm still worried about your safety, too. I feel like I should stick around. If you don't mind." He pressed his body into mine gently. He felt fully present. So did I.

"I don't mind. I have a plan for how to use Polly's blog to set up a meeting tomorrow. No more running around, no more clue solving. Let's find Beckman, the Panthéon Sketches, and, maybe, my father's notebooks. Please stick around." I pressed back into Nate and let him touch me. Kiss me. He was right. He was good at intense, and I was satisfied for once that we weren't some average couple on your average romantic weekend in Paris. The elevator doors opened on my floor. "This is my stop." We both got out.

"You're leaving?" The clock said 3:00 a.m., and Nate was pulling on his jeans in the dark.

"Going back to my room. I have to make some calls back to the States. I didn't want to wake you."

"Nate, are you sure you're okay?"

"Yeah. I was thinking about what you said, about ego and insecurity. Please don't ever introduce me to George Lucas. I couldn't take it if he turned out to be . . . not the guy I think he is." He leaned down and kissed my forehead. "I'll be by with coffee in the morning. Try to get some sleep. Sound good?"

"Very good."

"The Polly setup is perfect. It will work. I'll see you at ten. Big day."

Nate slipped out, but his words echoed in my head. I had some calls to make, too.

I reached for my phone and texted Mike: Closing in on Panthéon Sketches. Long story but appears to be in possession of old friend of my father's. Can you call me for name? Don't know motivation but making contact tomorrow. Will be safe. Don't worry.

Then I sent another: Thanks for your faith in me. I got this.

Then, I dialed California.

"Mom? It's Joan."

"Joanie, what a surprise! How great to hear from you. I just walked around the Rose Bowl with Candy, who says hello. It's a beautiful day here in Pasadena. High seventies and perfect." When did my mother get old enough to mention the weather on every phone call? "What's it like there?"

"Damp and gray, but I don't mind."

"Of course not, you're in Paris. You get to see all the women in their great coats. Is anyone actually wearing that honeysuckle pink they're calling the color of the year?"

This was valuable information to discuss at three in the morning.

"Nobody, except the under-ten set and Polly. She had a honey-suckle scarf on today, and it looked fantastic on her, of course." It still amazed me that my mother could care about the color of the year and the future of third-wave feminism in equal measure.

"Oh, I'm so glad you're spending time with Polly! She'll make you smile again." Then there was a pause on my mother's end and some recognition of the hour. "You never call when you're out of the country. Wait, it's cocktail hour here. What time is it there?" I could hear my mother pouring herself a glass of wine as she spoke.

"It's the middle of the night. My sleep schedule is all messed up, jet lag. Wide awake at three a.m. Thought I'd send some emails, catch up on work."

"Did you take the melatonin like I told you?" My mother had become one of those people who believed melatonin was the answer to all the world's problems, even if it wasn't sleep or stress related. She also felt that way about hydration and a good book. Panaceas all.

"I will," I lied. There was no way to ease into the out-of-the-blue discussions, so I plunged in. "Mom, the reason I'm calling is because I've run into a bit of a situation here in Paris. It's professional, but it's also personal." The last thing I wanted to tell my mother was that the Panthéon Sketches had been stolen from my hotel room. The maternal freak-out factor would be too much for me to take at the moment; plus, she was someone who had schlepped a lot of artwork in her time and never lost a piece, so I fudged the details. "Remember that I told you the potential buyer of the Panthéon Sketches was a possible acquaintance. Well, I still don't have all the details, but I'm ninety-nine percent sure that the buyer is a guy named Peter Beckman. He used to be in a band called the Ravens. I think you and Dad knew him. I've had some . . . communication with him that I need to ask you about. Does that name ring a bell?"

Is there a silence that is deader than dead silence? A hollow silence? An echoing silence? Because the void on the other side of the phone line was palpable, like my mother had dropped off the planet and was drifting in deep space. "Mom? Are you there? Are you okay?"

I heard breathing but no words for another half minute. Then my mother, the iconic Suzi Clements Blakely, the definition of American cool, calm, and collected, sounded off in a string of expletives I didn't even know she had in her vocabulary before putting the phone back up to her mouth. "I can't talk about this over the phone."

"What? What can't you talk about?"

"It's, it's . . . ," she stuttered. "I have a lot of anger toward him. He really, really let me down when I lost your father. He could have called. He owed me, that's all I'll say. He really owed me, and he didn't deliver. I can tell you all about it when you get home, but not over the phone."

"Mom, I'm in a little bit of a time bind. As I said, it's a situation—and not a good one. He is holding on to the sketches and refusing to return them, so I need to secure payment. Or lose my job. His behavior seems to be connected to his relationship with Dad somehow. Maybe even you. I need your help." The Daughter Card ought to get her to open up. I hadn't asked for help in years. "Who is this guy to you?"

More silence, then my mother spoke in a collected voice. "Peter Beckman was, is . . . like a bright burning firework, you couldn't take your eyes off him. He was magnetic. Onstage and off." *Oh, God. Maybe I don't want to hear about my mother's relationship with this guy,*

I thought. "He was very close to your father, at times like a son or brother to him. But he could be very destructive and hurtful to those around him. Your father was so patient with him, so supportive. He got him sober, kept him clean, seemed at times to put him ahead of, well, us even. You and me. Peter used to suck your father in. They had similar backgrounds, both with very restrictive religious parents that messed with their heads. Both were artists who could get totally lost in the work. Both had substance issues. Both wicked smart."

"What do you mean that he let you down? How?"

"Your father was a good, good friend to Peter Beckman. He even testified at some ridiculous trial for him as a character witness. Beckman was drunk and out of control on a plane and destroyed a drink cart or something. Not only was he thrown off the plane but he was thrown in jail, and your dad was there for him. He missed our anniversary once to go see this guy in jail after he'd been sentenced. But when your father died, I never heard one thing from him. Not one. I could have used . . . his support. He owed me that." My mother wasn't a scorekeeper; she didn't tally up who did what and when. Instead, she welcomed people into her life when they were there and wished them well when they ventured off. She was forever introducing people she hadn't seen in twenty years like they were the best of friends in each other's lives every day. It was a quality I admired. I was surprised that Peter Beckman's alleged snub was even an issue. Maybe she was more conscious in the aftermath of my father's death than I had given her credit for. "It hurt."

I paused because her pain was real. Then said gently, "But he did reach out, Mom. Those letters you stockpiled, my grad student Kiandra found a bunch of letters that I believe are from him. You'd never opened them. Did he call you 'Suzannah'?" There was a sharp intake of air from my mother, answering my question. "And did he sign his letters with a drawing of a black bird, a raven?"

"Yes." Disbelief.

"Well, he wrote six times over two years. In these letters, he claims he has something of Dad's." I had seen the scans of the emails that Kiandra had sent. They were legit even if the details were vague.

"I can't believe it. All these years, I thought . . ." She drifted off and then, "He wrote letters? What kind of nonsense is that? I have a phone."

"From what I can tell, he seems like a bit of a drama queen. Prefers complicated to clean. Fair to say?"

"That's an understatement. What does he have of Henry's?"

"I can't say for sure. I'm not trying to be mysterious. His, um, writing style is obtuse on purpose. But I think it may be Dad's notebooks. At least some of them. Or pages of them." There, it was out. For a second, I thought my mother might question my sanity, because, honestly, what rational reason could there be for him having all those notebooks?

"Oh, Joanie. Really?" My mother softened considerably. Her voice filled with hope, as I knew it would. *Damn*, I thought, *this guy better have at least one notebook.* "How do you know? Are you sure? How is that possible? It's possible, right?"

"I guess so. Somehow. I'm supposed to meet him tomorrow." I didn't add "if he reads Polly's blog" or "if he shows" because the whole tale was too long and too sordid. I was dying to tell her about Jacques and the hairdresser, and about Nate, of course. But I had to stay focused. "Is there anything else I should know about Peter Beckman, Mom? I don't want any surprises, because there is a lot on the line for me at work with this transaction. And if he does have the notebooks, I want to be . . ."—*What? What did I want?*—". . . solid in my approach. Something's not a hundred percent aboveboard with him."

"He's a romantic." Not the answer I was expecting. I was thinking more psychopath or narcissist. My mother explained, "When he was sober, he was a true romantic. And when he wasn't, he was even worse, darkly romantic, theatrical, in deep all the time. I don't know what else I can tell you. It's been such a long time. Listen to his music. He's in there."

My mother's voice ended on an up note, like she was going to say something else but decided against it.

Oh no. Don't make me say it. But I had to. "Mom, I have to ask, did anything ever happen between the two of you?"

"Joanie, I can't talk about this over the phone."

My phone rang again. I felt like I'd slept for about four minutes with a vise screwed to my head. "Mom? What is it?"

"It's not Mom. It's Mike." I checked the clock. I'd actually slept for four hours, so it was late in Los Angeles but a reasonable time in Paris. "Sorry to call so early, but I want to make sure I understood your texts."

"You're right. I've owed you a call. I didn't know what to say because there were so many loose ends."

Mike didn't need details. "Where are we now? I have to let the museum know first thing tomorrow LA time that the sketches are gone. I can't keep this from them any longer than that."

"I know. Here's what I can tell you. I think I know who has the sketches and it's personal. Like, very personal. I'm going to need you to check someone out."

"Who?"

"A guy named Peter Beckman. But let me give you some background first . . ."

From PasadenaMeetsParis

Allô, allô, allô, mes petites!

Happy Sunday. I hope some of you are sleeping in, but I'm guessing a few of you are early birds and up getting that worm. Let's start off this beautiful day with a café au lait and a croissant and a touch of mythology and the mystic, shall we? Imagine taking a long walk through the park to get in touch with our primitive roots. Maybe we'll see the silhouette of a blackbird against a blue Paris sky and it will remind us of why we love this city. Or serve as some sort of augury for encounters to come. If I remember my Classics, a blackbird flying East or South was favorable. I feel something good is in the air, don't you?

On Saturday at Chez Polly in the 16th, Mon Mari and I welcomed one of my dearest friends for brunch. Nothing could have made me happier than to share the day with Joan Bright Blakely. We laughed, we ate (Recipes and photos posted demain!) and we toasted to friendship. My husband was not amused by most of our "trip down memory lane" moments, except the bit about the saddest senior prom ever at the all-girls school we attended. He did love the amazing tale that Joan spun about a recent art world theft starring a Cute Geek, a Mystery Man with a Past, and a Romantic Hotel that shall not be named. More details on that when I can make it public but let me tell you that someday it will be a page-turner.

Joan and I caught up on all the news from Pasadena while she had a blowout fantastique at the Salon Franck Provost. A special merci to our anonymous patron who treated us to an afternoon of beauty. What a luxurious treat for two working women.

As I mentioned last week, Joan is in town for her own top-secret art world business. I'm not supposed to spill the beans but I can tell you it involves priceless sketches from a well-known painter who is particularly beloved here in Paris. (Hmm, that's a lot of Ps.) Joan was gushing over her prize. But she has had time to look up old friends, like famed critic and collector Jacques de Baubin of Atelier Artemesium, a fan and BFF of her parents, the late Henry Blakely and the lovely Suzi Clements Blakely. Imagine Joan's surprise when she arrived at the gallery in Montmartre only to see a photo of her parents in the window, circa 1980. And who is the mystery rocker in the photo? Oh, Joan knows. If you haven't been to Jacques de Baubin's lovely gallery, put it on your schedule. It's a treasure, as is he.

Joan is sleeping in this morning, but she plans to be at Notre-Dame by sunset. The cathedral has special meaning for Joan as one of the settings for her father's famous *Joan Bright & Dark* "urban art" series. "I want to experience the quiet of the cathedral and the St Joan statue lit by candlelight to remind me of my dad. This whole trip has been about memory." While she's not sure how long she'll be in Paris or where the City may take her, Joan has this to say about her next move, "I want to be able to part with these sketches with an honest heart and then move on to my next creative discovery, be it a notebook or a masterpiece—or both." Joan is a poet, isn't she? Maybe she will see her own blackbirds filling the skies around Notre-Dame. A raven, perhaps? Let's hope so. For we defy augury.

Did I mention that no one looks more at home than Joan in a black motorcycle jacket and blue-black trousers? Timeless.

xxoo Polly

Chapter 18

"When a tree falls in the forest and no one hears it, it's nature. When a tree falls in the forest and someone applauds, it's art." My father said that to me once, as he was packing up his big black cases and hustling out the door of our Central Park West sublet during his monthlong public art project called *Castle Burning*. I was on the brink of thirteen at the time and had no idea what he meant. Every night for the month of October, my father turned Belvedere Castle in Central Park into a fiery red, smoldering, flaming commentary on spiritual starvation in New York City. The castle was his tree, and Central Park was his forest. The project was underwritten by the National Endowment for the Arts along with other various cultural entities in the city and had taken years to put together, both in funding and creation. The logistics of making a nineteenth-century Gothic folly appear to ignite into flames every night in the middle of one of the world's most beloved parks were massive.

My father had spent a full year in his studio in Pasadena hand-crafting the flares, building the light boxes, molding the gel lights, experimenting with light bulbs, from argon to xenon, and perfecting the smoke effect. Moving vans took the guts of the installation to New York City and it was another three months on-site constructing the housing for the flares and the lights, and then constructing the optical illusions that would conceal the mechanics of the piece. Computer software for running such a complex show was in its infancy, so actual people did most of the effects work. It was an all-hands-on-deck affair. I swear, even my mother picked up a hammer at one point.

But it was all worth it, my mother said, to spend six months in the glorious apartment with the stunning view donated by a wealthy benefactor. Fall. Manhattan. The colors of Central Park. In October of 1993, *Castle Burning* was the talk of New York City, and to my eighth-grade self, it felt like living right in the middle of the action.

Though critics praised the intensity and power of my father's vision, early reviews from spectators lamented that *Castle Burning* was not spectacular enough. Viewers expected something bigger, more dynamic. Where were the fireworks? Where was the soundtrack?

When a morning-show host put that question to my father, he snarled back, "This isn't Disneyland. This is New York City. It's not effects; it's an experience. We make our own magic."

And with that, Henry Blakely became an art folk hero, and *Castle Burning* became this phenomenon created by my father but enhanced by the public every night for a month. After my father's comment, the good citizens of New York woke up and showed up and made their own magic. That night, as my father and his crew lit the flares, fired the electric lights that glowed from blue to blood, and created the smoke that engulfed the granite structure on the rock outcropping, the Gay Men's Choir appeared and started chanting Gregorian hymns. Dancers performed spontaneously. Fireworks from mysterious sources lit the sky. Other nights it was string quartets and gymnasts and bonfires of Monopoly money. Or gospel choirs, jugglers, hip-hop troops, mimes, spoken-word poets, and martial artists taking over the grounds around Belvedere Castle as the place "burned." Sometimes the fire department was called because some well-meaning tourist thought the place actually *was* on fire. In celebration of so many false alarms, one night the FDNY put on their own glorious show with fire hoses and bagpipes. For a month, the people of New York made the art their own, while the castle burned. They were the applause in the forest.

And, needless to say, Chief Marketing Officer Suzi printed up T-shirts with the line "This isn't Disneyland. This is New York City," which became hot sellers and eventually collector's items.

That's what my father was explaining to me on that breathtaking fall afternoon: "Art is everywhere. And it's never static. It changes with every pair of eyes, every interaction. We all have a responsibility to create art. Remember that, Joanie, because it's true of life, too."

That year, my parents pulled me out of my private Pasadena school, much to the chagrin of the nuns who would miss their annual Blakely Christmas tree lighting fundraiser, and enrolled me in PS 334 on the Upper West Side, a K through 8 public school for "gifted" kids, though most of them looked pretty normal to me. PS 334 was the perfect place to ride out an alarming growth spurt and some Shannon Doherty bangs as I lurched into puberty. The anonymity balanced out the loneliness.

My parents hired a high school girl named Rachel to be my friend and escort me around the city in the afternoon. That fall is when my obsession with Joan of Arc started, as there are quite a few Joans all over Manhattan, from a nearby statue at Riverside Park and the Bastien-Lepage masterpiece at the Met to a charming former junior high school near our apartment called the Joan of Arc School.

I loved a nineteenth-century French tapestry depicting Joan's life that hung at the Cloisters the most. The bucolic scenes made her look like a warrior version of Laura Ingalls Wilder, at least that's what I thought, as the Little House books were my only reference point for this medieval French farm girl challenging the king of England. Rachel and I spent many afternoons taking the long subway to the upper reaches of Manhattan to see the other gems at the Cloisters, but I kept returning to the tapestries. I was beginning to understand the importance of symbols in art and in life.

But it was also the beginning of my understanding of what Joan of Arc meant to my father. We weren't churchgoers, but I'd gone to Catholic schools my whole life, so I knew enough about faith to see that my father relied on Saint Joan for strength and sobriety. He manifested that belief through his art and through symbols like the coin in his pocket. When he noticed my interest in his patron saint, he took up the quest with me. We spent weekends in antique bookstores around the city, from Greenwich Village to the Upper West Side, hunting for a rare first edition of a children's book from the late nineteenth century about the life of Saint Joan by a French painter and illustrator Louis-Maurice Boutet de Monvel. Though the text was rather dry, the drawings of Joan were magnificent, filled with rich colors and a use of matte black that my father admired, like Japanese woodblock prints of that era. The book had brought Boutet de Monvel worldwide fame in his day, resulting in commissions from wealthy art collectors and collaborations with fellow artists. (I think my father admired his career trajectory as well.) In the days before Google, we wandered from one tiny store to another, spending hours in each other's company, buying dozens of other books, and stopping for hot chocolate before we walked home slowly through the park or ducking into Chinese restaurants and eating the sesame noodles my mother would never let us order because they were, according to her, "a calorie wasteland." We never found a copy of Boutet de Monvel's masterpiece, but it didn't matter to me.

It was my favorite year. Life changed for my father after that, for all of us really. Suddenly Henry Blakely was famous, like stopped-on-the-street and asked-for-autographs famous, something he'd never been before. Fellowships and awards came rushing in with cash prizes and medal ceremonies. There seemed to be an endless stream of commissions that took us to places all over the world for a month or two every summer. There were museum retrospectives and magazine covers. It was new territory for him and a role reversal for my previously more-famous mother, but my father stepped up to the task. He understood that he had an obligation that was bigger than his own work.

And that's what I was thinking about—our obligation to art, audience, Joan, experience, New York, tapestries, and faith—when I walked into Notre-Dame at sunset holding Nate's hand. I was reminded of Jacques's comment that the crowds made *Joan Bright & Dark* a masterpiece every night. I thought that everything I had known or believed was coming together in that moment, from the Panthéon Sketches, my father's work, and the cool gray walls of the twelfth-century church to my own reaction upon seeing the simple, elegant Joan statue in the north portico of the famed church. *I am not afraid. I was born for this.* Ha, Joan's own words seemed like a spiritual overreach, but I was emotional. I felt on the verge of tears.

Nate, on the other hand, was in full 007 mode. He was decked out in a leather jacket and on high alert. He dropped my hand, turning around slowly to take in the full scope of the interior of the church. "Wow."

"I know. Notre-Dame is something. Is this your first time here?"

"Yes. My previous trips to Paris included too many meetings, not enough time. And I'm not really a church guy."

"Well, then you've missed a lot of history." My hand caressed his sleeve. The leather felt smooth, supple. "Did you buy this today?"

"I needed one. You know, when in Paris."

I did know. "Of course."

Notre-Dame de Paris. Our Lady of Paris. When my father used this spot for *Joan Bright & Dark*, he examined both the feminine and the masculine sides of Joan. She called herself the maid but dressed in men's clothing. Her spirited leadership of the army compared to her ban on the prostitutes that normally followed the troops. Her devotion to Saint Catherine and Charles the Dauphin. My father had tried to capture that dichotomy using both light and sound. The statue of a pious Joan, hands in prayer position while holding her flag, was bathed in electric light using the colors of the famed rose windows as inspiration for his installation and bathed in sound by a chorus of a hundred women in men's suits. Standing there with Nate surrounded by the noise of tourists and the whizzing of their cell phone cameras, I wished I could go back to 1980 when there was, according to a piece in *Art in America*, "silence, then singing, then glorious light." There was no silence today, but a little glorious light seeped in through the stained glass.

I turned to Nate, who was fixated on the engineering of the cathedral, and the look on his face brought me back to a moment years ago. "I remember how all the guys in our study abroad art history class laughed when we came here with our teacher and he said the words 'flying buttresses' like a million times." I turned to see Nate laughing. "That's mature."

"Some things are always funny, no matter how old you are."

"You know the second trial of Joan of Arc happened right here in Notre-Dame."

"The second trial? I thought she was guilty, then burned at the stake during round one?"

"She was. Guilty of heresy and burned at the stake by the Church during the first trial. But twenty years later, after some rebranding and soul-searching, Joan got a retrial. In absentia, of course. The Trial of Nullification. The one where the Catholic Church said, 'Sorry. We take it all back. It's totally cool you dressed like a man and led an army and said that God asked you to do it.' That happened here in, like, 1450-something. Then she was canonized here almost five hundred years later."

"Why'd it take so long? The haircut?"

"That was it. Unflattering optics." I paused, and then added, "It can take a while for the truth to emerge."

I heard a voice. "Joan? Are you Joan?"

—

It wasn't Blackbird. It was Beatrice Landreau, the art agent and crook who had skipped town for the weekend, setting all the events of the last seventy-two hours in motion. The first thing I noticed was that her hands were empty. No black portfolio filled with sketches, no envelope. Beatrice, who had clearly aided and abetted Blackbird in his theft of the museum's valuable artwork, had the nerve to stand before me in a rather chic trench coat and freshly groomed hair. I was hoping she'd be more wild-eyed with a touch of crazy so I could forgive her and write off her bad judgment as a desperate financial move. But when I saw that she was an attractive woman in her thirties sporting a Chloé tote I'd been eyeing, a wave of anger passed through me. *She took the sketches and the bag I wanted!* I channeled my mother, hissing a decibel level that was both threatening to those close at hand and inaudible to the crowd at large. "You have some nerve showing up here empty-handed. Don't even try to pretend you didn't orchestrate fraud and theft. I will call the police right now if you don't produce the Panthéon Sketches," I said, shaking my phone in her face.

Beatrice gave no ground. She was unapologetic: "I have proof of a wire transfer from my client to the museum for the price of the Panthéon Sketches. Sold legitimately. The piece is in good hands. That matter is settled. Your work as the courier for these works has been successfully concluded."

Even her charmingly accented English bothered me, so I responded by dramatically swiping the paper out of her hands. It appeared to be a wire transfer, all right, from a business account to the museum account for the agreed-to price. The transfer was from an entity called Fortnight Studios, not Beckman himself. I handed it to Nate so that he could serve as a second set of eyes—had I missed anything? "Well, it's not exactly settled and concluded, because we haven't addressed the matter of you setting me up, stealing a valuable collection of drawings, and, let's not forget, trying to run me over. So settled and concluded? Not really."

"That's seems like very harsh language. These claims are preposterous."

"Not harsh, really. You've damaged my professional reputation, you endangered the museum's, and now, it appears, that you've moved into engaging in emotional blackmail." My usual reasoned restraint give way to an uncontrolled anger. It felt foreign and scary. But also exhilarating. She was not going to get the best of me.

Beatrice blinked. "It can all be explained. But not by me, by Monsieur Beckman. Please, he is waiting for you."

"Is he here?" Nate said, whipping around. "Where is he?"

"No, he's not here. I will take you to him."

Nate piped up, "We're not going anywhere with you. Or your buddy, Beckman."

Beatrice would not be swayed. "There is a car waiting for you. Monsieur Beckman wishes you to get in. I'm to escort you to Monsieur Beckman's compound in Rouen. I have been instructed to provide no explanation, as he would like to explain it all himself."

I listened. I understood. And, honestly, I was relieved that it was Beckman, and this charade was almost over. I assumed I'd still lose my job for hiding the theft, but at least the Panthéon Sketches were safe. And, the museum would get its money, so insurance didn't have to pay out because of some long-lost friend of my parents. But I was no less furious at being played by the likes of Beatrice, in her trench coat and attitude. Plus, the word "compound" had Branch Davidian overtones. "You think we're idiots? Why would we get in a car with you?"

Beatrice looked me straight in the eyes for the first time. "Because he has your father's notebooks. And he wants to give them back to you, personally." She was taunting me with memory.

"How do we know he really has the notebooks? I mean, come on, Beatrice. From my limited experience with you, all I know is that you're a lying crook." That got her. "Why shouldn't we call the police right now?"

"You're not going to call the police. You don't want the hassle." Frenchie had a point there. "Look at this." She handed me her phone.

"What's this? Proof of the hundred calls I made to you this weekend that you failed to return?"

"No, a video of Peter Beckman and your father's notebooks. Shot this morning after you didn't show up at Impasse Ronsin, clearly the final meeting point. He would like to return the notebooks to their rightful owners." She handed me her brand-new iPhone, and again I found myself annoyed by her reports of a dire financial situation. Apparently, lacking financial liquidity didn't impede some Parisians from acquiring the very best and latest fashion accessories and technology.

I hit "play" and saw the face of an aging rocker, in his sixties and still handsome, all warmth and enthusiasm, as if he were hosting an episode of *From the Vaults of VH1*. It was Peter Beckman, rebel front man of the Ravens, now with neatly trimmed hair and wearing a fresh black T-shirt and a necklace with a little silver medal around his neck, a Saint Joan medal. He was sitting in a richly decorated room surrounded by black-and-white notebooks. He waved his hands over the pile. "Hi, Joan. Sorry about all this. Come to Rouen for a few days. Let me explain. Bring Nate! See you soon." Then as an afterthought, he held up the purloined black portfolio and said, "This is a gem. Thank you for bringing the sketches to France." I hit "play" again, to make sure I hadn't dreamed what I had seen.

"*This is a gem?*" I shook my head. "Unbelievable. He makes it sound like the events of this past weekend never occurred and we're just headed out for a holiday visit. How do I even know those are my father's notebooks? Those could be props and this video just another invitation to the next stop along this goose chase. You can buy those black-and-whites anywhere."

Beatrice responded, "I have seen them. Why not see them for yourself?" Again, she fingered her phone. "Here. Regarde."

I swiped through a series of photos of interior pages of the notebooks. At least that's what they appeared to be, but Beatrice wasn't exactly a photographer of the highest order. "A little bit of focus would have helped your case, here."

And yet, they looked authentic. *How is it even possible that Beckman got his hands on a* truckload *of notebooks?* I looked at Beatrice's smug mug. I wanted to slap her. Or tackle her and steal the Chloé bag. Instead, I made a small, pathetic sound. My father's notebooks were, were . . . alive.

Nate held my arm back firmly and asked a sensible question: "I find Beckman's behavior careless, at best. Is this what he is like, completely blasé about the suffering his actions bring about in other people's lives?"

Beatrice nodded. "Yes. He is full of light." She motioned with her hand. "Shall we?"

There were a million reasons not to get into the black Mercedes sedan parked on a nearby side street: safety, sanity, and potential conflicts with international law. But Nate summed it up best: "At this point, we kind of have to, don't we?"

We did.

Like everything else over the past few days, the attention to detail was impressive. At Beatrice's insistence, we stopped at the hotel to collect our luggage and check out "in case we found ourselves in Rouen for a few days." As if an afterthought, she added that Monsieur Beckman would be picking up the tab for our stay at the Hôtel

Jeu de Paume to offset "the inconvenience." Then we were asked if we had any food allergies so Cook could adjust the dinner menu before we arrived, so apparently, death by *accidental* poisoning was off the menu. Finally, Beatrice presented each of us with rain boots and heavy socks in our correct shoe sizes because, she told us, walking about the grounds of Fortnight Studios was quite delightful, even in the rainy season. She actually used the word "delightful." She then proceeded to give us a rundown of where we were headed, what to expect, and the timeline. Never did it register that this field trip to Rouen was out of the ordinary. Clearly, this was not the first time she had done work for Monsieur Beckman, as she insisted on calling him. I wondered: *With this slick of an operation, what other ruses have these two pulled off?*

As we drove, Nate fired off a series of logistical queries at Beatrice about the location of the compound, the exact distance from Paris, and the availability of Wi-Fi upon arrival. She gave vague answers to each question, basically responding to everything Nate asked with, "You shall see."

As we reached the outskirts of Paris, the industrial area where Paris stops being magnificent and starts to look like any working-class city in Northern Europe, Beatrice instructed the driver to pull over at the corner, and sliding out of the front seat, she said, "This is my stop."

"You can't get out of the car. We don't know this guy," Nate said, pointing to the driver. I admit I was panicked, too.

"Monsieur Beckman will be waiting. You have no reason to worry. Tati is an excellent driver." Before she closed the door, she leaned into the car and said, "Monsieur Weller at the WAM has already been informed that the sale of the sketches has gone through at the agreed-to price. I will file all the necessary paperwork and send copies to the US. Please sign these." Beatrice thrust a clipboard of papers through the window, neat little stickers demarcating the signature spots. Stunned, I signed and handed them back to her. "Thank you for your trust. Good to do business with you." With that, the heavy German-engineered door slammed shut, and Beatrice Landreau and her questionable business ethics disappeared down the street, no car, taxi, or Metro station in sight.

"She must be sleeping with him," Nate said, thinking the same I was. "Or is heavily medicated. *Thank you for your trust.* That's a good line. I'll have to remember that the next time I steal a patent or stiff a vendor."

I laughed, "No, Nate, thank *you* for your trust."

"This whole operation has veered into *Twilight Zone* territory."

"I'm texting Mike. I don't want him to wonder why the heck I've been torturing him all weekend when the museum tells him that the Panthéon Sketches were officially bought and paid for. At least I'm off the hook for larceny under false pretenses, and perjury, and anything other law I might have violated." I typed quickly. "How does this sound? *Dear Mike, thank you for your trust.* And, also, he should know we're in a car speeding toward possible occult practices."

Nate waited a second and then said, "Yes, he should probably know that."

"I'm going to text Polly, too. I want someone in France to know that we are still in France."

"Good idea. I'll set the tracker on my phone and alert my assistant, so at least authorities will be able to find the bodies." Nate could tell I truly was nervous, so he added, "I think we'll be fine." He shifted in his seat to get comfortable for the remaining ride to Rouen. "Tell me where we're going again?" It was a good distraction.

"Rouen. It's about an hour to the north of Paris along the Seine and the capital of Normandy." I was playing tour guide again. "It's an old city, critical to the history of medieval England as well as

France because of its location. Timbered houses, churches, and, of course, where Joan of Arc was imprisoned and burned at the stake."

"Have you been here before? Of course you have."

"Yes, when I was in college." I'd managed to convince my American roommate, Breezy from Greenwich, to spend a weekend in the city because she had heard "there were beaches nearby." Much to Breezy's dismay, we spent the day visiting Joan of Arc–related sites, and by the time we got to the dank tower that had served as Joan's prison cell, Breezy's only comment was "This place smells. I'm thirsty. Come find me at that café near the train station." Breezy and I had dissimilar interests.

Though even I had to admit, the town was a bit of a letdown, an industrial city going through a rough patch economically, and I had no desire to find a hostel and spend the night. The main cathedral was still in rough shape from World War II, and it appeared that renovations were not on the horizon, evidenced by a lackluster fundraising effort supported by donation tins at the entrance and the sale of Joan of Arc prayer candles. The old town was certainly old, but not charming. I had expected more of an homage to my namesake, a robust marketing scheme that lured in tourists, but the effort was half-hearted. Joan was an afterthought here, fine for a day trip but not a weekend getaway spot. It surprised me that someone like Peter Beckman made his home there.

Presumably, Beckman was drawn in by the surrounding countryside, neat, green, and heavy on the agriculture. The car sped on for a while, and I noticed that Nate had popped his earphones in. He was staring out the window like he was trying to memorize the scenery in case we needed to make our way back to Paris in the middle of the night. Blindfolded and bound. Maybe he'd watched too many Bourne movies. I patted his arm to get his attention. "What are you listening to?"

"Peter Beckman's album from '93. *Yes, It's Me.* It's good, really good. I'd forgotten how raw these songs are. Someone really did a number on him."

Listen to the music. It's all in there, my mother had said, or something like that. And 1993, the same year as *Castle Burning*? That's a coincidence. "So, did I mentioned that I spoke to my mother last night? There's something you should know about her relationship with Blackbird."

Chapter 19

We pulled through the gates at Fortnight Studios, a bucolic Haute-Normandie estate spread out before us. Cue the milkmaids. "All right, I have to admit, this looks like one of those really upscale properties that advertises in the *New Yorker* in those little tiny ads in the back of the magazine. Do you think that's the spa building?" Darkness was falling, but lights throughout the property illuminated a handful of half-timbered structures, some new, some ancient, but it was hard to tell which was which, tucked in among a meadow, a vegetable garden, and what looked to be a hedgerow beyond the structures. The houses and gardens were maintained to a level between "overgrown" and "overdone." *It was quite delightful.* Damn Beatrice.

"Are you nervous?"

"Yes." So nervous, I was grinding my teeth while I was awake. "What if this is a hoax?"

"If this is a hoax, I'll . . . I'll . . ." Nate was a lover, not a fighter. "I'll be really mad. I know hackers, Joan. We'll get back at this whole crowd."

Small signs pointed visitors to the studio and the guesthouses off to the left. We turned to the right, taking the winding gravel driveway through a grove of trees, where a stunning stone house, in just the right state of disrepair, stood before us. It looked to be truly old, like fifteenth century, with a pitched roof, crumbling facade, and a dark maroon door. The front light was on. The driver, who hadn't said a word the entire trip, grunted as he stopped the car, "Raven House."

"I feel like Willy Wonka is going to emerge from that door with a cane," Nate whispered.

"He might."

The door opened before we could knock, and a woman called Marianne let us in. She spoke to us in Franglais with a precise set of directions. "Pleased to meet you, mademoiselle. Entrez and I'll show you to your rooms. After you refresh, then rendez-vous ici. Alors, food and drink in the library avec monsieur, oui?"

I looked at Nate. "Here we go."

We'd been sitting in the entry hall, as instructed, for ten minutes before Beckman made his appearance. Some nerve, I thought, making us sit in the wildly uncomfortable antique chairs instead of the library, all so he could make an entrance down the front stairs. The guy we thought might be a criminal mastermind really *was* Willy Wonka. I checked the texts I had sent to Polly and Mike, assuring them we were safe, but asking them to keep their phones on all night, in case "something came up." I thought that phrasing came off neutral and not paranoid. The sound of footsteps caused me to look up. A tall, fit man danced his way down the stairs, excitement on his face. It was the face I'd seen in the video.

Peter Beckman was magnetic, like my mother said. I had met my fair share of rock stars, and usually they were smaller and shyer in person, their onstage persona not adapting well to the real world, making them awkward offstage, never comfortable being out of the spotlight. But not Peter Beckman, maybe because he hadn't been onstage in two decades. All the energy he once used for performing he now harnessed for everyday life. He was the front man of his front hall. Dynamic, graceful, and so crazy handsome. I felt a charge when he took my hands, welcoming me to his home, a connection of some sort. That annoyed me.

He didn't attempt to hug me, but he did study me. "Joan of California. Wow, it's like looking at, at . . . 1979."

Fuck him and his memory lane. "Mr. Beckman, I'm not my mother. I don't know you, and given what you have apparently put me through in the past days, I don't care about you. But if you do have my father's notebooks, I want them now."

"Whoa." Beckman took a few steps back. "Got it, Joanie. You're . . . conflicted. There's a lot going on here."

"I'm not conflicted. I'm fucking mad. You hijacked my life and my work for . . . *theatrical effect*?"

Now Nate chimed in. "And you did try to run Joan over . . . which is *unacceptable*." Not exactly a strong sentiment against attempted manslaughter, but I saw a kind of awe pass over Nate's face when he realized exactly whom he was addressing. His rock hero.

"Nate, you're the man." Beckman grabbed Nate's hand and pumped it up and down, congratulating him like he'd just saved a litter of puppies from a burning building. Neither of us bothered to ask why Beckman even knew Nate's name. He'd been watching us, *with* us, for days. "I'm so sorry that happened in front of the hotel. That was some kind of coincidence, huh? Out-of-the-blue bad driver. I had nothing to do with it, truly. Wait until I tell you the whole story and I will, I promise. And you can ask me all the questions you want. But for now, let me say thank you for coming. I'm sorry for the subterfuge, Joan, but I hope I can make it up to you. Marianne showed you to your rooms? Everything to your liking?"

"Fine. Lovely. Thank you." Anger couldn't override breeding. Marianne had shown Nate and I to adjoining rooms in what appeared to be a new wing of the house designed to look original. Our rooms were like suites at a luxury property with four-poster beds and fresh flowers, a lit fireplace and sparkling candles on the mantel, and a huge modern bathroom stocked with lavender-scented amenities. We'd only spent five minutes freshening up, but I'd touched all the sheets and towels because I couldn't help it.

"What can I get you? Water, wine, champagne?" Beckman said as he dramatically opened the heavy wood doors into the library.

"The notebooks, please."

I didn't need to see a single page to know that the black-and-white notebooks stacked neatly on the library table were my father's. I recognized the handwriting on the outside immediately: #14, #26, #39. The numbers written in black Sharpie in the same spot on every book, lower left-hand corner, not the white box in the middle. I had to touch them all to make sure they were real.

There was no small talk. "How? How are these here? I mean, just how?"

Beckman went for a straight answer. "Read this." Beckman reached into a cheap plastic sleeve, one that could have been bought at any office supply store, and carefully removed a piece of paper, one that had once been folded into quarters. It was a handwritten note on what looked to be hotel stationery, dull white and worn, like it had been opened and refolded many times before being preserved in OfficeMax's finest. I looked closer at the engraving. It featured a stone building with arches, like the drawing in one of the clues. The lettering underneath said "St. Michael's Seminary, Newton, MA." It was my father's writing for sure:

10 September 2001

Becks . . .

I need you to take these notebooks with you back to Paris. Do whatever you want with them—hide them in a closet, read them at bedtime, just don't lose them. In ten years, I'm going to ask you for them. Give them to me then, but not beforehand.

I'm not done yet. I'm still doing my thing and I don't want to start wrapping up my creative life because some museum or some school wants these in their library. Don't let me give up, Becks.

Keep them safe. And keep yourself safe. Ten years, Becks. Ten years.

Henry

I read the letter three times to make sure I understood the significance. I passed the folder to Nate. *I'm not done yet.* There were tears in my eyes.

Beckman stood silent until Nate finished. "Your father gave them to me, Joan. The whole trunk. We'd been at the retreat, you know, the one he had every year, the sobriety renewal one? At the old seminary outside of Boston. It was the usual suspects. Those of us your father had collected over the years—artists, writers, musicians, a couple of fallen actors for good measure, a few Jesuits and university profs to keep us digging deeper. Every year he had a theme, and that year it was 'Why Are We Still Fucking Here?'"

Nate laughed despite himself; I couldn't bring myself to laugh, though I could hear my father's voice saying that sentence out loud clear as day.

Beckman continued, "It was a good one, deep. We talked a lot about gratitude. For most of us, it was a miracle we hadn't killed ourselves during the course of our addictions. And then we talked about staying relevant, not just present, but relevant. Our creative purpose. One of the speakers, this professor from somewhere, really pushed us to take stock in where we were and where we were *going* with our work. 'Don't stop yet. Don't let your work slip into insignificance. Your time isn't passed,' he said. 'Continue to enhance the human experience.' I think that got to Henry. He'd been talking about turning over his papers to a museum, and it must have started to feel like his career was ending, that he was signing off and slipping away. All I know is that I when I left the seminary on the night of the tenth to fly back to Paris, I opened my door, and there was this note and a trunk full of notebooks. Frankly, it was kind of a pain in the ass to check them in and cost me a small fortune in overweight fees. But Henry asked, so I had no choice but to take them. I was in the car on the way back with the damn trunk that had taken a few hours to pass through customs when I heard the news."

I snapped out a question. "Why? Why would he do that? Why would he give *you* his life's work? He wouldn't even let my mother bring them home from Boston." I remember her asking him repeatedly when we were in Maine about shipping the books back with everything else that was coming home to California from that installation. She had tortured herself over that for years, why hadn't she insisted? Why had Henry resisted? "I've been struggling to remember if my father mentioned you once in my lifetime. Why are you the guy he asked to hold on to the notebooks?"

"I asked myself that a million times. Reread his letter. It's in there. I think, I think . . . he knew something was up. I felt it then, and I still believe that. 'Keep them safe.' That's what Henry wrote. That seemed weird to me at the time. I mean, they're notebooks in a trunk. My plan was to put them in a spare room and forget about them. And then, after what happened, it seemed prophetic."

That sounded like my father. He wasn't psychic, but he did listen to the universe in a way that was otherworldly. I was silent, but Nate wasn't. "You know, you could have made sure they knew the notebooks still existed. Joan and her mother. They deserved to know. It's been ten years."

"I tried, man. I sent letter after letter to Suzannah. But I got nothing back."

"A few letters over the course of a couple of years isn't trying very hard for a guy who has clearly orchestrated much more complicated deceptions, like the one you put Joan through," Nate said quietly. "How about trying an email once a month? Or call a lawyer? That's what lawyers are for. You should have had your lawyer contact their lawyer. Or pick up your phone. Or get on a plane. Like a normal human being. It's been ten years."

And there was the catch, really. Because I knew what Nate didn't, that people like Peter Beckman aren't normal. "After that day, I don't fly anymore. And I don't really work like that. Neither did Henry."

"Please. We're not talking about producing some pop album, we're talking about a grieving family. And some intellectual property of value to the world at large. You could have called."

My mother's words echoed in my head. *He could have called. He owed me.* But before I could pile on, Beckman replied to Nate with a light tone, brushing off his accusations as if he was talking to a small child. "My whole job as an artist is to create a big production out of something. It's in the job description: create a mountain of magic out of a molehill of crap. It's what I do. It's what Henry did."

This riled up Nate. "I get it. Your artistic sensibility is way too refined for straightforward interaction," Nate snapped, the stars in his eyes now gone.

"When I couldn't reach Suzannah initially, I decided I'd do what my friend had asked of me. Henry asked me to keep the notebooks for ten years. So that's what I did. It made sense to me at the time and it still does. I did what Henry asked." Peter carried on, turning to me to explain. "I spent years in a protracted legal battle with my label, my bandmates, and my distributors. Agents and managers took advantage of me. And it soured me on the whole idea of that whole world. Plus, I prefer to take care of business myself. It's more *honest.*"

But Nate wasn't done. "Was it more honest to bring Joan to Paris under false pretense and then stage a robbery, threatening her safety and career? How is that more honorable than picking up the phone?"

"Stop. Please, stop. Thank you. I'm standing right here, so I don't need defending . . . ," I said, resting my hand on Nate's shoulder, but looking over at Beckman, "or whatever justification you're spouting. I can't believe you didn't think my father's death changed the equation."

The two men fell silent, as if there was no response solemn enough to follow my statement.

I was still trying to process what I'd read and heard. My mother and I had spent the summer of 2001 preparing to turn over my father's papers to the museum, to begin the process of building his legacy as my mother saw fit. It had been her idea to start the Henry Blakely Library and find a permanent home for his source materials, the notebooks being the centerpiece, of course. My father *appeared* to be in agreement, at least that's what I recall from our conversations that summer. He was enthusiastic, engaged. At least that's what I recalled.

But it was a decade ago and the circumstances of his death changed every memory I had of him, good or bad. Every memory turned bittersweet and foggy, like they were filmed through a lens covered in Vaseline, sharpness dulled. Maybe to ease the pain.

Had one weekend away with his buddies changed his mind about the library? Or had he been reluctant all along, not wanting to stand up to my mother. I made a mental note to ask Tai about his recollections. He had been new at the WAM then, but involved in the acquisition of the papers and the new piece of art. Maybe my father was dragging his feet. "I have so many questions about everything, including why and how I'm here right now. But I need some time alone with my father's work. Can I get that?"

"Of course," Nate answered.

"Yes, anything you need. And, Nate, I appreciate your passion."

Beckman turned to me. "I'm sorry, Joan. I'm sorry about your father. I miss him every day. But now that you're here, I hope you'll give me more time to explain. I'm . . . not always so good *in the moment* . . . one-on-one." Beckman's tone was on the edge of sincere, but I knew it was a lie. If he wasn't good in the moment, my mother never would have called him a bright burning firework. "Now, we're going to leave you alone, Joan. I'll have Marianne bring in a glass of wine and some food." Beckman walked around the room, flicking on a few extra lights, enhancing the dramatic shadows on the rough-hewn walls, revealing a room of beauty and comfort.

In the back corner, there was an exquisite statue of Joan of Arc, probably hundreds of years old. I'd never seen it before, in a photo or in person. On a beautiful wooden book stand next to the statue was the Panthéon Sketchbook, looking like it had always been there. Beckman saw me staring at it. "We'll talk."

He clapped Nate on the shoulders in an exaggerated gesture of masculinity. "Come on, mate. Do you like music? I'll give you a tour of the studio. Had Cage The Elephant in last week. Have you heard their stuff?"

"I have. Good band," I heard Nate say as they walked out of the room, trying hard to maintain his distance, but I knew Beckman would win him over with one look at the studio.

But me? Not so sure.

As soon as the door closed, I finally let out a deep breath and closed my eyes, to allow myself to feel anything, as if I were going to get a sign from above. I'm not sure what I expected. Spontaneous tears from the Joan statue? Sparks from the notebooks? Hearing voices like my namesake? There was the smell of dried lavender, the crackle of the fire, and a knock on the door as Marianne entered with food and drink. I shook to attention.

"I'll put it here," she said in accented English, indicating a table in the corner. "Not near the special books."

"The special books?"

"Yes, that's what Monsieur Beckman calls them. The special books. He works with them in his studio most of the time," Marianne said. "Merci, madame."

Works with them in his studio? What could Peter Beckman be doing that had any connection to my father's work? Maybe Marianne's meaning was lost in translation. Or maybe Beckman's reason for keeping the notebooks was less about his old friend and more about himself. I added that to my mental checklist of questions about what I now thought of as the Blackbird Era.

I had a million thoughts racing through my head, like the fact that my father didn't want to be immortalized before he was gone, but right now, I needed to focus on one sliver of time: the *Bright & Dark* years.

I approached the table and searched for the books from 1978 to 1980. I estimated where that era might be in my father's numbering system, knowing that he made many more notes in his early working days than in his later days. That last summer, while I was cataloging, I remember him tapping his head and the left side of his chest, explaining, "It's all in here now. Not so many calculations, lots more educated guesses. I had no faith in my work when I was younger. Now I do." I started at #14 and hit pay dirt at #19, opening to a page with a rough sketch of Sacré-Coeur and the statue of Joan.

My father's notebooks weren't diaries. He didn't write down his feelings or what he was wearing, like a teenaged girl. I didn't find anything along the lines of *Why doesn't Suzi like me more than Peter? There were so many cute girls at the party!*

They were a collection of images, numbers, maps, lists, pertinent words and phrases, and other small inspirational quotes. But nothing that confirmed what my mother had told me.

Still, having just been in Paris, seeing his hand-drawn renderings of the famous Frémiet statue or the alcove at Notre-Dame was poignant. I found the page that Beckman had included in the last clue, the drawing of my mother at Impasse Ronsin. I took it all in, finding new meaning in his notes that read *faith before reason; blood red, diamond white; glowing from within; alone with her God; young, young, young; strength, strength, strength. I am not afraid.* I paged slowly through notebook #19 and opened notebook #20. A few newspaper clippings fell out, yellow and brittle, along with an envelope. When I flipped the envelope over, I found that it was addressed to Suzannah, but not in my father's handwriting.

I opened it right away. A magazine article and a letter to my mother from Beckman. I read the letter first:

25 December 2003

Dear Suzannah . . .

It could not be a colder, drearier day here in Rouen. Of course, I am thinking of the Christmas we spent together in Mexico in that tiny fishing town. What was it called? We drove all night through the Sonoran Desert, a terrible idea, and stayed in that hotel with no hot water. Remember that wild processional that came down the street with the piñata Baby Jesus and the traveling manger starring goats, cows, chickens and Mother Mary in sequins? You, me, cerveza, fish tacos, stars, sun, beach, saltwater skin, poinsettias, sunsets. Merry Christmas to you.

Are you still sad? I'm sure you are.

I spent all of December working with a semi-talented band who is trying to re-create the magic of their first album but they've lost touch with the pain and poverty and heartbreak that made their songs mean something before they were famous.

Success has separated them from humanity. They have it all, they want for nothing, they have nothing to give but strings of words that are meaningless and will certainly be a gold album because of a clever hook or two. I guess if you string together enough clichés, meaning emerges. But I don't know. Is that what happened to us?

That never happened to Henry. Always moving forward with human hands, bright eyes.

I've decided that this is my last letter to you. I can only guess that you are coping with Henry's death through silence and contemplation and caring for your beautiful daughter, Joan of California. I will respect that. Please know that you may reach out to me at any time and that the gift I have for you—and it is a gift—is yours whenever you are ready to receive it. In the meantime, I will keep it, safely and reverently.

> If the gilded light should fade
> When you hear good men have strayed
> Here's memory that tells me so
> Here's golden hair that falls below
> I'll touch the line of her chin
> Like steel & glass from within

Sweet Maid.

The letter was signed with the blackbird I had come to expect.

Was this a draft of one that he sent to my mother? Or never sent? This letter was new to me, not part of the packet that Kiandra had scanned in Pasadena and then sent to me. For whatever reason, Beckman had kept a copy, then stashed it in the notebook.

Then I opened what turned out to be a magazine clipping. It was a two-page spread from *Paris Match*, the French version of *Us Weekly* but slightly more substantive because it was French, after all. My mother had a subscription for years sent to our Pasadena home. She told me it was a great way for me to practice my French, but I know she paged through the magazine as often as I did. That subscription really fueled her Kate Moss animosity.

But these pages were from an issue dated February 1980, long before my high school French days. According to the caption, the photo spread was taken at an after-party for an Yves Saint Laurent show. The usual YSL suspects were pictured, like his muses Betty Catroux and Loulou de La Falaise, but on the second page was a photo of my mother and Peter Beckman. Clearly, the two were together, a couple. My mother was wearing some sort of safari-inspired getup with belts and buckles and epaulets, draped in bangles, rings, and beads, finished off with an animal-print silk scarf tied over her blond hair. She was leaning up against a tall, clean-shaven Beckman, who'd obviously been styled for the evening, in a paisley shirt and velvet jeans. Beckman was smoking, my mother had a drink in her hand, and they were both beautiful. The cheekbones on the two of them. So, so beautiful.

I looked at the date on the clipping again: February 1980. According to the "Love at First Sight" myth I'd been told all my life, that was five months after my parents met that night at the Motel, four months after my parents were married, and two months before *Bright & Dark* happened. I was a Paris honeymoon baby, maybe already in my mother's belly. But in this photo, my mother looked like she belonged to Beckman, completely. I was stunned.

Had Beckman meant for me to find the envelope?

The last time I saw my father, he was in the barn of the house we were renting in Maine, wearing his trademark white coveralls, drinking coffee, and shouting instructions over the music, a Grateful Dead bootleg. The barn, his summer studio, was meant for quarter horses, but he'd turned it into a workshop with welding equipment, cutting tables, circular saws, lathes, and all the raw materials to create *Light/ Break #46*, a sort of psychedelic Stonehenge made from steel and illuminated with mirrors and stained glass prisms. Now that the commission was complete and celebrated with a Labor Day cocktail party and unveiling at sunset with two hundred guests and the banker who paid for it, it was time to pack up and head home. My father was supervising his assistants, Tom and Zane, on what he wanted to shipped back to California, what could be donated to a local trade school, and what could be trashed. Whenever he had finished installing a commission, he was lighthearted, effervescent; the intensity of the creative process gave way to a kind of larger-than-life spirit you could see in his laughing and joking, even singing. I guess it was joy.

I was headed to Boston on the airport shuttle, flying out of Logan that night for LAX. My work for the summer was done, too. I had packed the notebooks as instructed for my father to take with him. My notes were on my new laptop, a graduation gift, ready to be part of the package handed to the museum when needed.

In a few weeks, I'd be in Istanbul, kicking off a year of study and travel, working on my own interests and leaving my family far behind. At least, that was the plan in early September 2001. I gave Tom and Zane a hug and told them I'd see them back in Pasadena. They wished me luck and safe travels.

Then my father gave me a squeeze, tighter than usual. That joy again. "Thanks for everything, Joanie. We had fun, didn't we? Love you."

"Love you, too, Dad." One last hug and then I gave a little wave as I exited the barn. "Bye." And I never saw him again.

I've thought a million times about that day in the barn, why I even went down there to say goodbye. There were a lot of comings and goings in my family, and we weren't particularly sentimental about farewells. I could have left a Post-it on the fridge, but it had been a long, wonderful summer in Maine, and I felt compelled to acknowledge the end of our time there. Even though the shuttle was waiting, I ran down the path through the blueberry bushes to the barn to say goodbye. I've been grateful every day since that I did. *Thanks for everything, Joanie. We had fun, didn't we?*

"Joan?" It was a whisper from Nate, entering the library after a quiet knock. "It's late, nearly midnight. You missed dinner. Come to bed." He stood behind me and rubbed my shoulders. "Are you okay?"

I wasn't. "I may not be Henry Blakely's daughter."

"I don't know what to say."

"Me neither."

"You like him." I was sitting on the side of the bed, trying to put on my nightgown with arms that weighed about a thousand pounds. Nate sat in the chair by the fire. I'd filled him in on my discoveries, the highlights and the lowlights. I couldn't manage to communicate the dread in the pit of my stomach, so I asked about his dinner with Beckman instead. Nate told me they talked about music, of course, and Nate's work, which Nate said Beckman grasped quickly. But not about me or the Panthéon Sketches or Paris because, as Nate said, that wouldn't be fair to me.

As Nate spoke, it reminded me of how easily he mixed with the crowd of photographers and drivers at the art gallery. I couldn't help but compare him to Casey, who stood at alert in the company of other men. My ex exuded competition; Nate exuded competency and curiosity. A sweet sensation of pride welled in me, despite the circumstances. His antagonism toward Beckman had softened, for sure. "You actually like him."

"I don't have a stake in this at all, Joan. It doesn't matter whether I like him or not. And I don't have to trust him like you do, if you want to understand what happened ten years ago or three days ago. But remember, in my business, it's common for me to work with difficult personalities who have strong visions of exactly what they want. Not many have gold records, so that's a little impressive." He shrugged. "He's a complete egomaniac, but he's not bad."

I was too drained to go too hard on Nate. "Great. You were all 'He tried to kill you' and now you're on his side?"

"I'm on yours. Always." Nate paused to let that sink in. "Clearly, he believes that he did you a service. I tell you this, based on the number of big radio hits for other bands that he played for me today in the studio, whatever money he didn't make as a seminal punk band in the eighties, he's making up for it now. I think he could buy ten more collections of Joan of Arc sketches if he wanted."

I managed to laugh. "The museum blew it. We should have charged a million, straight up, and all gotten bonuses." I fell back into my pillow; I'd never get up now. "What day is it?"

"Sunday. Almost Monday now."

"Don't you have to go to Sweden on Monday?"

"Switzerland. But I pushed it back."

"You can go if you need to, Nate. I mean, I don't want you to go, but I know that you have work. And this has been a really long one-night stand."

'That is true." Nate sat beside me and rubbed my back. "Sleep now. I'll bring coffee in the morning. I'm going to my room. I have to do a little work, re-arrange a few things." He kissed me softly. "If it counts for anything, I like Shook Up Joan. She shakes me up."

Chapter 20

The coffee next to my bed was stone-cold. Nate must have put it there hours ago. I felt like I had slept the sleep of the dead. I rolled over and checked my phone. It was nearly eleven, and there were a bunch of missed calls from Polly. I should have checked in with her once more last night. She probably thought I was being held hostage in a Normandy barn. I hit the screen, and the phone promptly died. I needed a charger.

The smell of fresh-baked bread got me out of bed. Then I heard the clattering of pots and pans in the kitchen. And voices coming from a different place, maybe even outside.

I opened the shutters and looked across the lawn. There were two tall figures standing in the garden, gesticulating broadly with voices raised.

One was Peter Beckman, and the other was my mother.

"What is happening?"

It wasn't the most dramatic entrance, but when I took in the scene in front of me, it was the only phrase that popped into my head. Sitting at the farmhouse table in the kitchen that was part sixteenth century, part *Traditional Home* photo spread, was Nate, drinking coffee and chatting up Polly, who was standing in a striped apron at the stove sautéing something like she was the lady of the manor. Marianne played sous-chef, arranging a sideboard of ham, quiche, roasted vegetables, bread. A full offering of all kinds of citrus caught my eye, brightly colored oranges and grapefruit, sliced and arranged on a white platter. The sun was streaming in through the lace curtains, bringing light and warmth. The kitchen looked so cozy, the disconnect was annoying. I snapped. "How did my mother get here?"

Nate immediately got up and poured me a cup of coffee, handing it to me while holding back any details. Polly, to her credit, was raising her hand in admission.

"It was me. I'm so sorry. I thought you knew or at least had some idea. Your mom called me from LAX and said that she had spoken to you and you needed her. She said she got my number from my mother, who was thrilled that Suzi Blakely had called her about anything. Your mother was on the plane to de Gaulle before I could check her story," Polly conceded, then handed her wooden spoon to Marianne and said in French, "Can you watch these? Don't let the mushrooms get too soft."

Polly crossed the kitchen to hug me. "In my defense, I did try to call, but I guess you were immersed in your own mystery here. Nate here has been filling me in a bit. I'm glad you found the notebooks. I can't imagine what that feels like. And, it sounds like the museum got its money and you can keep your job. So that's great. But seriously, what are we all doing here?" She looked at sous-chef Marianne to see if that comment got a rise, but the Frenchwoman remained focused on the mushrooms.

I took a seat at the big table. "I was hoping to find that out today, like right now. But it looks like some old business is getting taken care of. I can't believe my mother is here."

Nate remained silent, but I was guessing that he, too, could not believe my mother was now involved.

"Your mom told me that she and Blackbird there were an item back in the day. Is that true?" Polly resumed her position back at the stove.

"You probably know more than me at this point. But I think so." I could see the two of them out the window, the volume of their conversation lower but still intense. I hadn't seen my mother this animated in ten years.

"Eighties punk music wasn't really my jam, but I can see he has a vibe your mom would like." Polly played the cello in high school, and the only CDs that ever seemed to be in rotation in her car were by Yo-Yo Ma, En Vogue, and Arrested Development. Punk was definitely not her jam.

"Yup." It was clear that Nate hadn't told Polly that Beckman might be my real father, or I don't think her tone would be so light. I didn't want to go into details in front of Marianne, but I appreciated Nate's discretion. I took a slug of coffee. It made a difference. "What happened when she walked in? How did Beckman react?"

"He was speechless," Nate said.

"She was not," Polly added.

"He recovered quickly, and then they disappeared to work it out."

Polly picked up the story: "First, they went into the library and she did some yelling. Then they went into the studio and it was quiet for a bit. But they've been outside yelling at each other for a good fifteen minutes. I'm surprised they didn't wake you up sooner. It's only funny because on the trip here from the airport, your mother must have said a million times that she has learned to accept whatever life may throw in her path. Apparently, not so much."

I looked at Nate. "Does she know all about Blackbird, the clues, and the whole Paris treasure hunt?" Nate looked at Polly.

Polly nodded. "I could only fill her in on what I knew, but I did. I hope you don't mind. It was a long drive from de Gaulle," she said.

What did it matter who told her what and when? This was happening and I couldn't control the unfolding. "Thanks. Saves me the trouble."

Polly poured me more coffee. "She seems pretty mad about the notebooks. And he seems pretty happy that she's here."

Right then the back door opened.

"Joanie! Here I am!" My mother rushed to hug me, her enthusiasm more befitting a surprise visit for a bridal shower than a potentially awkward family moment. Her coat was cold from the damp air outside, and her eyes were red like she'd been crying, but her energy was strong. "It was like the old days. I hung up the phone after talking to you, packed, and was at LAX in a few hours. By the time Charlie, you know the driver I use, by the time he dropped me off, I had a plane ticket and Polly on the other end picking me up. How great is it that Polly could make this happen?" My mother, gracious as always, gave Polly a little squeeze. She unwrapped several layers of cashmere and sat down at the table next to Nate.

That was my cue. "Mom, I don't know if you've met Nate. This is Nate Redmond. He's my . . . seatmate."

"I think you're more than that, Nate." My mother held out her hand to be shaken. "I'm sorry about earlier, rushing in without introducing myself. I'm sure you can understand, given the circumstances. I'm Suzi Clements Blakely. Thank you for being here." My mother charmed, and Nate shook hands on command.

"Your tea." Beckman placed a teapot and mug in front of my mother. Whatever had been discussed outside, he looked triumphant, like he'd won this enormous prize and now he was going to bask in the victory. "Food will be ready soon, sleepyhead!" Beckman announced, looking at me like I was a college kid back home from term. That did it.

"Can I talk to you a second, Mom? Privately."

"Let me finish this tea. And, Polly, I'll take one of those croque monsieurs. A half. Did you make those? They smell delicious. And how about some fruit? Thank you so much." My mother settled in like a frequent guest who expected excellent hospitality. Nate made another round with coffee, and I was beginning to sense that coffee was Nate's one and only food skill.

Accommodating my mother, Polly switched into service mode. "I put mushrooms in them. It's my signature." Leave it to Polly to feel the need to improve on a classic French dish. "Joanie, what can I get you? Nate, do you want of these, too?"

I exchanged glances with Nate. I needed to talk to my mother about the notebooks, about Beckman, about that photo from *Paris Match*. And then we needed to hear the whole story about why and how Peter Beckman pulled off the heist of the Panthéon Sketchbook. But it appeared that Suzi Clements Blakely's agenda was our focus, and she wanted brunch. My questions would have to wait, but not for long. "Sure, I'll take the other half of my mother's."

The random collection of humans in this beautiful kitchen in Normandy made me think of the meals that often happened at our house in Pasadena when friends of my parents would come for dinner, then end up staying over for brunch. My father, if he wasn't at his studio, would make omelets and squeeze orange juice. My mother would lay out fruit, nuts, yogurt, granola. A guest might take over setting the table with plates, linen napkins, and silver. I remember Judy Chicago wandering around our yard, assembling an arrangement for the table from olive branches, pomegranates, and late-winter roses. Impromptu, but perfect. You never knew who might be there or show up. This moment had the same feel.

Beckman was serving himself at the buffet Marianne had set up, clearly pleased at the scene, too. Like this was what he had planned all along.

—

The only time in my life when my mother got completely furious with me was New Year's Day 1997, when I returned home from the Rose Parade clearly hungover and miserable. Following a grand Pasadena tradition, I had spent the New Year's Eve of my senior year of high school camping out on the Rose Parade route, in anticipation of Polly's triumphant ride down Colorado Boulevard. Also in a grand Pasadena tradition, I drank too much schnapps to counteract the cold and paid for it the next morning. It was a miserable night on the hard ground, once the thrill of being on the loose at midnight with thousands of other high school kids had worn off. I slept through most of the parade and arrived at home needing a shower, a hot breakfast, and permission to lie on the couch the rest of the day, but my mother went nuts.

To say I wasn't in the fast lane in high school was an understatement. I was the kind of teenager who really enjoyed her duties as president of the French Club. My idea of a good time was staying up late to do the cooking before the crepe sale we sponsored every Valentine's Day. I was hardly a party girl, so the fact that my mother, who had, in fact, been a party girl on an international scale, came down on me so hard that day was surprising. My father had simply chuckled a bit, handed me an aspirin, and offered to make me an omelet and some coffee. But my mother's response was more befitting of finding me in a crack den than hungover from some New Year's Eve overindulgence.

"Do you want to end up in rehab? Is that what you want? A ninety-day stay at Las Encinas?" she screamed, referring to the celebrity rehab in town. She then proceeded to list every celebrity offspring that had gone offtrack and ended up in jail, therapy, family court, or Vegas for a quickie wedding. The litany was impressive, like she'd been gathering information from *Hello!* magazine for years to throw back in my face. I was shocked that she had thought through this all so deeply.

During her rant, I hung my throbbing head, assuring her I didn't have a problem, didn't need rehab, and wasn't headed down the same path as So-and-So's kids who we used to ski with in Aspen, and she backed off. And I haven't had another shot of schnapps since 1997.

After the death of family friend's son from an overdose years later, I realized that my mother wasn't mad at me; she was scared for me. I wasn't exactly a coal miner's daughter. My childhood, with its exposure to all sorts of glamour, glitz, and bad behavior, was privileged in ways that are hard to explain to civilians who've never experienced a backstage pass or private elevators in hotels. What I had was access to a very fast life if that's what I wanted. A couple of phone calls on a Saturday night, and I could have been out clubbing until dawn thanks to the upper du jour and in recovery by nineteen. But my mother didn't have to worry. She and my father had done a good job scaring me straight with their endless tales of friends who never really lived up to their potential because their vices got in the way. Plus, being in control was more addictive to me than being out of control.

As my mother and I stood in the library, looking at my father's notebooks, the anger and the fear welled up in me like it had so many years ago in my mother. I was mad, but I was also scared. I had so much to tell her, about Paris and Jacques and everything that had happened over the past four days, but first, I had to get to the bottom of a few issues. I wasn't sure I wanted the answers to the questions I was about to ask.

"I like Nate. He's adorable. Is he your adventure? Or something more?"

"I think my adventure." I felt disloyal admitting it, but there it was. Nate was a *Revenge of the Nerds* rebound situation, and I'm pretty sure I was the girl he'd one day refer to as You'll Never Believe What Happened to Me That One Time I Went to a Conference in Paris. "I'm not ready for anything more right now."

"Well, I approve of whatever he is."

As always, her approval resonated with me. I opened notebook #20 and removed the envelope. "I dug around in the notebooks yesterday. I needed to understand what happened during the *Bright & Dark* time period. I found this." I handed her the photo and the letter.

She read slowly and studied the picture for a half minute or so. Finally, she spoke. "Peter's a poet, isn't he? I take it you have some questions for me."

"Yes. Let's start with why you've been lying to me my entire life about the great love story of Henry Blakely and Suzi Clements?"

"Now, Joanie . . ."

"This photo was taken weeks before *Bright & Dark* and months after you allegedly fell madly in love with my father in Pasadena and married him on the spot and moved to Paris. Is that whole story bullshit? What really happened between you and Beckman and"—I hesitated—"my father?"

"You make some valid points."

"Come on, Mom. *Valid points?*"

She knew she was in deep. "I owe you an explanation."

"Yes, you do."

"Why don't we take a minute here to breathe and appreciate the moment."

"Jesus, Mom."

"Joanie, take in the fact that the notebooks still exist and so do we. We are all in this room together. Isn't that something?"

I had no time for metaphysics. "I don't want to breathe or appreciate anything. I've been calm for thirty years, always doing the right thing, being the good girl. I'm exhausted from walking the straight and narrow. You said you couldn't talk to me over the phone about this, but you're here, so, please, tell me. I don't need the nitty-gritty. Big picture it for me." God knows, I didn't want the details. I could see, from Beckman's expression when he looked at my mother in the kitchen sipping her tea and shaking her blond hair, what the details might have been from thirty years ago.

"Fine. I just got off a plane and read the riot act to Peter, but if you want to hash this out now . . ." My mother sat down in a wing-backed chair near the window. She sighed dramatically and paused, as if I might step into the void, call the whole thing off, and give her a big hug. No such luck.

"Hash away."

"Oh, all right. I met Peter Beckman backstage at a Rolling Stones concert in 1978. Obviously, I was there with Jerry. The Ravens were the opening act, at least for a couple of cities before they were fired for, well, basically being drunk most of the time onstage. But the show I saw at the Palladium was their first on the tour, and they were amazing. Most of the people in the crowd weren't even paying attention, but they did an unbelievable set. It was nothing like I'd ever heard before and really nothing like the Stones, so it was no surprise that they were booed offstage in later cities. But there was a connection between Peter and me that night. It was like a lightning bolt. Like a song, really. For a few months, we saw each other whenever we could. I was really working a lot then, traveling all the time, so it was hard to maintain. But he was on my mind—always. After a few months of . . . intensity . . . we called it off.

"Then about a year later, I was in LA for fun, and I ran into Peter Beckman at a diner on Fairfax late one night. His band was working on another album. It was like a second strike of lightning between us. I blew off work and stayed in LA for two weeks. It was unpro-fessional and really unlike me. The night before I had to fly out to a shoot in Miami, we went with some of Peter's friends to this motel in suburbia that some brilliant artist ran as studio."

"Wait, so not even the Rod Stewart birthday party bit of this story is true?"

"Oh, no. That was true. But I went with Peter, not the Swedish model. Anyway, Henry was working like crazy to have the money to stage *Bright & Dark*. He'd been on the Stones tour when he met Beckman. They hit it off, both being from Southern California, blah, blah, blah, you know. I had never heard of Henry Blakely, but Peter wanted to see this motel setup, so out we went. I mean, I thought Pasadena was where grandmothers in pearl chokers went to die. That night I met your father." Her voice shook a little.

"While Peter was off doing . . . a lot of things in dark corners, I sat in the courtyard and talked to Henry. He told me about Paris, his plans, his work, and I was completely taken. Peter was this young, raw talent; Henry was mature, complete. If Henry had said to me that night, *Don't ever leave*, I wouldn't have. And I think if he and Peter hadn't been such pals, he might have. But they were like brothers, the serious older brother and the wild younger brother. So, yes, I stayed with Peter, but I knew Henry was my future.

"The Ravens were starting a European tour, and I made up this excuse that I had to be in Paris all winter. Peter thought it was so that I could be closer to him, but really it was to be in Henry's orbit. To be part of his world. I told my agency to book only European jobs. I rented a little flat near Henry's studio. When Peter was in town, we all went out together with a big crowd of artists and musicians, and we were invincible. Henry called us Impasse Ronsin. Do you know what that is?"

I nodded. I thought of the photo I'd seen at Atelier Artemisium. *Maid, Prince, and Silent Knight.* That must have been during this time period. "Yes. I know what that is."

"Of course you do. You know everything. You always have." My mother carried on. "Peter was in and out of Paris a lot. I couldn't have cared less. I didn't know how Henry felt about me, and I was hedging my bets. If the mature genius didn't want me, I'd stick with the bad boy. But Henry did. We fell in love. Hard. Neither of us had told Peter; it was really my responsibility. That photo in *Paris Match* was taken the night I did." My mother picked up the clipping and stared at it like it was coming to life. "Peter was loaded and the evening ended badly and I blurted out that Henry and I wanted to be together. He did not take it well." There was a long pause, but then she snapped back. "But God, I look great, don't I?"

I smiled. "You do."

"It was messy, Joanie, and I'm not proud. I was deceptive and desperate. I set a trap for Henry Blakely, and he fell in. Peter Beckman was the collateral damage."

I took another sip of coffee to settle myself. "Is Peter Beckman my father?"

"No. He's not. I can promise you that. Don't ever wonder that again. I know for sure you are Henry Blakely's daughter." She was emotional. "Of course you are. Confident, mature, focused. You buckle down and do the work, like your father. You look like me, but inside, you're all him. Joanie, your father and I wouldn't have misled you about something like that."

I was relieved, incredibly relieved at the news. Deep down, I knew what she said was true, particularly the last bit, about not misleading me. Especially about my father. My father valued honesty and integrity above all. You could see that in every aspect of his work. The relief was physical. Much to my surprise, I started to cry. My mother rubbed my back, a comforting gesture from my childhood. But she wasn't off the hook yet. "Then why did you lie about getting married at Pasadena City Hall? I've heard you tell that story a million times. Wait, is November fifteenth even your anniversary?"

"It is. We did get married on November fifteenth, just not in '79, but in 1980, when I was eight months pregnant. We lied because . . . well, your grandmother Adele would have died if she knew I was pregnant out of wedlock. You know how she is. So proper, so snobby. That sort of thing mattered to her. And it was a bigger deal back then than now. When we got back from Paris and I knew I was expecting, we made up the story. That we'd met, fallen in love, and married quickly but kept it a secret. You could lie a lot more easily in those days. It was great. No Internet, no social media. Adele Clements wasn't doing a lot of fact-checking. She may even really know the truth. But it served both of us well."

"And Dad went along with it?"

"I'm not even sure your father was aware of the timeline. Once *Bright & Dark* happened, it was like a whole different era for him. He didn't sweat the details like I did." My mother rose and walked over to the desk piled high with my father's notebooks. She ran her hands over them like they were fine silk. I understood her need for tactile reassurance. *Yes, they are really here.*

But she still hadn't answered all of my questions, some of which had nothing to do with Peter Beckman at all. "Why did you disappear after Dad died? Why did you leave me all alone to cope with everything? You stopped caring about the details at all."

I surprised her. She was silent for a bit and then answered. "I am ashamed that I let you down like that. I know I should have been there, but I couldn't be. People describe losing a spouse like losing a limb, a physical part of your body. But your father's death, it was like being gutted. And then losing my spirit. And it was such an awful death. I couldn't make the pain go away, not with Xanax or therapy or even you. At the time, I thought I was doing you a favor, giving you a role. But I know that was a lie of convenience. I'm sorry."

"And when I married Casey?

"I tried to support the marriage because you wanted to be married. But I knew then and I should have told you that Casey was nowhere near your level intellectually or socially, and he medicated his wounded ego with pot, or weed, whatever they call it now. And booze. Plenty of that. I didn't know about the other women, but I'm sorry to say it didn't surprise me. At the time, I didn't want to drive you away by criticizing Casey. You were fragile, too."

"I'd use the word 'scared.'" I took a job that kept me in a cubicle for a decade, instead of pursuing what I loved: travel, history, and art. I still live in the house you grew up in, alone with the ghosts. And when my lousy husband humiliated me, I went deeper into my cubicle and turned out a few educational videos on obscure museum practices instead of acting out. When I told my mother so many years ago that I was marrying Casey, she remarked that it was like my life was on hold and accelerated at the same time. "I'm not scared now."

"I'm glad. If I could go back to September 12, 2001, I'd do it all differently. I'd be the person your father married, instead of the widow I became. I was so unprepared to be alone."

I had never heard my mother explain her behavior so succinctly.

"Mom, the other day, you were furious at Peter Beckman on the phone, and you had a right to be. He lied to us for ten years about Dad's notebooks. Who knows how that could have made a difference? Now you're chatting him up in his kitchen like it's a happy reunion."

"Joanie, please know that I hold resentment. About the notebooks. About his lack of communication. And there's no reasonable explanation for his interference in your life. No matter what tale he's going to tell us—and I'm sure he will come up with some dramatic retelling of his part in this weekend."

"Marianne said something about Beckman working with the notebooks in his studio. Any idea what that's all about?"

"Who knows? Maybe the notebooks act as some sort of sobriety reminder, like a daily practice." She shrugged. It was a plausible notion. Presumably this afternoon, we'd get our answers.

My mother continued. "I have a lot to work out with Peter. My plan is to stay here and talk all of that out with him. It's not something I can wrap my head around in an hour's conversation and then get back on a plane. There's a lot here to unravel." My mother straightened up the desk rearranging the notebooks, her attempt at stage business, trying to avoid eye contact. She moved a pile of books from one side of the desk to the other and said, "The truth is, we'll never know if having these notebooks would have made a difference in the last ten years. You saw the letter from your father, right?"

I nodded. "I don't know what to make of it."

"Neither do I. Why would your father want the notebooks hidden away? Away from me."

Exactly what I had predicted: she was hurt.

"But that appears to be what your father wanted. And, Joanie, if he hadn't given these notebooks to Peter Beckman, if he had checked them onto that plane, they would be gone forever. Not just ten years, but forever."

I hadn't thought of that. Not once. I was focused on what we didn't have, not what we did. "I guess that's true."

"Maybe we weren't ready for your father's notebooks in 2001. Maybe we needed time to grieve and rage and make a lot of bad decisions before we were handed this gift of his genius. Peter gave us that."

Fuck it. She was right. We could have squandered the currency of the notebooks by immediately handing them off to the WAM in the fervor of national grieving, letting them out of our hands to gather dust in some archive before we could appreciate what was really in them and what they meant to us personally. Still, I was cautious. "I like to think that we earned the return of these notebooks the hard way. Let's not give Peter Beckman too much credit here. He seems to fancy himself some kind of benevolent bystander. That's not how life works."

"That's not how your life works, but for him, everything works out somehow. But look at this life he leads with nobody to share it with. His bandmates are gone. Your father. No wife or kids. It's a lonely life here." I had my suspicions about his loneliness, especially the Carla Bruni decade, but I didn't want to rub that in. "I want to try to give him some benefit of the doubt, now that I've yelled at him. That felt good."

"It looked dramatic. But I think he thought he'd won."

"Enormous ego. Always and still." She looked drained, like the travel had caught up with her. My mother picked up the photo from *Paris Match* again. "It's been thirty years since Peter and I last saw each other. That's unfathomable to me when I look at that photo. That was yesterday. In my mind, it was yesterday. We've both changed a lot, maybe even completely."

My mother continued, "Remember that night in Ojai when you came to tell me about Casey, and we laughed and laughed?"

I nodded.

"That fixed something in me, reset my purpose. You know?"

I did know. I felt it, too. I looked at the notebooks again and thought how truly remarkable it was that they were all here intact. "How did Dad stay friends with Beckman? And why did Beckman stay friends with Dad after all that went down?"

"You know men. They don't fuss, emotionally anyway. Like I said, they had a lot in common to begin with, and eventually that included sobriety. Honestly, Peter must have known I would move on someday. I was too good for him," she half joked. "But I did really, really hurt him. I only saw Peter once or twice after Paris. It was too awkward for your father and too painful for Peter. But your father did. He gave me updates like 'He's doing great' or 'Making money and happy.' I never asked for follow-up."

A memory exploded in my brain. "That time you came to Paris during my junior year . . ."

"And you went to Germany?"

"Yes. I should apologize for that. I've thought about that nonstop since this whole incident began. There was so much I never asked Dad about *Bright & Dark*, and maybe I would have learned more if I had stayed. But, on that trip, didn't Dad say he was going to go out to Normandy to meet a friend? Was the friend Beckman?"

"Yes. It was. And he did. You left. He came here. I stayed in Paris. Your dad took the train out for the day. Think about that!

You might have met Beckman, because undoubtedly you would have chosen his offer over mine."

She was right. I would have picked the train adventure with my father over Paris shops with my mother. "This whole mess could have been avoided." The second the words were out of my mouth I realized I'd never really been involved in anything messy. Sure, the split from Casey was awkward and embarrassing, but it wasn't messy. He cheated and left. I changed the locks within forty-eight hours. Very neat, very clean. I never understood until now. I missed the messy bits and went right for the clean choice. "So now what? Are you here to see me, get the notebooks, or check out Peter Beckman?"

"Can I say all three?" Her voice became playful. "He looks good, doesn't he? Like Sting good."

"What did he say when you showed up this morning?"

"He said, 'I was hoping you would come.'" And just like that, Suzi Clements was back. *Like steel & glass from within.*

My mother and I spent most of the afternoon reacquainting ourselves with Henry Blakely through his notebooks. We didn't do much talking. Talked out, I guess, but occasionally we'd share a page with each other. My mother loved the scale of his later work and the places they'd been together while he created it. She'd hold up a page and say, "Look, the piece he did in Sydney. That was a massive installation." Or, "I'd almost forgot about the Vegas exhibit. I thought I'd never find my way out of that mall, but they paid him a boatload." At one point, she dozed off in the leather chair next to the fire, jet lag catching up to her.

I spent more time in Paris with the *Bright & Dark* notebooks, even finding a few copies of the photos Jacques had shown us stashed in the pages. Everything was so fresh in my mind; I could see the installations now.

At some point in the early afternoon, there was a knock on the door and Beckman stepped into the library. The scent of baking apples wafted into the room. "Hey. Everything okay?"

"Yes," my mother said, waking like Sleeping Beauty.

"Everything's fine," I echoed, not sure exactly how to feel about this man who my mother had crushed but my father trusted with his work. I still needed to hear a full accounting from him directly.

"Quick update. Someone named Jean-Michel arrived. He appears to be Polly's husband or very good at role-play. Polly says he's here for extra security, so don't worry. If someone sues us tonight, we're in good shape. Otherwise, I'm not sure he's going to be much help. But I like his shirts. Marianne is teaching Polly how to make a traditional apple cake so she can photograph it for her blog. Can you smell it? Nate and I are walking into the village. Do you need anything? Bread? Cheese? Decorative lace?" We both shook our heads. "Okay. Well, don't make any plans for tonight. I have a surprise for all of you."

I started to laugh, like we were cooking up some wild Monday night in the French country. "Okay, I'll cancel the fire-eater."

"Drinks and explanations at six. I know I owe you that, Joan. Then we head out for Local Night at a spot outside of town with great food and live music. I know the band playing there tonight. I think you'll like them. Be ready to rock and roll. Sound good?" He made a point to look at me. I nodded.

"Can't wait," my mother responded.

He's producing his own confession, I thought. "Hey," I called to him as he was shutting the door. "Marianne said you usually work with these notebooks in your studio. What kind of work?"

"You'll see. Soon enough," Beckman paused, a little mirth leaving his face. "À bientôt."

Chapter 21

No doubt, the library had been staged for full effect. Marianne had lit candles, placed three large pewter vases with fresh flowers on various tables, and set out a tray of drinks and small plates. The fire was lit, music was on low, and everything, including the people, sparkled. Despite my efforts to remain angry at Peter Beckman, I felt caught up in the party atmosphere, almost like it was the opening night of a show. Anticipation was thick.

Nate and I waited for the others to filter in. I'd had a chance to tell him about the conversation with my mother and the news that Beckman was not my father, but I had concerns he might be my new stepfather. "If my mom had to remarry, it would be to a retired bank manager, not a genuine rock star," Nate said.

Polly and JM arrived at the library minutes before six, dressed for dancing at a country club engagement party, with looks that included pressed blue jeans and blue blazer for him and a navy-blue sheath dress for her, her pregnancy showing now for real. I had considered wearing my magic black dress again, mainly for Nate, but also for me, as it had become like couture armor. But JM appeared to have arrived with a week's worth of outfits for Polly, so she loaned me a sparkly top and some dramatic earrings, two items she herself was never going to wear, and she made that clear.

"Remember these?" she said as we got ready in my room, as we had so many times before in our lives. "You wore this top when we went to that club in Saint-Germain junior year. The really smoky one with the cheesy Europop, but they let American girls in for free. I dug it up for you." Polly's memory of details was astonishing. I barely recalled the club, never mind my outfit.

When Nate saw me in jeans, sequins, and loaner heels from my mother, he gave me the thumbs-up and the pointed to his own dancing shoes, L.L.Bean moccasins. "They've never let me down."

Beckman waltzed in and poured himself a Diet Coke from the bar. He was in another version of all black, but, tonight, he looked cleaner, shinier, like he truly was ready to rock and roll.

My mother was the last to arrive, well after the appointed hour. The decades fell away as she stepped into the library, the low lighting on her side. Somehow, in the rush to get to LAX, she had managed to pack her Elie Saab jumpsuit that I'd seen her wear on several occasions over the past few years on her rare nights out. The fit was stunning. I think the photo from *Paris Match* had inspired her, because she piled on a few extra layers of jewelry and created a head wrap out of an Hermès classic silk scarf. She circled the room to greet everyone with kisses before picking up an aperitif from the silver tray.

No one was more impressed than our host. "Worth the wait, Suzannah. Always worth the wait."

"This is a bigger audience than I had bargained for, but I welcome you all here tonight. To new friends and old." Beckman lifted his glass in a toast, and the rest of us automatically responded. I was losing the battle of neutrality. "Joan, I lured you here because it's been ten years since your father gave me the notebooks. And the time was right to return them to you and to you, Suzannah." He made a grand show of acknowledging my mother. No doubt, he'd been rehearsing this monologue for days.

"Forgive me, Joan. But I thought you needed a shake-up," he said, now leaning down next to me, like a Shakespearean actor begging his point. "And that's what I do. I shake people up. I rattle their brains. I push their buttons. And I get them to put down on paper or on a vocal track how they really feel. But first, I knock them off their feet."

Nate's assessment rang in my head: *He's a complete egomaniac.* "You don't even know me. How could you possibly know what I needed?" I said.

"Luther."

"You know Luther?"

"Of course. Met him several times with your father. We've talked once a year since your father's death. I usually call him in September to check in." Beckman announced this like keeping in touch with my dead father's best friend made complete sense.

"Does Luther know you have the notebooks?" I hoped the answer was no. I couldn't imagine Luther keeping that information to himself while watching my mother and I struggle day-to-day. He would have told us, wouldn't he?

Beckman shook his head. "No, because your father gave them to me to keep for ten years, not Luther. He must have done that for a reason, right? I like to think it's because I'm an artist, not a lawyer. But we'll never really know." Clearly, Beckman took his role as Keeper of the Notebooks seriously. As resentful as I was about his withholding the information from us, as one art courier regarding another, I did admire his loyalty to the mission.

"What do you and Luther talk about?"

"You. Your mother. Your dad. Life. I like to check in on you, Joan." Beckman paused to let that sink in. It did. Then he picked up his story: "When I got sober, I realized that I had, for lack of a better word, a gift that didn't need booze or drugs. Disruption. It's why I started the Ravens, it's why I still write, and it's why I'm here on this planet. *Why the fuck am I still here?* Henry asked at that retreat. This is why."

I needed to challenge that heroic self-portrait. "So instead of creating chaos in your own life by using, you create chaos in other people's lives?"

There was tension in the room. "Fair enough. Well put," Beckman said, pausing briefly to acknowledge the truth. But Beckman was in the zone. This was not a conversation; it was a performance. He continued, "Some artists I work with are two or three hit albums into their careers, and they are lost. Lost. They can't get in touch with the wanting, with the desire, the raw emotion that made their music great in the first place. Their success has made them numb, in so many ways. Cogs, complacent cogs. So, when they would show up here to work with me, some record company executive watching every move, I began inserting small experiences of chaos into what would otherwise be a predictable trip to write and record the next album. It started small, sending them off to write in Paris or London for a few days, but *in disguise*. I would put them up in crappy apartments, take their computers and phones and gaming crap away, and give them only a few bucks to spend. I wanted them to remember what it was like to walk the streets without a bodyguard or screaming fans. They could be regular people again, *feel* again.

"Then I began to make the experiences more complicated: paying beautiful women to turn them down in bars or hiring street kids to steal a wallet and see how they got out of it. Sometimes, I arranged for childhood friends to show up with baggage and vitriol, or former lovers to disarm them. Anything to knock these arrogant rock stars off their pedestals. They would have no idea. They'd think it was a getaway weekend, but it was all orchestrated from the get-go—the creepy cabdrivers, the bar fights, the spontaneous open mic nights that were setups. I found that I was good at planning stuff like this and eventually developed a roster of players who could be counted on to help—hotel clerks, bartenders, street kids, pretty girls, fake policemen. You know, people will do almost anything for money . . .

and a signed CD. I never ask anyone to do anything completely illegal, just *unsettling*."

"So was Beatrice part of your crew?" Nate asked.

"Yup. Beatrice has become a reliable foot soldier. She's has been
in on a bunch of these. In various roles. This one was literally right
up her alley." Beckman paused for a second as if he was remembering
an intimate moment with the young art agent. *Of course, he'd been
involved with Beatrice. Her reverence for him a sure sign of a broken
heart.* "Here's the thing, Nate, it works. Bands would come back from
these four- or five-day 'retreats' and be energized again. Able to tap
into something real that they had lost. You know the British band
Synnex?"

I shook my head. It had been a long time since I'd known any
hot bands. Maybe never. JM, on the other hand, broke into a chorus
that included some beatboxing, not only indicating he had knowledge of Synnex but shocking us all. Polly begged him to stop, but
you could tell she loved him for it.

"That's right, JM. Love that hook! I wrote it! Boy band with a
rock edge. You know their whole fourth album that was a monster
hit? It all came out of one crazy weekend in Paris. First, we purposely lost their gear, and then I sent them on a wild-goose chase for
their stolen guitars, but only after I canceled their credit cards. They
walked for miles, bummed rides, hopped Metro turnstiles, hung out
in cemeteries and dive bars. Totally changed them. Full creative re-
charge. They came back to Fortnight ready to work."

"That's genius," said Nate. "How come I've never read about this
in any article on disruption? It's all we talk about in my business.
That's something a tech journalist would love to write about."

"Nondisclosure agreements as soon as they stepped onto the
property. My business manager tells everyone it's because I'm a recluse and I'm terrified of press. But that's not it at all. If an artist
knows they are going to be messed with, it doesn't work. I don't want

this to be Club Med for Madness. I want the experience to be authentic, so the deal is that they can't tell anyone afterward. Or else I won't go into the studio with them again. A few get pissed and walk out, never to return. One pop diva did that after I dognapped her Maltipoo for, like, twelve hours. Beatrice was in on that one, too. She loves dogs. But ninety-nine percent of the bands get over it. We've turned out some great music." Beckman was clearly proud of his own mythology, a creative guru with special powers.

"This is all fascinating. Thanks for the TED Talk," I said, frustration growing within me at his hubris for thinking I was akin to some boy band with too many followers. "And you thought that I, someone you'd never met and didn't know at all, needed the 'Peter Beckman treatment.' Are you kidding me? I'm not a client. I'm not a band searching for musical identity. I'm an actual person that you don't know at all. You screwed with me *and* my career for your own amusement. What is wrong with you?"

"Joan, I do know you. I've been following you since you were born, and much more closely since your father's death."

My mother was about to jump in, but I shut her down. This was my conversation to have. "And because you had a few phone calls with Luther and set up a Google Alert on me, you think you know what I need?"

"Actually, I used an old-fashioned clipping service, like it's 1985. But they do it digitally now. That's how I came across your blog a couple of years ago, Polly. You mentioned Joan in a post. But now I read you for fun. You really make me laugh, Polly. I loved that post last month on the best stalls at the flea markets for lamps. I printed it out and used it like a road map two weeks ago."

"I'm so glad to hear that. I bet you got some good deals! I sense you can negotiate!" Polly said, clearly pleased. Then she noticed my look and ceded the floor, like our debate club days. "Oh, I'm sorry, Joan."

"Thank you, Polly. I want to be clear, Peter . . ." The name did not sound comfortable on my tongue, after days of Blackbird and Beckman. "I don't need a stranger to orchestrate an adventure for me so I can get back in touch with my feelings. I'm in touch with my feelings, and, sure, over the last ten years, many of my feelings have sucked. But I've dealt with them. You had no right. It was disrespectful." This was more than I wanted to say in a crowded room, but now it was out there, and I felt unburdened. I caught Nate's eye. He didn't turn away.

"I loved your father, Joan. I'd be dead by now without him. No question. OD, suicide, something tragic." Beckman crossed in front of the enormous fireplace for effect. "And I loved your mother. Deeply. Differently. But you nearly killed me, too, Suzannah. But, somehow, between the two of you, you saved me."

"All this, the interest in the Panthéon Sketches, the running all over Paris, the clues, the meetings with Jacques de Baubin, this was your plan to save me?" I asked.

"Well, 'save' is a strong word, but yes. Thanks to my Google Alert, as you called it, I read your quote in CandysDish about wanting a reinvention sabbatical in Paris, or some nonsense like that. I thought, 'That's my in. I can be a part of that.' Plus, I felt I owed it to your dad."

"That's a pretty big debt: $350,000." I quoted the sale price of the sketches I'd seen on the paperwork.

"I'd have paid twice as much, for the art and for you. But, sorry, JM, I didn't want to send a letter through a lawyer. Or an email. It needed to be bigger. What I'd done for pop stars I could do for you. But make it matter more. I discovered the WAM had the Panthéon Sketches in their archive, and everything clicked for me. Paris, Saint Joan, *Bright & Dark*, Joan Bright Blakely."

Beckman let that last sentiment sink in. It worked. I wanted to hear more. "I contacted Beatrice. She has a certain skill set that really came in handy this time. Once, she put this auto-tuned teen diva in a real haunted castle for a few days. It was brilliant. Scared the crap out of her, and her next album was nominated for three Grammys."

Again with the self-congratulations. Peter Beckman may not have been onstage for the past two decades, but he had retained the need to hear his own voice. "When you refused to be booked in the hotel where we had a front desk contact, we had to come up with a plan B to get the sketchbook. But then Polly hinted at the name of your hotel in her blog, and it was almost too easy. Claude was an old friend and has a very sketchy past. He's a great guy. He pulled a bunch of extra shifts to execute the heist. We got lucky there. You went out to dinner with Nate on the first night, and he sprang into action. We thought you might never leave your room, but night one, you were out the door because of this guy here," Beckman said, pointing to Nate with two finger guns. "He lifted the sketches from your secret compartment. That was a fake police officer. Totally fake! An actor! Did you know that?"

I knew Claude was suspicious, but Inspector Agnier? No wonder he only left me messages at the hotel desk and never called my cell. Because he didn't exist, and his callback number would have proven that. And now I understood how Beatrice afforded that Chloé bag. None of this could have been cheap. "This was all so elaborate. And, I'm guessing, expensive."

"It was a few key people in key places. And throwing some euros around."

"What about the clues? Why those sketches from my father's notebooks? Why those locations?"

Beckman was thoroughly enjoying himself now, like he had made it through the roughest part of the evening. "Well, starting at the Panthéon was a no-brainer. I needed to make the first clue pretty obvious or else the whole setup would have failed. And then I chose spots that had some history for me or your father. I thought the hair salon was a bit of fun. I wanted to signal that this was more of a lark than a threat. When you went to Polly's for her help, I knew you'd nail it. Great apartment, you two," Beckman said to JM and Polly, who looked like they were guests at the best murder-mystery party ever. "I mean, from the outside. Don't worry, I don't have someone on the inside in your building."

"Thank you. You should come by for lunch the next time you're in town," JM said. Beckman said he would. I was losing control of this.

"And Jacques de Baubin? Did you pay him?" In the same way I couldn't bear the thought of Luther knowing about the notebooks, I wanted my conversation with Jacques to have been pure. But I'm sure he could have used a few bucks.

"Jacques was delighted to be a part of my scheme. It was all in good fun for him. He only wanted to meet Henry's daughter."

I was relieved. It was as Jacques had said, he was an old man and wanted to meet me. "Did you consider my job at all?"

"Yes. And I hope you lose it."

Now I understood my mother's reaction on the phone when I mentioned Beckman's name. I also wanted to howl out a string of expletives aimed at his condescension and ego.

My mother spoke first. "Peter, that's too far."

"I'm sorry. It's that you have so much more to give the world than tours to donors and carting art around the world," Beckman waxed on, more motivational speaker than mastermind, defusing the tension. "There was one thing I didn't plan on, though: Nate here. You did that all on your own, Joan. You, too, Nate. Well done." Beckman high-fived Nate, who, caught off guard, reluctantly played along.

"Did you arrange for the first-class upgrade?" I asked, needing to know how much I owed to Beckman and how much I owed to the gate agent.

"No, I don't have an airline in yet. But if I did, I would have taken credit for Nate."

"I didn't sign a nondisclosure agreement. I could blow your cover."

"Oh, no, you signed one," Beckman said. "Remember when Beatrice asked you to sign off on the transfer paperwork? There was an NDA in there."

Son of a . . . "But Nate didn't. He could expose you."

Beckman rolled his eyes; Nate shook his head. "Who would believe me, Joan? I'm not the celebrity daughter in this story." He was right.

Beckman nodded. "I can tell you this: I wrestled every day with what your father asked me to do, to hold on to the notebooks for as long as I did. You read the letter. Yes, circumstances had changed, but I believe Henry's wishes would have been the same if he knew he was going to die. He wasn't ready for the work to be seen in hindsight. I felt compelled to honor your father." Finally, Peter Beckman looked like a man with some humility. "And, admit it, Joan, you had some fun."

Yes, I had.

Beckman looked at his watch. "Okay, kids, time to go. Let's load up the van. It's party time."

It must have been the music that carried away our concerns, because I looked at the collection of faces on the dance floor and maybe, for the first time in ten years, I was awash in happiness. We were in a bar on the outskirts of Rouen, and Peter Beckman was onstage with a backup band that had appeared out of thin air playing a cover of "Brown Eyed Girl." It was one of my mother's favorite songs, although that probably goes for most American women of a certain age. As soon as the first few notes started playing, she dragged us all onto the dance floor—me, Nate, Polly, and JM. We were dancing and laughing and singing along like we were closing down a wedding. Typical Americans.

Nate had some dance moves that I was going to have to get to the bottom of later. The L.L.Bean mocs delivered. I liked that he sang along to every song, too.

Once again, we'd been part of an elaborate scheme, but this time, the intentions were good. After a dinner of simple, rich food, most of which Beckman didn't touch, he excused himself from the table. The conversation was lively, and the place was packed, so it took us all a moment to realize that when the lights went down, it was the former lead singer of the Ravens who took the stage. Beckman, in his black shirt and black jeans, could have been opening for the Stones again. I looked at my mother's face. She was already in deep. Polly leaned over and said into my ear, "Man and guitar. Oldest pickup trick in the book, and it's working on me. Pregnancy hormones, I guess."

"Oh, please."

"I meant JM was going to get lucky tonight," Polly explained. "The all-black look is not my thing. Give me a man in a blue blazer. Now, that's hot."

"Bonsoir, mes amis!" Beckman shouted, a line I thought was a little hackneyed, but the locals ate it up. Clearly, they knew who he was, and I got the feeling that this appearance wasn't quite as spontaneous as he wanted us to believe. He was thorough in every detail, as I'd come to know. This was a total setup for my mother's benefit.

Beckman and the band played a full set, starting with early Ravens tunes that got the crowd up on their feet and kept them there. Nate was like a teenager, grabbing my hand and rushing to the front of the stage. Polly and JM surprised me with their enthusiasm, bobbing up and down at the edge of the dance floor, entangled in each other. She was right about those hormones. My mother stayed at the table, watching Beckman, but not giving anything away. She was no groupie.

Then Beckman moved into a few songs off his solo albums,

heavy with meaning. He barely took his eyes off her as he sang the lyrics about his crushed soul and his lonely existence. She stared back a little too intently for my liking. Nate, too. I thought he might cry, he was so overcome with the moment.

Honestly, people had to get ahold of themselves.

Then Beckman announced with some gravitas that he was going to play a few songs from a new project and asked everyone to take their seats. "This is something I've been working on a long time. Like ten years. But I've never played the songs in public. I call it *Bright & Dark*. It's about love and friendship and faith and loss and redemption. You know, Life's Top Five. At first, I thought it would be an epic album, my last big solo project. But then it became something more. Something breathing, three-dimensional. I knew it was play, a rock opera, whatever you want to call it. I knew it had to come alive. Tonight, I want to play a few songs for you." He nodded at my mother, who nodded back. Did she know? I don't think so. He repeated his speech in French, and it sounded even more beautiful. Then he said, "This one's called 'Sweet Maid.'"

I looked at Nate, who was definitely moved now, because it was essentially the clues from our Parisian treasure hunt set to music. The melody was beautiful, and he sounded like a troubadour telling the tale of losing the girl while finding Saint Joan. Then Beckman played a kind of rock anthem, which included my father's equation for moonlight in the verse, and a catchy hook that repeated "Light it up. Watch it shine."

Finally, he picked up his acoustic guitar, sent the rest of the band offstage, and told the packed house, "This one is called 'Palladium.' It's written as a duet, but tonight I'm singing it solo. Someday soon, though, I'll find me a girl to sing this with." Then he launched into a heartbreaking ballad about two beautiful people who fall in love in an instant, but not forever. Exactly the way my mother said it happened.

My mother was a puddle, a jet-lagged, gorgeous puddle.

While the crowd gave Beckman a standing ovation, JM, ever the lawyer, leaned over to me and said in English, "Make sure Peter Beckman buys the rights to this story from your mother. And make sure you get a piece of the show. Because these songs are pretty good."

By the time the band revved up the Van Morrison as an encore, I had already put a reminder in my phone to call Luther. The way this night was going, I was pretty sure I might forget by the morning.

"I'm putting this in my Top Three Nights of All Time List. That was like rock and roll fantasy camp but for real." We were back in my room, peeling off layers of sweaty clothes from a nonstop hour on the dance floor, and Nate was on a high. We'd danced off the alcohol, thanks to my mother. Once Beckman spotted her out of her seat, he must have decided that the music couldn't stop. He and the band played a set of covers straight out of 1978, inspiring Nate to shout at me several times over the music, "Considered the greatest rock and roll year of all time." We didn't sit down again until Beckman loaded us back into the van, and we collapsed.

Now, emotionally spent but physically exhilarated, I unbuttoned my shirt slowly. "So, tonight was worth all the running around in Paris?"

"Yes. Even the time you accosted me at the conference in front of my peers and accused me of theft. I forgive you for that." He pulled me toward him from behind, his hands at my hips. I felt his bare chest against my skin.

"What are the other two nights on the list?" I said, wanting to draw him out.

"Well, one was my first great coding breakthrough, and the other is not appropriate for someone as refined as you." He turned me around. Nate was still in his jeans, and he reached into his front pocket. "Here, I picked this up for you today." He handed me a coin, like the one Jacques de Baubin had, with Saint Joan on one side and an inscription on the other. "The church in the village was selling them for a euro. I bought one for myself, too. We can all use a little reminder to keep the faith every now and then, right?"

I rubbed the coin in my fingers, deeply touched. "Thank you, Nate. Thank you so much." We kissed.

"I have to go to Geneva tomorrow. I can't put it off any longer. My sister is freaking out that I missed so much of the conference, and believe me, this whole trip to Rouen was a little hard to explain to her. If I don't meet with this Swiss company this week, we could lose the deal. Polly and JM are going to drive me to the airport on their way back into Paris." My face must have fallen, because he reached for my chin. "I know. I don't really want to go, either. So, while you were talking to your mother, I made a few calls. I thought we could meet in Copenhagen for a long weekend, then fly back to LA together. You can see your father's piece at the Arken, which you haven't seen in a while. I can buy some hard-to-find *Star Wars* Lego sets. And we can wander around and do nothing together for a few days. Can you get some time off?"

Probably the rest of my life if David Weller gets wind of what really happened, I thought. But at the very least, I was in the clear for the next ten days. I'd assumed I'd stay in Paris, but now, fleeing to Denmark with Nate seemed like the perfect plan. I nodded. "Aren't you sick of me yet?"

"Not yet. Now, I didn't say we'd spend the entire trip on the Blakely Family Memory Lane Tour. I feel like I've done my time on that front. But one afternoon at the museum would be a fitting way to . . ." Nate faltered. To what? *Wrap this all up? Say goodbye?*

"To celebrate?" I offered.

"Yes. Exactly. To celebrate."

"I would love to meet you in Copenhagen."

"We'll work out logistics tomorrow."

"Yes." And now I had a few ideas on how to make sure that this night was at the top of Nate's list. "How about a shower? A very unrefined shower?"

Only Beckman was in the kitchen when I went down for my morning coffee. He was sitting at the table in a plaid bathrobe, reading the paper and petting a giant calico cat that was sitting on his lap. He could have been anybody's dad, in the morning light. He looked up. "Hey."

"Hey. That was something last night. I was impressed." There was a pot of French roast already made with blue ceramic mugs set out next to a white pitcher of milk. I poured myself a cup and then asked, "Do you need a refill?"

"Yes, thanks." He folded the paper and scooted the cat away, ready to talk. "I'm glad you enjoyed it."

"My mother was very happy. And so was Nate."

"And Joan? Was she happy? Or only impressed, which is not exactly a rave review."

"Remember, I'm not here as a fan, Becks. More as a hostage." I used my father's nickname for him intentionally; Blackbird sounded goofy now, and Peter sounded all wrong. He'd always be Beckman to me. "I have other interests. Like protecting my mother. And my father's memory. Your music was beautiful, and I look forward to hearing the rest and figuring out what happens next."

"So, does that mean you've forgiven me?"

"I have a lot to work through still. What I know now it that I'm ready to move forward."

Beckman looked a tad too proud.

"Do not give yourself complete credit."

"Partial credit, though. I'm taking partial credit."

"We still need to talk about rights to that material."

"Peas in a pod. Your mother already mentioned that. Sharks, the both of you." He was kidding.

I was not letting him off the hook. "It is her life you're exploiting."

"I object to the word 'exploiting,' but, yes, we can negotiate terms. Have Luther call me." He stood up to cut himself a wedge of bread. "Is every moment with you so intense?"

"Well, Pot, or should I call you Black?" We could both laugh at that. "Can I ask you something?"

"Of course."

"Of all the pages in all the notebooks, why did you include the Disneyland page? The *It's Not Really a Small World After All* sketch. I understand all the others—the sketch of my mother, the archway of the retreat center—but how did you decide on that drawing?" It had been a piece of the puzzle I couldn't solve.

Beckman answered without hesitation. "Your father talked about that day all the time. It was really important to him. It changed his life."

Shock. "Disneyland changed his life?"

"Not the theme park. The experience." He studied me. I could tell he was taking my emotional temperature. I waited. Then he continued. "Your father had been drinking again. For months. He'd fallen off the wagon, as you amateur drinkers like to say. Really, it's more like falling into a deep pit of hell when you start drinking again after years of sobriety, but that's off topic. Anyway, like he told me, he'd blown it, straight up succumbed to his demons. He was hitting the bottle at his studio, missing all kinds of deadlines and dates. I guess he missed your birthday and had a huge fight with your mother, right?"

I nodded. I had some idea about the lapse, but a PG version fit for teenager. But I was surprised my father would have confided in another person about that awful night. That was deeply personal.

Beckman continued, "He told me Suzi served up an ultimatum:

stop drinking or she was leaving and taking you to New York. So he stopped. Never touched the stuff again. That was the year he started the retreat, as insurance to stay sober. That trip to Disneyland was what he needed to remind himself."

"Of what?"

"Of all he had to lose. He found clarity of purpose that day. *It's Not Really a Small World After All* was all about personal responsibility. I'll never forget, he said to me once, 'Becks, it's not really a small world after all. It's a fucking enormous world. Enormous.' He got that. Your dad understood the enormity."

The most incomprehensible fact about the universe is that it is comprehensible. "When did he tell you this?"

"Joanie, there was some truth-telling at those retreats. That's all I'm going to say about that."

I guess my mother was wrong. Maybe men do fuss emotionally. "I never knew most of that."

"Well, that's the way it is, really. We only know what others want us to believe."

We all stood out on the gravel driveway to say goodbye to Polly, JM, and Nate—me, my mother, and Peter Beckman—like some sort of aging blended family still not over the uncomfortable phase. My mother was standing next to Beckman with a kind of closeness that only familiarity brings. She was swathed in layers of cotton and cashmere, her hair pulled up in a messy bun and her eyes bright as she leaned into Beckman's fit frame. I thought about what my mother had said when she saw the *Paris Match* photo. "In my mind, it was yesterday." I wasn't really old enough or wise enough to appreciate the passage of years in the same way, but I had the sense seeing him again had made time stop for a bit. Beckman and my mother shared the same ease standing in the driveway as they had shared at that

YSL party in Paris long ago. Well, I guess the three of us would sort a few things out over the next few days, including their relationship status.

Nate and Beckman shook hands and did a lot of promising to be in touch. My mother gave Nate a big hug and thanked him for being such a gentleman.

I'd said my proper goodbye to Nate earlier, so I focused on Polly and JM. "Thank you for taking care of my mother and me on this trip. You guys are the best. What a story you'll have, Polly."

"This is too good for the blog. You need to sell this to Hollywood. I won't breathe a word about all the fake art theft shenanigans or the missing notebooks or the Svengali overtones, now that I know Peter Beckman is a regular reader. But I am pretty proud that I put this whole thing in motion when I nearly revealed your hotel room on the blog! When the next movie about your life comes out, I hope Gabrielle Union plays me. Look at your mother. She looks so happy!" And, of course, we did look because Polly commanded it and she was right. There was no denying the contentment on my mother's face. "But I'm totally posting those photos of the apple cake and mentioning that wild night at the bar. A punk icon in Rouen. I think the baby's going to have a rocker's soul, don't you, JM?"

JM agreed. "Anything you wish, my dear."

"I have no doubt your baby will be a brand someday," I said.

Polly was touched. "Oh, merci, merci."

"Joan, come back and see us. And call that lawyer."

"Will do and I already sent an email!"

Nate appeared next to me. He whispered in my ear, "See you soon. Text if you need me." I gave him a quick kiss on the cheek, and the three of them loaded up into the car and drove off with the crunching of tires and a toot on the horn.

Then it was only us: the awkward family. Beckman started to suggest a few group activities, but I had already made my plans, so

I declined. "I'm heading into Rouen. There are a few places I want to see today."

"Need a ride?" Beckman asked.

"No, thanks. I'm going to walk."

"A pilgrimage?"

"Yes," I answered. "A pilgrimage of sorts."

"Want some company?" my mother asked.

We walked and we walked, from the fields surrounding Fortnight through the industrial part of the city into the old part of Rouen, filled with Gothic architecture, Renaissance spires, and an air of medieval mystery, heightened by navigating through the winding streets lined by half-timbered houses and stone shops. The city looked a little better off than it had ten years ago, but the cathedral was still in want of repairs. We had no particular itinerary, except to take it all in slowly. The day was cool and cloudy, but my mother was prepared with wraps for both of us. I bought two pairs of cheap gloves from a vendor so we could be outside for hours.

We wandered past open-air markets selling everything from local produce to cleaning supplies. Past cafés and squares filled with tourists and locals. At a market, we stopped for a pressed galette of ham and cheese wrapped in a paper cone to eat while we walked. We talked about memories, about my days in Paris last week and my parents' time in Paris years ago. I told her about Guy from Galerie Luna who wanted to show her work, and about lovely Jacques feeding us and showing me his book of snapshots. Finally, we stood wordlessly gazing up at the old stained glass windows preserved and restored in the modern Church of Joan of Arc. The contrast was striking and effective.

Now we were parked at an outside table in a café off the Old Market Square. I ordered hot chocolate and a plate of sablé Breton cookies. My mother opted for red wine.

"How long are you going to stay?" I tried to make it sound like travel small talk, instead of telegraphing my concern about the vortex that was Peter Beckman. I didn't want my mother getting sucked in, too furious and fast to be saved.

She wasn't fooled. "Not forever, if that's what you're worried about. And clearly you are."

"It's your life, Mom, but I still don't trust him."

"Oh, neither do I. He's a performer, a poet. And now that's he's sober, he's clearly a control freak. This whole experience, experiment, whatever you want to call it, has made me realize that the last thing I want at my age is someone calling all the shots." She broke a piece of buttery cookie and popped it in her mouth. "I mean, the Wizard of Oz routine has a certain appeal, but not for the long haul."

"I thought you were sunk, the way you were looking at him last night. And the way he was looking at you." On cue, I noticed several passersby, women in their early fifties, pointing at my mother, snapping photos with their phone. It didn't happen often these days, but occasionally.

My mother noticed, too, sitting up straighter but keeping her eyes on me as she confessed. "I do feel like I've been in cold storage for the last ten years. But not anymore. Not after last night." Then she gave her shoulders a little shimmy-shake and did that Suzi-patented wink that I could never manage.

"Okay, Suzi . . ." My face reddened like a teenager. "Got it. Totally understand. Thanks for sharing, Mom."

She was very pleased with herself, and I was worried she was going to give more details, but she surprised me. "He's pretty unbelievable onstage, isn't he?" I nodded. He was. "But really I was thinking, 'If he can do that at his age, why can't I do my thing at my age?'"

"So you're going back to full-time groupie-hood?"

"No, strutting my stuff. I miss being in the limelight, Joanie. I know that was never your thing, but it was mine. I loved modeling, playing the part with the hair and makeup and clothes. I want to be relevant again, not famous, but I want to at least show up in my own life. Wasn't that why your father gave Beckman the notebooks and said to keep them for ten years?"

"True. Henry Blakely wasn't ready to become a biannual think piece in the *New Yorker*."

"I so get that. If the notebooks' reappearance means anything to me, it's that I'm not done yet. I was jealous of Peter up there, staying true to himself after all these years."

"So, what does that mean? Staying here and working out of Paris?"

There was a definitive head shake. "Oh, no. I can't compete with the Frenchwomen my age. I've had too much sun, and they have a genetic advantage. And really, whatever this is with Peter, it's temporary. Or, let's at least say, not full-time." She paused for effect to take a sip of wine and look out over the street. "But, what do you think if I move to New York? Get a little place in the Village. Be part of the scene again, if there is a scene in the Village anymore."

"According to my sources, the scene all moved to Brooklyn in 2009," I said, then saw how determined she looked. She meant it. "Seriously? Back to the Village?"

"Yes. Seriously. That's what I was thinking about last night. There must be an Eileen Fisher catalog shoot I can get in on. I can call my good friend Ralph, see if he needs a young grandmother in the Holiday campaign. Of course, I'd have to detox, do a cleanse, a month of boot camp, and, you know, whatever it takes to look my best, courtesy of Dr. Injectable. And my agent will have to call in a few favors to get some new decent portfolio shots. But I've still got it, right?"

I was stunned and thrilled at the revelation. "Oh my God, yes. A million times yes. You should totally do that. New York. Modeling. Everything. Jump back in."

"It will mean some changes. As long as we're selling the Motel, maybe it's time to sell the house in Pasadena." She said it gently, as if I might crumble at the suggestion.

But as soon as it came out of her mouth, the mantle of responsibility was lifted off my shoulders. I felt a lightness immediately, freedom. "I've been thinking the same thing. I love the house, but now it's too much for me." I didn't want to admit that Casey had soured the last of the good vibes I got from the place. Plus, I needed a change. "We both need to move on. We should do it on our terms, though, not on Beckman's."

"Agreed."

Then I added something of my own delicate situation. "There's something I've been thinking for a while, since that visit to Ojai. Maybe we need someone outside the family but inside the art world to run the Henry Blakely Foundation. Especially now that we have the notebooks back. There really is a Henry Blakely archives now. And I don't want to be the de facto person in charge anymore. I think Tai would be a great choice. He's a scholar, knowledgeable about Dad's work, and we know him, he knows us, so he'd be respectful but bold and thoughtful in his approach. He's eager to strike out on his own, apart from the WAM. I think we should talk to Luther about structuring the foundation with a paid position for Tai and an assistant or two, even if it means selling some of the artwork at the house for an endowment. Plus, Tai adores your personal style."

Without hesitation, my mother chimed in. "Brilliant. Oh, Joanie, you're brilliant. I loved your Dad, but I'm not the best person to carry on his artistic legacy. I was good at managing him, but not his place in history."

"Me neither. Frankly, after this last week, I've sorta had it up to here with his artistic legacy."

"Cheers to that!" We clinked glasses, attracting the attention of the table of Germans and the waiter who asked if we needed anything else. My mother asked for some water without bubbles and the check in her decent French.

I carried on, "And, not to give Peter Beckman too much credit, but I think it's time for me to leave the museum. That is, if I don't get fired when I tell David Weller what actually happened, which, of course, I have to do."

I could tell that pleased my mother. She'd been a bullhorn about leaving since the departure of Casey. But she played it cool. "What will you do?"

"Travel, for sure. Go back to school, maybe for an MBA in arts management. Then, a gallery of my own, someplace new. I'm ready." Then, without any buildup, I told my mother what I'd kept hidden from Nate. "I heard from Casey."

She perked up. "When? About what?"

"Well, I saw him at LAX when I was flying out. There he was with the whole family, off to Belize for his art show, apparently, and he looked . . . not happy. Kinda terrible actually, which made me kinda happy. Then, the next day, I got an email from him. He wants to see me again and see if we can 'heal together.' That's what he said: 'I've thought about you a lot since seeing you at the airport and I think we should talk so we can heal together.'"

"Sure, a few months of full-time fatherhood and a lame offshore art opening and now he wants back into the Blakely Family fold." I was surprised she knew about his exhibit. "Polly told me in the car about the show and the airport sighting. We did some digging. The reviews were meh."

"I know. I checked, too, after Polly told me. He doesn't want to heal together; he wants to self-promote using my name. Like old times. He's lost a little of his art-world cred."

"I would say a lot of his credibility. So transparent."

"He went on to say that he'd made a big mistake, wished he done everything differently, and seeing me made him realize that I had always been the calm in the storm. He actually wrote, 'You were my North Star.' I mean, really . . ."

"That's no Peter Beckman lyric. What a . . . I don't even know the word for him."

"Coward?"

"Did you respond?"

"At first, no. But then I sent him a brief note. I wished him well in his future endeavors, because I thought that sounded like a college rejection letter. I ended with the request that all communication should go through my lawyer and, once we'd finalized the sale of the Motel, that would be the last of our contact."

"Did you hear back?"

I shook my head. "No, I shut him down. And you know what? It wasn't hard at all. I'm glad that I didn't waste one more minute with him. Not one."

"Here's to you."

We toasted again, with the dregs of our beverages, as the water and the check arrived. My mother pulled out twenty euros to cover the bill and handed it back to the waiter, who smiled with something more than gratitude. An appreciation for her effort on all fronts, from her attempt at French to her roots' maintenance to her command of navy and beige.

I thought about what my mother had said about Beckman, about not handing over control at her age. We had something in common. My future felt like my own. "I have to admit, I'm relieved. I thought I'd be spending Christmases here with the two of you like some sort of adult third-wheel child."

"You'd never be a third wheel anywhere but, really, I wouldn't worry about holidays yet. I mean, I'm not leaving right away. Remember, ten years of cold storage, so I think I'll stay a few weeks at least and enjoy all that France has to offer."

Pretty sure France was a metaphor in that sentence. "Okay, see, I can't have this conversation with you."

My mother laughed. "You would have made a terrible rock and roll groupie."

"Thank you." I missed Nate. "I'm more a Sweater Vest Girl than a Tight Leather Pants Girl."

The sun was almost gone and the temperature was dropping. I looked around the streets, filled with so much history, ancient and contemporary, and knew one thing for sure: I was wiped out. My pilgrimage was over for now. "Can we grab a cab back to Fortnight? I've walked far enough for today."

January 2012

It was cold and rainy in Southern California, the perfect evening for a cashmere pashmina, a glass of red wine, and a fire. And that's exactly the situation I found myself in on a Sunday night, not cozied up at home but back at the bar at the Langham Hotel, once again taking refuge from a tricky domestic situation. Although this time, it wasn't my ex-husband moving out of the house; it was me. The boxes labeled, the paintings in Bubble Wrap, all that was left was the moving trucks to arrive on Monday. So rather than sleep in a ghost house filled with memories, I checked myself into the hotel, booked a few spa treatments, and headed to the bar.

Next week would officially be the start of something new. But tonight, I was keeping my eyes open for something familiar.

The bar was quiet. When it rains in Southern California, no one leaves the house, terrified of slick wet roads, inexperienced rain drivers, and terrible traffic: all justified fears. The light crowd meant that I spotted him right away as he walked in, the guy with wet hair in one of those puffer coats that had taken over America, with a small gym bag over his shoulder. Exactly as he'd said: he was here most Sunday nights. He caught me staring and stared right back, long enough to register my identity and give me a nod and then a bit longer to take in the fact that I was alone at the bar and waiting for him. He headed in my direction, but first stopped to say hello to the regulars, order from the bartender, and direct the drink to be delivered to where I was sitting. He was in no hurry.

Neither was I.

It had been almost a year since Casey had delivered his news, and the rush of panic and frantic searching for self—and other items—dissipated into an understanding that eventually I'd figure it out. The decade between my father's death and now was a long slow grief train, and the shotgun wedding, a marriage built on hopes and falsehoods, the safe but uninspiring job were all cars on that train. I didn't realize how much baggage I'd accumulated until I let it all go. Now I was at a place where I knew where I was coming from, where I was headed. Conjunction junction. Now that. As long as. With.

In a first things first move, I quit the museum. Or I was sort of fired because I had to confess to David Weller how I'd lost a piece of artwork, withheld the truth about it, and then took some risk, both personally and institutionally, to get back the Panthéon Sketches. Even though the fake theft resulted in a sale, I knew that the real story of what went down in Paris might come out, and Mike Dembretti and his security business would take the fall if I didn't explain my part in "the misunderstanding." David proceeded to tell me how valuable my contributions had been in the past, but now seemed like a good time for me to move on. He hoped that this conversation wouldn't, in any way, affect our future relationship. I assured him it wouldn't.

After a short deliberation, my mother and I listed the Pasadena house. It was a real estate feeding frenzy that signaled the long economic downturn was over. A pristine midcentury modern with a pedigree resulted in multiple offers over the asking on the day it listed. The decision to sell was easy when I returned from Europe with my dignity and confidence back intact and my mother returned with my father's notebooks and a renewed zest for life. With Luther's help, we made a number of financial and foundational decisions we should have made years ago. The Henry Blakely archives would be donated to the Wallace Aston Museum.

Thanks to the sale of several pieces of art from my parents' collection, there would be an endowment to cover a website and educational outreach programs, and a dedicated scholar, Tai Takashita. Tai was thrilled to have the opportunity to shape the cultural scholarship, and I was thrilled that my father's legacy was in such good hands. "Do you think I can add 'thought leader' to my LinkedIn profile?" Tai has asked over our celebratory dinner with Anders, now publicly his boyfriend, as the added title and money had given Tai the courage to come out to his family. It had gone poorly, but Tai was hopeful that his parents would come around. In the meantime, he was proceeding with his life. Tai reveled in the fact that he and my mother had very similar taste, so it made all conversations about branding and design work a snap.

For the tenth anniversary of my father's death, my mother did two interviews, one with CBS Sunday Morning the other with the *Los Angeles Times*. Both were moving and dignified and returned my mother to public life. On September 11, 2011, we skipped the formal ceremonies and made the trek to Marin County, where we asked the private collector who owned *It's Not Really a Small World After All* if we could come see the piece. He was touched and very accommodating, inviting us into his home afterward, where we talked for hours about Henry Blakely. The collector put us in touch with his brother, a film agent in New York. Now there was a deal in the works for a documentary about my father's work. My mother, Tai, and I would executive produce, and David Fincher would direct. Suzi Clements Blakely had her eye on an Oscar nomination.

She was splitting her time between Manhattan and Rouen because Peter Beckman didn't fly, so transatlantic ocean liners were their transportation mode of choice, and an East Coast city made more sense than Ojai. It was both a shock and a comfort that she had found someone to share her life with, even if it was Peter Beckman. Clearly, she was drawn to men who lived on the edge of genius and sanity, and that's a pretty short list of eligible bachelors available to an aging supermodel.

I might never fully trust Peter, but I fully believed my mother deserved some life back in her life, and I didn't have the energy to judge. *Bright & Dark: The Musical*, currently being workshopped at a regional theater in Connecticut, was set to debut at the Public Theater in New York the following summer. I had followed through with JM's suggestion, and Luther had negotiated the life rights and a piece of the show. Beckman, who claimed not to have any lawyers, seemed to round up a few for the contract negotiations, but it was cordial, and he was generous. As Luther reminded me, "He has to be, or it's ten years of work down the drain."

I had promised to be at the premiere, God help me. I couldn't decide if I wanted it to be a flop or a rave, but either one or the other because a lukewarm review and half-packed houses would kill my mother. She wanted that story told.

Once the house was sold and my job was gone, decisions came quickly and easily. My share of the house sale made it possible to buy a work-live space in the downtown LA Arts District, which both Tai and Luther assured me was going to be hot, hot, hot. I had decided to open my own version of Atelier Artemesium, a gallery, shop, and gathering spot. But with Wi-Fi and an espresso bar, because Luther and I ran the numbers and I'd never make it otherwise. According to Luther, conversation was a fine idea, but not income generating. My shop would be on the ground floor of a converted flour mill; my loft on the second floor. There was parking underneath, a brew pub and yoga studio down the street, and a taco truck on Saturday nights. For now, that was all I needed. Well, almost all.

For the past few months, while architects drew up plans, contractors submitted bids, and workers arrived to finish off the space, I put Kiandra in charge of on-site construction, communication, and scheduling. I'd been on a buying trip—from Cuba to Kyoto to Cairo—looking for relics, antiquities, any pieces that brought strength to the buyer, touching on faith, hope, healing, everything from neon signs to ancient amphora to modern triptychs. I'd commissioned a metal artist in North Carolina to create a series of coins, like the ones my father and Jacques kept in their pockets, like the one Nate had given me. I wanted to create a shop organized around the creative principle that objects held meaning, both personally and spiritually powerful.

The devotion I'd seen to Saint Joan had taught me not to dismiss the mystic, how something as simple as a well-rubbed coin could hold someone's life together.

The art buying itself had been a thrill, literally a visceral experience that raised my heart rate and flushed my skin, propelling me from one country to another. All those years of research at the museum had informed both my eye and my head. *I was good at this.* Tai called it my Eat, Pray, Art phase, and that sums it up perfectly. Hopefully, there would be many more such trips if I prayed hard enough to the art gods and my publicity team. I'd be part shopkeeper, part gallerist. My existence, my choice.

The last stop on my world tour had been Paris. I saw Polly, JM, and the baby, a camera-ready bundle swaddled in all white, named Genevieve Marie-Jean Davis-de La Fontaine. So many, many syllables. Like a pro, Polly had successfully incorporated haute-Parisian parenting into her blog, confiding in me that she considered Genevieve to be as powerful a tastemaker as her contemporary, Harper Beckham. "Did you see my Instagram post with Genevieve in that pink-and-white-bunny sweater? Well, it sold out the next day at Jacadi!" Polly crooned. "Take that, Posh Spice." JM mouthed the word "hormones" to me, but I give Polly more credit than that.

I also popped in to see Guy at Galerie Luna and told him the whole story behind our visit to the opening that night. He was astounded and delighted to have played a part, asking about Nate and how he was enjoying his photo. As I left, he insisted I give my mother his card. He said again that it was time for a Suzi Clements Blakely retrospective, and Galerie Luna was eager to show my mother's vintage photos as well as anything new she might have, especially now that she was going to be spending so much time in France. I passed along the information. She was on it. Between the musical and the show, Suzi Clements Blakely would be having a moment next year.

But my primary reason for stopping in Paris was to see Jacques de Baubin, to show him my plans and get his advice. It was another long afternoon that segued into evening, filled with memories, wine, and laughter. When I was leaving, he took the beautiful oil painting of Joan of Arc off the wall, the one he'd bought in a Paris flea market and the one I had admired on that first evening, and he handed it to me. "Take this, Jehanne. For strength."

"I can't."

"Please."

I agreed to take it, but only for a price. Jacques nodded, stating, "We are both in the art-buying business now, so that seems fair." I took the painting and wept, for the last time, I think, about my father.

On Monday, I would hang that painting on the wall behind the desk at Artemesium LA, and the Sam Francis on the wall of living room in the loft above, and I'd be home. But tonight, I had some old business to attend to.

"It's nice to see you again, Joan Blakely."

"And you, Dr. Andrews."

"Please, call me Mason. I'm off duty." He leaned toward me as he took the bar stool next to mine. I thought he might kiss me, but no. He was settling in, pulling the bar stool closer. Yes, freshly showered from the gym, with a warm, rummy scent. "Well, what have you been up to? It's been a minute."

Ten months and seventeen days since he kissed me at my hotel room door. "I followed the doctor's orders."

"I see." He was more than amused; he was flattered. "You are a very good patient. And I must be a very good doctor. Because you look to be in excellent . . . health." Mason looked straight into my eyes, then let his gaze wander over my shoulders, clavicle, and below. Lightning. The months of travel had loosened everything up about me. My hair was longer, my skin brighter, my smile quicker. There was a little less black in my closet and a little more color. I did feel like I was in excellent health, especially tonight.

The bartender placed a beer and bowl of nuts in front of Mason, and he took a swig and handful. "Thanks, Dougie." Then he turned his attention to me again. I felt heat in my chest and was pretty sure I was blushing. "As I recall, I suggested a couple of Advils and a rebound guy. Is that correct?"

"You did."

"And . . ."

"Very solid medical advice. Which I heeded."

"And the ex? Still gone?"

"Very. He remarried."

"The baby mama, I presume."

"Unbelievably, no. Some other woman. Apparently, in addition to having a second family, he was also having an affair. It was in the *New York Times* last month with a giant photo of the whole happy wedding party riding down a dirt road in Montana on a hay wagon." And a paragraph of gory details that mentioned my name, Marissa and the twins and, of course, the late Henry Blakely. Somehow Casey found a real estate heiress with a chain of cupcake stores in the New York area to marry him and be absorbed into his self-absorbed life. So much for being a "father to his sons," as the announcement mentioned the happy couple would be splitting time between Greenpoint and Eagle Rock. I felt sorry for Marissa and the twins.

I had run into Amy at the post office, pushing a double stroller and sucking on an iced latte, after reading the wedding announcement. When I asked if she had been invited to the ceremony, she explained, "No. It was very small. Mainly Brooklyn people." So even loyal Amy and Dave had been dumped for trendier friends. I didn't feel sorry for them.

"More proof that you did the right thing, locking him out of your house. Now, do I need to know anything about this rebound guy?"

"Nah." There was no need to tell him about Nate or Paris or any of that right now. He didn't need to know about the five days in Copenhagen that had been one long perfect dream of laughter and letting go, wandering the streets during the day and soft sheets at night. Nate decided that he should live his whole life in Danish modern, and I vowed to start a food truck featuring open-faced sandwiches on dark rye bread with smoked fish and dill. The beer was cold and delicious, as were the oysters. We took in a few galleries and design studios, learned everything we needed to know about Viking culture, and ordered room service a few nights because why not. Nate worked here and there, early mornings, late afternoons, because that was a part of him. I walked and wandered and brought him coffee every day.

We had saved our trip to the Arken Museum for our last full day in Denmark, a sparkling blue day that called out for exploration. We took the train from Copenhagen Central Station to the town of Ishoj, a small beach town a half hour outside of the city where the museum was located on an island. The building was designed to look like a deconstructed shipwreck—a clean, crisp Scandinavian shipwreck, of course. Stunning. The short walk from the station to the museum took us along the water's edge, surrounded by green marshes, a crystal lagoon, and white sand. I had spotty memories of being at the museum for the dedication almost twenty years ago, which seemed impossible as I watched children wading out into the water. Today I would remember.

Light/Break #22 is a classic Blakely, one of his signature three-dimensional experiences in sensory deprivation, an empty giant box with a hole to the sky. For *#22*, my father intended to re-create deep space, not in some hokey planetarium light show fashion, but a full-body experience as the box becomes filled with color, allowing the viewer to understand the materiality of light and, in the case of *#22*, the vastness of space. During the cycle, the edges of the room disappeared; the walls glowed with projected color that changed so seamlessly, the viewer barely noticed the evolution from bright white to purple to orange to dark green to deep black and back to bright white. The opening to the sky was washed in that brilliant Danish blue light my father had worked so hard to get exactly right. On this day, my father's sky and the Danish sky matched exactly.

We stood together holding hands for thirteen minutes as the colors cycled, our perception of the edges of the room falling away the longer we stood there. In the deep black light, I had the sense I could be anywhere and yet only here.

Only when the light returned to bright white did Nate speak. "We can know a star without touching it. Isn't that what you said this piece symbolized?"

I nodded.

Nate squeezed my hand. "Now I get it."

I think we knew it then, that what we had, the adventure of it all, would never survive an everyday life of buying groceries or doing laundry, but we held hands anyway. We had a sweet, sad, wonderful goodbye at luggage carousel number 4, when Nate kissed me for the last time and whispered in my ear, "Thank you, Joan."

And I whispered back, "No, thank you."

Maybe someday, I would tell this handsome smart doctor about Blackbird or the black dress or the occasional texts from Nate when he spots what he calls a "Joan in the Wild" and sends a photo of some artistic depiction of my patron saint that he's stumbled upon in his travels, but I doubted it. He might meet Nate at the premiere of *Bright & Dark* because Beckman would insist that Nate attend, and I wouldn't mind if he did. But even then, I'd keep the backstory to myself. Not because I thought this Mason wouldn't be around for long, but because I wanted to savor my own little messy business, something else I learned from my mother. "There's nothing you need to know. Except that you were right in your prescription."

"I'm glad to hear it. Thank you for the faith." More food arrived, some exotic fries with dipping sauces, a slider plate of some sort. It all smelled wonderful, rich and smoky. I was starving.

We both let the food sit there, delaying the gratification. Mason leaned forward. "And now, look at you. Here you are."

Yes, here I am.

Acknowledgments

My working title for this book was *Joan of Art* and I still think of it as *Joan*, even though I love the current title. I'm thrilled and relieved that my fictional Joan has finally arrived in the world, emerging like a champion to restart her life after a period of loss and upheaval. Go, Joan. Many thanks to my editor, Rachel Kahan, who believed in *Joan* from the beginning. Your faith and insight were invaluable. I'm honored to be part of the William Morrow imprint and appreciate the hard work and kind support of: Jennifer Hart, Ariana Sinclair, Tavia Kowalchuk, Elsie Lyons, Shelby Peak, and Kyle O'Brien.

More thanks to my agent, Yfat Reiss Gendell of YRG Partners, who provides equal parts encouragement and tough love. Onwards, sister.

This book evolved over many years and I'm grateful for people who asked me repeatedly, "How's that Paris book coming?" Writers need nudges and I have mine in longtime supportive friends, family, and colleagues. For this book, a special thanks to my go-to text chain when I needed a boost, the women of 47 Sexy Sagehens: Daniela Stepman Abbott, Louise Felton Brown, Karah Koe Curtis, Kristin McQueen, Lyn Cunliffe Reeder, and Rachel Horton Pusch. The Sagehen Sisterhood is strong.

The sisterhood of women in fiction is also strong. Cheers to the writers and wonderful women of Friends & Fiction for their early and ongoing support: Mary Kay Andrews, Kristin Harmel, Kristy Woodson Harvey, Patti Callahan Henry, and Mary Alice Monroe. And the many writers, booksellers, and book advocates I've gotten to know over the years, both in person and on social media. We lift each other up.

My Satellite Sisters community is filled with wonderful people and readers who have supported my books for over a decade. Thanks to the self-appointed Satellite Sister Street Team for spreading the word. And a special debt of gratitude to librarian extraordinaire, podcaster, and Satellite Mister Ron Block. Thank you, Satellite Sisters and Misters!

Finally, a salute to the men in my life that helped make *Joan* happen. My father, James Dolan, had a deep reverence for Saint Joan and inspired portions of this story. I think he would have enjoyed this tale. My son Colin Treidler joined me on my research trip in Paris, climbing the steps of Sacré-Coeur, exploring the Panthéon crypts, and suffering through my rusty French in restaurants. Thank you for your curiosity, Colin. I'm grateful to my son Brookes Treidler for my author photos and so much other creative advice over the last few years. It never occurred to me how handy it would be to give birth to a professional photographer. I'm very proud of you, Brookes. And, as always, love and thanks to my husband (and sweater vest inspiration), Berick Treidler.

About the Author

Lian Dolan is a *Los Angeles Times* bestselling author of fiction and nonfiction. Her previous novels are *The Sweeney Sisters*, *Helen of Pasadena*, and *Elizabeth the First Wife*. She has written regular columns for *O, The Oprah Magazine*; *Working Mother*; and *Pasadena Magazine*. She is also the host of *Satellite Sisters*, an award-winning podcast she created with her four real-life sisters. A graduate of Pomona College, she lives in Pasadena, California, with her husband, two sons, and a big German shepherd.